FORT WORTH PUBLIC LIBRARY

W9-AHA-166

For weeks, her spirit felt restless, as if some monumental occurrence was on the verge of overpowering her. Reverend Brown often said when the good Lord had a mission for a body, He'd give a warning with a strong stirring in the person's bones. In her youth, Willow did not understand. Now her stomach fluttered, her flesh tingled, and her mind burned. If the good Lord didn't have something special in store, she didn't know what was wrong with her. Something extraordinary was on the horizon, and if she searched her mind hard enough, she'd figure it out.

A f   gedly handso   inating.

Th

FICTION DOUGLAS 2006
Douglas, Dominiqua
Love lasts forever

Shamblee

SHAMBLEE BRANCH

LOVE LASTS FOREVER

DOMINIQUA DOUGLAS

Genesis Press, Inc.

Indigo Love Stories

An imprint of Genesis Press, Inc.
Publishing Company

Genesis Press, Inc.
P.O. Box 101
Columbus, MS 39703

All rights reserved. Except for use in any review, the reproduction or utilization of this work in whole or in part in any form by any electronic, mechanical, or other means, not known or hereafter invented, including xerography, photocopying and recording, or in any information storage or retrieval system, is forbidden without written permission of the publisher, Genesis Press, Inc. For information write Genesis Press, Inc., P.O. Box 101, Columbus, MS 39703.

All characters in this book have no existence outside the imagination of the author and have no relation whatsoever to anyone bearing the same name or names. They are not even distantly inspired by any individual known or unknown to the author and all incidents are pure invention.

Copyright© 2006 by Dominiqua Douglas

ISBN: 1-58571-187-X
Manufactured in the United States of America

First Edition

Visit us at www.genesis-press.com
or call at 1-888-Indigo-1

DEDICATION

To My Folks

ACKNOWLEDGMENTS

I thank God for the words, the desire, and the gift. Without Him, I would never have written the first word.

I also want to thank my family for teaching me how to read and encouraging my love of books. Their love and support brought me from reader to author. My friends and my first readers inspired me to put my fingers to the keyboard and view the blank white computer screen as a space for infinite possibilities.

Finally, to the reader, I hope you will enjoy Thor and Willow's journey as much as I have.

CHAPTER ONE

Stone Mountain, Georgia
October 1985

Thor Magnusen sat alone in the downstairs den of his isolated split-level home as the wide screen television hummed and vibrated with colorful images and excited voices. In the darkened room, he sat transfixed. Gaze riveted, he leaned closer to the set. At the bottom of the screen, a digital display counted down the seconds. His heart pounded an erratic beat as the moment of his greatest disappointment appeared before him.

Crack!

The sound of breaking bones exploded in Thor's ears. He winced. Although he'd played the football game almost a year ago, his flesh burned with remembered pain. His throat constricted in frustration. Bitterness settled in the pit of his belly, creating a sour aftertaste. The shining moment for the Atlanta Falcons' backup quarterback came and went in less time than the blink of an eye.

He wasn't sure why he tortured himself by watching the video repeatedly like clockwork. The play had been classic. He called it, his teammates responded, and the ball soared from his hand with the grace and determination of the team's namesake.

The tackle from the defensive lineman had been like no other. The powerhouse drove him into the ground, pummeling him like a butcher with a pound of steak. Nothing in all his experience prepared him for the excruciating pain that followed.

Standing six feet one and weighing one hundred ninety-five pounds, he didn't have an ounce of fat on him. His body was a fine-tooled mass of muscle and withstood countless tumbles. Hell, he had played the game since childhood. He took his licks dry-eyed and like a man, but a cracked collarbone and an arm broken in two places brought tears to his eyes. Later, when the doctor told him he would never throw again, no tears came. He froze.

Months later, he remained unchanged.

Sports announcer John Madden appeared on the screen, and Thor stopped the tape. He could only stand so much torture in one sitting. Rising from the leather recliner, he muffled a yawn. Outside, gravel sputtered in his driveway and music blasted. He groaned. He was not in the mood for company.

Jim Croce's "Bad, Bad Leroy Brown" came to an abrupt halt as an engine died. Two doors slammed and a voice called out, "Thor! You might as well open up, 'cause we're coming in anyway!"

Normally, he had no problem with turning his older brother, Cal, away with a promise to call him later. He doubted his luck today. The "we" business bothered him and meant only one thing. Their father was out there, too.

"Thor!" Bo, the Magnusen patriarch, shouted with the gentleness of a drill sergeant.

Escape was impossible. A dejected sigh pushed from his chest as he plopped onto the recliner. "It's open!"

"What the hell are you doing?" His father burst through the door. He stood a few inches shorter than his youngest son, but still presented a powerful figure. Sandy brown hair mixed with gray peeked from his Atlanta Braves cap. Piercing blue eyes glowed with concern, as angry red dots colored his weathered cheeks. Hands resting on his waist, he loomed over Thor. "I've been calling you all day. You don't know how to return a phone call?"

Thor shifted uncomfortably under his father's unrelenting stare. The dark room gave him a slight shield, but that came to a quick end when Cal flipped the switch for the overhead lights.

"Hey!" The sudden brightness stung his eyes. He squeezed them shut to alleviate the pain.

"Hey, yourself!" Cal kicked Thor's outstretched legs as he went to the entertainment center. He pushed the eject button on the VCR, and the tape oozed out. "Surprise, surprise."

"What's that?" Bo questioned.

"Nothing!" Thor's eyes shot open. He bolted from the recliner and grabbed the video from his brother. After shoving the tape inside a plastic case, he stuck it on the bottom shelf of the entertainment center. Waves of sandy brown hair flopped into his eyes, as he stood upright. He brushed the locks aside with the back of his hand. "It's nothing, Pop."

"He's lying." Cal's tone carried accusation. "It's that damned tape of the game again. He can't answer the telephone because he's stuck, knee-deep in a pond of self-pity."

"No cursing." Bo pointed his finger at first one son and then turned to the other. "And you, when will this end?"

The corner of Thor's mouth twisted with annoyance. In less than five minutes, their interrogation began. *Great, just what I need,* he thought. His brows knitted together in one firm line. Biceps bulged as he folded his arms across his chest. Staring down the two men who raised him since he was five and still tried to lord over him twenty-three years later was no easy task, but he attempted it anyway.

"I'm not feeling sorry for myself! Football is the only life I ever wanted, and it's gone. I'm sorry if I'm not dealing with it the way you two want."

Bo regarded Thor in silence as Cal rolled his eyes. "There's more to life than football."

Thor's eyes narrowed. "Not everyone wants to spend his life hiding behind a book, Cal."

"Who's hiding?" The brothers stood nose to nose. "You're the one all holed up in your house, refusing to answer the phone, and repeatedly watching a stupid tape. No matter how many times you watch it, the outcome will be the same. He sacked you hard! It wasn't your fault, so move on already!"

Heart pumping wildly in his chest, Thor's hand tightened into a fist. His brother's words rang true, but he didn't want to hear them. Hell, he hadn't even invited him over. Why did he have to put up with this?

Why can't they just leave me alone?

"Cal, that's enough." Bo's hand closed around Thor's clenched fist and held firm until his grip relaxed. "We didn't come to yell at you."

"Oh, no?" His voice dripped of sarcasm. Hurt flashed in his father's blue eyes, instantly shaming him. He pulled his hand free from his father's and shoved his hands into the front pockets of his jeans. "Sorry, Pop. Why did you and the professor come over? I can't believe you drove out here just 'cause I didn't answer the phone."

"We worry about you, knucklehead!" Cal thumped Thor's forehead. "I'm going up for a beer. Anybody want one?"

They declined his offer. As Cal bounded up the short staircase to the main floor, the hardwood floors creaked under his weight but father and son barely noticed. Bo eased himself onto the matching leather sofa, and patted the space beside him. He didn't speak until Thor joined him.

"We're worried about you, son. I know I raised you to love football, and maybe I was wrong in that, but I know that I didn't raise you to be stupid."

"Great, now my father is calling me stupid, too. Thanks a lot."

"I didn't say you were stupid, but this hiding out isn't the brightest thing you've ever done. Sure, you can't be a quarterback anymore, but you can still play. Even if you don't want to play anymore, there's still a life to live. I never thought I'd see the day when one of my sons would quit."

"I'm not a quitter." A spark of anger coursed through him.

"I'd say you're doing a damned fine impersonation of one if you don't get off your ass soon," Bo countered.

"Don't curse." Cal rejoined them in the den. Pulling the top off the can, he jutted his chin toward his brother. "We're going to Allatoona Lake. Come fishing with us. Forget about the game…your shoulder… everything. Relax and have some fun."

The offer was too good to be true. The Magnusen family had owned a cabin near the lake in Cherokee County for over a century. At their grandfather's knee, Thor and Cal learned the history of the land and their family. The cabin and the surrounding woods filled his heart even more than his own little hideaway on Stone Mountain. Fresh clean air and free-flowing streams were only part of nature's gift to him. The place with the countless memories of family outings represented happiness to Thor, and maybe he needed a healthy dose of that.

His first real smile in months curved his lips. "When do we leave?"

=∽∾∽=

A smattering of stars glittered like diamonds in the indigo sky. Yet, an oppressive cloak of humidity weighed heavily in the night air. Fall settled in Georgia, promising a healthy downpour of rain. Thor inhaled a slow, deep breath. The sweet familiar fragrance of pine and the intoxicating scent of the coming shower washed over him. He closed his eyes, tipped the rocking chair back, and allowed the peacefulness of his family's cabin to comfort his soul.

The screen door creaked open. Footsteps plodded across the porch. A deep sigh followed. "Smells like rain," Cal announced. "Feels good, doesn't it?"

Thor's eyelids lifted. One eyebrow arched with suspicion. His brother stood with his back to him. At six feet four inches and graceful athletic ability that most envied, the older man could have pursued a career in professional basketball, but chose books instead. Cal's passion for history far overshadowed anything he could have obtained on a basketball court.

In his role as older brother, Cal always made sure Thor understood the importance of education and grasped the lessons that the past taught. Like any younger sibling, Thor listened to his brother's every word until the thrill of a touchdown pumped wildly in his veins and pushed everything else aside. The fleeting reminder of past dreams brought the usual ache back to his chest. Unhappiness threatened his tranquility.

He grunted, "Sure, it feels just great."

Moving from the edge of the porch, Cal settled his backside on the wooden railing. Concern gave his voice a quiet edge. "Is the air bothering your shoulder?"

Subconsciously, Thor's hand went to the old wound and rubbed hard. "It's all right. Is Pop asleep?"

"Nah, he's going through Gramps' old trunk."

"Oh, yeah? I can't see you missing the chance to go through that heap of junk. Go back. I'm not about to walk off and disappear into the woods."

"I'm not out here 'cause I'm afraid of that. Pop is fussing like an old woman. He told me he didn't need any help and threatened to tan my hide if I didn't join you outside. Can you believe that?"

Thor released a grunt. That was as close to a laugh that he could get. When their father was in action, there was no stopping Bo Magnusen. Yeah, Thor believed their father's threat. "I'm sure he didn't mean anything by it," he said, noticing the tightening of Cal's jaw. "He'll let you in on whatever he's doing when he has a mind to."

"I'm not worried about that." Cal waved his hand in the air in a dismissive gesture.

"So stop bitching," Thor gibed. Even in his present dejected state, picking on his brother was a pastime that was too enjoyable to pass up.

"I'm not. Where do you get off calling Gramps' stuff 'a heap of junk?' Do you realize the value of what's in that trunk?"

"I hadn't thought about it. I guess some of it has to be worth a pretty penny."

"You *are* a knucklehead!" Cal reached out and thumped Thor's forehead again. "Hollow, just as I suspected. They must have hit you harder than I thought. Boy, I wasn't talking about monetary value, I'm talking about the value of our family's lifeblood. You remember the stories that Gramps told us about these woods and this cabin? What happened during the Trail of Tears, the War Between the States and everything since then…why, this place could be a landmark!"

"Quick, somebody notify the historical society," Thor quipped, dryly.

"You just don't get it. I guess they did knock all the sense out of you on that football field. I always thought you were smarter than that."

"Now hold on a minute!" Thor stood so abruptly the rocking chair skidded back a foot, and its sharp edges scraped against the house. "This place is important to me. Just because I don't revere it like you do doesn't mean that I don't understand what happened here. I heard Gramps' stories and may even have a few of them memorized, but what does that prove? That stuff is in the past. Get over it already, Cal."

"That football game is in the past, too," Cal commented quietly. "I don't see you getting over that anytime soon."

A sour taste settled in Thor's mouth and overrode the caustic retort that lay on the tip of his tongue. Shoving his hands into the front pockets of his jeans, he brushed past his brother and stormed off the porch.

A few seconds passed and Cal's heavy footsteps retreated. The accusing slam of the screen door followed, echoing like cannonball fire in the otherwise still woods.

Grudgingly, Thor admitted maybe Cal had a point…a small one. His dreams of quarterback stardom were dead. The realization hurt, but moving beyond the pain proved too difficult to fathom. The dream had been his whole life; he hadn't wanted anything else. *What am I supposed to do with my life now?*

Like Cal, he enjoyed reading about history, but not enough to teach it. Coaching football to a bunch of snot-nosed kids as his father suggested was the last thing on his list. Has-beens became coaches. He wasn't ready to walk down that road—yet.

The screen door creaked open behind him again. His father's warm voice called out, "Thor, come back here, boy. I wanna show you something."

He joined his father on the steps and nodded toward the palm-sized treasure in the older man's hand. "What is it? Did it belong to Gramps?"

"Yeah, in a way." Bo's large, lined hands ran over the object he held. An earnest expression settled on his face. "Your Gramps isn't the sole owner of what I have here. It belongs to us, the Magnusen men before us, and those to follow after we're long gone. This is our legacy, son. This tells us the story of who we are and what we aspire to be. It doesn't come from cheering crowds on Super Bowl Sunday, but from inside of us."

Bo and Cal sounded like broken records. "I know that, Pop, but you don't understand—"

"I understand, and empathize with your situation, but what *you* don't understand is that you're not the first man to have his dreams taken from him, and you won't be the last. It happens. It happened to your great-great-grandpa Anders, and that's how we came to be in Georgia in the first place. His goal wasn't to settle here, he came looking for gold but didn't find any."

"So why didn't he just leave?"

"Eva, your great-great-grandma, was pregnant again. Since the first one was stillborn, he didn't want to risk that happening twice," Bo explained. "So, he stayed put and made a life here."

"He could have left after the baby was born; they didn't have to stay here."

"Anders didn't see it that way. I guess a part of him still believed that he'd find gold in these woods someday, he just had to keep looking."

His father's point soared over his head. "And?"

"The knucklehead doesn't get it, Pop," Cal informed them from behind the screen door. The door screeched open. He moved onto the porch and sat behind them on the rocking chair. "Gold prospecting doesn't compare with a Super Bowl ring."

"Shut up," Thor bit out.

"Both of you cut it out." Bo inhaled a sharp breath. "Later, Anders found something else that replaced his earlier dream of being a gold miner. Here." He placed an old timepiece into Thor's hands.

Light spilled from the cabin onto the watch. "Is this gold? It must be worth a fortune."

"I've never seen that before." Cal leaned in to get a closer look. "Where did you get it?"

"From the old trunk." Bo gave Thor a long, hard look. "You're right. It's gold, and it is valuable, but that can't be judged by dollar signs."

"Pop, you kept a family heirloom like that tucked away here at the cabin?" Cal questioned. "Why? It could have been stolen!"

"It wasn't."

Thor unfastened the latch. Bold black Arabic numbers from one to twelve encircled the white face of the timepiece. Both hands of the watch pointed straight up. In the bottom center was a small circle of numbers beginning with zero and ending in sixty, which should have counted off the seconds, but its tiny hand was motionless.

"It doesn't even work." Thor moved to hand the pocket watch back to his father.

"No, you keep it and think on this—like the Good Book says, there is a time and a season for all things. Anders realized that when he found that old timekeeper in the woods and it changed his life. If you let it, it just may change yours, too." Bo smiled and patted Thor's shoulder as he rose from the porch. Taking a deep breath, he looked at his two sons before glancing at the surrounding woods. "Smells like rain. There's always good fishing when the rain is coming down. I'll see you in the morning."

The door closed behind Bo, and in an instant, Cal was beside his brother, reaching for the timepiece. "Let me see that."

"No." Thor kept a firm grasp on the pocket watch and rose from the step. "He told me to keep it. You can look at it later."

Cal's eyes widened in surprise. "Well, looky here. Does this mean you're learning how to listen to your elders?"

"It's possible, but only to the smart ones."

"Knucklehead," Cal murmured in an affectionate tone. "Going fishing with us tomorrow?"

"Maybe." He eyed the watch thoughtfully. The old timekeeper captivated him. Funny thing was, he didn't understand why. "I wanna play around with this a little before I turn in. I may not wake up in time. If I don't, go on without me."

"Sure." Cal called over his shoulder as he went inside the house, "Goodnight."

"Yeah, you too."

Caught in a haze of pondering his father's mysterious advice, Thor stood alone for several minutes. The watch resembled most pocket timepieces. The round metal fit snug in the palm of his hand. The lettering on the outside was hard to make out in the dim light, but the shiny gold finish gleamed brilliantly in the moonlight.

He popped the latch again. The little door swung open with a soft groan. A faint smile crossed his face. He understood the old watch's aches and pains.

The hands of the clock still stood at midnight. The tiny hand to count off the seconds refused to budge, too. He held the watch up to his ear and shook. The clock didn't tick, but something rattled inside. He decided to have a closer look.

Leaving behind the humid fall night, he wandered inside the cabin. His footsteps carried him through the living room, floorboards creaking under his weight. The familiar sound comforted him. Everything about the cabin represented the truest aspects of home. His father and

Aunt Greta were born in the back bedroom. Cal accused Thor of not honoring his family's history, but that couldn't be further from the truth.

Clutching the watch in one hand, his other hand trailed across a pale blue and gray quilt draped over an antique rocking chair. His grandmother made the quilt, and his great-great grandmother rocked her firstborn daughter in the chair. He paused for a moment on the threshold between the living room and the dining area. His thoughts wandered to the Magnusen family that first drew breath in that cabin. *Who were they? Where did they draw their courage? How did they survive during the conflicts of their times?* The questions became too much. He released a long sigh and realized that he'd never find the answers to those questions.

He glanced down the darkened hallway to his left. Beyond the living room, dining room and kitchen, his brother and father lay fast asleep in two of the cabin's three bedrooms. Careful not to disturb them, he moved through the open dining area to the kitchen behind it. On habit, he flipped the switch near the backdoor before grabbing a handful of tools from the drawer underneath the sink and heading to the square, wooden table in the center of the room. Light reflected off the few modern appliances that contradicted the cabin's timelessness. The dazzling fluorescent glow aided him in his investigation of the broken watch.

Deep in thought, he hunched over the table as he examined the timekeeper. A heart within a heart adorned the front cover. The marking had been done with care, and Thor traced the image with his forefinger. Energy surged through him, and he came close to tossing the watch. Curiosity got the better of him. With his thumb, he turned the watch over. A sentence was engraved on the back.

Whispering, he read, "Love lasts forever."

The three words seemed simple enough, but their effect on Thor was not. Warmth filled his chest, and his heart began to race. He swallowed hard and tried to ignore the odd sensations. Sure, the heirloom was strange, but that was because he had never seen nor heard of it before, that's all. It certainly wasn't worth him freaking out. Having convinced himself, Thor shrugged off the moment and disassembled the timepiece.

His nimble fingers slowly spread the tiny parts of the watch onto the table. Ever since he was a boy, he always wanted to know how things worked. He often took his toys apart and put them back together again. While Cal was a thinker, Thor had always been more prone to take the hands on approach.

As he worked with the family heirloom, Bo's words came back to him. The time for glory had passed him, and he was in the season of transition. Twenty-eight was far too young to pack it all in, but the road before him remained hazy and confused. What path should he take, and would it be the right one? Offers for a better future weren't knocking at his door, yet he wasn't without choices. No matter how dismal the future looked, everyone always had a choice. What was his? Even as he fitted the watch's innards back together, the question rattled in his mind.

Morning came with the cry of a distant rooster, jolting him from his thoughts. He rubbed his eyes as he stood and stretched. A healthy dose of caffeine seemed the best solution for a sleepless night. He started a pot of coffee. Minutes later, the rich aroma began to fill the room. His father and his brother entered the kitchen, looking refreshed from a good night's rest and decked out in fishing gear. Thor smiled in greeting and grabbed the watch from the table. Resting his backside against the counter, he polished the watch with the edge of his blue denim shirt.

"You pulled an all-nighter?" Cal asked. "That must be some watch."

"It's not so bad once you get it working."

"Did you?" his father asked.

"I think so. I haven't set it, yet. I left my watch at home, and the clock above the stove needs a new battery."

Cal glanced at his wristwatch. "It's half past six. Are you going to bed now?"

Thor turned the dials on the watch to set it. He held the watch to his ear and frowned. The ticking sounded distant and not as strong as it should have been.

"Nah, I'm not tired."

"Well, if you're coming with us, get your gear," his brother advised while he poured the fresh coffee into a thermos. "We're ready to head out."

Thor shook the watch. "I'm not going fishing. I'll take a shower instead, and then go for a walk. Whereabouts are you and Pop fishing? Once I get this thing fixed, maybe I'll head out that way."

"North end of the lake," Bo answered. "We'll take your gear in case you show up."

"Thanks."

A quick shower refreshed him. With the pocket watch held firmly in his hand, he began his slow hike through the woods.

Rain bypassed them during the night and took the heavy humidity with it. The air was light and refreshing. Rays of sunlight beamed down from the cloudless sky and brought warmth to the fall morning. The scent of maple blended in with the woodsy smells of pine and oak. Thor soaked everything in as his feet followed an old trail that led to the small creek, which had once been the source of water for his family's cabin.

The lack of sleep took its toll on him. Stifling a yawn, he sat at the base of one of the maple trees and leaned back against the trunk. Determined to fix the watch before he succumbed to a nap, he opened the catch and stared intently at the timepiece's stern face. The time read an hour later than when he had set it.

"Seems right to me," Thor murmured softly. Just to be sure, he held the watch up to his ear again. This time, the ticking was loud and clear. "It's good to know there are still some things I can do." Slumber overtook him soon after.

A soft melodious hum roused him from his impromptu nap. Thor felt more relaxed than he had in months. The sound of plopping water accompanied the lilting, feminine voice that drifted in the air. Where he napped was private property. Hikers never ventured that far onto their land. His Good Samaritan instincts kicked in, and he followed the sweet voice, having decided to help the lost soul find her way.

As Thor followed the sounds, he noted differences in the woods that he knew like the back of his hand. The trail wandered off in several haphazard directions. He frowned. A nap in the great outdoors wasn't what it used to be. Waking up disoriented irritated him.

The voice grew stronger. His pace quickened in time to the melodious tone. He reached her just as she dipped the second pail into the water. Pausing briefly, he allowed himself a few moments to appreciate the view she unwittingly provided.

She seemed about average height for a woman. It was hard to tell for sure since she was bent over. Wearing a long, coarse brown skirt, her clothing appeared outdated, but the rounded curve of her backside was timeless. Breath lodged in his throat. His imagination conjured an image of her without the cumbersome garments. Masculine approval swept through him. "Mmm."

As she rose to her full height, his heart raced in an unexpected resurgence of primal male interest and expectation. Long, glossy black hair fell in a single braid down her back. The tips of the wispy tendrils brushed against the waistband of her skirt and brought his attention to the small width of her waist. Unable to wait another second to see the face he instinctively knew was beautiful, he coughed once to alert her to his presence.

"Hey."

She stumbled at the sound of his voice. Quickly and with the gracefulness of a ballerina, she righted herself and stood tall. Surprise shone in her large, dark eyes, her sensual, full lips parted. The beautiful stranger inhaled a sharp breath and answered with husky warmth, "Mr. Anders. Good morning."

Anders? Thor wondered about that only briefly. Drinking in the sight of her consumed him. Long black hair dramatically framed her creamy milk chocolate complexion. Rounded olive black eyes appeared radiant with life, pain, and compassion. Her face was an expressive mixture of curiosity and dread before an unreadable mask froze her features.

The swift transformation concerned him. He longed to put her at ease. "It's okay, really. If you're lost, I can show you how to get back to the main road."

The mask slipped. Confusion lurked briefly in the depths of her eyes. She stooped to pick up the other wooden pail and moved with hesitation away from the banks of the creek. "Mr. Anders, I'm not lost.

I am here to help Miss Eva prepare for the baby. Miss Olivia sent me over this morning. I can go back…"

She spoke as if she knew him and stared at him as if he'd lost his marbles. He rubbed the back of his head. Maybe Cal was right. Maybe the lineman sacked him harder than he thought.

"Sir, are you feeling all right?"

"I'm fine. At least, I think I am. Miss…?"

Her eyes widened at that. She then quickly lowered her lashes and moved down the trail that Thor thought he used earlier. Struggling with the full pails, she took great pains to sidestep him. He ignored her apprehension and moved quickly to reach her. His right hand shot out to take the bucket. Their fingers brushed. The initial contact was startling.

Electricity sizzled from the single touch. The pail dropped from their hands. Water splashed. Thor jumped to avoid it.

"I'm so sorry, Mr. Anders, sir."

"It wasn't your fault." She looked primed to bolt. His hands on her shoulders stopped her. "Please, I'm the one to blame. I scared you and I apologize."

"You apologize?" Disbelief lit up her eyes. "To *me*?"

"Yes," he said with a warm smile as he reluctantly dropped his hands. "I have better manners. I should have offered to carry them both in the first place."

"Mr. Anders—"

"Why do you keep calling me that? My name is Magnusen. Thor Magnusen to be exact."

"You sure do favor him," she murmured mostly to herself. Her head tilted. Large eyes squinted at him. "I can see now that you're not Mr. Anders."

"No, I'm not," he agreed with a ready smile. "So what's your name?"

"It's Willow, sir." A small smile touched her full lips before slowly fading away.

"Nice to meet you, Willow." He took her hand and shook it gently. He then bent forward to grab the handle on the forgotten bucket at their feet. "May I?"

He extended his hand for the pail she still kept a firm hold on. Another quizzical expression crossed her face before she gave him the pail. "Show me where you're camped out. Maybe I can help you and your pregnant friend."

Willow gave him another look that said she questioned his sanity. Instead of voicing her thoughts, she nodded once and said, "It is this way, sir."

CHAPTER TWO

Willow Elkridge walked with her head held high, her back straight, and her thoughts on the man who walked quietly beside her.

He said his name was Magnusen. Thor Magnusen. Thor. God of Thunder. According to Viking history, Thor was the strongest of all the Norse gods and defended them against the forces of evil. Lightning flashed whenever he wielded his ax-hammer. A quick temper warned all who crossed his path. She shuddered. *Now that's a strong title to live up to.*

Glancing surreptitiously out of the corner of her eyes, she decided that he was far too beautiful to be a deity of violence, pain, and destruction. His hands, clutching the handles of the buckets, were sturdy, long-fingered, and comely. Worn Kentucky jeans molded to his muscular thighs like a second skin. The matching shirt hung loosely on him but did little to hide the breadth of his shoulders and chest. His rolled sleeves revealed the strength of his corded forearms and the faint dusting of baby-fine light brown hair.

Her heart pounded under her breast. Heat coursed through her. Surely, it was indecent to mark his form so closely. Common sense prevailed. He was Mr. Anders's kin after all. A woman of color knew better than to fall for the charm and fancy of a white man, no matter how comely or friendly he seemed. Whether slave or free, succumbing to such an attraction only led to heartbreak and quite possibly death. Her urges would be best held in check lest she forget her place or her aspirations.

The lesson from the impromptu lecture did not sit well in her head. Against her better judgment, she stole another glimpse. This time, his face captivated her.

What a magnificent face it was! Compelling blue eyes set off his ruggedly handsome features. His skin, darkened by the sun, had been surprisingly soft to the touch. His lips were full and curved into a generous, warm smile upon her blatant perusal. Shame overtook her, and she stumbled on the path.

"Are you okay?" The rich timbre of his voice wrapped around her like a velvet cloak.

"Excuse me?" Willow fought desperately to rein in her confusing reaction to him.

"Did you hurt yourself? Maybe I should look at your ankle. You might have twisted it or something."

"My ankle is fine, sir." His concern for her well-being was another pleasing aspect to the baffling man. Mr. Anders would have never offered to look at her ankle, and she would not have wanted him to if he had. Even if their blood was the same, the two men were distinctly different; nothing alike at all.

"My name is Thor." His dark blue gaze bored into her and his warm smile returned. "Please, don't call me sir. It reminds me of my father."

His response baffled her. Even Reverend Brown, the white man who took her in after her parents died, never spoke with such boldness. Calling a white man by his birth name was unheard of. No matter his age or station in life, she knew that such familiarity was unacceptable. Her brows knitted together, and she said nothing more.

"Let me hear you say it." His enthusiasm reminded her of a playful pup. He tilted his head down as he looked at her in a breathtakingly charming manner. "Say it, Willow...Thor."

Her name on his lips caused her steps to falter. She righted herself before she could embarrass herself further and shook her head in refusal. The spark of attraction burned brightly between them. Was it all sport for him? She dared not take that risk.

"You'll call me Sir, but not by my name. Why not?"

"You know why not," she responded in a choked whisper. "It is not seemly for me to do so."

He came to an abrupt halt in the middle of the trail. A confused frown furrowed his brow. "What? Not seemly? What are you talking about? Of course you can call me by my first name. These are modern times, you know."

"These times are indeed modern, but not quite that simple as you well know, sir." Swallowing hard, she glanced at the surrounding thicket. The cabin stood only a few yards away. Her reprieve from her chores had ended. She beckoned for the pails. "If you please, I must carry these now."

"No." A muscle flicked angrily in his jaw. "I said I'd carry them, and I will. Besides, they're too heavy for you. Now what's this about the times not being simple? They're simple enough for me to call you Willow, isn't that right?"

"Well, of course," she muttered as her irritation grew. He knew darn well that it was fine for him to be less familiar with her. Why must he persist in teasing her?

"Well, if I can call you Willow, and by your own admission, I can... Well, by my own admission, you are to call me Thor."

"I cannot, sir."

His gaze darkened and his mouth thinned with displeasure. "Then I'm not moving an inch."

"As you wish, sir," she countered, holding out her hands again. "The water, please."

"No." He shook his head like a spoiled child. "I said I'm not moving. I'll have to move to give you the buckets, and I'm not gonna do it. Not unless you call me by my name."

"This is nonsense," she muttered underneath her breath.

His eyebrows lifted a fraction. "Indeed it is. Finally, we agree on something."

"Sir—"

"No, we can stand here all day if you want. I have nothing to do but enjoy the breathtaking view."

She glanced around. Only tall oaks and rigid maples surrounded them. Long branches hid the beauty of the cloudless blue sky and the beaming golden sun. Brown and red leaves replaced the lush green variety. Fall was comely indeed, but not quite breathtaking.

"I wasn't talking about the woods, Willow." His voice deepened suggestively as his gaze pierced her.

She swallowed hard. With desire burning bright in his eyes, she had no doubt as to his meaning. Her pulse quickened in spite of her earlier warnings to be cautious. He invoked a response in her like one she had never felt in all her twenty-one years. Miss Eva often said that a look from Mr. Anders left her feverishly excited. Now Willow understood why.

"Willow," he whispered her name softly like a gentle breeze. "Just say it once. I promise to behave myself then."

"Do you solemnly promise?"

"Scout's honor."

Yet, another peculiar phrase passed from his lips. She wondered if he often spoke in riddles or had her highly-strung senses addled her brain. No matter, he had the water she needed. She had no choice but to accept his promise and take him at his word.

"Thor." Her voice sounded unnaturally low and husky.

Head bowed and peering at her through lowered lashes, he gave her a smile that singed her flesh. "See, Miss Willow, that wasn't hard at all."

His remark dumbfounded her. By the time she collected her wits, he had disappeared up the trail. Lifting her skirts, she hastened after him.

When she reached him, the color had drained from his face. His bright gaze swept over the cabin and the surrounding elements. Suddenly, his handsome features clouded over with uneasiness. His rich voice shook noticeably. "Oh, my God. What happened here?"

"What's wrong?" His change in demeanor troubled her.

"The cabin is wrong. Where's the rest of it? What's that barn doing over there? Where did these chickens come from?" The two pails thudded to the dusty ground. He looked east and west. "What happened to the road? Why is all this dirt and gravel covering the pavement?"

Willow moved cautiously toward him. "That's the road right there." She pointed to the ground.

The cabin door opened. Eva, her petite frame consumed by the width of her womb, stepped outside. "Willow, I thought I heard you… Anders didn't tell me that family was coming."

Eva welcomed Thor with the warmth of her smile. She stepped down the steps with more energy than someone her size should have had and slipped her arm around his. Leading him toward the cabin, she continued to talk.

Willow grabbed the two pails and followed them. Even though she was not close enough to hear his reply, she sensed his bewilderment. A change came over him when they stepped into the clearing. Maybe now he remembered what was acceptable and what was not in the modern times of 1860 Georgia.

—◦◦◦—

"Anders should have told me." The brunette steered him inside the one room cabin. "I would have had something more than collard greens and hot water cornbread prepared. Maybe we can get one of those chickens to fry."

Wide-eyed and staring, he mumbled, "Don't go to any trouble for me, ma'am. I'm fine."

"Call me Eva." Fluttering about, the pregnant woman talked up a storm.

He tuned her out, just the essentials registering. He mumbled, smiled, and nodded in all the right places, which seemed to please her while his brain tried to make sense of his surroundings.

Despite the extra foliage along the way—there were more trees than he ever remembered seeing, and all sorts of flowers and plants everywhere—the trail had been the same distance from the creek to the cabin. He was damn sure about that! But the cabin…wasn't the same.

The changes were startling. The family sanctuary now consisted of one moderately sized room. A solid-looking wall hid the hallway, leading to the three bedrooms and the very important bathroom. The sofa, easy chair, and television were gone, too. The fireplace consisted of the same multi-colored stone blocks and the numerous family pictures on the mantel had vanished, leaving only one framed photograph. He moved slowly to get a closer look.

"That's Anders and me on our wedding day." Eva glowed with love and devotion. "I told him it was too extravagant, but he was determined. You know how you Magnusen men are when you get your mind set on something; just about as stubborn as a mule."

Thor offered a polite chuckle. Her close proximity forced him to maintain a calm, cool façade. Deep down, unease threw him off kilter. He breathed a sigh of relief when Eva moved away from him to speak to Willow. The feminine voices played like a soft melody in the background while his eardrums pulsated with an erratic beat. Something strange, peculiar, and just not right was happening here.

His gaze strayed to the photo again. Staring intently at the image, recognition dawned on him. *I know that picture!* The image hung prominently in the cabin. Gramps often used the photograph to emphasize stories about…their great-great-grandfather Anders and his wife, Eva…

Anders and Eva?

Oh, God. His hand began to tremble. *This can't be happening.* Cal, ever the practical jokester, was playing a dirty trick on him. That was it! While Thor napped, Cal and Pop hired a couple of actresses and rearranged the furniture to shock him into getting his head back on straight. That had to be it.

His world felt safe again. He breathed deeply and set the framed picture back on the mantel. Smiling, he looked at the women. Their conversation was over, and Willow stood a step or two closer to him. His gaze connected with her dark, searching eyes. He winked broadly at her to let her know he was in on the game, but her reaction surprised him. Instead of admitting defeat with a wink of her own, she gasped and whirled away.

The cool heat of Eva's stare as she witnessed the minuscule interaction baffled him. He was flirting; big deal. Willow was a beautiful woman, even if she took her acting performance to heart. Besides, he had the strongest suspicion that the attraction was mutual. Trick or not, he aimed to explore it, thoroughly.

"You didn't say if you were passing through," Eva murmured in a chilly tone, "or thinking to stay for a spell. And since Anders didn't mention you were coming…well, we don't have much room to spare."

Now both females were really letting the ruse go to their heads. Eva actually had the disapproving stare down to a science. Thor came close to applauding their performance but thought better of it. Being a jock, he had never acted in a play during his school years, but he could ham it up with the best of them.

"I haven't decided, yet. Depends on how delicious dessert turns out to be." He aimed a wolfish grin in Willow's direction and turned to his left.

The bathroom was just down the hallway. *The façade Pop and Cal rigged is a neat trick, but no matter how much they want to shake me up, they wouldn't get rid of the toilet.*

Thor pressed his hand against the wall and pushed. In that instant, his world shifted completely off its axis.

The hallway, leading to the bathroom, was nothing more than a wall with a rifle rack. The cabin truly consisted of only one, solitary room. Maybe he really did suffer from too many hard tackles on the football field.

The room wavered before his eyes. Dizziness washed over him. His eyes closed to ward off the worst of it. Then, a pair of arms wrapped around his waist, preventing him from falling.

"Just lean on me." Willow's voice came clear and sweet at his side.

Gratitude flowed through him at her unsolicited assistance. Thor willingly followed her advice. Her warm and comforting body brushed against his and provided the stability he needed. She guided him across the room and into a rocking chair. A cry locked in his chest when she took her soothing touch away. Slowly, he released the air from his lung. Before he opened his eyes, he realized another truth. The rocking chair was the exact same chair his father rocked him in when he was a little boy, except this chair held no scratches and scars from generations of use. No, this one was brand new!

Eva stood before him with a tall glass of water in her hand. The disapproval in her eyes warmed to concern. He gladly accepted her offering, sighing as the cool liquid refreshed his parched throat.

"Thank you, ma'am." He showed his appreciation for both women with a faint smile.

"When was the last time you ate?" Eva questioned. After he drained the glass, she took the empty glass from him. "You seem faint. Are you sick? I have to be careful, considering I am with child. I don't mean any disrespect, but if you are ill…"

"No, ma'am, I'm well. Physically, that is. I'm not sure what's going on with my head."

"Would you like more water?"

"I'm fine, Willow, but thank you. I'm sorry for interrupting your day like this. I wasn't expecting this... I...um...I'm feeling a little confused about some things. Maybe you could help me. Either of you, I suppose."

Willow went to the center of the room and pulled two chairs from the wooden table, setting one near Eva and claiming the other for herself. Her dark gaze peered into his eyes. The obvious interest in his plight mesmerized him. If they weren't playacting and Eva really was his great-great-grandmother, he was in a heap of trouble.

Nineteenth-century Georgia had no tolerance for sincere affection between the races. With electricity charging him whenever Willow was near, he sizzled enough to cause a blackout. That was if Edison had discovered the current's many uses, yet.

"What's gotten you confused?" Willow ignored a sharp look from Eva. "I thought something was amiss back at the creek."

By the demure lowering of her eyes, he recognized her meaning immediately. She referred to his cockiness on the trail. God, if this was the eighteen hundreds, he was lucky she hadn't bolted from him on sight. The looks he gave her were far from chaste and bent more toward downright suggestive. If she feared all he wanted was a roll in the hay or would demand that from her...

Oh, damn!

Blood pounded a tempestuous beat at his temples. Everything confused him and didn't make a lick of sense! He couldn't just assume it was the eighteen hundreds. Maybe he hiked further away from the cabin than he previously thought. Maybe the lack of sleep had muddled his thinking and sent him on a different path.

Caught up in his internal debate, he forgot about the women and searched his brain for alternate possibilities.

Unfortunately, there were none. No other cabin in the world had that framed photograph, and the Eva in front of him looked too damned much like the Eva in the picture to be a fake. She was the real deal, which meant that the impossible had happened as he sat in the current home of his great-great-grandparents.

"Miss Eva, didn't Doc Sully leave some laudanum on his last visit? Maybe he could use some for whatever's ailing him."

Thor shook his head, vigorously refusing the drug. He needed his mind clear if he hoped to make any kind of sense of his present situation. "Really, I'm fine now. I haven't eaten in a while. I didn't realize that 'til just now."

Eva gave him an understanding smile and nodded. When she moved to stand, Willow patted her hand and said, "You should rest. I can fix him a plate."

"Wait!" Thor said quickly. Both women regarded him with puzzled expressions. He understood that sentiment all too well. His soft words reassured them. "I can do that myself, Willow, but first...well, what's the date? I've been traveling so long that I've plumb forgotten it."

"Why, it's October twelfth," Eva answered.

"And the year?"

"1860," Willow supplied when Eva's mouth dropped open. "I think I'd better fix you that plate now."

"Thanks."

Willow spun on her boot heels and headed for the kitchen area. Once or twice, she glanced over her shoulder in his direction. Their gazes connected. Thor sensed that she was worried about him. Her concern touched him.

"How can you forget the year?" A stunned expression remained frozen on Eva's face. "I apologize for that," she added quickly. "Of course, an empty stomach can make a body forget many things. I suppose you have not forgotten how you are related to Anders? I know he doesn't have any brothers, but you look so much like him. . ." She stirred uneasily on the chair. Her head lowered and she glanced away for a brief moment. "You see, he doesn't talk about his family. Just that save for me and our little one," she said, patting her swollen abdomen with a mother's pride, "we're his only family in the world, but here you are."

"I'm a distant relative." *About a century away, give or take a couple of years.*

"I noticed the resemblance right off. I imagine Willow did, too."

"Yes, she did," he murmured softly. The mouth-watering aroma of home-cooked collards and hot water cornbread drifted toward him. A hearty growl erupted from his stomach. Heat flooded his cheeks. "Excuse me, ma'am."

"Anders's roars like that, too." She dismissed his embarrassment with a wave. "We have fresh water from the creek and lye soap. You can wash up over there." A chamber set rested on the nearby chest o' drawers. "Clean towels are in the top drawer."

"Thank you, ma'am."

"Please, call me Eva. We are family."

Returning her smile, he rose from the chair then made quick work of washing and drying his hands. When he faced the women again, he found that the table had been set for three. Each plate held a heaping portion of greens with the fragrant hot water cornbread on the side. Thor briskly rubbed his hands. He couldn't wait to dig in, but he wasn't about to forget his manners.

Going first to Eva, he pulled out a chair. She thanked him with a smile. He moved around the table to do the same for Willow. Surprise glittered in her black orbs for only a moment before she too sat.

In a husky tone, she murmured her gratitude. "Thank you."

"It was my pleasure." He claimed the empty space beside her.

Eva bowed her head once everyone settled. She thanked God for their meal and for the latest addition to the family. The prayer ended with a request for Anders's safe return home. "Amen."

"Would you like coffee?" Eva asked.

"No, thank you. I'm fine with the water."

Thor shoveled in a few forkfuls of collard greens and broken pieces of bread. His taste buds exploded with delight. He expected the food to be bland, but it was far from it. Salted pork and smoky bacon were flavorful in the greens, and the hot water cornbread was moist and delicious. The meal reminded him of Sunday dinners with his grandparents. Although he was concerned about the change in century, the feeling of being at home comforted him.

"This is delicious!" He paused to look at the quiet woman to his right and his great-great-grandmother who faced him. "I haven't had good food like this in a long time."

"I wish I could take the credit, but Willow deserves the honor. She is a godsend for me while Anders is away."

He wanted to bestow more praise onto Willow, but her demeanor changed. Instead of being comfortable and relaxed, her back was now rigid and straight. Her luscious full lips thinned into a straight line. Tension oozed from her and he wondered if he was the cause.

Their earlier conversation came to mind. The modern times of 1860 were nothing like his own. His flirting could have meant something more to Willow, something unkind and violent.

In this time, white men often took what they wanted, including women, without fear of repercussion. Bondage often sealed the fate of non-white women. Judging by the size of the cabin and its furnishings, he doubted if his ancestors had the money to afford slaves, but looks could be deceiving.

What if Willow feared his attraction to her? The thought of forcing himself on her made him sick to his stomach. The food weighed heavy like lead in his belly. What remained on his plate lost its appeal.

He shoved the plate aside. A red haze of anger and disgust at the sadistic institution of slavery flared through him. On impulse, he turned to her and blurted out, "Are you a slave? Are they holding you against your will?"

CHAPTER THREE

"No, sir," Willow spoke quietly but firmly, "I am not a slave. I am free."

"Thank God for that!"

His dark gaze penetrated her with its intensity. In the next breath, he pushed himself off the chair and thundered from the cabin. The door rattled on its hinges, as it slammed shut after him.

"What on earth!" Eva blew heavily, fanning herself with the wave of her hand as she stared at the closed door. "What do you suppose that was all about?"

"I don't know."

Willow rose and took her plate to the metal bucket beside the back door. The leftovers from her mid-day meal dropped into the tin pail. Her automatic movements gave her mind the freedom to deliberate over Thor's actions and words.

His inquiry had been exact. Passion burned in his eyes and vibrated his voice. Did he find the tradition of human bondage deplorable and inhuman? Could he be an abolitionist, willing to fight the evils of society with conviction and dedication?

The grating of Eva's chair across the wooden floor ended Willow's silent questions. Releasing a slight laugh, she shook her head at her fanciful notions. Just because the man demanded answers from her in such an intense fashion did not by any stretch of her active imagination mean that he was a member of the anti-slavery movement. More than likely, abolition meant nothing to a man such as him at all.

"What are you doing, Miss Eva?" Willow turned away from the tin pail to find that her friend had risen and held an empty plate in her hand. "I'll take that. You rest yourself. Doc Sully said that you need plenty of rest. So just sit down in that rocking chair over there and—"

"And what? I declare, I'm so bored just sitting and rocking all day.

I wish this baby were here already. I'm tired of waiting."

A quiver of fear trembled in Eva's voice, overshadowing her impatience. Willow set the plate on the table and then gently rubbed her friend's shoulders. "You'll be just fine. The baby will be here in a little while, and all will be well."

"I get so scared sometimes. When the baby stops moving around, I think that it's gone like the last one."

"Hush now. You shouldn't think like that. Everything will happen the way it's supposed to. Now go over there and rest. I'm here to help, and I can't do that with you underfoot."

Willow folded her arms across her chest and watched while Eva followed her suggestion. Once the mother-to-be settled in the rocking chair, Willow finished her task of cleaning up the dining area. She pushed the remains of Eva's meal into the pail and then turned to Thor's plate. Most of the food had been eaten, but not all.

The man had shoveled the meal in as if he hadn't eaten in weeks instead of days. She couldn't see herself tossing his plate to the pigs, considering how hungry he had been earlier. She draped a napkin over his plate and set the plate on the stove to keep it warm.

Tending to the remains of Thor's meal made her thoughts drift to him. A few minutes had passed since he stormed from the cabin. Despite his flirtatious manner, he appeared to be a gentleman. Surely, he would not leave without saying goodbye.

Her stomach fluttered unhappily. An urgent need to see for herself that in his whirlwind of emotion he had not left overcame her. She grabbed the pail of leftovers and called out to Eva, "I'll be right back."

Willow paid little attention to the squealing pigs as she tossed their food into the trough. If her lack of conversation saddened them, she failed to notice. Shading her squinting eyes from the afternoon sun, she searched the yard for any sign of Thor. Silently, she cursed her limited eyesight and her forgetfulness. Remembering her spectacles would make life more manageable.

"Looking for me?"

Her skirt brushed against him as she whipped around. Willow's flesh tingled from the caress of his breath, so warm against her cheek. Heat flowed from his body to hers even though a few inches separated them.

Willow lifted her chin to look boldly into his eyes. His earlier wild disposition appeared subdued. Concern, confusion, and a hint of avid interest filled his intense stare.

Her heart pounded. Never had one person baffled and affected her so. This stranger's power over her senses frighteningly excited her.

"I—I was feeding the pigs."

"Liar."

He reached for the pail, his hand sliding over hers. Strong, caressing fingertips lingered on her knuckles far longer than necessary. A tingling sensation coursed through her hand and caused her to gasp in surprise. She stepped back and turned away.

The handle of the pail clattered. From the sound, she knew that he had set it on the ground. He crossed in front of her. His hand tugged on the fence railing of the pigpen, testing the wood's sturdiness. Soon after, he pulled himself up and sat on the wooden plank.

"I saw you looking around after you fed the pigs." He leaned forward, resting his forearms on his thighs. "Listen, Willow, I hope I didn't offend you at the creek. I have a habit of acting on impulse."

"You didn't scare me." His quiet admission oddly flattered her. "Your candor surprised me is all, sir."

"Please, don't do that. Don't call me Sir. Call me Thor."

Her breath lodged in her throat. "Even with freedom, there are still some liberties that are not extended to me."

An unpleasant scowl darkened his face, but he nodded in acceptance. "What about in private? You don't have to be so formal with me. It's not necessary."

"Very well." She found herself trusting him. Looking down at the tuffs of grass near her feet, she murmured, "In private."

Willow dawdled near the fence. With her task of feeding the pigs completed, she had no real reason for remaining outside. Yet, she couldn't leave.

The earlier questions about his possible involvement in the antislavery movement tormented her. She wanted desperately to get answers for them. The unknown strengthened her hesitation.

What if he were a spy? The movement demanded secrecy. She

dared not let anything slip. If he were not for the cause, many lives would be endangered. Perhaps, it would be best to leave her questions unanswered.

Words of departure rested on the tip of her tongue, then she discovered him watching her. The heat of his gaze burned into her straight through to her heart. She couldn't look away even if she wanted to.

"I'm sorry for my actions at the table. You set a fine meal, and I almost ruined it. It's just that…well, I needed to know."

"Why?"

"I don't have a real reason." He broke his stare to look at the trail. "I've been out here trying to figure out what happened and what brought me here. I keep waiting for Cal to wake me up and tell me to quit dreaming. But when I look at you and this place," he said, turning his gaze to her again, "I know this is all real. I just don't know what I'm doing here, Willow. I just don't know."

"You're Mr. Anders's relation, you said. Aren't you visiting him and Miss Eva?"

"Maybe that's it," he said quietly, "But I know they'll be fine. I can't see them as the reason for this hurdle through time."

"Hurdle through time? I don't understand."

His eyes darkened. The piercing stare returned. "I think you do. You may not realize it all at first, but deep down you know that I'm not like most of the men around here. I'm not like any of the men you know."

"Sir!"

Thor jumped from the fence. He didn't touch her, but the look on his face told her he wanted to. Roughly, he shoved his hands into his pockets.

"I didn't mean it in that way, Willow. I meant in how I act. To you, I must seem forward and brash. I'm not shy about my attraction to you despite the difference in our skin color. My time made me the man that I am, and I'm not ashamed of it. I just wish I knew why I'm here."

His statements bordered on insanity, but the truth resonated in his declaration. He simply was unlike any white man she knew.

His clothing resembled the general store's offering, but the material was finer, softer. His shoes were odd, white with a slash of red on both sides. His way with words...the intensity of his emotion... Everything about him left her dumbfounded.

"I don't know what to say to ease your mind. How did you come to be near the creek if you hadn't intended to visit Miss Eva and Mr. Anders? Isn't Mr. Anders your kin?"

"I stayed up all night, working on a watch my Pop gave me. He and my brother, Cal, went fishing and I took a walk. I sat down near the old creek and checked the pocket watch. It was still working when I fell asleep. The next thing I know, someone's humming," he answered. "Yes, Anders and Eva are family, and since I'm here now, I guess I'm supposed to visit them."

"You said that your time was different. What did you mean by that?"

"I'm from the future. The year was 1985 where I come from."

"That's over a hundred years from now! Maybe you should come back inside to finish your plate."

She spun on her heel, intent on grabbing the pail and going back inside the cabin. His ramblings were almost un-Christian.

Nineteen hundred and eighty-five?

Time travel was simply impossible! Passage from the South to the North was hazardous enough. His journey must have been harrowing for him to fabricate such tall tales. Surely, a heaping plate of collards and hot water cornbread would settle him and calm his senses.

Willow never reached the bucket. Thor grabbed her arm and whirled her around to face him. "I'm not so hungry that I'm hallucinating. I can give you proof."

She looked pointedly at his hand. After he released her, she met his gaze and said, "Proof."

"Okay. Can you read?"

He hesitated, ready if she took flight. When she didn't move, he stuck his hand into his back pocket. A flat, black pouch made of leather rested in the palm of his hand. He opened it and pulled out a small, square card.

"Look at that." He gave her the unusual object. "It's a driver's license. There's my birthday. Nineteen fifty-seven was the year I was born. See my color photo. That's my identification. I have a few credit cards in here, but they won't mean as much as my driver's license. Do you believe me now?"

"I've never seen anything like this before. I've never heard about anything like this," she murmured.

Willow held the card close to her face. Her gaze absorbed the information that the tiny license held. A thumb-sized representation of Thor's face swam before her eyes. His features were fierce and his blue eyes twinkled.

Quickly she memorized the details before handing the card back. "I suppose I believe you, but I don't understand it. If you are from the future, what are you doing here? Now?"

"I don't know!" he exclaimed in a hoarse whisper. "I think the watch brought me here. I went back to the creek to look for it, but it wasn't there."

"Well, one thing's for sure, you can't tell anyone what you've told me and that includes your kin. Talk about coming from the future would raise hackles up on some folks. They'd lock you up or maybe something worse."

He gave her a faint smile. "We'll keep it between us then. I knew I could trust you."

The warmth of his voice sent quivers up and down her spine. Her thoughts spun and her senses reeled, leaving her dizzy and confused. She needed to put some distance between him and the wanton urges he stirred inside her. Stooping down, she grabbed the pail by its handle and swiftly turned to the rear of the cabin.

"I'd best go back inside now. Your plate is warming on the stove should you get hungry again."

"Thank you, Willow."

"You're welcome…Thor." Then she hurried inside the cabin.

—⟨⟨⟩⟩—

Thor apologized to the women for his earlier abrupt departure, and then spent the day communing with nature and reacquainting himself with manual labor.

The afternoon sun was warm and its golden beams, energizing. Strangely invigorated, he searched for something to do. The pigpen needed mucking. He grabbed a shovel and went to work. Thor soon found himself working harder than he had since the football training camp of nineteen eighty-four.

The rambunctious pigs rutted and frolicked around him. His rubber-soled athletic shoes failed to provide the necessary traction. Outmatched by the mud and the playful pigs, he slipped. Loud squeals of protest echoed in the quiet air. The women rushed out of the cabin to investigate.

Thor guessed he must have looked a sight to the women. Flat on his behind in a pile of mud with pigs running back and forth in an uproar, he couldn't fault them for laughing at his predicament.

"Oh, my!" Eva pressed her hand against her mouth as her body shook with mirth. Shaking her head, she waved her hand at Thor before disappearing inside the cabin again.

Willow handled her humor less prettily. Giggles shook her hourglass frame until tears fell from her eyes. While wiping her eyes and pausing to breathe, she slowly made her way from the cabin to the pigpen.

Her attempt to hold her laughter in check and regard Thor with a solemn face lasted all of two seconds. Upon her arrival, Thor tried to stand only to trip over one of the excited pigs. He landed on his backside again.

"Be careful!" Her warning held the distinct tinkle of laughter.

"Was that for the pigs or for me?" he asked with a deep chuckle.

He rolled onto all fours and crawled to her. The fence supported his effort to stand. Air lodged in his chest. The sparkle of amusement in her black eyes and the flash of dimples did the impossible. She appeared even more beautiful than the first time he saw her. His mouth parted, but words failed to come.

In response to his unwavering gaze, her laughter faltered and then abruptly died. As rapid as an electrical storm, awareness charged the air between them. The tip of her pink tongue darted, moistening her full, sensual lips.

Her voice was hoarse and void of humor when she spoke to him. "Both."

"Excuse me?"

His senses blasted into overload. Her womanly scent, sweet like honeysuckles, filled his nostrils. His mouth watered. An ache to taste her burned inside his gut. The thrill of anticipation made him forget his earlier question.

Her olive black eyes shone with an invitation that Thor couldn't refuse. He pulled himself over the fence. His intentions must have been obvious as she stepped back and shook her head in disapproval.

"You mustn't." Desire and regret filled her tremulous whisper. Her mouth parted to say more, but the sound of pounding hooves, jangling harnesses, and a boisterous voice drowned them out.

The interruption brought a disappointing end to the special moment. Thor watched in silence as Willow moved away to pat the pair of horses and greet the driver of the wagon with a smile. A surge of jealousy soared through him as her lips curved in genuine affection. Through narrowed eyes, Thor glared at the visitor as he climbed down from the wagon.

The man was about twenty years older than Thor. Chestnut brown hair with flashes of silver peaked from underneath his wide-brimmed hat and fell to the top collar of his coat. Lines etched from the corner of his eyes and Thor couldn't be sure if they were from humor or worry. Although the sun browned his face, the man was white, and he returned Willow's greeting with a smile.

"I believe you left something this morning." The stranger pulled a pair of glasses from his pocket and handed them to her. "I'm surprised you were able to find your way without them."

"Thank you, Reverend." She hesitated and glanced at Thor before sliding the glasses on. "I hadn't realized I'd left them until I had come too far to go back. You didn't have to bring them. I'll be home tonight."

He shook his head. "Not tonight. I saw Anders in town just a while ago. He'll be staying over. Yates told him he'd get his full pay if he finishes adding on the extra room before the week is over. Anders asked me if you could tend to Miss Eva until he comes home. I told him I was sure you could, but of course, the choice is yours."

"Of course, I wouldn't want Miss Eva to be here alone."

"I thought you'd say that." The man grabbed a parcel from the rear of the wagon and gave it to her. "Olivia packed some of your things just in case your stay is longer than one night. She included your lessons, and she was most particular about those sonnets. I'd get to studying if I were you." He turned his attention to Thor, looking at him as if he just noticed the younger man. "Now who might you be? You have the look of Magnusen. I reckon you must be kin."

"Reverend Brown, this is Mr. Thor Magnusen," Willow introduced in a rush.

Brown's eyebrow twitched, and he nodded his head once. "Thank you, Miss Elkridge. I 'spect he can tell me the rest. You'd best let Miss Eva know that her Anders won't be with her tonight. Tell her I'll bring the supplies in directly."

"Yes, sir." Her wide skirt whistled as she turned away and left the men alone.

Thor's gaze followed her until she was inside the cabin and then he looked at the Reverend. Judging from Willow's behavior, the man was decent enough, but that didn't quiet his annoyance at their casual relationship. What was the man to her? Why did they share the same home?

Thor edged closer to the man and his wagon. With his arms folded across his chest, he strained to maintain an even disposition while jealousy gushed inside his veins.

"Reverend Mitchell Brown." The older man extended his hand with the introduction. "I suppose I'm pleased to meet you, Thor Magnusen, but by the looks of you, I haven't decided, yet. Anders didn't mention to me that he was expecting his kinfolk to visit."

"It was a spur of the moment decision," Thor answered him after shaking the man's hand.

"Oh, I see. Well, come on," he invited with the wave of his hand, "help me unload the wagon. We can get acquainted while performing a good deed for our fellow man."

Thor sauntered to the rear of the wagon. He had no problems with helping around his ancestors' home. He would do whatever he could for however long he was there. Until he found that damn watch…

A cool chill swept through him at that thought. How long would he be there? Back in time with his family was strange enough, but what if he never found the timepiece? Hell, what if nothing happened when he found it?

"Something wrong?" Brown rested his large hand firmly on Thor's shoulder. "You're looking peaked around the edges."

Thor pushed his questions aside for later. He offered the older man a thin-lipped smile and shrugged. "Nothing wrong, sir."

"Good. Let's get to work then."

Lumber filled the wagon bed and a medium-sized crate squeezed against the side. The crate held supplies for the home. At a glance, Thor read the labels for wheat flour, sugar, cornmeal, and coffee. Other items rattled and sighed as he lifted the crate from the wagon's floor and headed for the cabin. Before he could take more than a few steps, the Reverend swiftly relieved him of the wooden box.

"I'll take this inside. You can get started on the planks."

The older man crossed the yard and moved toward the cabin. Irritation bristled inside of Thor at the man's manner. Of course, the good Reverend wanted Thor to start with the heavy work while he rested inside with the ladies and ate a plateful of Willow's fine cooking.

"Figures," he mumbled, his voice heavy with sarcasm.

Thor rolled up his sleeves and went to work. Removing lumber from a wagon proved to be easier than cleaning out a pigpen and not as smelly. The repetitious movement even calmed his racing thoughts. Perspiration dampened his brow. The strenuous activity gave him the peace of mind to think things through rationally. As he piled the wood in front of the pigpen, he thought back to his nap and the events that occurred right before and right after it.

He remembered staying awake all night to think about his life. Football was out and something had to replace it. The something hadn't been revealed to him, but when morning came, he felt a renewed sense of purpose. No, his life wasn't completely over and would get back on track again.

After declining Cal's invitation to go fishing, he took a short walk to the creek and the next thing he recalled was the sound of Willow's voice, floating to him and waking him from his nap.

They walked to the cabin. Did he have the watch then? He must have left it near the creek, but he searched that area, including the trail from the creek to the cabin. Nothing! Where was the watch? Had it vanished?

"Dammit!" The curse fell from his lips just as he tossed a plank onto the ground.

"What did that piece of wood do to cause you to curse it?"

Reverend Brown's voice came just behind him. He turned to find the man looking at him with a thoughtful expression on his face. Intelligent dark green eyes narrowed, as a thin layer of tension coated the air with the sentiment of suspicion rising up strongly between the two men.

Thor rubbed a hand over his injured shoulder. "Nothing much at all, Reverend."

"See to it that you're careful," Brown advised. "Anders paid a good deal of money for that wood. He wouldn't appreciate his kin treating it with such disregard."

"I'm unloading this carefully enough, considering I've done over half of it alone."

Brown laughed at that. "Well, if you're all tuckered out, sit down a spell. I can handle the rest."

"I've got it," Thor growled.

The two men formed a system as they worked side by side. Reverend Brown handed a plank to Thor, and Thor set it on the ground. Their sweat soaked shirts clung to their backs. After minutes of working in silence, Brown suggested a brief break. Both men quickly discarded the wet garments, hanging them on fence poles before going back to work.

"You passing through or planning to stay a spell?"

"I haven't decided yet." Thor glanced at the older man as he grabbed more lumber. He suspected that Brown didn't trust him and figured that the man had just begun his interrogation. "Why?"

"I'm not one to beat around the bush, Mr. Thor Magnusen. I saw how you were looking at Willow, and I won't allow it."

Thor refused the last piece of wood and drew in a ragged breath. He snarled in contempt, "You planning to keep her all to yourself. Is that it?"

Sudden anger blazed in Brown's eyes. "I am a man of God, Mr. Magnusen, and Willow is like a daughter to me. My wife and I took her in when she was just barely eight years old. I've raised her like she's my own, and I'll be damned if you mistreat her!"

"I wouldn't!" Thor growled back and then in a softer voice, added, "I respect Willow, and I genuinely like her."

Surprise doused the flames of anger in the reverend's eyes. He stared at Thor with open curiosity. "I think you may mean that."

"I do," he quickly responded. "I—I... well, I'm not from around here, and I view things differently than most. I do not intend to hurt her in any way, and I do honestly respect her. I think she's a kind, gentle woman."

"She is also a determined young woman with a loving heart. Remember that and you won't have any trouble from me."

"That'd be hard to forget." Thor took the last piece of lumber from the Reverend and set it on top of the rest. "There's a lot of wood here. What is Anders planning on doing with it?"

"He's adding another room to the cabin." Reverend Brown grabbed their shirts from the poles. He tossed Thor's to him and then pulled on his own. "Come 'round this way. I'll show you."

They walked to the west side of the cabin. Reverend Brown gestured with his hands while he spoke. "He's building a bedroom or two over here. With the baby coming, he's thinking about planting his roots for a firm foundation."

The rooms would be right where Thor remembered them. Awe filled him at seeing the cabin in such a young state. He never realized just how much he took for granted. He frowned.

"What's wrong? You think you could do it better?"

"No, I was thinking about something else. Anders has some fine ideas for this place. I'd be honored to help him in any way I can."

"If I know him, he'll take you up on it." Brown reached inside the pocket of his shirt and pulled out a corncob pipe. "Want a smoke?"

Thor declined with a quick shake of his head.

"I shouldn't, but I like the smell." Brown stuffed the pipe with tobacco and raised it to his lips. He scratched a match against the side of the cabin to light his pipe. After inhaling deeply, he smiled. "Where are you from? You don't sound like a Yankee, but you think like one in some respects."

Thor thought it best not to lie, but to fudge a little around the edges. "I'm from Georgia; down by Atlanta."

"Anders never mentioned having family down that way, and I've known him since he and Eva came into these mountains about two years ago now. I think he might have mentioned some family, don't you?"

Thor lifted his shoulders in an offhand manner. "Maybe, maybe not…our family is further apart than most."

"You don't say."

Thor shrugged again and looked at the woods around them. The talk of family made him lonesome. Somewhere in time, his father and his brother were fishing. Would he return before they missed him? Would he ever find his way home? They irritated the hell out of him, but they were family. He loved them. Sadness filled him at the possibility of never seeing them again. He tried to swallow his despair and directed his gaze at Reverend Brown.

"Yeah, it happens. Distance can separate a family in more ways than one."

"I reckon it can," the Reverend murmured. He took a whiff of his pipe. "Considering your views on things, I can see how your family would have parted ways. Are you active in the movement?"

Thor hesitated, regarding the older man closely. There was no malice in Brown's disposition, but the hint of suspicion had returned in full force. He tried to read between the lines but wasn't sure if he was doing a good job. Thor recalled only a handful of movements in the late nineteenth century. Pro- and anti-secession were a couple, while pro and anti-slavery were two more. He decided his best bet would be to ask for clarification. "Which one?"

"Miss Willow Elkridge is a woman of color, yet you say that you respect her. I believe that you mean it."

"I do."

"Do your beliefs extend to those in bondage, or just to beautiful young women who please your fancy?"

Thor nodded in response and in understanding. His eyes narrowed as he gave the reverend a long, hard look. The questions hadn't been asked out of idle boredom, and now Thor was curious. After a quick glance around the woods, he moved closer to Brown and quietly asked, "Are you an abolitionist, Reverend, or are you more than that?"

Reverend Brown walked around the wagon. Thor followed him. When Brown reached the wagon, he grabbed the reins and climbed onto the seat. Looking down, he smiled.

"I think you already know the answer. I had my doubts about you at first, but my eyes are opening. The good Lord sent you this way for a reason. If you're looking for answers, come by my place tomorrow. Willow will show you the way. Giddy-up!"

The man, his horses and wagon disappeared into the woods with Thor staring after them. A chill of anticipation swept through his body.

Tomorrow.

CHAPTER FOUR

Willow set the lit lantern on the floor of the porch and placed her book of sonnets, notepad, and pencil beside it. Careful of the lamp, she padded in sock-covered feet to the porch's edge. Closing her eyes, she inhaled the night. This was her favorite time. Dark and quiet, the world slept while nature came to life.

A blanket of stars glittered in the sky, illuminating the forest's antsy critters. A distant owl hooted to his friends, and a wolf called to its pack. In the underbrush, crickets chirped their songs, eagerly adding to the night's melody. Even the pigs, a few yards away, joined in. When the sounds came together so beautifully, the velvety warmth of tranquility wrapped around Willow, almost making her forget the world around her and the lack of peace it held.

Her mouth twisted into a wry smile. Even if she wanted to, she could not forget. Turmoil and danger were her constant companions. Her life in the small community a few miles north of Canton was fairly safe, but hazardous pitfalls loomed outside the boundaries.

The cloak of night protected her and the small number of people the Browns allowed her to assist on their road to freedom, while the light of day presented the chance of exposure and punishment. Her thoughts were constantly haunted with longing for the day when all of God's people would be free.

A sudden tingling sensation crept over her. Pulling her shawl close around her shoulders, she opened her eyes to find Thor watching her. Stepping back, her lips parted in surprise.

"I thought you were settled in the barn. Miss Eva has another quilt if you need one."

"Wait," he called when she turned to open the door. "I don't need extra cover. It's warm enough."

She tilted her head in a nod. Her gaze wandered over him from head to toe before she faced his piercing stare. His clothing seemed to mold to his flesh. Awareness of his masculinity, the breadth of his chest, the corded muscles in his neck and the thickness of his thighs made her mouth go dry. Her pulse raced, and she swallowed hard to ease the dryness of her throat.

"Mr. Anders's pants and shirt were a perfect fit. Are the shoes comfortable?"

"Everything's fine." He took a step toward her as he pointed at the steps. "May I join you? I see you have your studies; I don't want to disturb you."

"No, please."

She inhaled deeply to calm her racing heart, but the opposite happened. His woodsy scent filled her senses and nearly blinded her to everything else. She felt lightheaded, hot, and out of sorts. None of that warranted sending him away.

"You're not disturbing me."

She claimed the space beside the lantern and her materials. Trying desperately to ignore him and her frightening reaction to him, her fingers fumbled with the book while she busied herself.

He lowered himself to the bottom step. Moonlight cast a shimmering glow over his face. Dim shadows hid the rest of him. He spoke to her in a deep, husky whisper. "What are you studying?"

"I'm reading the sonnets by Mr. William Shakespeare."

"Oh, really?" A curious smile appeared on his face. "I read a few of his plays in college. I've even seen a couple of them performed."

"Do tell!" Excitement and wonder coursed through her. She leaned toward him without realizing it. "Miss Olivia said that she saw the like up in Boston. She said there was a stage and an orchestra played in the pit below, and the costumes were beautiful." She sighed wistfully. "And at the end, the audience stood up and clapped for at least five minutes. It sounded wonderful. Did you enjoy it?"

A hint of sadness flashed in his eyes. His mouth tightened slightly, and he shook his head. "Not as much as I should have. Next time, I'll be more attentive." He looked away from her for a moment toward the sky. He took a deep breath and sighed. "Tonight is nice, isn't it?"

His behavior baffled her. He seemed upset, but Willow wasn't sure what caused it. Had her words upset him?

"Very. No clouds in the sky to hide the stars. I love nights like this." She spoke softly, hoping to ease the tension between them.

"So, do I." Thor leveled his gaze on her and gave her a smile that warmed her down to her toes. He pointed at her book, and she handed it to him. As he thumbed through the pages, he asked, "Do you have a favorite?"

"I like Sonnet Twenty-seven," she said with a shy smile.

He turned the pages until he found it. Then he handed the book to her. "Would you read it to me?" When she hesitated, he added, "Please."

"Weary with toil, I haste me to my bed..." She read the words slowly at first, nervous at reading aloud for a stranger. As she reached the middle of the poem, her voice became stronger and her shyness faded. Glancing at his reaction, she saw that the words touched him, and when she came to the sonnet's end, the remainder of her timidity disappeared altogether. "'...For thee, and for myself, no quiet find.'"

"I liked it. Your presentation was impeccable."

Her face grew hot at his bold compliment. "Thank you."

"You're welcome. I suppose I have taken enough of your time." He moved to rise but stopped. "What is it? Is something wrong?"

"I just...well, you weren't fooling with me about being from the future, were you?"

He stood and moved up the steps to sit beside her. His expression darkened with heartfelt intensity. "No, Willow, I was telling you the truth. I'm not from this time."

"I didn't think so. You were polite, even if you were a might brash." She laughed softly and then lowered her head, observing him through lowered lashes. "You truly treated me like a woman. I thought you were making fun at first, but then I could see that it was your way."

His fingers brushed gently against her cheeks then slid underneath her chin. With tenderness, he tilted her head so that their eyes met. "You *are* a woman. I treat *all* women with respect, Willow. I would never make fun of you."

He pulled his hand away. The loss of his touch created an immediate void, leaving her empty and cold. "Is the future so different? Is that why you can say those kinds of things to me?"

Dots of scarlet stained his tan cheeks. A faint smile tugged his mouth, and then his expression became solemn. "The future is a different place in some ways and still the same in others."

"How?" She leaned toward him. "Please, tell me that things will be better than this."

"Life will be better. Slavery will end, but not before the death of thousands."

"Oh, my!" she gasped, a hand covering her mouth. "When will this happen?"

A frown darkened his brow. A muscle flicked rapidly at his jaw. "I'm not sure if I should say. I saw a movie this summer with my brother. A kid went back in time and wrecked havoc on his parents' lives. He did and said some things he shouldn't have. It was just a movie, a fantasy really, but a lot of it made sense. There's the time space continuum to think about."

She listened closely, but his words left her confused. Her voice quivered with bafflement. "I don't understand; a movie? What is a time space continuum?"

He took in a deep breath. "I'm sorry about that. I was talking about a movie I saw and…you have no idea what I'm saying. You don't know what a movie is, and as much as I'd love to explain it, I probably shouldn't. I wish I could, but I have to be careful." His knuckles grazed her cheek. "What if something changes because of what I've said to you or what I've done?"

"Something has already changed," she whispered. His gentle touch filled her with longing. She reached out and clutched his hands. "I feel like I've changed. I feel things I've never felt before."

He looked down at their hands, turning them until their fingers entwined. "You're not afraid of me, are you?"

"No."

He tilted his head to look at her. "I'm afraid of you," he whispered hoarsely.

"Of me? Why?"

He shook his head and refused to answer. "I don't know why I'm here, and until I do, I have to be careful." He pulled his fingers free and raised her hand to his mouth. His lips brushed against her knuckles, and then he lowered her hand to her lap. "Goodnight, Willow."

"Goodnight, Thor," she whispered to his retreating back.

———❦———

The rhythmic pounding of the hammer rattled the windows. Willow jumped at each heavy thud. A sleepless night set her nerves on edge, and the constant noise only added to her irritation. She removed her spectacles to rub her tired eyes.

Ignorant of Willow's plight, Eva greeted the morning with happiness and looked out the window with the curiosity of a child. Holding the curtain aside with one hand, she beckoned to Willow with the other. "Come look. Do you suppose Thor has any idea what he's doing?"

Willow pushed her eyeglasses back on and joined Eva at the window. "I suppose he does," she mumbled, hungrily drinking in the sight of him.

Thor's sandy brown hair curled and clung against his forehead. The muscles in his arm bunched and relaxed with his movements. His hand was steady and sure with each strike of the hammer onto the nail. His concentration focused intently on his task, and she remembered how he had focused on her the night before.

For a moment, she envied his project for having his complete attention. Instant shame washed over. *Imagine being jealous over wood, a hammer and nails!* Abruptly, she turned from the window and began cleaning up the breakfast dishes.

"You're in a mood this morning." Eva closed the curtain to look at Willow. She pressed her hand against the small of her back and wobbled to the table. "I imagine you're tired of having to clean up after me. I can finish. I never expected you to do so much."

"No, Miss Eva. I'm not upset about doing this. I don't mind. Besides, you'll have plenty enough to do when that baby arrives. Cooking a few meals and washing some dishes don't really compare."

"I'm so happy that Anders changed his mind about moving away." Eva took her sewing box and moved to the rocking chair near the fireplace. "I couldn't imagine having the baby without you and Miss Olivia around to help me."

Willow paused in wiping off the table to smile at Eva. "We're happy that you stayed, too. Reverend Brown was afraid that he'd have to talk some sense into Mr. Anders otherwise."

"No!" Eva exclaimed with a laugh. "We're all fortunate that never took place. I declare, in some instances, Anders holds dear to every word the Reverend says, but in others, he closes his ears. He wouldn't have taken kindly to being told what to do. He'll listen to Reverend Brown in matters of religion and the good Lord, but Anders is much too stubborn to allow anyone to dictate our lives. It's a good thing the good Lord blessed us with another chance."

Willow nodded in agreement. "The reverend says He moves in mysterious ways. It was for you to stay."

"I always felt it was." Eva riffled through her sewing box until she found the piece she wanted to work on. A shift small enough for a baby, but large enough to see the child through several growth spurts. As she threaded her needle, she said, "He will move for you, too."

"Who will?" Willow asked. Now that she was done with cleaning the dishes, she moved toward the window again. The hammering tapered off, and she wondered what Thor was doing. If he was looking for his pocket watch again, hoping that it would take him back to his time and his world.

"The Lord will. He's given me a family. He will do the same for you."

Willow sighed and turned away from the window. "Now, Miss Eva…"

"Don't 'Miss Eva' me," the other woman scolded. "You're a young woman and you're far too pretty to hide away with the Browns for the rest of your life. One of these days one of those freed men will come through these backwoods and sweep you out of here."

"A free man of color," Willow murmured. She tried to visualize it, but the only face that came to mind belonged to Thor. While amalgamation was known, it certainly was not encouraged. She released another deep sigh and frowned. The complications of life never ceased to diminish. Here it was the first time she ever envisioned marriage and a man of her own, and it was someone she wasn't free to have. Even in love, freedom was elusive.

"Yes, a nice handsome man," Eva continued on, carried away by her thoughts. "Maybe he'll be an educated man, having gone to that college in Ohio."

"At Oberlin." Willow clarified for her.

"Yes, Oberlin. Perhaps, he'd be a man of the cloth like the reverend. I know he'd give his blessing to a union such as that." Eva tossed her sewing down onto her lap when Willow didn't respond. "Willow! I know you think about it. Every woman does. A handsome man, big and strong like my Anders, who will love you and cherish you as long as you both shall live. Surely, you want that, too."

Willow swallowed hard and lowered her eyes to study her clenched hands. "I've never thought about it."

"I think you'll have pretty babies, and our children can play together."

"That would be nice," Willow said quietly.

The possibilities Eva presented were too painful for Willow to consider. They awakened desires she tried hard to ignore. The nighttime discussion with Thor left her longing, and Eva's words filled her with despair. She couldn't listen to her friend's wishes and predictions for a moment longer.

Willow turned her back to Eva and grabbed the pail at the back door. "I think I hear the pigs calling. I'd best feed them before they jump out of the pigpen. I'll return directly."

"Thank you. While you're out there, could you ask Thor to come inside for a moment?"

Willow dipped her head in a slight nod and with pail in hand, slipped out the back door. She made quick work of tossing the leftovers into the trough.

Since the pounding stopped, she had no idea where Thor wandered off. The area around the cabin presented a number of hiding places, and although he seemed to know his way around, the idea of him going off alone bothered her. Leaving the empty bucket at the rear of the cabin, she went in search of him.

"Thor!" she called out, subconsciously using his first name without hesitation. It simply rolled off her tongue as if it belonged there. She pushed through the brush on the west side of the house and called again, "Thor!"

From out of nowhere, a hand shot out and clamped over her mouth, silencing her. Her mind floundered as icy, cold fear left her frozen in shock and alarm.

—◦◦◦—

Thor's hold on Willow was solid. She squirmed and gave him a good elbow to his ribs until he whispered against her ear, "It's me!"

The words obviously did little to reassure her. She wiggled again and landed another jab to his midsection. Afraid that she'd hurt herself, he pulled her behind a large oak and whipped her around to face him. He braced his hands against the tree trunk to box her in.

It took a moment for recognition to set in. When it did, her black eyes brimmed with hurt and accusation. The display of emotions plagued his heart. *Didn't she know she could trust him?*

"I'm sorry I scared you," he whispered, "but you don't have to be afraid of me."

"Why did you grab me?" Her eyes watched him and suspicion radiated from her.

"Ssh." He pressed a finger to his mouth for emphasis. "I thought I heard something. With you calling for me, I thought I'd lose them."

The tension slowly evaporated, and she exhaled. Her tone matched his whisper. "What did you hear? Was it a wolf? Mr. Anders ran off a pack months ago. He'd be fit to be tied if he learns they came back."

Thor shook his head. He gestured with his hand for them to squat. Once the bushes hid them, he answered her. "Not wolves. I heard voices. I couldn't make out what they were saying. When I came out here, everything got quiet."

"Did you see anybody?"

"I think I saw a glimpse of a man, but I'm not sure. You stay here. I'll go look."

He moved to stand, but she stopped him by taking his hand. A frown marred her forehead. "Let me."

"You shouldn't go out alone. We don't know who's out there. I'll go."

"I live here, Thor. I go back and forth in these woods all the time. I'm safer here than I'd be anywhere else in these United States! I'll go first. If I need help, I'll call you."

He wanted to disagree, but the stubborn set of her jaw told him to prepare for a serious battle of wills. Besides, he followed the voices out of curiosity, not danger. As long as he was close enough to see her, he could compromise. "Okay. You can go first."

"Thank you." Annoyance flashed in her eyes, belying the words of gratitude.

Thor bit back a smile. The thinly disguised sarcasm tickled him. He admired her spunk. Bowing slightly, he gestured for her to proceed. She rose and moved through the weeds and bushes. At a considerable distance, he followed.

A crow cackled as it sailed overhead. A frog croaked in reply. Even the whistle of a whippoorwill joined in the chorus. Thor heard it all, but the noises came from a distance. His gaze locked on Willow, as he made sure no harm came to her.

She moved gracefully through the shrubs. Her hands brushed aside weeds while her feet stepped over rocks and logs. The sight of her slight body, moving so carefully and sure, sent urges through Thor. He wanted to protect her, yet he enjoyed her independence. Holding her in his arms even for a brief moment gave him a glimpse of Heaven. The desire to embrace her properly ripped through his insides and made coherent thought nearly impossible.

As he followed her trail, he wondered about her odd effect on him. Thor wasn't a novice, and he certainly couldn't be classified as a monk. With his looks and position on the football team, he never had to look for female companionship. Girls flocked to him, but none stirred him; not deeply.

After a few weeks of passionate exchanges, the novelty wore off.

Football beckoned him and he heeded its call. The pattern began in high school and didn't change until the tackle took his dreams away. In that one game, Thor lost the ability to play on the field and the desire to play off it.

Until now.

Willow did things to him. Her plight, in the unfriendly 1860s America, worried him. He was scared for her. Blacks were making progress in 1985. *The Cosby Show* was number one on television, and Thurgood Marshall sat on the Supreme Court bench. There was also a female talk show host who wasn't doing too shabby either.

1860 presented a different story. The Fugitive Slave Act of eighteen fifty made all people of color easy pickings for bounty hunters, marshals, and a number of jerks wanting to make a quick buck. He remembered reading about that from his college American History class. For all he and Willow knew, she could be walking into a trap. *What if a bounty hunter was luring them into the woods to imprison her?*

Frightening images of Willow bound in chains and whipped until her flesh was wet with blood flashed before his eyes. Her beautiful olive black eyes lifeless, her sense of humor and kind spirit stripped from her. His fear turned to anger and his temper flared. He quickly looked around for a weapon to protect her. Spotting a fallen branch to his right, he bent to retrieve it. The whippoorwill whistled again and another replied.

Listening, Thor held himself still. He was raised in these woods and participated in plenty hunting trips. He knew the difference between human whistles and those from birds. The similarity was close, but humans made those calls.

His grip on the branch tightened, and he rose to his full height. Through narrowed eyes, he watched Willow's every move and those of the surrounding woods. He moved quietly. His hearing tuned to the woods. The natural sounds diminished as Willow's soft whisper carried back to him.

"It's okay to come out. Come on. You're safe."

A deeper masculine whisper replied, "What about that young massa? We saw him with you."

"He won't hurt you," Willow replied. "He's with me." Without turning, she beckoned with her hand for Thor to come to her. "Thor, let them see you."

Thor moved briskly at her call. His hold on the branch loosened, but he didn't think to drop it. He was too busy looking at the trio who surrounded Willow.

A young man, probably in his mid-teens, and a girl and a boy who were a few years younger stared with large brown eyes at Willow. Their clothing was little more than rags, and none of them had extra luggage with them.

Their faces were round even though their cheeks were sunken. The boys' skin was bronze while the girl's complexion was darker like chocolate. The resemblance between the three was startling and left little doubt they were siblings.

As he reached them, three pairs of eyes watched him and Willow with thinly disguised fear and wariness. On instinct, Thor moved to her side and placed a protective hand at the small of her back. She stiffened at his initial contact and then relaxed, pressing lightly against his palm.

"I won't hurt you," he reassured the trio quietly.

"He's not a patroller," Willow quickly added when the children remained silent.

"Is he a station massa?" the young girl asked. The biggest boy gave her a hard look, and she moved behind him.

Willow shook her head. "He's not, but I know one. I can get you to him. How did you find these woods? This path is off the track. Did you have a shepherd?"

The oldest boy nodded, his brown-eyed gaze boring into Willow. "Our shepherd told us to go on ahead. He told us to follow the Drinking Gourd."

"The Big Dipper?" Thor slowly deciphered the coded conversation.

"Yes," Willow answered him. "Why did your shepherd tell you to go without him? Patrollers rarely come up this far, but it has happened. He shouldn't have left you alone."

"He had no choice, miss," the boy said. "A few nights ago, the other runaway with us got scared and said he was going back. The shepherd didn't trust him, so he went after him. He told us to keep going, and we'd see the light, and sho'nuff we did! We saw the lantern on the porch and knew we was on the right track."

"The lantern?" Willow repeated softly.

Thor glanced at her. A worried frown creased her brow. "What's wrong?" he asked her.

She ignored his question and kept her focus on the children. "When was the last time you ate?"

"About two nights ago."

She inhaled sharply and nodded. "It's another two miles to the station. Can you make it?"

"Miss, we can do whatever we needs to do to make it to the Promised Land. We come from down by Macon and don't have no plans for stopping until we get to Canaan."

She gave the boy a tender smile. "I understand. Follow me."

"Willow." Thor's hand wrapped around her elbow to stop her from leading the group away. "Where are you going? You don't have to take them anywhere when there's food inside. Let's go back to the cabin."

Her eyes grew large as she vehemently shook her head. "I'm forwarding them to Reverend Brown's place. They can't eat at your kin's cabin."

"What?" He almost yelped in surprise. "Why not? It's right here. You heard him. They haven't eaten for two days. They may be dehydrated, too. We can feed them here, and then take them to the reverend."

"They can't eat here! Please, Thor. Go back to the cabin and watch out for Miss Eva. I won't be gone long. Tell her I'll come back as soon as I can—"

"Why can't they eat here?" He refused to release her even as she tried to twist free.

Her mouth tightened. Through stiff lips, she replied, "Mr. Anders won't allow it, and I won't ask Miss Eva. She'd say yes, I'm sure of it, but it wouldn't be right of me to ask. Now, please, let go."

Thor flinched as if she struck him. *My great-great-grandfather won't allow her to feed three hungry kids?* What kind of man was he? The stories he learned at his Gramps' knee led him to believe that Magnusen men were honorable, compassionate, hard-working men. If so, where did Anders fit in? He couldn't have been included in the tales Thor's grandfather once told.

Reluctantly, he dropped his hand from her elbow and nodded. "I understand. Tell me the way, and I'll take them to the reverend's."

"I can't let you do that. This is not play, Thor. If a patroller catches you with them…"

"You said they rarely come this deep into the forest," he reminded her when her voice trailed off. "Besides, it's less dangerous for me than you. I could lie. You couldn't."

"But you don't know these woods—"

"I grew up here," he said softly. "I can find it. Just tell me where his place is and if there are some special words I should use. I'll get them there safely, Willow. I promise."

"Miss Eva wanted to speak with you," she attempted one final protest.

Her stalling tactics irritated him, but he couldn't help the smile that spread across his face. She was a beauty when her hackles were raised. "Eva can wait. They can't."

"But what should I tell her?"

"Tell her you couldn't find me. That's why you were gone for so long. You looked for me and gave up. When I come back, I'll tell her that I went for a walk and got lost."

A look of alarm streaked across her face. "What if you do get lost?"

"I won't." One hand lightly cupped her cheek. His voice dropped to a low whisper meant for her ears only. "I won't get lost. I'll get them to the station master safe and sound, and I'll return before nightfall. You'll see me tonight because I'm not about to miss one of Mr. William Shakespeare's sonnets as read by Miss Willow Elkridge."

A soft sigh passed from her lips and the dewy-eyed expression on her face was almost Thor's undoing. To his relief, she fought for control over the attraction they shared and won. After taking a deep breath, she gave him directions to the Brown farm. With his wary charges at his heel, Thor became a shepherd. He looked over his shoulder once to wave at Willow before leading the trio of runaways into the woods.

A wry chuckle rumbled from his chest as realization set in. A former quarterback for the Atlanta Falcons was now a conductor for the Underground Railroad. If only his Pop and Cal could see him now.

CHAPTER FIVE

The trail to Reverend Brown's place reminded Thor of the path to his father's favorite fishing hole. Of course, a century brought some changes to the backwoods hideaway, but not many. Sugar maples with their low branches populated the way just as he remembered, except these weren't as tall as the ones he knew. Dark green leaves, with a hint of red and gold along the edges, tapped Thor's shoulder as he walked under the trees. Fanning the foliage aside with a wave of his hand, he glanced over his shoulder at his solemn charges.

The two younger children regarded him behind eyes bright with unrestrained curiosity while the oldest boy kept his face void of expression. Offering the trio a friendly smile, Thor's footsteps slowed until he walked beside the children. "How long have you been on the track?"

"A while, sir," the oldest answered.

"You'll reach your Promised Land soon. What are your names? Y'all can call me Thor."

Regret hit him as soon as the words left his mouth. The first meeting with Willow came to mind. At first, her refusal to call him by his first name seemed coy. In hindsight, he understood her caution. In his desire to put the children at ease, he probably did the opposite. He opened his mouth to rescind the offer, but how was beyond his grasp. Once it was out there, he couldn't very well take it back without looking like a total jerk.

The boy's brows furrowed together. Skepticism haunted his eyes, as if he didn't trust Thor's introduction. The silence lingered for several seconds before he seemed to accept that he could trust Thor at his word. "I'm Nat. This is my brother, Clay." He pointed to the boy at his right and then at the girl to his left. "Charity's our sister."

"Pleased to meet you." Thor greeted them all with a cordial smile. "How old are you? You seem rather young to be out here. Couldn't your parents make the journey with you?"

"I think I'm fifteen or maybe sixteen years. They're twelve," Nat responded, answering again for his siblings. "Our Papa was sold and our Mama. . ."

Thor's breath caught in his throat as Nat's voice faltered. The boy's face twisted into a frozen mask of heart-wrenching pain. Thor didn't have to ask to know that the children's mother was dead, and he didn't want to guess how it happened.

He reached out his hand to offer comfort, but Nat flinched. Thor dropped his hand and shoved it into his pocket. Words of sympathy escaped him, and he didn't know what to say. Having lost his mother at the young age of five, he could guess how the children felt. Words didn't fill the void the loss of a mother created.

Charity's hoarse whisper ended the silence. "Mama cried and cried when they took Papa away." She took Nat's hand and peered across him to look at Thor. Her brown eyes watered and marked her sadness at the memory.

Clay closed in on Nat and looked up at Thor. Unshed tears glistened in his eyes, but none fell. In low, husky tones, he added the rest. "Massa Henry didn't like how Mama was carryin' on so he told her to hush up. When she didn't, the overseer took her to the whuppin' tree. Overseer Charlie whipped her 'til he got tired, and then they cut her down from the tree. She didn't make it through the night."

Thor shuddered at the torture their mother had endured. Looking down at the child who walked beside him, he admired Clay's ability to recount the events of his mother's death without shedding tears. If the circumstances were reversed, he doubted if he could have done the same. Hell, he could barely recall a memory of her now without choking up.

Anguish lodged in his throat. No one had the right to treat another with such cruel indifference. Unable to stop himself, his hand pulled free from his pocket and closed warmly over Clay's thin shoulder. "I am terribly sorry for what happened to your mother. I wish there was something I could do."

"You are, sir," Clay said, craning his neck to gaze at Thor. A thin-lipped smile made the boy looked far older than his twelve years, and then it disappeared altogether. He lowered his eyes and directed his attention away from Thor.

Before he looked away, Thor read the confusion and the grief etched in Clay's eyes, and it pained him. Guiding them to Reverend Brown's station wasn't enough. The knowledge that slavery would end did little to quell his growing outrage. Abraham Lincoln wouldn't pass the Emancipation Proclamation freeing slaves in the seceded states for another three years, making no mention of the slaves in the border states. Slavery wouldn't officially come to an end for at least another five years.

Bile lodged in his throat at the thought of the number of people who'd suffer the same as these children's mother, if not worse, during that time. The need to do more pulsed wildly in his veins, but he was at a loss. What could he do? Could he slip onto plantations and lead more slaves to freedom? Was it feasible? Reverend Brown said he'd find answers at his place, and now he was leading these children there. Had the reverend known he'd feel this way? Maybe he traveled back in time to lead these children to freedom and maybe others, too.

The sudden snap of a twig jerked Thor and his charges to attention. Stark fear glittered in the three pairs of eyes that cut to Thor. His stomach clenched, and he forced himself to focus. They needed him to keep a clear head. Animal or man could have made that noise. Either way, Thor would handle it. The reverend's place couldn't be more than a mile away. There was no way he'd get them that close to the refuge to be led astray. *Dammit! I'll see them all the way.*

—◦∞◦—

Leaving the lantern on the porch was a grievous mistake, Willow thought. Her frantic pacing wore a path in front of the fireplace. *I should have been more careful!* A lantern on the porch was a clear signal to runaway slaves that the building was a safe haven for them. If Mr. Anders had been at the cabin instead of Thor, she would have been in a world of trouble.

My distractions put those children at risk! She must not lose sight of what's important. She had to keep her mind clear of diversions.

"Really, Willow, it was a simple mistake!" Eva said. "No harm was done. Mind you, I still cannot understand why you didn't invite them here. We have plenty."

"Mr. Anders wouldn't have been pleased, and I couldn't ask you—"

"You should have asked me!" Eva clutched the arms of the rocking chair and pushed herself into a standing position. She crossed the room until she stood in front of Willow. Reaching out, she took Willow's hands and squeezed. "You fret far too much. Anders isn't here, and he would never have known those children were fed in this cabin. He's not a heartless man, Willow. He's just cautious. He wouldn't have minded those children having a plate of greens."

Willow looked at their joined hands. Their friendship was special, but there were things that Eva just didn't understand. Anders wanted no part of the Underground Railroad. Nor would he willingly participate in the abolition movement. He had told the reverend in no uncertain terms neither he nor Eva would become involved. Reverend Brown had forwarded the information along to her.

She knew what Eva said was true. Anders had a good heart. He doted on Eva as if she hung the sun, the moon, and the stars. Nobody grieved more when their first child was stillborn. His heart was full when it came to his family, but not when it came to outsiders. For them, he was as emotionless as stone.

Willow gave Eve a faint smile as she squeezed the other woman's hands before releasing them. "I reckon I should have asked you, but in my heart, I know I did the right thing. I'm not sure about the other though. What if he and the children get lost before they reach the reverend? For all we know patrollers are after them."

"If Thor said he'll find it, he will. Magnusen men are excellent trackers."

"I know that Mr. Anders is familiar with these woods, but Thor may not be."

"Thor?" Eve's brows drew together to form a slight frown. Resting her hands on her distended abdomen, her head shook in disapproval. "You seem rather familiar. I didn't want to comment on it before, but

Willow, you mustn't be fooled by his charming smile and attentive manners."

"And I must remember my place," Willow added with a knowing nod. "I understand, Miss Eva."

"Now don't be that way. You are my dearest friend! You know as well as I do, some liberties just aren't allowed. At least not here in Georgia," Eva stressed. "I wouldn't want to see you heartbroken over something that could have been avoided. Thor is a handsome, delightful man, but he's white and you're not."

Eva's words did not surprise Willow. Just below the surface, she harbored similar thoughts. Anders's relative, with his warm, inviting eyes and charming behavior, tempted her in ways she never imagined.

Willow endured a restless night because thoughts of him haunted her mind. His secret about being from the future created a bond between them. She couldn't help but be concerned for his safety and curious about his experiences.

When he looked at her, tingling sensations rippled throughout her body. Nothing had ever sent her in such a tailspin. Most definitely if he was not there last night, she wouldn't have been distracted. The lantern would not have been left on the porch all night, and the runaways wouldn't have seen it.

Willow swallowed hard, digesting Eva's comments as well as her racing thoughts. Her friend spoke the honest truth! Pining over Thor would only lead to heartache and more mistakes. She'd best keep her thoughts free of him and her mind focused on her goal of freedom for her people.

—◦◦◦◦—

"Relax," Thor instructed the children under his breath.

The word was just barely out of his mouth when a dirty, grizzled white man stepped from behind one of the dogwoods. A rifle rested idly in his hands, but his body language was on alert. A tattered brown hat rode low on his forehead, and the man pushed it back with his large paw of a hand. He chewed steadily. He spat tobacco juice from the corner of his mouth. "Well, looky here."

"Hello," Thor replied as his hand tightened its grip on the branch. "Whereabouts you headed? There's some good fishing down by the river."

"Ain't out here for no fishin'." He spat again, wiping his mouth and dark beard with the back of his hand. "I'm huntin'."

Thor shrugged even though he understood the stranger's double meaning. The man's beady eyes glazed over as he stared at the children, especially when he looked at young Charity. Thor crossed over until he was a buffer between them and the bounty hunter.

Deliberately misunderstanding the man, he said, "No good game been in these parts in a long while. Wolf packs tryin' to take over and run off the deer and such. If I were you, I'd head back toward the Etowah. The river might lead you to better prospects. You'll find none here, friend. You can believe that."

"Better prospects down by the river, you say?" The man grunted. He tried to look past Thor, but each time he moved, Thor blocked his view.

The stranger spat more juice onto the ground and glared at Thor. Moving the rifle to his other hand, he cocked his head to the side. "I ain't huntin' for no game, *friend*. Runaways bring a good price per head. Word's out that they hide up in these foothills, and I mean to find me some."

Thor worked hard to maintain an even temper. A muscle quivered angrily at his jaw, but other than that, his control didn't waver. Returning the bounty hunter's stare, his lips twisted into a cold smile. "Well, the day's passin', and I have things to do. Good day."

Thor gestured with a quick jerk of his head for the children to move ahead of him. They complied while he stood still, keeping his eyes trained on the other man. "There's some Cherokee who still live up this way. I've heard some tales about them and the hunts they've been on. Unlucky white men out here alone have disappeared in these foothills. I keep those younguns close by for protection. Be careful some old chief don't mark you as easy pickings."

Color drained from the bounty hunter's face. He pulled his gaze from Thor to dart suspiciously at the woods. His brows pulled togeth-er. "You ain't funnin', is you? I don't cotton to Injuns, and I ain't ever heard nothin' about some still hidin' up in these woods."

"Then you're not from around here, are you?" Thor asked quietly. "You can heed my words or ignore 'em. The choice is yours."

"I'm quick enough with a rifle. I ain't scared of no Injuns—"

"Hey." Thor raised his hand in mock defense, silencing the other man. "Your rifle probably can take care of one of them. If there's only one, you more than likely won't have a thing to worry about. I heard some birdcalls that sounded a might suspicious a while back. Maybe it wasn't the old chief and his braves. All I know is I'm gettin' out of these woods as fast as I can. I came up here with my full head of hair, and I aim to keep it."

"Which way was the calls?" The bounty hunter looked from side to side. His head jerked wildly as if he heard whistles zigzagging over-head.

Thor bit back a cynical grin. The bastard didn't mind hunting scared, unarmed people, but when he could be marked as prey, he was ready to turn tail. *Damn coward.* "They sounded north of here, but that could have been a trick. You never can tell with Indians."

"I didn't hear nothin' on my way up here. Y'suppose they'd circle 'round?"

"It's not likely. I imagine if you hit the trail hard and go back toward Canton, you'd outrun 'em. They don't pounce on the main road. They usually get their game off the beaten path, so to speak. Better hurry though. It'll be nightfall before you know it."

"Ain't that the truth!" The man spat another mouthful of brown juice then tipped his hat to Thor. He turned and took off as if the hounds of hell were yapping at his heels. The echo of snapping twigs crackled in the woods.

Thor watched the man's retreat. Only when the sounds of the other man's departure grew quiet did Thor move. Wary of calling out to the children, he pushed quickly up the trail. His heart beat erratically in his chest as his worry increased with each step. When he didn't spot them immediately, he feared that his trick backfired. If the bounty hunter had a partner, Thor would never forgive himself. *I have to find those children!*

Tossing the branch to the ground, he covered the mile with the fluid gracefulness he once used on the football field. His muscles soared at the unexpected use. Energy surged through his body.

His feet sidestepped rocks and leapt over fallen logs. He ignored all of it, concentrating only on the path. The children were within earshot when Willow gave him directions to the Brown place. He hoped when he silently told them to keep going, they headed for Brown's spread and not for some obscure hiding place in the woods. Otherwise, it might take hours to find them.

The endless sea of maples, dogwoods, and oaks halted. At the clearing, he paused to catch his breath. A well-traveled road stretched and curved from the east, leading to a two-story farmhouse. The wagon he unloaded yesterday sat in front of a medium-sized barn.

Quickly, he scanned the house for the sign Willow said would mark Brown's home. Sure enough, it was there! White bricks bordered the top section of the chimney as a signal to runaways that they could find temporary sanctuary there. He breathed a sigh of relief, but doubts lingered.

The homestead vibrated with an eerie silence. Nothing moved or stirred. Thor edged away from the woods, crossed the road and headed for the house. As he walked, he glanced around. Where were the horses, the chickens, and whatever else the Reverend kept on his place? Hell, where was Brown or his wife, Olivia? Why was it so quiet?

He started to go to the front door, changed his mind, and swerved to the right. He peered inside a window and nearly jumped a foot when a hand clamped over his shoulder.

"No, need to look any further. God's lost sheep have been found, my boy. Like a good shepherd, you followed the right path. Now come with me. We have much to do."

"Like what?" Thor allowed the reverend to pull him away from the window and lead him to the barn. "The wagon's empty. What do you want from me now?"

"You're brash. I like that." Chuckling, Brown gave Thor a hard pat on his back. "True, the wagon's empty, but I could use some help in here. There's a meeting tonight, and this place could use a good cleaning."

"You've got to be kidding!" Thor exclaimed as they stepped inside.

The barn was much larger inside than its outside appearance. For the most part, the space was clean. However, a few piles of horse dung littered the walkway. Thor's stomach turned at the smell. He wasn't sure which smelled worse, horse droppings or squealing pigs?

Frowning, he gave Brown a hard look. "I suppose you expect me to do something with that."

Brown laughed again. "I take care of my own mess, son. I want you to check the kerosene in the lanterns and make sure there's enough. I also want you to listen because what I have for you isn't meant for the rest of the flock that will be gathering here tonight."

"Wait a minute before you keep going on with the code words, there's something I need to know."

The older man folded his hands across his chest. "I'm listening. What's on your mind?"

"I just want to make sure for my own peace of mind that the kids got here safely. Nat, Clay and Charity *are* here, right?" His eyes met Brown's green-eyed gaze head on. The stubborn set of his jaw demanded a straight answer.

Brown dipped his head in compliance. "They made it here. Olivia is tending to them now, feeding them, and giving them proper clothing."

"Good." Another sigh of relief passed from Thor's lips. "I sent them ahead without me. I wasn't sure if they made it. Will they be safe during the meeting?"

"No one allowed on my ground would harm a hair on their heads," Reverend Brown vowed. "Now are you ready to hear my message for you?"

Thor nodded. "I'm ready, but I think I know what it is. You want me to help on the Underground Railroad, and if that's it, consider me enlisted. Just tell me what you want me to do."

—◦◦◦—

"You won't rest until he returns, will you?"

Willow let the curtain fall and turned from the window. Swallowing the lump in her throat, she shrugged. "I suppose not. He should have come back by now. I don't know what could be keeping him."

"Maybe you should go to the reverend's to see if Thor and the children made it there safely."

"I can't leave you alone. Your baby could arrive at any moment, and you shouldn't be alone when the pains start." She went to the stove. The warming stew claimed her attention. As she stirred the flavorful dinner, she added, "I'll stay with you until Mr. Anders returns and then I'll leave."

Eva nodded and went back to mending her husband's shirts. Willow watched her friend for a moment. Creating a home and raising a family consumed Eva's world. The worry over whether or not the child growing inside her would arrive safely was the only negative thought to enter Eva's mind. She never lived in fear with Anders by her side.

Willow didn't begrudge Eva for her content life. If the world were a simpler place, perhaps her focus could be on the joys of taking care of a family. Since the world wasn't simple for her, she mustn't fill her mind with idle thoughts of what ifs. She must reconcile herself to the present.

Willow returned to the stew. The meal didn't require further attention from her. In another hour or so, it would be ready. She covered the pot with its lid and joined Eva at the table. Sifting through the pile of clothing, she found another shirt of Anders in need of repair.

Neither woman spoke. A companionable silence filled the one-room cabin. Mending was a mindless task for Willow. Her fingers looped the needle in and out of the material. When one hole was patched, she searched for the next piece to sew. This repetitious movement gave Willow the freedom to expand on her earlier thoughts of liberation for her people.

For weeks, her spirit felt restless, as if some monumental occurrence was on the verge of overpowering her. Reverend Brown often said when the good Lord had a mission for a body, He'd give a warning with a strong stirring in the person's bones. In her youth, Willow did not understand. Now her stomach fluttered, her flesh tingled, and her mind burned. If the good Lord didn't have something special in store, she didn't know what was wrong with her. Something extraordinary was on the horizon, and if she searched her mind hard enough, she'd figure it out.

A fleeting glimpse in her mind of dark blue eyes and a ruggedly handsome face mingled with a rich, deep voice invaded her ruminating.

Thor.

"Blessed be!" she muttered under her breath.

"What is it?"

Willow shook her head. "Nothing, I'm just having a harder time with patience than usual. I'm fine, Miss Eva."

The other woman held Willow's gaze as if searching for more than her words said. Then she directed her attention to Anders's shirt.

Without the strain of Eva's close observation, Willow's thoughts returned to Thor. He was just a man, one who certainly had no place in her life. Surely, she could make her goals without thoughts of Thor Magnusen intruding upon them.

Very well, she thought with a stern jab of the needle through a buttonhole. *Remember the movement.* She silently repeated the three words until thoughts of Thor drifted away, and the plight of the three children from the woods came to the forefront.

The two boys and girl were family. The resemblance was too strong to be otherwise. *Where did their flight from bondage begin? Did they have parents, and if they did, what happened to them?*

What would the children discover in Canada after their ride on the Freedom Train ended? Would they find a kind family to take them in, or would they have to make it on their own?

Willow knew that the network of abolitionists who assisted in helping slaves escape to freedom would provide for the children's welfare, but the children needed more than money. They'd need love and guidance, too. *Who would provide for their emotional needs?*

"Did you hear that?"

Eva's voice, hushed with an undercurrent of excitement, interrupted Willow's thoughts. Disoriented at having her thoughts jarred abruptly, Willow shook her head. "I didn't hear anything. What did it sound like?"

She moved to stand, but Eva waved in a dismissing gesture. Eva's chair scraped across the floorboards as she pulled herself up and waddled to the door. Her slender, pale hands patted her hair into place, searching for any loose tendrils.

Eva then pinched her cheeks a couple of times before answering Willow. "It sounds like Anders." She pulled the front door open, and a wide smile parted her lips. "He's home!"

"Blessed be," Willow said aloud with a soft laugh. Eva's love for her husband was certainly a remarkable sight.

While Eva greeted Anders, Willow stored the mending inside its box and set it on the floor near the fireplace. After wiping the table down, she prepared a meal setting for two. By the time she was done, Eva returned with Anders.

"Good day, Mr. Anders." Willow forced a demure smile as she moved away from the table to gather her belongings. Despite her deep affection for his wife, Anders's staunch disregard for the anti-slavery movement stung. The reverend tried many times to convince him of the moment's importance, but nothing shook him. Willow wondered how a man loved his wife with his whole heart, yet that same heart held no compassion for others in dire circumstances.

He returned her greeting with a jerk of his head. "Willow."

She draped her shawl around her shoulders and tucked her things inside the crook of her arm. Looking at Eva, she said, "The stew should be ready in a minute or two. I suppose I'll see you in the morning. Bye, Miss Eva, Mr. Anders."

Eva's face fell. "I thought you'd have dinner with us. I wanted you to be here when I told Anders about Thor."

Willow's heart pounded at the mention of Thor. "You don't need me for that, Miss Eva."

"Who's Thor? I heard that there have been strangers in the area." Anders demanded when Eva opened her mouth to protest further. "Is he a friend of the reverend's?" His voice clipped with a steel-tipped edge. "I appreciate his help with the lumber, but he knows better than to bring his friends around here. I told him my views on that—"

"Anders, please," Eva hushed him. "Thor is not one of Reverend Brown's friends. He's your kin!"

"My kin?" Disbelief riddled his expression. "You must be mistaken, Eva." He shrugged out of his jacket and set it on the back of a chair then strode to the chamber set to wash his hands. "None of my kin would be caught dead down here."

"He is a relation," Eva argued. She looked at Willow for support. "Tell him. Didn't you mistake him for Anders when you first saw him?"

"I did," Willow agreed. "I didn't have my spectacles, but there was a resemblance. At the creek, he told me he's a Magnusen, and he later said that he's a distant relation."

Anders finished drying his hands and faced the women with a frown. "I don't know any Magnusen by the name of Thor. Where is he from?"

"He said down by Atlanta." Eva tottered across the room to take her husband's hand. "It's possible that you wouldn't know him since he's from so far south. You favor so much you must be related."

Anders's frown softened at the touch of Eva's hand. He glanced at the table and then looked at Willow and his wife. "Well, where is he? The table's only set for two."

Willow's stomach clenched as unease swept over her. Her eyes darted to Eva and the woman's face was void of color. Clearing her throat, Willow answered in a strained voice. "He's over at the reverend's. I'll tell him you're back."

"Willow, wait!" Eva spoke with sharp conviction. "What were you saying about strangers, Anders? What did you hear in town?"

"I heard bits and pieces from here and there. No one said anything about another Magnusen in the area."

"Then, they weren't referring to Thor," Eva said quietly. "Could the strangers have been slave patrollers?"

His mouth tightened into a grim line. "You know I wouldn't ask something like that."

"You should," she gently reprimanded. "Willow crosses two miles of woods between here and the Brown farm just to help me. If bounty hunters are roaming the woods looking for people of color, she isn't safe. That should concern you some."

He colored fiercely. "It does. I don't want anything to happen to her, but no one said anything about bounty hunters or patrollers. They just said strangers, and that can mean anyone. Since people are starting to come to Brown's meetings, I didn't think anything of it. Willow, I can see you home—"

"That won't be necessary. Miss Eva needs you," Willow said. "Besides, I know a safe way to get home. Reverend Brown and I often change my route. I'll let Mr. Thor know that you're home and dinner is ready. Have a good evening."

Before they could voice disapproval, she slipped out the door and headed for home.

—◦◦◦—

The afternoon spent with Reverend Brown was grueling. The man whipped out the history of the abolitionists' role in the Underground Railroad as well as key code phrases at a rapid-fire pace.

Thor concentrated hard to keep up. The impromptu class quickly reminded him of his first football practice with a real coach instead of Cal assuming the role. The immediate recognition of the similarities made the jargon easy to remember. He didn't foresee any difficulties that would prevent him from assisting the reverend to the best of his ability.

Willow appeared.

Her sudden emergence was an instant distraction. Her gentle, melodious voice called out a greeting that drew his gaze to her. As she left the doorway of the barn and glided toward them, Thor instinctively realized she represented a powerful complication.

Thor swallowed hard when she reached them. "Hi, Willow."

Her liquid ebony eyes darted once at Brown before her gaze settled on him. "Hello, Mr. Thor."

Silent, forbidden thoughts languished between them. He intrigued her just as she fascinated him. Thor knew it. With every fiber of his being, he knew she found the draw irresistible but fought diligently to ignore the temptation. He waged against his primal impulses, too. What would happen when the fight left them and they were left alone? Could common sense defeat the inevitable?

Reverend Brown's harsh cough broke the spell. Willow's face tightened as she looked away. Thor drew in a ragged breath, riddled with irritation and frustration. Turning his back to them, he grabbed a nearby pitchfork and shoveled hay into the horses' stalls.

"Olivia could probably use some help with the younguns. They've eaten, but I suspect there's more that could be done to help them."

"I understand," Willow answered. "I have a message for him, and then I'll go inside to help."

Her light footsteps brushed across the barn floor like a quiet whisper. Thor stiffened when she reached him, and the heat of her body burned against his back. His knuckles became white as he gripped the pitchfork and faced her. "Is Eva still asking for me?"

Several wisps of jet-black hair escaped from the single braid hanging down her back and caressed her high cheekbones as she shook her head. "Not exactly. Mr. Anders is back, and he wants to meet you. I told him I'd tell you."

"Thank you." His tight expression relaxed into a smile. "Thank you for the message."

"You're welcome," she returned with a soft curve of her mouth. "Dinner's ready over there, too. It's not much. Only rabbit stew, but it is filling."

"Rabbit stew?" He cocked an eyebrow. Another of his grandmother's concoctions came to mind, and his stomach unleashed a hearty growl. Chuckling softly, he rubbed his stomach. "That sounds tempting, but I aim to stay for the meeting. If I'm lucky, I suppose Anders will leave enough for a plate."

"The meeting?" She directed her dark, questioning eyes to Reverend Brown. "There's a meeting tonight?"

He pierced Thor with a hard stare of disapproval then he cleared his throat. "There is. Thor encountered a patroller while forwarding the baggage. It's prudent that more guidelines are set forth. From now on, either Anders or I will escort you to and fro. These woods are no longer safe. Now Olivia is waiting, Willow."

"I know she's waiting." Her voice was quiet. Her chin set into a stubborn line.

Dark lashes slipped over orbs that Thor noted were brimmed with hurt. He ached to comfort her but sensed anything he said would only fuel her pain. She knew the workings of the Underground Railroad, and he wondered why Brown excluded her from the meeting. From the series of questions that etched across her expressive beautiful face, he knew she wondered the same.

With determined strides, she spun from Thor and went to the reverend. Her husky voice stammered with disappointment. "Wh-Why didn't you tell me about the meeting, Reverend? Why did he know and not me? I want to help, too. This is important to me."

Reverend Brown rested his hands on her shoulders. He spoke to her in warm tones that hinted his superiority. "I understand that, but as I've told you before, your involvement must be kept to a bare minimum. Let's not have this discussion again. Those children are waiting, and the light of the sun is slipping away. Don't be disrespectful just because a stranger is watching."

Willow's throat worked as she swallowed down his words. Her humiliation drifted to Thor and sickened him. She left without looking back, and he didn't blame her.

His regard for Brown diminished. Thor's hand closed to a fist. The urge to strike out on Willow's behalf gripped him. The pitchfork fell at his feet as Thor stormed from the stall. "You didn't have to humiliate her," he bit out. "She didn't deserve that."

Brown pulled a pouch from his coat pocket. He took his time as he filled his corncob pipe with tobacco. When he finished, he rolled the pouch up and stuck it inside his pocket. The pad of his thumb pressed the tobacco while he bored his steely green eyes into Thor. "You've known her for a little more than a day, and you're telling me what she doesn't deserve. Son, I've known her all of her life. I know—"

"I'm not your son," Thor growled through gritted teeth. He jerked his head toward the door. "It doesn't matter how long I've known her. She deserved a better answer than the one you gave her. You had no right to patronize her, either alone or with me as a witness. She wants to help. Let her."

"I reckon you have all the answers, don't you?"

"I know the difference between right and wrong," Thor retorted. "The way you talked to her just now wasn't right. She's a woman, not a child."

"A woman you say?" The older man's eyebrows raised inquiringly.

Thor rolled his eyes. "Not that again. You made your feelings clear, and I agree. Nothing will happen between Willow and me."

"I wasn't referring to that," Brown explained in a quiet voice. "I know she's a woman, but she's young. There are ways in the world that she does-n't know a thing about. I 'spect Olivia and me may have been wrong to shelter her so, but the wrong was born of love, so we'll have to answer to God for that."

"Love? I find that one hard to believe."

"I imagine you do," Brown replied, "but consider this... What do you suppose would have happened if Willow had led those children here instead of you? Do you think that sour bellied marauder would have lis-tened to her tale of rampaging Cherokee on the hunt for white men's scalps? Do you?"

A stab of ice-cold fear pierced Thor's heart and rendered him numb. His mind went crazy as images of alternate possibilities flashed in his head. Remembering how the bounty hunter's eyes glazed over twelve-year-old Charity, the man would have drooled at the sight of Willow. If she had guided those children in place of him, the patroller would have taken all four of them back with him. No doubt the bastard would have brutalized both females along the way.

Another thought seized him. If he hadn't traveled back in time and changed the course of events, Willow would have been with the children instead of him. The color drained from his face. He groaned. "Oh, God."

"You understand." Reverend Brown's mouth set to a grim line. "I don't speak harshly to harm her, but the less she knows, the better off she is. Maybe you've seen it. She's headstrong and smart, and that can be an advantage. However, for her, until things change, it isn't. I do what I do to protect her...from herself and anything else that's liable to cause her harm."

—◦∾◦—

Reverend Brown's words stabbed Willow's heart. He was adamant about what role she took with the movement, but he had never shamed her. To have him do so in front of Thor embarrassed her. Her face grew hot with renewed humiliation. Pounding blood roared in her ears and tears stung her eyes. Willow blinked the offending moisture away, took a deep breath and entered the place she thought of as home.

A slight woman with fiery red hair and warm brown eyes welcomed Willow with a smile. "Hello, dear. You're back just in time. Dinner is almost ready."

"Thank you, Miss Olivia," Willow said. "I'm not hungry. I hope you don't mind if I excuse myself to assist with the baggage. The reverend said you needed help."

"You look a little pale, and I've never known you to refuse chicken and dumplings." Olivia left the kitchen and moved to stand in front of Willow. She pressed the back of her hand against Willow's forehead. "Your forehead isn't hot, but that doesn't mean anything. Are you feeling under the weather? "

Willow shook her head. "No, I'm fine. I'm just not hungry is all."

Olivia nodded slowly. "The food will be here for you whenever you're ready for it. The children are resting. I haven't time to see if I have anything that will fit them. Could you go through the trunk and take some things in there to them?"

"Yes, ma'am. I'd be happy to."

Willow left her belongings in her room and then headed down the hall toward the bedroom the Browns' shared. She searched through the trunk at the foot of the bed. After finding garments she thought would be suitable for the children, she closed the trunk and moved to the far wall. Her fingertips glided along the wooden partition until they found the faint break in the wall that disguised the hidden catch. Using her palm, Willow pushed against the secret hitch. The opening to the concealed room parted with a soft hiss, and she slipped inside.

The children jumped as the bottom of her shoes tapped across the hardwood floor. Candlelight flickered in the compact room, enveloping it in a dusky glow. Willow stepped closer to the burning flame and knelt beside the bed where the children lay. She gave them a tender smile and whispered, "It's only me. I brought some clothes for when you continue on your journey."

"We have to leave now?" the young girl asked.

Willow shook her head. "No, you'll stay here for a few days to build your strength and what not. These clothes are for when you leave."

The oldest boy took the garments from her and mumbled a barely audible, "Thank you."

"You're welcome. Were you sleeping?" she asked.

This time, the smaller boy answered. "No, ma'am. The Missus told us to stay back here and be quiet. We're tired, but we ain't sleepy. Do we have to sleep now?"

"You don't have to do anything you don't want to," Willow told him. "Would you mind if I sit here with you for a while and we talked?"

The younger children's eyes grew large as if they wanted to say yes, but they didn't utter a word. Instead, they looked at their older brother who sat quietly with his back against the wall. He gave a slight nod, and the girl quickly added, "We don't mind."

Willow brought a chair from against the wall and set it beside the bed. She sat down and laced her fingers together in her lap. "We didn't have time for introductions before. My name is Willow. What's yours?"

"I'm Charity," the girl quickly responded. She pointed at her brothers. "This is Clay and that's Nat."

"Are you brothers and sister?" Willow asked, amazed by the younger children's eagerness to converse. Nat was quieter than his siblings, but Willow sensed that he hung on every word.

"Yessum," Clay responded. "We're twelve and Nat is about fifteen or sixteen."

Willow bit back a chuckle. "You say that like you've been asked that before."

"Thor asked us—"

"Ssh!" Nat hit his brother's arm. "You know better than to call a white man by his first name."

Clay's bottom lip poked out as he rubbed his arm. "He said we could."

"White men say a lot of things. That don't mean he means 'em.

Look at what happened to Mama and Papa."

Thor's defense was on the tip of Willow's tongue, but was forgotten at the mention of the children's parents. She slid to the edge of her seat and leaned forward. "What happened to them?"

"Massa Henry sold Papa and Overseer Charlie whipped Mama to death," Clay answered, his voice tight with anger. "Massa Henry say he never sell any slave, but he sold our Papa. He woulda sold us, too. But we ran."

Willow's throat constricted, and her heart convulsed in sympathy. A slave trader abducted her mother when Willow was a young girl. Hearing the galloping hooves of a stranger's horse, Bessie instructed her daughter to hide underneath the porch while she went inside for her husband, Elijah's gun. Bessie never reached the firearm. The wiry stranger tossed a rope around Willow's mother and dragged her after him. Bessie fought hard, digging her heels into the ground. In the end, her fighting was in vain and the man disappeared with her.

By the time Elijah and the reverend returned from a hunting expedition, Willow had been overwrought with tears. Her father coaxed the horrific tale from her, and when realization hit, his ebony eyes blazed with anguish and revenge. He thrust Willow into the reverend's arms. Elijah made the reverend promise to watch over her. He then reloaded his rifle and left. Willow never saw either of her parents alive again. A day didn't pass when she didn't mourn them and promise herself that their deaths weren't in vain.

The isolation she felt at losing her parents at such a young age returned as she gazed at the children huddled together on the bed. Willow decided that she wouldn't allow them to go through the same. Whether Reverend Brown liked it or not, the flames of determination weren't doused by his harsh words. She would help these children, and she knew just how she'd do it!

First, Willow would find out where their father was sold. Disguised as a slave, she would steal onto the plantation, rescue him, and reunite their family.

CHAPTER SIX

Instead of trekking back to his great-great grandparents' cabin to appease his growling stomach, Thor accepted Olivia's invitation to join them for dinner. The meal was a simple affair, which quickly put him at ease. Olivia and the reverend treated him like part of the family, encouraging him to eat more and telling him that he could use some extra meat on his bones.

The conversation was light and engaging and almost calmed his sole interest except for one small factor. Willow's absence loomed over him like a thundercloud in the midst of a tornado.

When dinner ended, his plan to look for her came to an abrupt halt. Reverend Brown beckoned Thor to join him on the porch. His growing irritation at the delay faltered and died as he stood in awe of the twenty plus men and women who came from all directions of the sparsely populated area, heading for the barn. Thor remembered that during this time, the settlers lived far and wide in rural parts, and Canton served as the central hub. Seeing more than a dozen participants impressed him.

With the light from the sun long diminished, their kerosene lanterns created a bright orange trail. The reddish-gold glow from the lights matched the compassion he sensed from Brown's eager followers. Thor's awe for the man crept back over him.

He looked at Brown in wonder and asked in a quieter voice. "Are you responsible for all of them being here?"

"I can't take credit for their kind nature, son. Our cause attracts shepherds from near and far. Under the guise of prayer meetings, they come. Friends and family recruit new members. Each meeting has a little more than the last, but today's number is nothing short of miraculous. I suppose they feel the savagery of human bondage just as strongly as those children you helped today. They're here because their souls won't let them rest if they were anyplace else. If you plan to sit at the meeting, you'd best come on with me now. Olivia will join us when she's done cleaning up."

Thor followed Brown off the porch. The barely contained excitement of the people in the barn drew him in even as his concern for Willow's whereabouts grew. He lagged behind Brown once they entered the barn and stood in the doorway. Half in and half out, he could hear the man's words while keeping watch for Willow.

"Good evening to you, ladies and gentlemen. Praises be to God for such a large gathering. The Missus and I weren't expecting this many of you, but we wouldn't dare turn any one away. In fact, we are truly thankful because there is safety in numbers and we have never needed this more than we do right now."

Reverend Brown's calm, soothing tones caused a hush to fall over the crowd. Once the building quieted, he instructed everyone to bow his head while he gave thanks to God. The prayer ended with a chorus of Amen, and then an endless supply of questions interrupted the stillness of the night.

"What's to happen, Reverend, if Georgia secedes from the Union? My cousin just came down from South Carolina, and he says that's all they're talkin' 'bout up there. He says that if Lincoln wins the election, they're leavin' the Union for sure!" one excited voice called out. "That'll cut us off from our brothers up North."

"Yeah, Reverend!" another voice added. "We're starting to have troubles with the all-fired patrollers slipping in and out our woods! There's bound to be more of them if Georgia secedes, too."

More voices piped in with questions. Apprehension overrode the earlier shroud of compassion. Thor turned his attention from the Brown home to look over the heads of the concerned abolitionists to focus on the reverend. How would Brown handle the tension and legitimate fears of his followers?

"What's to come, you ask?" Brown questioned, slightly raising his voice over the low grumbles of concerns. "Some of you asked the same question when the Fugitive Slave Law passed ten years ago. Didn't you learn anything then? The patrols increased for a time, but then the lazy scoundrels became lax. Our forwarding of precious baggage never ceased. If anything, the number of occupants on the Gospel Train grew larger. The Lord was on our side then, and He will not fail us now. We'll have to become more cautious, but we will not limit our efforts until our goal is met!"

The knowledge of the future sprang to the forefront of Thor's mind. The rest of Brown's moving speech dwindled to a low hum. Thoughts of the War Between the States and the number of men who fought and died consumed him. His chest ached as he remembered the total number of fatalities would far exceed the amount of American soldiers lost in both World Wars and Vietnam combined. Suddenly, the space in the barn became too tight, too constricting. He needed air and slipped out of the barn to inhale a deep, ragged gulp.

His reaction surprised him. He'd read about the Civil War for school and for leisure. Cal and he often discussed it. They even agreed to visit the famous battlegrounds with Gettysburg first on their list.

The detached way he once viewed the war would never return. Some of those men in that barn would die on a battlefield not more than a year from now. Reverend Brown could be in that number, and so could he if 1985 didn't call him back. Thor muttered an oath and sagged against the barn.

"The meeting doesn't interest you?"

Willow's softly asked question startled him. Shaken back to his present environment, Thor pushed away from the barn. By the light of the moon, he looked down into her dark, compelling eyes. "I needed some air. The reverend's speech is powerful…"

"But?" she asked with a tilt of her head.

Words lodged in his throat. He shook his head and walked past her to the porch. Her footsteps followed, and he found himself still unable to speak.

She crossed in front of him. Her cool hand took his and squeezed. "I watched from my bedroom, and I saw you leave the meeting. You moved slowly like old man Atlas with the world on his back. Would you tell me what's wrong? Does it have to do with the future?"

Her boldness encouraged him. He pressed his hand against the curve of her smooth cheek. A dreamy sigh passed from her lips, but she didn't move away from his touch. The pad of his thumb brushed her satiny skin.

He responded in a broken whisper, "It's everything, Willow. Your future, my past, and our present. All of it is driving me crazy. I don't know what to do about any of it."

"What do you want to do?"

"This."

Before she could escape, his arms encircled her small waist and pulled her against his chest. He caught a brief glimpse of surprise in her liquid eyes before his mouth closed over hers.

Thor began the kiss with exquisitely slow precision. He was patient, giving Willow time to adjust to the taste of his mouth on hers. Her full, moist lips softened and parted. He couldn't resist her silent invitation if he tried.

A kilowatt jolt of electricity surged through him as the kiss deepened. His tongue explored the warmth of her mouth. He reveled in her natural sweetness. With a tentative stroke, her tongue brushed against his. The slight sensuous movement shook him to his core, and he felt like he'd been electrocuted by her innocently erotic caress.

"Willow," he groaned against the shell of her ear after the kiss ended. She shivered within the circle of his arms, and his hold tightened. "I thought I was scared before. Now I'm terrified."

—◦◦◦—

Thor's words dumbfounded Willow. The deep timbre of his low moans sent a multitude of shivers up and down her spine. The rigid muscles of his back rippled underneath her hands as he pulled her closer. A small ache formed in her lower belly. Wild sensations flowed through her, leaving her dizzy and weakening her resolve to avoid the man who caused them.

"Thor," she moaned when he ended their embrace. She didn't want the delirious emotions to end.

Does he not enjoy them, too?

"Ssh." He pressed a finger against her lips. Taking her hand, he led her to the side of the house hidden from the barn. His hands settled at her waist. He lowered his head so that their eyes met. "I don't know what to do anymore. I shouldn't have kissed you, but I won't apologize for it."

"I don't want your apologies. I liked it."

"Oh, God," he growled in a harsh whisper. "Willow… please, don't tell me that."

"Why not?"

"Because it makes me want to do it again, and I shouldn't. You understand, don't you?"

Willow nodded. They became quiet. Slowly, her senses returned. She remembered her earlier decision and stepped free of his hold. Wrapping her arms around herself, she walked to a fallen log and sat. She wasn't surprised when Thor joined her.

"For me to act on my attraction to you is. . . well, it's wrong. I don't know what I'm doing here or how I got here. I could fall asleep tonight and wake up in my own time tomorrow."

"I know, Thor, and I understand. I shouldn't have said what I did either. I am not lacking in morals. Please forgive me if my behavior contradicted that."

He reached for her hand. "There's no need for forgiveness. I enjoyed it," he added with a throaty chuckle.

His touch, warm and protective, threatened to confuse her again. She snatched her hand away, stood, and turned from him. "I suppose we shouldn't speak on it again."

He was quiet for a moment. When he finally replied, his voice was low with resignation. "I suppose you're right." The log creaked as he shifted his weight. Twigs crackled beneath his footsteps, and then the heat of his body enveloped her as his sweet breath whispered against her ear. "It's getting late. I should get back to the cabin. I'm sure Anders and Eva are wondering what's keeping me. Goodnight, Willow, and pleasant dreams."

His finger trailed a whispery soft path down the side of her arm before he moved away. Willow turned on her heel and went after him. His comments about his journey through time worried her. If he woke up in another place, she wanted him to remember her.

"Thor!"

He halted his retreat and waited. She circled in front of him. His gaze never wavered as he stared down at her. "Yes?"

"I wish you knew how or when you'll return to your time."

"So do I. It would make things a lot easier all around."

"Well, I just wanted to tell you how pleased I've been to know you." Her hands shot out to rest on his broad shoulders. Standing on tiptoe, she leaned forward and brushed a chaste kiss across his cheek. When she pulled back, tears blurred her vision, casting him in a watery haze. "Goodbye, Thor."

With tears streaming down her face, she ran inside the Brown home and closed the door firmly behind her.

On wobbly feet, she pressed down the hall to her bedroom. The quaint confines offered the comforting solitude she desperately needed. Goodbyes battered her soul and saying goodbye to Thor made her heart ache. The finality of her words was beyond his understanding. She planned to leave that night and now, she must accept that upon her return, he might be gone.

More tears rolled down her cheeks. She rubbed them away with the heels of her hands and sniffled. Crying wouldn't change the facts. Besides, even if he remained in 1860, there could never be anything more between them than friendship. The excitement that pulsed in her blood at his nearness must be ignored. Her goal to reunite the children with their father must take precedence over the tingling sensation of Thor's soft lips on hers or his hard, muscled arms wrapped around her.

The memory of her first kiss rocked her. Trembling fingers pressed against her mouth as she closed her eyes and relived the savory taste of Thor's lips and the woodsy scent of his body.

A shout roared from the barn, and her eyes shot open. "Blessed be!" she muttered. That quickly, thoughts and longing weakened her. She wasn't a hypocrite, but continuing to think of Thor would deem her one.

Daydreams and wishes were a senseless waste of time. More pressing matters warranted precedence, and their names were Nat, Charity, and Clay. The children needed their father, and she needed now more than ever to prove that she could play a vital role in the anti-slavery movement. Who in this township knew more about the ravages of slavery than her? Who lost their parents to the vicious cruelty of bounty hunters? Slave patrollers did not hesitate in taking Bessie and Elijah Elkridge's lives. Outwitting them as she walked the woods did little to repay the pain and loss her parents' deaths caused. No, she wanted more. She *needed* to reunite the children with their father. Surely, afterward the reverend would understand that she was no longer the little girl who clung to his hand, but a woman fully capable in guiding her people to freedom.

Willow pulled off her clothing and slipped into the disguise she stored away after speaking with the children. Dressed as a boy, it would be easier to creep through the woods. Her hair posed a problem, but she couldn't bear the thought of cutting off the long braid. She coiled the ropy mass on top of her head, holding it in place with a few pins. One of Reverend Brown's old worn hats fit perfectly over her hair and completed the ruse.

With that chore complete, she sat down behind her desk. Using strong, sure strokes, she dipped her pen into the vat of ink and drafted a letter to Olivia and the reverend. Once they were fast asleep, she'd leave the letter on the dining room table and steal away into the night.

—◈◈◈—

Something in Willow's luminous eyes haunted Thor, but he couldn't put his finger on it. The nighttime hike to his family's cabin absorbed most of his concentration, forcing his concern for Willow to take a backseat for the moment.

The bright full moon and the glittering stars provided a natural beacon to guide his path, but he still preferred the large expansive beams that came from electrical lights. Adjusting to the current century was easy enough, but he sorely missed the little modern conveniences like electricity and indoor plumbing.

When he reached the cabin, he noticed the groundwork for the additional rooms. A breath lodged in his throat at the sight. As if in a daze, he ran his hand along the wooden planks. He marveled at how fresh the wood looked in comparison to its appearance in 1985. The pride Anders held in his work was evident in how everything was laid out. Thor felt a momentary twinge of disappointment at having never noticed before.

"Who's there?" The click of a rifle followed the deadly quiet voice.

Thor raised his hands and moved away from the cabin. "It's Thor."

The rifle clicked again. A figure stepped from the shadows. The man stood an inch shorter than Thor, but other than that, the similarities were startling. His eyes were the same dark, piercing blue, and his hair was the same sandy brown.

Lowering the firearm to his side, the man moved closer until they stood only inches apart. "So, you're the Thor Eva's so fond of. I can see the resemblance, more or less. You took your time returning. Did you get lost from Brown's place to here?"

So, this was his great-great-grandpa Anders. Thor accepted Anders's outstretched hand and gave it a firm, hearty shake. "Sorry it took me so long. The reverend needed help with a few things."

"Eva held dinner for you. She's asleep now, so if you're hungry, make your plate quietly." Anders's steely gaze fixated on him.

"Thanks but I'm not hungry. I had chicken and dumplings at the Browns."

Anders nodded once. He moved away from Thor to lean the rifle against the cabin. Resting his backside against the porch's edge, he folded his arms across his chest. "You've spent a considerable amount of time over there. What did he need help with?"

"Just a few things around the place. Odds and ends."

His ancestor bent over and grabbed a blade of grass from the ground. Rising, he stuck it in his mouth and chewed. "Eva says you're from down by Atlanta. I didn't realize the Magnusens had traveled so far south."

Thor stiffened slightly. Anders wanted to play twenty questions. *Okay*, Thor thought, *let's have it.*

"We've been there for quite some time."

"For how long?"

"All my life. I can't really speak for what happened before I was born."

"Your folks didn't talk much, huh?" Anders shoulders relaxed. The piercing gleam in his eyes relented. He appeared almost relaxed and as if, he trusted and believed Thor. "I suppose all Magnusens have that in common."

"It would seem so."

"Tell me about the work Brown had for you. He's a nice enough man, but he's involved in things that are best left alone. While you're staying here, I'd rather you not take part in his other activities."

"Why not?"

Anders broke eye contact with Thor. Looking away, he spit out the grass and then bent down to grab another blade. When he straightened, he gave Thor a hard stare. "Some things are best left alone. Only devilment befalls a man for treading where he doesn't belong."

"But how can a man disregard souls screaming in agony?"

"It's not that simple," Anders countered. "Things are boiling to a fevered pitch. I won't be in the thick of it. With the baby coming, I have to put *my* family first and tend to their needs."

Thor sighed and ran a weary hand through his short mass of hair. Even if he disagreed with his great-great-grandfather, he understood the other man's reasons. "There's no point to arguing."

"No, there isn't."

"Give Eva my regards. I'll be over at the Browns." Thor looked down at his shirt and pants. "These are yours. Mine got dirty in the pigpen yesterday. After I change, I'll be going."

"Wait. Never mind about my clothes. They fit. Wear 'em. I can only wear one shirt and one pair of pants at a time anyway. We'll take care of your clothes when we do the wash. When you see Willow, tell her I'll take care of the chores here tomorrow and she can stay at home."

Anders's attitude irked Thor. The other man spoke as if Willow was nothing more than Eva's maidservant. His jaw tightened, and in a voice heavy with sarcasm, he replied, "Sure thing. Will do."

On the return trip to the Browns, he strode quickly through the woods. He slapped the overhanging branches and fading leaves off his shoulder. The nocturnal beauty of the woods went unnoticed.

Annoyance and a slow building anger fueled his movements and came close to blinding him to the world around him. A few yards away, a twig snapped. Thor's stride came to an immediate halt. He held himself still and listened.

The game of watch and wait lasted for what felt like an eternity. Through narrowed eyes, he searched the woods for a sign of anything. Nothing stirred. *When did I become such a wuss?* Of course, nothing stirred! He was the only person fool enough to be in the woods at that late hour. He dismissed his overly cautious behavior and took a step forward.

The evidence hit him. The fragrance of honeysuckles mingled with the scent of pine, oak and maple drifted to him. The delicate aroma assailed his nostrils and Thor breathed it in. A knowing smile spread across his face. He called out softly, "Willow."

No response, but he wasn't surprised. Why was she in the woods at this late hour anyway? Why was she hiding from him?

He planted his hands on his hips and looked around. "I'm not leaving until you come out, so if you're prepared to stay out here all night, I'm prepared to wait. It may get awful cold, though. I hope you're bundled up. I wish I was."

The rich timbre of his voice lingered with a sad note. She'd probably be unable to resist, but just in case, a little improvisation might be necessary.

Balling his hands into fists, Thor blew into them. "Whew!" he exclaimed as he shivered. He then wrapped his arms around himself and rubbed briskly. "Yeah, it's getting nippy out here, but I can handle it. I won't catch a cold. Well, I hope I won't."

More silence answered him. Giving up wasn't an option. With bounty hunters running rampant, there wasn't a snowball's chance in hell of him backing off. He wouldn't leave her out there alone, so if she wanted to play, he'd be her playmate.

A fleeting image of passionate play flashed before his eyes. Hot bodies pressed together and slow, moist kisses came to mind. A sense of urgency rippled through him. His body hardened in response.

Sudden anger at the direction that his thoughts took him flared deep within. Through clenched teeth, he bit out, "Willow! Enough's enough! Come out now, or by God, I'll come in there after you." He paused a beat. "So, what will it be? Willow—"

"Blessed be!" She stepped from behind the large trunk of an oak. "You'll wake the dead!"

"It's the living I'm more concerned with," he retorted. His gaze roved over her, and he shook his head. Men's clothing covered her from head to toe. The masculine garments did little to hide her femininity. He wondered why she wore the clothes in the first place. Thor moved to her and snatched the hat from her head. Holding it up between them, he asked, "What's the meaning of this?"

Her hand shot out to retrieve the hat. He held it over her head, just out of her reach. "Give it back!"

"No. Not until you tell me why you're dressed like that."

Irritation blazed in her eyes. "This is ridiculous and childish, too!"

"I agree." He tossed the hat to his other hand, still out of her reach.

"Thor!" Her small hands balled into fists, but she made no move to strike him.

Anger livens her up, he mused. Oh, she was a beauty no matter what expression she wore, but fury added another dimension to it. Black orbs glittered dangerously under the light of the moon. The usual soft tones of her voice gave way to husky indignation. Her breath came out in short gasps and drew his attention to her chest. Despite the bulky jacket, he remembered the round, ample curves that lay underneath.

"Why must it always come down to this?" she asked.

"To what?"

"To using your manhood against me! You did it with the water buckets, and you're doing it now! I thought you were different, but you're not! You're like all the rest. You take what you want, not giving a care to anyone else!"

The hardness of anger slipped from her eyes. Thor caught a glimpse of hurt and disillusionment before she whipped away. Her words slammed into his chest and knocked the wind out of him. Tension crept in through the trees and became a long, thin cord between them. Words left him, but he refused to accept that excuse.

He cleared his parched throat and went to her. "Here's your hat."

She turned around to grab the hat before giving him a good view of her back again.

Thor groaned. This would be difficult, and what's worse, he deserved it. He swallowed hard and moved to stand behind her. Without a moment's hesitation, his hands closed over her shoulders and gently squeezed the tight muscles they encountered.

"I am so sorry," he said with quiet emphasis. "I was only teasing, and it got out of hand. Seeing you dressed in these clothes threw me, and when you wouldn't answer me, I lost it. Forgive me."

"Are you asking for my forgiveness or demanding it?"

"Begging," he said in a low, apologetic tone. "Please. I won't make the same mistake again."

"I forgive you," she murmured as she turned to face him.

Eased by her forgiveness, his earlier curiosity returned. "What are you doing out here dressed like that in the middle of the night?"

"I can't exactly say."

"I suppose this means you lied to me then. You haven't forgiven me."

"Blessed be!" she muttered. "What does one thing have to do with the other?"

"If you've forgiven me, you would trust me," he said sadly, spreading the guilt on thick for effect. "If you trusted me, you'd tell me. You're giving me the run around again, so that can only mean one thing."

"No, please don't think that," she said soothingly. "I do trust you. It's just that... Well, if I tell you, you may try to stop me, and I won't be stopped."

An eyebrow raised in surprise. "Stop you from doing what exactly?"

Her chin lifted in a gesture of defiance. "From doing what I must to preserve a family!"

"A family?" Thor sputtered. "Whose family? What are you talking about?"

"I'm talking about Nat, Charity, and Clay. They told me what happened to their mother. Her death was horrific, and it's abominable those children had to witness it."

"Yes, it was, but I don't see how dressing like a man and running around in the woods in the middle of the night will change that—"

"If you would hold your tongue and not interrupt."

"I won't say another word." He made a show of buttoning his lips and waited.

"Their father is very much alive, and once I bring him back to them, their family will be whole again!"

"I don't believe it," he said underneath his breath.

"Believe it! Don't try to stop me either because I won't stand for it. I can do this, Thor. I know what it's like to be without a mother and a father. Those children don't have to experience that."

"Are you trying to convince me or are you just telling me?"

She looked taken aback. "I'm just telling you. I will do what I set out to do! And you won't stop me either!"

"Did I say I wanted to? It sounds like a good idea. In fact, I like it so much that I can't think of anything I'd like more than to join you."

"But you can't! You can't sneak on and off a plantation like I can!"

"No, I can't. I can take us right up to the front door."

"I'm not sure about this." Uncertainty clouded her expression.

"I wasn't asking you." Thor shrugged. "Either I go with you, or you don't go at all. The choice is yours. I'll wait right here while you make your decision."

CHAPTER SEVEN

The smirk on Thor's face was maddening. *You are truly an insufferable man!* Willow's breath came in huffs, and she turned away.

She paced from one large oak to another. Her mind wrapped around him and his proposition. *The nerve of him! He certainly leaves me with few choices.* Just when she believed he was unlike all the men she knew, he proved there were some things about men that never changed. They all believed they made the rules and that was that. She was mad enough to spit.

"What's it gonna be, Willow?" he asked in his deep, soul-stirring drawl. "Time's a-wastin'."

"I know it is," she mumbled. A twig snapped in two beneath her foot. She furiously kicked the remainder of it as hard as she could.

Her bottom lip trembled with agitation. Truly, her choices were limited. No child should be without a parent. Sparks of excitement rippled through her at the thought her planned rescue mission. She *had* to agree to his terms. Her shoulders slumped in defeat. She had no choice.

"Time's a-wastin'," she muttered, throwing his words back at him. "Let's go."

She stomped through the woods without sparing him another glance, but still felt his steady gaze on her. Her heightened sensations told her he was fully aware of her anger, and it bothered him. Of course, it didn't bother him enough to change his mind and let her go alone.

"Willow." His low voice interrupted the terse silence. "We're partners on this."

"Partners?" She sniffed in disdain.

"Yeah," he replied. "Of course, it wouldn't be right for me to just let you go off all by yourself, but that's not the only reason for me going with you. I believe in your cause. I know what the future will bring and…well, even if I didn't know, I'd still want to help you."

His stalled comment about the future made her breath catch. She desperately wanted to know. Against her resolve to limit civil conversation with him, she spared him a glance. "What will the future bring?"

"I thought you understood. I can't tell you."

"Telling me won't change a thing. I promise. I won't mention a word to a soul."

"It doesn't matter. Besides, the future has already altered. Going with you now is a big risk, but it's about the only one I'm willing to take."

"It's because you don't trust me." She directed her gaze back to the dark path before them.

"That's not true. I trust you, Willow. It's just that I'm not sure how this time travel thing works, and then in that movie…" A loud sigh passed from his lips. "Well, it feels like I'm running a play without a playbook. I'm playing everything by ear here, and I don't want to mess up. It's not just my future I'm thinking about. So many little things can be affected just by telling you something that I consider to be insignificant."

"You said the future's been changed. How do you know? What happened to change it?"

"I think I saved your life."

The hairs on the back of her neck stood on end. "When?"

His large, warm hands closed over her shoulders. He bent slightly until their eyes were level. "This afternoon on the trail, an armed bounty hunter roamed the woods. If I hadn't been here, you would have been with the children instead of me, or maybe you wouldn't have been there at all. You left the lantern on the porch because of me, but they would have been in the woods alone anyway because their shepherd left them. Who knows if they would have found the reverend on their own? Maybe my being here saved you all. Maybe that's why I'm here, to keep you safe. In all honesty, I don't know if my presence is making things better or worse, but I do know that the bounty hunter wouldn't have let any of you go."

"He would have killed us." Her blood ran cold at the certainty of it. Anders's warning about strangers and the reverend's latest restrictions came together in one bone-chilling whirlwind. While she initially fought Thor's participation in her quest, she was certainly glad of it now.

During her talk with the children, they mentioned nothing about a slave patroller. She knew of the godless men who hunted Negroes like animals. Many of the precious cargo passed through the Browns' home spoke of the narrow escapes they had. Her hatred ran deep for the men who relentlessly pursued runaways. With guns, dogs, and whips, they exercised horrific tactics. If somehow she had discovered those children wandering in the woods and been alone on the trail with them instead of Thor, only God could have saved them.

"Times are changing." His hand gently caressed her cheek. "Everybody's getting desperate."

Willow nodded. Change stirred in the air. Brown and his followers moved with untold necessity. The same urgency fueled her desire to help. "You didn't answer my question. Would he have killed us?"

"There's no real way for me to know that, but it's possible. I didn't like the way he looked at Charity, and I know he would have…" The muscles in his jaw clenched. "Whatever would have happened wouldn't have been good. If he hadn't hurt you then, he would have sold you somewhere, and I don't think you would have survived that."

She bristled. "I'm not weak—"

"That's not what I meant," he growled as she tried to jerk free of him. "You're so stubborn and willful! It drives me nuts, but I wouldn't harm you because of it. I can't say the same for slavers."

Willow nodded. She wouldn't have kept quiet if somehow she landed on an auction block. There was too much of her parents' passionate nature inside her. Reverend Brown tried to mold her into a docile young woman, but a part of her refused restraint. She was usually able to hide it, but not with Thor. He saw through her defenses and broke down her walls without any difficulty. His ability made no sense to her, yet, she wasn't afraid of it.

He continued to stare at her. "Now do you see why I couldn't let you go alone? If something happened to you, I wouldn't be able to stand it."

His voice made her insides melt. The heat from his hands burned through the layers of wool and cotton to scorch her flesh. She moistened her bottom lip with the tip of her tongue. His responding groan vibrated through her. Her mouth hastily slanted across his.

He closed his arms around her, crushing her to his chest. The wild thud of his heart beat in unison with hers. When his tongue parted her lips, she gripped his shirtsleeves. Her knees weakened as he explored her mouth and overpowered her senses. She never wanted the kiss to end, but far too quickly, he pulled away.

"We can't keep doing that."

Her mouth still tingled, and an ache throbbed in her lower belly. These sensations were dangerous but too tempting to resist. Thor and the longing he created within her were too powerful to deny, yet too consuming for surrender. In order to rescue the children's father, they would need their wits about them. Submitting to desires of the flesh was not an option. She couldn't lose control like that again. Too much was at stake.

"It's not that I don't like kissing you," he said while she remained quiet. "God knows, that's not the case. I like it too damned much if the truth must be told."

"I understand. We'd better keep going."

—◦◦◦—

Shit! Why is she so damned understanding? Thor fell into step behind Willow, and her rounded backside immediately drew his attention. Baggy trousers did little to lessen her rear's appeal. His hands itched to mold themselves to the curves brushing against the worn material. During their embrace, her slender thighs pressed hard against him and created a yearning to the depths of his soul. Her unintentional sexiness put all of Calvin Klein's models to shame. Willow Elkridge simply drove him wild.

The Magnusen cabin appeared in the clearing. He caught her hand as she moved to go past it.

"What?" she whispered. "Did you change your mind?"

"No, but I wanna stop here. We'll need money."

"Mr. Anders won't give us any."

"Maybe; there's only one way to find out for sure. You can stay out here. I'll be right back."

"I'll go with you if you don't mind. I left a note for the reverend and Miss Olivia. I may as well tell Miss Eva good-bye just in case…"

Thor nodded. The danger of their adventure couldn't be forgotten or ignored. This was definitely a life or death mission.

"Maybe. She was asleep when I left, but I'm pretty sure Anders won't keep quiet when he sees us at his door. She'll wake up and you can say what you need to."

As they approached the cabin, he reluctantly released her hand. He rapped his knuckles against the door. "Anders, it's Thor."

Low noises rustled on the other side of the door and drifted out through the open windows. Unintelligible whispers sounded. Light glowed from inside the cabin. Soon after, the door opened. Anders stood in the doorway with a candle in his hand. His eyes glowed with suspicion. "Weren't you going to the Browns?"

"There's been a change in plans. I need to ask for a favor."

Anders squinted as he looked past him. "Who's that with you? Come to the light so I can see you."

Willow stepped to the doorway. Anders held the light up to her face and moved it downward.

"Why are you wearing men's clothing? What mischief are you into now?"

"It's not mischief, Mr. Anders." She turned to Thor. "I told you this was a bad idea."

"Let's just wait and see. Anders, about that favor—"

"What do you want?" the wary man asked. "I told you before. I won't do anything that would bring harm to my family."

"I know that," Thor replied through clenched teeth. "I'm not asking you to do anything."

"Well?"

"I want some money," Thor bluntly stated. "What I mean to say is that I want to borrow some."

"For what?"

"Anders, please!" Eva appeared beside her husband. Waves of rich brown hair flowed onto her shoulders. A plaid robe stretched around her swollen abdomen. She held a glass of milk in one hand while she beckoned with the other. "Please, come in, and we'll see what we can do."

"Eva," Anders clipped, "we don't know him from Adam, and we don't know what he plans to do with the money. He says borrow, but that don't make it so."

"He's family, and that's good enough for me."

Eva gestured with her hand for Thor and Willow to enter. Thor followed Willow inside. A burning lantern glowed from the center of the table. The mother-to-be sat and invited everyone to do the same. Once they all sat down, she gave Willow a long, hard look. "Why are you dressed like a boy? That's unseemly, Willow!"

"It's a disguise. It's safer for me to travel as a boy and easier, too."

"Travel? Where are you going?"

"Down south, onto a plantation."

"You mustn't!" Eva gasped. Color drained from her face. "You can't go down there."

"She won't be alone," Thor replied. "I'll be with her."

"Why are you going?"

"We know why they're going," Anders stated quietly, "and that's why he came here asking for money."

"I asked to *borrow* money. I don't expect a donation. I know your feelings on this subject."

"But you can't do it," Eva protested. "It's too dangerous. Both of you could be killed! Does Reverend Brown know about this?"

"No, ma'am, he doesn't know," Willow said. "This is something that I have to do. I can't keep watching in the background."

"That's not all you do. You have helped many runaways. You don't have to put yourself into this kind of danger to keep helping them. I don't understand this at all, Willow. Anders, go get the reverend so he can talk some sense into her."

"Don't," Thor said. "She's made up her mind, and so have I. If Anders leaves, we'll go right now."

"But what about my baby? You promised to be here. I don't know if I can do this without you."

"Eva, stop begging," Anders said.

"I'm not!" Tears streamed down her cheeks. "But I will if that's the only thing that will make her see reason!"

Willow rose from the chair and knelt beside Eva's chair. She patted her friend's hand. "Don't cry, Miss Eva. I wish you could understand why I have to do this. Those children aren't orphans. They have a father. I'm going to get him."

"What children?" Anders gave the three of them a hard look.

"Three runaways passed through the woods, and we showed them to safety. Don't worry. They didn't come inside." Thor stood. "Willow was right. We shouldn't have stopped here. Eva, I'm sorry you're upset. We know the risks. Alone, she'd be in grave danger, but I promise to do everything I can to keep her safe."

Anders shook his head. "Not dressed like that. Slave owners have fancy clothes. They don't travel in a flannel shirt and a pair of thread-bare britches. And they certainly don't travel without money."

He grabbed a tin can from the mantel. He pulled out a leather pouch and spilled its contents onto the tabletop. Silver and gold coins clattered into a good-sized heap. He retrieved several pieces and handed them to Thor. "You can use these. I have a suit coat, pants, and boots you can wear, too. The money isn't a loan, but the suit is. I was married in it, and I want it back."

Words lodged in Thor's chest. He nodded and accepted the coins. "Thank you."

"Don't thank me." Anders removed a handsome black suit with a crisp white shirt from the wardrobe. "Return safely so that Eva can find some peace. We don't have a valise, but this bag should be big enough to hold a day's change of clothing and a few supplies like soap, a razor, coffee, beans, and jerky. I suppose you can say the trunk is on the way or something to that effect. You can try on the suit out in the barn."

The pants fell past Thor's ankles and turned out to be a better fit than the britches. He walked a few paces in the barn, adjusting his feet to the fit of the spit-polished boots. Anders leaned against the barn door and watched.

"The pants never did fit me right. The suit was a gift from Eva's father. I couldn't complain," Anders explained. "How are the boots? I expect you'll be doing some walking and probably some running, too."

"The boots fit like they were made for me." Thor pulled the suspender straps over his shoulders. "I'm surprised by your generosity. Why the change?"

"I'm careful, not heartless. The situation is getting bad on both sides. Straddling the line and being neutral should protect us, but I have a feeling it won't for very long. I'll have to make a choice."

Thor tested the weight of the jacket before he shrugged into it. "It looks like you made it."

"Because I'm helping you? Maybe so. Eva loves Willow. If something happened to her, Eva would be heartbroken. I can't let that happen. Besides, you are family. Nobody but a Magnusen would be stubborn and foolish enough to sneak onto a plantation with the intent of reuniting a slave father with his runaway children."

Thor smiled faintly. "I suppose that's true." He took off the suit and shirt, carefully folding them and placing them into the bag. As he changed back into the shirt and pants he previously borrowed, he noticed the thoughtful expression on the other man's face.

Anders reached inside his pocket. "I found this on the road today. It was just lying there, blinking in the sun. Something made me pick it up and pocket it. I don't have much use for one of these things, though. I can tell the time of day by looking at the sky."

Anders opened his hand and extended it toward Thor. A shiny gold timepiece rested in his palm. Thor's throat constricted. *Could it be? Nah.*

There was only one way to know for sure. Thor inhaled a quick breath. He took the watch and held it to the lantern. The clasp opened easily. The clock ticked without hesitation. Unable to put off the inevitable, he flipped the watch over. The inscription winked back at him.

Air rushed from his lungs. "Love lasts forever."

"It's true," Anders said. "Good times and bad times come and go, but it's the love that remains. I didn't always know that."

The timepiece held Thor transfixed. His key to the twentieth century rested in the palm of his hand, but was it really? If so, did he want to take it? What about Willow? She needed him, and he didn't want to let her down. Hell, he didn't want to let himself down! He endured his share of disappointment and failure. If he could risk the dangers of stealing a slave from a plantation in 1860, there was no doubt he could face his future in 1985.

He extended the watch. The timekeeper would be safe in his great-great-grandpa's hands. "Here. It's too expensive. I have your money. You keep this."

"I was thinking about trading it, but nobody in these parts has any use for a fancy timepiece like that. You use it to complete the picture. Who knows? You may need it yourselves."

Thor hesitated. When Anders's stance didn't change, Thor grudgingly accepted the timekeeper. Uncertain of what set the thing off and hurled him back in time made him edgy. Maybe the watch didn't work on its own. Maybe variables like location and state of consciousness mattered, too. As long as he refrained from napping under the tree near the creek while in possession of the watch, he should manage to stay put. He hoped for some control. He refused to think of the repercussions without it.

"You'll get it back when we return."

Anders replied to Thor's promise with a nod. "Do you have anything in case you run into trouble? I hear patrollers are starting to roam again and they're never empty-handed."

Thor shook his head. "I don't have a weapon. I suppose I could buy one."

"Don't waste the money on that. Use one of my pistols. Like the clothes, I want it back."

"Of course."

—◦◦◦—

"We have some decisions to make." He and Willow followed the trail away from the Magnusen cabin. "With the money Anders gave us, we can either take the train or use the stage. Which do you prefer?"

"It doesn't make a difference, but wouldn't using either of them bring attention to us?"

"I don't see how it could. The return trip will be the hard one to make. Getting down there will be the easy part since we're together."

"I suppose so." She chewed her bottom lip. "Well, Thor, I can't decide. Whichever you want is fine with me."

"Have you ever been on a train?"

"I've heard about them. Miss Eva rode the train when she lived in Boston. She said it was a nice ride if you had the money to afford it."

"We have the money—"

"But should we waste it on a train?" she asked. "What if we need it later to buy horses or food?"

"We'll have enough," he assured her.

"Sounds like your mind is made up. The closest railway is quite a ways."

"There's one in Canton. That's only a few miles."

"The railroad doesn't go through Canton."

He frowned. Canton's railroad had been around for a long time, but obviously not prior to 1860. Hiking through the woods to the plantation would take up a considerable amount of time. Time, he wasn't sure they had. Big Nat's circumstances weren't clean cut. What if he'd already been moved to another plantation? What if the reverend forwarded the children to the next station before their return? The questions nagged Thor and made him wish for faster transportation than what the nineteenth century offered.

"So, Canton *will* have a railroad one day," she commented softly.

Her attempt to lead him into a discussion about the future was cute. He wagged his finger at her. "Yes, it does and that's all you need to know about that."

"I suppose." She stifled a yawn. "But aren't there little things that you could talk about?"

"I'm not sure. I'll think about it some and let you know."

He glanced at the sky. To the east, the golden rays of sun had yet to make an appearance. Stars still glittered across the sky. Daylight promised to arrive before they knew it. Neither of them had slept.

Their movements had slowed. They needed rest.

"What were you planning to do about sleeping?"

"I hadn't really thought about it," she confessed, stifling another yawn. "Most of the runaways say they catch sleep when they can. I guess I was thinking of doing the same, but I wanted to get some distance first. When the reverend sees my note, he'll come after me."

"And when he finds out I'm with you, he'll come even faster. Since we can't take the train, we might as well get a horse."

"From where?" she asked. "Few folks in these parts have horses, and if they do, they're not about to give them up."

"Canton is about a half hour walk away. We'll stop at the livery station and see what happens. Time is important, and we have to get a good lead on Brown. Around what time will he get up?"

"Usually after a meeting like the one last night, he'll be tired. He won't wake up until after eight."

"And Olivia? Will she sleep in, too?"

"Sleep in?" she repeated slowly. "Um, no, she wakes up early every day, but I doubt if she'll see the note. She'll be busy with the children and getting breakfast ready. She won't take a moment until her chores are done."

"Do you think she'll miss you?"

"Not with Miss Eva as large as she is. Miss Olivia expects me to leave early and go to the cabin. If the reverend hasn't told her about my need for an escort, our secret will be safe for six or seven hours. Otherwise, she'll wake him immediately and they'll be after us."

"We should keep moving. After we get the horses, we'll ride for an hour or two, and then we'll find someplace to rest."

They arrived in Canton while the small town was fast asleep, and daylight was still some hours away. Having adjusted to life without the convenience of electricity, Thor read the names on the buildings by the light of the moon and stars.

A small general store sat in the center of the town with a tavern on the opposite side of the wide dirt road. A blacksmith lay adjacent to the store, but nowhere did Thor see a sign for a livery.

Willow's soft hand brushed against his. Her footsteps lingered a step behind. Her interest in their surroundings caught his attention and he paused, waiting for her to stand beside him. "You've been here before, haven't you?"

"Yes, but never at night. It's so quiet. I always thought the town breathed on its own, but I guess like the rest of us Canton needs its rest. Mr. Hammond is the blacksmith. Here's his place. Maybe we'll find some horses inside."

The blacksmith shop was dark, but a sign propped against the window said that the owner was upstairs in case of emergency. Thor headed toward the staircase. "Wait here for me. I'll be right back."

He raced up the creaky steps and knocked firmly on the door. A disheveled man appeared. The man squinted at Thor. "Yeah?"

"Are you Hammond, the blacksmith?"

"Yeah. You need something?"

Thor grimaced at the man's slow response. *What's the point of false advertisement?* "Yes, I'd like a couple of horses if you have them."

"I have some, but they don't come cheap. You'll have to pay for 'em."

"I have money."

"Hold on. Let me pull on some pants, and I'll meet you downstairs."

Thor found Willow waiting for him in the doorway of the shop. Eyes closed, she leaned against the jamb. From the slow fall of her shoulders, he knew that slumber claimed her. She should be near exhaustion with all the walking they'd done coupled with the lack of sleep. He'd have to find a decent place for them to rest.

He lightly cupped her face and whispered, "Willow, wake up."

Her eyelids fluttered open. Her eyes focused on him and she smiled. "Thor."

The innocent happiness of her response warmed his heart. No one had ever looked at him quite that way before. It made him feel special.

Creaking stairs reminded him of their surroundings and ruse. He dropped his hand. "The blacksmith is coming. Don't say anything. We'll pretend you're mute. Does he know you?"

"He's come to a few of the reverend's meetings. I've seen him, but I don't know if he'd recognize me."

"Keep the hat on and try not to look at him."

"I'll keep my eyes on the ground."

"The horses are back here in the stable," Hammond informed them. He held a lantern and waved it front of Thor and Willow. He then moved it back to Thor again. "The stable's this way."

Thor followed with Willow right behind him. The blacksmith led them to the rear of his shop. He unlocked the large double wooden doors and pushed them open. Horses neighed at the sudden noise and light. The efficient man spoke to the animals in soothing tones. The horses soon became quiet again.

"Here they are. The ones in the first couple of stalls are yours if you want them. The price is—"

"Hold on a minute while I take a look at them." Thor went to the first stall and bent to inspect the horse's legs. He didn't know a damn thing about examining horses, but hoped Willow did. She squatted beside him, and he whispered in her ear, "Is this one any good?"

She held up a finger and moved around the horse, examining its legs, shoes, and flesh. When she finished, she looked at Thor and nodded.

He waited for her to check the second horse. Upon her approval, he said, "I'll take them. How much?"

"They don't come cheap. I got them from a breeder from Charlotte."

Thor handed the man two gold coins. "Will this be enough?"

Hammond bit into the coins and gave Thor a wide smile. "It would be just fine. I'll even add a couple of saddles and blankets, too. Do you need anything else?"

Thor smiled at the man's eagerness. No matter the century, money talked. "A couple of canteens with water and some beef jerky. That will be enough. Thank you."

"You're welcome." The blacksmith chuckled, coins jingling in his pocket as he closed the doors behind them.

Thor and Willow left Canton and followed the dirt road south. Willow sat upright on the horse and guided it without any problems, but her shoulders slumped, and that was enough for Thor. "We'll stop soon," he promised.

"We should go a little ways more. Do you think you can make it?"

"I suggested we stop for you. You look like you're about to drop."

"I'm fine." She straightened her shoulders. "Do you know what you're doing on that horse? He's looking antsy."

Thor stiffened. He never did like horseback riding. Cal loved it, but he always hated it. Horses were unpredictable, and it was only a matter of time before the one he rode proved it. He grunted. "I can handle him."

She guided her horse closer. Her left hand reached out and covered his. Despite the leather gloves that prevented flesh-to-flesh contact, ripples of pleasure shot throughout his body. He sucked in air and tried not to react, all the while hoping she'd keep her hand there awhile longer.

"You're holding the reins too tight," she said in a husky murmur. Her thumb caressed the back of his hand in sweeping strokes. "Loosen your grip, and the horse will respond in kind. If you're gentle with him, he'll be gentle with you."

Thor obeyed her soft command, and sure enough, the horse calmed down. Her hand dropped to his thigh. Her light touch was enough to ignite a flame of desire within him.

"Relax. You're wound as tight as a tin drum. He can feel it. Calm yourself."

Calm myself? How in the hell was he supposed to do that when the mere touch of her glove-covered hand inflamed him? Her sweet, honeysuckle scent made him dizzy with desire. Her soft, husky whisper aroused him further and made him long to hear her cry out in passion.

She removed her hand, and he caught it. He pulled the glove off and raised her hand to his lips, brushing a soft kiss onto her fingertips. She exhaled loudly before tugging free.

"Thank you," he added and handed the glove to her.

She slipped the leather material onto her hand. "You're welcome," she replied under her breath.

They rode in silence for several more miles. Thor wondered where her thoughts took her. She seemed eager for the adventure, refusing to let fatigue stop her. Her zeal inspired him and presented another quality that attracted him to her.

Dammit, how he wanted her. He tried to push the longing out of his mind, but the solitude made it so damned hard to ignore. In 1985, he wouldn't have hesitated in pursuing her, but 1860 demanded that he kept his distance. It wasn't fair, but nothing in life was. He learned that a long time ago. Knowing the truth didn't make it any easier to accept.

"There's a station in Chicopee. It's almost forty miles from here. The Station Master there may know where Big Nat is."

"That's a long way," he replied. "There's no way we can make it there without resting. Let's get off the main road and find a place to sleep for a few hours."

This time Willow didn't attempt to dissuade him. She guided her horse off to the west side of the road, and Thor did the same. They found a spot hidden in a grove of bushes and trees. Both promptly fell asleep.

—◦∕◦∕◦—

Heavy pounding on the door shook the walls of the Magnusen cabin. Anders left Eva's side to answer the knock. He jerked the door open and greeted Reverend Brown's angry red face with a scowl. "Eva's birthing," he grimly announced and rushed back to his sweating wife.

Brown's footsteps struck the floor with heavy blows. He stood just behind Anders. "How long?"

"Since first light," Anders replied. "About two hours now."

"How close are the pains?" the reverend questioned.

"They're getting closer and closer," Anders said. "She's passed out a few times." He pressed a towel against Eva's glistening cheek. "I 'spect the pains are bad."

She reached for his hand. "They're not so bad. With pleasure must come some amount of pain. It makes us appreciate the little one we're being blessed with."

Brown rested his hand on her swollen abdomen. His fingers flexed against her quivering mound. "It's not right."

"What's wrong?" Anders and Eva asked in unison.

"The head isn't in the proper place. The baby will need to be turned." He gave Anders a hard look. "Can you do that?"

"I've done it for a mare, but… I'm not sure I could do that to Eva. Can you help us?"

Brown's mouth tightened. "I could prepare her, but Olivia has a better hand at this, than I. Go get her, and I'll stay here with Eva."

Anders stood and Eva grabbed his hand. "What about Willow? The reverend came here looking for her. Didn't you, Reverend? We can't take up time in your search."

"She's with your relation, isn't she?" Brown asked.

"Yes."

"I imagine your kin is keeping her safe. I came close to going past your cabin to look for her, but the good Lord spoke to me, and here I am. I'll stay and help you." He looked at Anders. "Hurry along. We don't have much time."

CHAPTER EIGHT

Anders found his patience sorely tested as late afternoon arrived and Eva lost consciousness again. The pain of the prolonged childbirth had shone vividly in her bluish gray eyes. He longed to ease her suffering. If he could bear her pain, he would. Anders hated seeing her this way.

"Why won't the babe just come? Why must my Eva endure such agony, and for so long?" he thought.

"We can't question the ways of the Lord," Reverend Brown said quietly, letting Anders know that he'd spoken his thoughts aloud. "Some things happen a certain way for a reason. The Good Book says there's a season and a time to every purpose under Heaven. You can find that in Chapter Three of Ecclesiastes."

"Can I find out the purpose of the pain she's in? Will it tell me why she's hurting so, and if she dies, will it tell me why?"

"You mustn't talk like that," Olivia scolded. She patted Eva's glistening forehead with a towel. "She can hear you."

"She's no doubt wondering the same thing," Anders said, bitterly. "All she's ever wanted was a healthy, happy baby to love and care for. Why can't she have that without this trouble?"

"Perhaps this birthing will cause you to cherish the child all the more," the reverend suggested, "and any other children you may have."

Dogged determination brought a grimace to Anders face. He shook his head. "After this one, we won't have any more. I'm not watching her go through this torment again."

"It isn't torture." Eva's eyes fluttered open. "I want more babies, Anders, and you'll give them to me."

He knelt at her bedside. Tears welled in his eyes. "I'm so sorry about this."

"It's not your fault. Birthing is rarely ever easy. It took almost an entire week for my grandmother to give birth to my Uncle Calvin. I suppose I should have warned you when I married you. Childbirth isn't child's play in my family."

Olivia raised the quilt to Eva's knees. "It's time to turn the babe," she announced. She quickly washed her hands before addressing the men. "Hold her down. If she passes out again, leave her be. Are you ready? Anders, she won't enjoy this a bit, but this will make the rest of the process much easier."

His jaw clamped down. "I understand." He moved to one side of his wife while Reverend Brown claimed the other. His hard gaze connected with the reverend. "You'd better pray."

"I never stopped."

—◦◦◦—

Whale-oil lamps and burning candles illuminated the dark, tense cabin. Perspiration saturated the bedclothes covering Eva, and Anders worked hard to make her comfortable. After Olivia turned the baby, Brown suggested several times for Anders to join him outside and leave the rest up to the women. Anders refused to budge. He feared that if he left Eva's side, he could lose her forever. A bite of fresh of air wasn't worth that risk.

"It's coming along nicely now," Olivia announced. "You're doing just fine, Eva. Bear down when I tell you to, and relax when I give the word."

"I will." Dots of apple red colored Eva's flushed cheeks. She gave Anders a watery smile. "Soon, we'll be parents."

He tried to make light of his uneasiness. Pressing a kiss to her temple, he whispered, "You've been saying that for hours."

"Anything worth having is worth waiting for," she reminded him. "This babe will be a prize for sure."

Sudden tension claimed her body. Anders grabbed her hand. Her fingers dug into his flesh with sharp precision. From her hold, he knew the pain was great. Damn near unbearable. Olivia called out instructions, and Eva followed each of them and remained conscious throughout.

"Keep pushing," Olivia advised. "I can see the head. This baby has a thick patch of brown hair. I can't wait to see the rest."

Anders resisted the urge to observe the arrival from Olivia's viewpoint. Eva needed his hand. He listened to the older woman's commentary and gathered the rest from his imagination. If Eva was right, the birthing would be over soon, and they could both see the babe then.

Please, God, let it be over soon.

"Relax now, Eva," Olivia instructed.

"Is something wrong?" Eva panted. Perspiration trickled down her ruddy cheeks. "Shouldn't I keep going until the baby is free?"

Olivia wiped her glistening forehead with a swipe of her sleeve. "You can rest yourself for a moment or two. The baby is fine just like he is. Anders, wet her tongue a bit. I imagine she's parched."

Anders reached for the almost empty glass of water that rested on a nearby table. His hand supported Eva as she rose slightly and drank the contents. She emptied the glass, and he asked, "Would you like more?"

"That was enough." She looked at Olivia. "Now?"

"My, you're impatient," Olivia scolded, gently. "Yes, now."

Eva bore down. Her hand clutched Anders's in an even tighter grip. Low groans passed from her lips. A faint cry followed the eerie silence.

Olivia told Eva to relax. The new parents shared worried glances. Knots formed in his belly. Anxiety made his voice harsh and demanding. "Olivia? We heard the cry."

"Everything is just fine," she said. "I'm making sure your daughter is presentable before she greets you."

"Our daughter." Eva released a deep breath. She extended her hands. "Please, Miss Olivia. Is she perfect? Let us see her."

"She's the spitting image of an angel." Olivia held a squirming bundle in her arms as she stood and gently placed the infant into Eva's waiting arms.

Anders peered down at his small family. His breath caught in his throat while he watched Eva fold the blanket away from their child's face. The door creaked open and heavy footsteps crossed the room. Anders paid Reverend Brown's entrance no mind. Awe held him still as a statue.

He stroked the baby's cheek. Her squirming paused as if she understood and acknowledged the love behind the tender caress. "Our little Dorothea is God's gift."

—◦◦◦—

As the days passed and Thor remained in 1860 with Willow, his confidence in his time travel theory strengthened. As long as all the variables weren't in place, the timepiece alone would not suddenly return him to 1985. Maybe it wasn't the watch that sent him to the past after all. The more time Thor spent with Willow the less he cared what caused the phenomena. His need to be with her grew with each conversation and every passing glance. Hell, just the sound of her breathing caused air to lodge in his throat. Most mornings, he awakened before her and simply watched her sleep. The smile she gave him as her eyes opened made him feel wanted. He wasn't wasting space. Finally, he served a purpose again, and that was enough. Returning to his time was a problem for later.

Riding at night and sleeping during the day became Thor and Willow's pattern. Thor hated that Willow slept on a ground covered with twigs and pebbles buffered only by a thin wool blanket. She never complained, saying that she didn't mind. It was only for a little while. Sleep was sleep no matter where or how they got it.

That wasn't good enough. The desire for proper sanctuary possessed him. He voiced the goal aloud as the sun peeked at them from the east and tinges of pink began to replace the midnight blue of the sky.

"We're stopping in the next town."

"Why? Are you hungry?"

"Fish and berries are filling. I don't mind what we eat on the trail, but I'm tired of how we sleep."

"You're as stubborn as an old mule." She groaned. "You know I'm not allowed in hotels."

"If I put up a fuss about it—"

"When the reverend rides through looking for us, he'd be able to find us for sure." She possessed the calm voice of reason.

Thor grunted. "You should have been able to sleep inside at that Station in Chicopee." The memory of their most recent stop burned a hole in his male pride. "Making you sleep in a barn! I should have knocked him on his ass!"

"Thor!" Her voice scolded him while her giggle told another tale. "The bales of hay were soft and pleasing. You said so yourself."

"I lied."

After riding for several more miles, Thor spotted what appeared to be an abandoned farm. A shack sat beneath a cluster of oaks, and a dilapidated barn stood several yards away. Weeds and wildflowers flourished in wild disarray. A rippling stream lay behind a row of bushes. His hopes soared at the sight of gushing water. Their canteens needed refreshing and a bath promised to ease the low throb in his shoulder.

"Looks like we have a choice."

"The shack is hidden by the trees. If someone comes, we could sneak off into the woods."

"The shack it is."

"It could be set up to trap runaways." Willow warned as she slid off her horse. "Don't rush inside. Be careful."

"I will."

His inspection of the shack found nothing suspicious. The interior bordered on imperfect. In a battle of safety versus appeal, safety won every time. After hours of travel, they desperately needed a safe haven. He called out for her to join him.

"The horses are tied up. I couldn't lift the saddles off." She handed him a canteen. "There's a stream nearby. If we hurry, we can wash up before the sun rises and then refill the canteens tonight before we leave."

"You're very efficient." He swallowed a gulp of water. The cool liquid refreshed him instantly. "Let me know before you bathe. I want to be close in case someone comes around. I'll take care of the saddles and water the horses. In the meantime, make yourself comfortable."

—◦◦◦—

Willow looked around at the dank surroundings. *Comfortable?* That was easy for him to say. The dirt floor hardly provided relief, but it was possible the extra blankets could help.

She found an old broom in the corner and swept a space for them. There was a small hole in the floor. She gathered some twigs to fill the opening. By the time Thor returned, vibrant orange and red flames flickered in the makeshift hearth.

"It's looks nice." He gave her a saddle and a blanket. He dropped his saddle on the ground near the fire, covering it with a blanket. "I checked out the stream. We'll have fish later."

"Are you hungry now?" She wondered if his comment was a hint for her to make breakfast. With few stops to eat, Thor's stomach growled loudly and often. She wondered if he had a bottomless pit inside him.

"No." He rubbed his shoulder. "Food is the last thing on my mind. I'll get the fish later. Are you ready to wash up?" An infectious grin curved his full lips. "I promise I won't peek. I won't mind if you do, though."

She knew better than to respond to his flirtatious teasing and silently walked beside him toward the stream. Whenever bathing time arrived, he made the same comment. At first, she wondered if he would peek. He never did. Now, she trusted his word, but that didn't stop the tingle from traveling down her spine at the mere suggestion of seeing his bare body. Clothing fit him far better than cotton and wool had a right to. Anders's wedding suit would no doubt add to his handsome features. She could hardly wait to see him dressed in finery.

The cold water and the threat of passing travelers made for a short bath and fast cleaning of her drawers and chemise. Willow pulled on her clean spare undergarments and hat. She shook out her riding clothes and stepped back into them. A light splash warned her that Thor was no longer decent and already in the water. Usually, she left him alone and moved to do so.

"Willow, wait."

Trepidation sparked through her. Her voice wavered with uncertainty. "Yes?"

"Turn around," he said quietly, "I won't bite." When she followed his bidding, he added, "I need your help. We should reach Big Nat and the plantation tomorrow. I may not have time to shave before then, and I doubt we'll find a mirror. Can you help me shave?"

"I've never done it." Her heart swelled at the thought. Having a reason to touch his face and stand close enough to breathe his scent created a doubly sinful temptation. She backed away. "I may cut you."

"It's not as hard as it looks. Besides, I trust you."

Although a few golden rays filtered through the overhanging branches, the sun had yet to reach its full glory. Shaving outside could trap them in full daybreak. Willow nodded once and said, "I'll do it for you at the shack. I think I saw a bucket in the barn. I'll come back and get water."

"No, I'll bring it with me when I come in." He paused and gave her a faint smile empty of the usual hint of flirtation. "Thanks, Willow."

She returned to the shack cloaked in nervous anticipation. Half a dozen reasons to rescind her agreement came to mind. *This chore is too intimate*, she thought, as her footsteps wore a path across the dirt floor. Since the kiss in the woods, she was careful not to reveal her attraction to him. Awareness grew despite her vigilance. This small task threatened to be her undoing. Then, the door opened and there he stood. One look into his eyes and her refusal died.

"I brought the water." He held up the bucket as he kicked the door closed. His heavy footsteps brought him to her. He handed her their bag of supplies. As he towered over her, he said, "We can't do this standing up. The fire you made is just right. We can sit near it."

They settled where he suggested. Firelight flickered beside them. Pretty colors reflected against his stubble covered jaw. She barely noticed the brilliant, dancing hues. Being this close to him left her breathless. He smelled fresh like the stream, yet his distinct male scent carried through. A sudden sensation of weightlessness made her balance falter. His hands closed around her shoulders, steadying her.

"Relax. It's really easy. I'd do it myself if I had a mirror." He watched her closely, as if gauging her reaction. "Maybe I will try it—"

"No, just tell me what to do."

His instructions were simple. After lathering his face with soap, she grazed the sharp edge gently along his jaw. Although his hands rested on his lap, she felt the weight of his stare as surely as if he touched her. Blood pounded her temples. Heat scorched her fingertips on his skin. By the time she reached the area bordering his mouth, her heart pounded wildly against her ribcage. At his sharp intake of breath, she feared he heard it.

"You're almost done." His voice sounded gruff with unspent emotion.

Trying to ignore the urgency building within, she willed herself to complete the task. When it was over, he looked more handsome than ever, and her nerves felt stretched beyond recovery. Thor took the razor and spoke quietly as he cleaned it.

"Lie down and get some rest. I'll watch the fire and put it out. If you need another blanket, you can use mine."

Too shaken to protest or accept his offer, she sat on her blanket and removed the hat from her head. Hairpins dug into her scalp for days. Some relief came at allowing her hair to go free. The low burning ache inside required more. With a shake of her head, the long braid uncoiled and fell to her shoulder. Her fingers pulled through the thick mass, separating the braid. Before she could blink, he moved beside her.

"Allow me."

His husky voice whispered like a low, rumbling sigh. She shivered in spite of herself.

He took the braid from her trembling fingers and stroked the hair loose. The liberated mane flowed down her back in coarse waves, but that didn't stop him from running his fingers through it.

"So beautiful and soft. I've wanted to do this since the first day I saw you. Your long, dark braid is a silent invitation for loosening it."

Her heart pounded rapidly in her chest. Almost afraid to look at him, she shifted around to memorize the look in his eyes. Shadows from the fire flickered across his face and made her think of danger. He was so handsome with his strong jaw, full lips, and dark blue piercing eyes. She should look away from him but felt powerless to do so.

"We should get some rest," he murmured. Yet, he made no move to leave her. Instead, he leaned forward and nuzzled her neck. "Willow," he moaned, "make me leave. Push me away. Tell me to stop."

Her hands lifted to his broad shoulders then slipped to the nape of his neck. Curls brushed her hands like tiny caresses. Her fingers rubbed his neck and he moaned. She leaned toward him. "I can't."

———◦◦◦———

Thor's voice quivered with Willow's surrender. He didn't know whether to shout for joy or beg for a reprieve. His gut vibrated with warning. *Do the honorable thing — the right thing— and get away from her. Move to my blanket, lie down, close my eyes and try to sleep.* The slight pressure of her soft fingertips on his scalp and the desire burning in her eyes entranced him. The only move he made was toward her.

His face lowered to claim her lips in a deep, imploring kiss. His mouth moved sensuously across her soft, pliant lips, silently demanding her to open to him. She did, and in his eagerness to taste her, his tongue slipped and found hers.

Tasting. Probing. Tantalizing.

She shivered against him and grasped his back. His hands slipped inside the thick, wild mass of ink black hair. Gently, he angled her head and kept her close so the kiss didn't break and wouldn't end as he continued to press his hot, open mouth against hers.

Thor lowered her onto the blanket. His knees nudged her thighs apart as he settled between them. Resting on one elbow, his other hand cupped her full breast. Through the thin fabric of the worn work shirt, his fingers kneaded and caressed her hardened peaks. His mouth planted a trail of kisses along her neck and down to the pulse beating rapidly at her neck. His tongue laved the pulsating flesh and low moans vibrated from the back of her throat. She clutched his head, and her thighs gripped his waist.

Rock hard, his arousal throbbed within the confines of his pants. Picking up the ages old rhythm, he rubbed his lower body against hers. She moaned his name in a pleading whimper. "Thor…"

Her cries inflamed him. He lifted his head from her neck to look into her glazed eyes. "I want to make love to you. If you want me to stop, say so now. Please, Willow, make me stop now."

"I don't want you to."

Desire shone vividly in her glassy eyes. Her tongue darted out to moisten her lips. Thor needed no further response.

He kissed her again, as deeply and thoroughly as he did the first time. She responded by pushing her tongue inside his mouth and tantalizing him with her innocent insistence. Her pelvis rocked against him. He groaned. The ache in his pants begged for release, but he made no move to do so. Her innocence forced him to take care with her. Instinct told her what she wanted from him, but he knew she had never gone that far before. Tenderness and patience would have to be his guide.

Tenderness is a given, but Lord help me with patience.

The kiss ended. The suspenders fell from his shoulders. She tugged his shirt free from the waistband of his pants. He allowed her to pull the garment over his head. The appreciative gleam in her eyes as she looked at his bare chest only fueled his arousal.

Her hands glided over him, caressing the hard planes of his torso and the clenched muscles of his abdomen. Her inquisitive fingers trailed the thin line of hair that disappeared inside his pants. When she tried to unbutton them, he closed his hand over hers.

"Not yet."

"May I touch you?"

Hitching a sharp breath, he nodded. Her hand found the rigid length of him. The heavy cotton material of his pants failed to diminish the insistence of her touch. His back arched as her hand stroked him, and he groaned.

"Do you like this?"

Thor shuddered. Unable to speak, he nodded.

"You're so hard," she said as she continued to caress him. "Like the iron spokes on a wheel."

She moved to the next button, but he was fast. He pushed her hand away and pressed his pelvis against hers. "Not yet," he muttered again with all the control he could muster. Her mouth puckered into a pout, which he kissed away.

While his lips claimed hers, his fingers plucked open the buttons on her shirt. The ribbons on her camisole were quickly untied and his hand slid across her warm flesh to caress the full, quivering mound inside. When the kiss ended, his head dipped to her breast. Open-mouth, he kissed her there. Her hips bucked against his, and she clutched his head. His tongue bathed the hard pebble. His hand stroked down her body to the apex of her thighs.

Not wasting time, he unbuttoned her pants in one fluid motion. His hand pressed against her damp undergarment, his fingers caressing her through the cotton barrier. His mouth watered in anticipation. He longed to taste her there. Planting kisses along her ribcage, his fingers continued to caress her. She bucked against his hand and clutched his shoulders, all the while moaning his name.

Thor quickly removed the remainder of their clothing. Willow whimpered in protest when he moved away, but those whimpers soon became moans of pleasure when he returned.

Intending to love every inch of her lithe, willing body, his large hands grasped an ankle. He brought her foot to his lips, running kisses along the arch. His teeth nibbled her toes, and she shrieked.

"Easy now." His voice was husky and soft, seducing her. "This is only the beginning."

His fingers grazed across her silky, smooth flesh from ankle to thigh. He smiled seductively as goose bumps covered her long limbs.

"Thor," she moaned, as he lowered himself between her legs. His tongue trailed paths along her inner thighs until she cried out to him again.

He inched closer to the heart of her femininity. Her sweet musky scent greeted him, increasing his desire to savor her. Unable to resist another moment, his mouth opened, and his tongue licked her slick folds.

Her hips bucked wildly. "Oh, Thor!"

Her response nearly pushed him over the edge. His mouth opened wider, and his kiss deepened. His tongue laved and devoured her spicy feminine juices, feasting on her in wild abandon. Her fingers dug into the bunched muscles of his shoulders and served to encourage him even more. Moving his mouth to direct his attention to her tiny nub, he carefully slid first one finger inside of her. She stiffened at the initial contact, and he withdrew.

Patience, he reminded himself, sweat beading on his brow.

His hands moved from her thighs and slid over her flat abdomen then rested on her full breasts. His thumbs and fingers rolled over her nipples, making her sigh and moan in barely contained passion. Delirious sensations swept through him, making him feel as if he was sent back in time for the purpose of bringing life to her passions and reawakening his own.

All the while, his ardent kisses possessed her. Thor took her little bud between his lips and tongue. He sucked gently at first. "Oh," she moaned, as his tongue's strokes became more insistent. She released a loud shriek as his mouth sucked harder.

Her legs trembled against him. Her hips jerked in time to his ministrations. Suddenly, she tensed and closed her legs around his head. Her first taste of passion captured her completely. Pleasure rippled through Thor. He was the first man to take her there.

As the waves of desire engulfed her, he continued to love her with his mouth. He craved the taste of her, instantly addicted to her wild response. She moved wildly beneath him, screaming his name, and digging her fingers into his flesh. Just when her movements stilled and she seemed breathless and spent, he entered her.

The barrier of innocence reminded him to control his instincts to bury himself within her. Her body tensed with his first thrust.

Patience.

Thor withdrew and eased inside her again. Slowly, he moved, allowing her to become accustomed to his penetrating arousal. Veins corded in his neck as he focused all of his attention on loving her with gentleness. His efforts paid off when she begged, "Please, Thor."

He buried himself deep within her, filling her with his hardness.

Her legs wrapped around his hips, and her pelvis bumped hard against his. His mouth closed over hers. Her tongue pushed inside his mouth and quickly found his. Thor drew it deep into his mouth, tasting her there just as thoroughly as he had tasted her before.

His previous sexual encounters had never been as exquisite as this. Their bodies melded together. He felt at one with Willow. An invisible cord stretched around them, making this more than a quest for physical release. His soul connected with hers. She was better than his boyhood and college fantasies. Willow Elkridge was all he ever wanted and more. Inside her arms, he discovered joy that he never knew existed.

His body became hot and slick with perspiration. She slid her hands slid down his back and grasped his backside. He pushed hard against her. Their hips moved closer, enabling him to sink deeper inside her.

She cried out in ecstasy. "Blessed be! I love you, Thor."

Her declaration mingled with the loud roar of blood filling his ears. Rocking against her, his release came hard. His voice was raw and hoarse. "Oh, Willow.."

Rolling off her, Thor closed his eyes and wrapped his arms tightly around her. In the otherwise quiet shack, their breaths came in ragged spurts until their heart rates returned to normal, and they slowly came back to earth.

Willow's slender frame curved against him in a perfect fit. Her thigh rested trustingly on top of his, and she sighed deeply. As he enjoyed the warmth of her body, her words came back to him. His eyes flew open.

She loves me.

A few simple words rocked his world and rendered him speechless. What should he say? He cared deeply for her. More than he ever cared for any woman but was it love?

Oh, God, we didn't even use protection. What if? It was too soon to consider that possibility after the joy of being with her. The need for words nagged him. He owed her that much.

He brushed damp tendrils from her face. "Willow?"

She mumbled an unintelligible response. Through parted lips, her breath tickled his chest in slow, deep caresses. She was asleep.

He shifted beside her and watched her. He was bone-tired and should do the same, but his eyelids refused to close. Even in slumber, her beauty captivated him.

Willow Elkridge was so much more than a pretty face. She embodied everything that he previously ignored in his determination to achieve his Super Bowl dreams. Selfless and loving, she willingly risked her life for someone else. Through her, he was learning what his family had been trying to tell him for almost a year. There was more to life than football.

"Oh, Willow," he murmured, pressing a kiss to her dewy, soft temple, "thank you for saving my life."

CHAPTER NINE

Sunlight streamed through the slats of the shack and beamed across Thor's face. He blinked awake with a yawn. Willow's sleeping form still curved against him. Careful not to disturb her, he reached inside the saddlebag and removed the timepiece from the leather confines.

Mid-morning was giving way to early afternoon. They had a few more hours of rest before their nightly journey began. He closed his eyes and drifted to the edge of slumber. A low noise rumbled in the distance. Thor sat up. Alarm shot through him. When she awakened and stared at him in surprise, he knew he hadn't been mistaken.

Dogs.

Muttering an oath, he rose from the blanket to investigate. His view from the window left him with nothing but a sour taste in his mouth. Barking thundered just south of them, but he couldn't judge the distance. Just that animals were coming fast. He quickly pulled on Anders's suit and grabbed his great-great-grandfather's pistol.

"What the hell is that?" He paused before going outside. "Are those dogs or the wolves you were talking about?"

She moved with urgency. Her fingers flew over buttons, righting her clothing and tying her bootstraps. While braiding her hair, she joined him at the door. "I can't be sure. Those wolves were wild. We'd better see to the horses."

"You stay here. There's only one pistol, and I have it. I'll check the horses."

Her hands briefly clutched his. "Please, be careful."

Shouts and louder barking greeted him as he headed toward the frightened horses. He checked the pistol and satisfied that it was ready. He spoke gently to the horses. Seconds later, a pack of hunting dogs raced past him and circled an oak, yapping wildly. A group of men on horseback followed. The leader raised his rifle and shot at the sky. The man yelled, "Come on out of there! You know I won't shoot. You're no good dead!"

"What's going on?" Thor asked. "What's in that tree?"

"A runaway." The leader fired another shot at the sky. "We can do this all day, but the longer you're in that tree, the worse it's gonna be! Get your ass down from there!"

The scene unfolded right in front of Thor's eyes. It was like being in the middle of the mini-series *Roots*, but this was different. This wasn't a television program that could disappear with the ease of changing the channel. This was real life, and there wasn't a damn thing he could do to make a difference or stop it.

A black man jumped from the oak's branches. He was shorter than Thor. What he lacked in height he made up with in muscle. His arms and shoulders looked rock solid and strong. The clothes he wore were little more than rags, yet he stood proud and tall. He didn't say a word to his captors and simply held out his wrists for the ropes that would bind him.

The man's face was immobile, and as Thor neared him, Thor noted only sheer force of will kept the man from acting on his rage. Their eyes met for a second. Raw hatred burned in the captive's eyes as their gazes locked. The intensity of the runaway's glare shocked him.

Thor averted his eyes to look at the leader. "What will happen to him now?"

"Oh, Big Nat will be shown a thing or two about what happens to runaways. Mr. Warren Eugene Davis don't coddle his property. This one will learn that fairly soon."

Big Nat?

Thor took a closer look at the captured man. He was older, darker and larger, but he bore a striking resemblance to the three children Thor led to Brown's refuge. There was no doubt about it. He had to be the children's father. *Talk about luck.* Now all Thor had to do was free Big Nat from the goons who had him.

A posse of armed men and snarling dogs surrounded them. Some things were easier said than done. He'd have to use a little creativity. "Mr. Davis, you say?" he asked the leader.

The man reared his head back and laughed. "I'm not Davis. I'm just the overseer's son. Grady Falls at your service."

"Oh." Thor made his voice sound disappointed. "I've been looking for the Davis plantation and have gotten badly lost. I hoped to make the man a business proposition. Do you think you and your men could show me the way?"

"Sure." Grady shrugged. "Those your horses back there? We don't have any extras to spare unless you're willing to double up."

Thor offered him a polite smile and shook his head. "That won't be necessary. Just let me get my things."

——◦∕∾∕∾——

Willow handed Thor his saddle, blanket and canteen as soon he entered the shack. "Did you hear?" he asked.

"We found him," she said, her expression solemn, "and not a moment too soon. They're taking him back to be punished. Probably whipped or beaten."

Tears glistened in her eyes and rolled down her cheeks. Thor went to her, brushing the wetness from her face. "I won't let that happen."

She nodded and sniffled. "We'd better get out there."

"Willow, wait." He stopped her from walking out the door. "Maybe you should go back to the Browns. Let me take it from here."

"I've come this far. I can't turn back now. I'll be okay, and don't worry, I won't say a word." She pushed a few stray tendrils inside the lopsided hat she wore and gave him her spectacles. "How do I look? If I keep my head down and stay quiet, think I'll still pass as a boy?"

His smile faltered. "Only to someone who doesn't know you."

Despite the curious stares of Grady and his assortment of armed white men, Thor insisted that Willow ride on horseback. She wanted to protest, but her role as a mute prevented her from voicing her opinion. Dark clouds looming in Thor's eyes worried her. Losing his temper could jeopardize their rescue mission, so she obeyed him and climbed onto the saddle.

"I didn't get your name," Grady called out.

"Folks call me Thor."

The men shook hands. "Pleased to meet you, Thor. Do you mind if Big Nat rides along with your boy? Usually, we make 'em walk. Davis wants us back before nightfall. We'll get back faster if he was riding."

There was a slight pause before Thor answered. "He can ride."

Without her spectacles, she could not read his face clearly, but the deep rumble of his response made up for what her eyes couldn't tell her. The idea of Big Nat riding with her displeased him.

Grady instructed one of his men to untie Big Nat's hands just long enough for the runaway to pull himself onto the saddle behind Willow. Once settled, they bound his wrists again and the party began their journey.

Willow had no knowledge of a lover's temperament, but she guessed Thor was jealous of Big Nat's proximity to her. His reaction flattered her, but it left her a little bewildered, too. Her feelings for Thor were strong. Big Nat was a stranger and could not compare to her time traveling companion. It seemed to her Thor should know that.

"He don't like me riding with you," Big Nat said in a low voice against her ear.

She stiffened and remained quiet.

"I saw you with him in that shack. I know you can talk, and I know you ain't no boy."

Her heart lurched. She stirred uneasily on the saddle.

"Don't worry," he quickly replied. "I won't say nothing to them about you, but you'd best be careful with that young Massa. Just 'cause they bed you don't mean they care about you. They don't care about nothing but what's between their legs. You just be careful with him."

She glanced around. The other men were busy talking to each other or listening to Thor and Grady. None of them was interested in her and Big Nat. "I know him well enough," she whispered, barely moving her lips. "He's not like the rest of them."

"He's just like 'em." Big Nat grunted. "Ain't no difference to none of 'em. When he tires of you, he'll go on to the nex' one. That's how they do it."

Willow's heart constricted at his prediction. She didn't want to believe Thor would cast her aside so easily. Especially after she surrendered herself to the delirious warmth of his touch. However, his departure was inevitable.

He came from a different world. A whole century separated them, and just because he was with her now, didn't mean he always would be. Whatever brought him to 1860 could just as easily reclaim him and send him back to nineteen hundred and eighty-five. Her love wouldn't hold him to her. Losing her parents at such a young age taught her that her love wasn't a restrictive bond. Just as easily as she lost her Mama and Papa, she could lose Thor. She needed to remember that and never forget.

"Why you dressed like a boy anyway?"

His question made her think of the children hiding out at the Browns. A faint smile crossed her lips as she pictured their young faces and their happy reunion with their father. Her smile widened as she spoke. "To look for you."

"For me?" he gasped. "You don't know me."

"No, I don't, but I know your children. Nat, Charity, and Clay are yours, aren't they?"

"Yeah," he responded slowly. "How do you know them?"

"I saw them on the Gospel Train. Thor," she said, inclining her head toward him, "was their Shepherd for a brief spell. He guided them to the station."

"Well, I'll be." Big Nat released a deep breath. "When?"

"Days ago. They told us what happened. I'm sorry about your wife."

"What?"

She glanced at him. His face was still unyielding and unreadable, but his eyes were completely different. She saw concern and grief reflected there. "The children said she passed on."

Willow wanted to say more, but thought better of it. She faced the road again and gently patted the long mane of the horse. A moment of silence passed between them.

"What happened to her?"

"She was upset because they sold you. The overseer became angry and whipped her. The children said she died the very same night. They ran away while the elders were preparing her for burial. They met another group of runaways and joined them. By the time we found the children in the woods, they were traveling alone. Their shepherd had to double back and told them what to look out for and what to do. You should be proud of them."

"I am. I thank you for watchin' over my children."

"You don't have to thank me. I'll get my thanks once you're reunited with them. That's why Thor and I are here."

"Is he good with that pistol?" Big Nat asked. "There's six of them and they're armed. I suppose we could take 'em."

"I'm not sure about that, not with those dogs. They'd set them on us for sure. We'll have to wait until the sun sets."

"We'll reach the Davis place before nightfall. If I make it in, I might not make it out. I've heard about Davis. He don't like his people running off. Grady Falls spoke the truth. I'm in for a beatin' or worse."

"Thor won't let that happen," she promised, "and neither will I."

"I don't see how you could stop it. Slaves told me he like to put on a big show. Folks come from all around to watch it. Davis won't change his ways on account of y'all."

After several more hours of riding, Grady announced that it was time for a break. The horses needed watering and he was hungry. Willow decided this would be the perfect opportunity to tell Thor about the Davis plantation. Maybe there was a way they could overpower Grady Falls and his men.

"How are you?" Thor cornered Willow between her horse and a tree. They were a few yards away from the others. He didn't try to mask his concern. "Have they offended you in any way or done anything to make you feel uncomfortable?"

"I'm fine. A little sore. I'm not used to riding a horse for so long. And you?"

He shrugged and averted his eyes. "I'm managing. It looks like we'll be at the Davis plantation before too long."

"I wanted to talk to you about that. Big Nat says that Davis is a horrible man. He thinks he'll be punished as soon as we get there," she said. "We have to help him, Thor."

"I know. I've been trying to think of something, but there's too many of them," He glanced toward the group of men sprawled underneath the oak. "If they fall asleep, we could slip off. Too bad I don't have a mickey."

"A mickey? What's that? It is a weapon? Maybe we can make one."

Tension left his face as he cracked a smile. "I wish it was that easy. It's something people put in drinks to knock a person out. I mean, it makes a person fall asleep or pass out."

"I know a few herbs that can do that. I'll look around for some."

"Don't. If they see you walking around, one of them will get suspicious. Stick close to me until we ride again."

"But, Thor—"

"No, it's too dangerous. I don't want you walking around alone. They're looking at us. Let's join them."

He hung back as if he was waiting for her to pass. Willow shook her head. "You have to go first. I'll follow you."

A frown creased his brow, but he didn't offer opposition. He moved briskly past the horses, and with a considerable distance separating them, Willow followed.

—◦◦◦—

Anders joined Reverend Brown on the porch. The spicy scent of the older man's corncob pipe flavored the air. The new father filled his lungs with the aroma and slowly exhaled. His appetite rarely craved the taste for tobacco, but there were occasions where he enjoyed the smell of a good pipe.

"How are the womenfolk?" Brown twisted his body to look up at Anders. "Asleep?"

"Not quite," Anders replied, joining Brown on the step. "Olivia is tending to Eva, and Eva still can't keep her eyes off Dorothea. The two of them are a sight to behold. I doubted if either of them would survive."

"I know," Brown said. "I could read it as plain as day on your face."

"Thank you for all your help, you and the missus. Eva and I wouldn't have fared better without you."

"We're here to help. That's what neighbors are for. Now that Eva and the baby are gaining strength, I'd best tend to Willow."

Reverend Brown stood and stretched. Anders watched his movements. The man was strong, but probably not as strong as he used to be. Looking for Willow would require a good deal of energy. He wondered if Brown could do it alone.

"As soon as Olivia's done, we'll be on our way."

"To look for Willow?" Anders asked. "You shouldn't take her along. It could get dangerous down there. It's no place for a woman."

Brown's lips curved into a faint smile. "Convincing Olivia of that took some doing, but I'll be looking for Willow on my own. Of course, you're welcome to come along."

Anders rose and folded his arms across his chest. He didn't want to be disagreeable, but he wasn't sure if he wanted to take Brown up on his invitation. Childbirth left Eva weak. In the days that followed, she still hadn't regained her strength. Leaving her alone felt wrong.

"That's something I'll have to think about."

Brown bit down hard on his pipe. "I imagine it is. I'm leaving first light. If you're meaning to join me, be ready when I pass by."

CHAPTER TEN

The Davis plantation bustled with energy. Shouts announced the groups' arrival. Thor watched in sick fascination as the antebellum South introduced itself to him. Black men, women, and children avoided his gaze. Some harbored expressions of disappointment as Grady led Big Nat toward the huge mansion. Others kept their thoughts to themselves behind stoic masks. None of them milled about, and when a balding, middle-aged white man and a petite young blonde stepped onto the porch, the slaves made themselves scarce, seemingly vanishing into thin air.

The reality of his travel through time punched Thor in the gut. Seeing slaves and actually being on a plantation brought his circumstances to the forefront of his mind. The movies didn't do it justice. There was nothing quite like being thrown into a world where he had all the answers and the knowledge of absolute right versus horribly wrong echoed loudly in his head.

Nobody had the right to dehumanize another human being. There were other ways to make a living and other choices for preserving a certain way of life.

Words of protest lodged in his throat. He opened his mouth to cry out on Big Nat and the other slaves' behalf, but never got the chance to voice his disapproval. The planter ignored Grady and the captured runaway to acknowledge Thor.

"Where are my manners?" Warren Eugene Davis asked, a charismatic smile on his face. He extended his hand. "Welcome to Pleasant Hill. We rarely have occasion to entertain guests. What brings you here?"

The man's charming manner failed to impress Thor. Hoping his reaction was hidden deep inside, he extended his hand, offered a wide smile, and threw himself into his role. "Your reputation for being an astute businessman has necessitated my journey to your plantation, Mr. Davis. Thor Magnusen at your service, sir. Folks call me Thor."

Davis grasped Thor's hand in a strong handshake. "Pleased to meet you, Thor. Do go on about my reputation. Are you on a selling expedition? I'm not in the market for anything new, and if you're trying to peddle that boy behind ya… Well, he's too small for the work I have around here—"

"No!" Thor stepped in front of Willow and blocked her from Davis's view. "I'm not here to peddle anything. Just to speak with you for a spell and discuss cotton."

"What's there to discuss? Cotton is a godsend and a necessity. Everybody knows that."

"Papa!" The pert blonde tugged on his hand. Ringlets brushed against her ivory cheeks almost on queue. Her rosy lips offered Thor a demure smile while her eyes danced with wanton approval. "He's come all this way. It would be rude to send him away."

"This business with the runaway must be dealt with," Davis grunted, "and I have other things to attend to."

"Papa, it's been so long since we've had nice company." Her breathy voice applied extra emphasis to the word nice. "We were about to sit down to supper. Surely, this young gentleman could enjoy a hot meal. It wouldn't be neighborly to turn him away."

The planter's face glowed with fatherly affection. "Mr. Thor Magnusen meet my polite daughter, Leah. I suppose I could listen to her this once. Won't you join us for supper?"

The delay gave them some time to think of a solution for Big Nat. He nodded. "I'd be much obliged. Thank you, sir. Thank you, Miss Leah. I'll be just a moment." He turned to speak to Willow.

"Never mind about your darky," Leah said. She descended the staircase with the gracefulness of a prima ballerina. Her dainty gloved hand slipped around Thor's bicep and squeezed. "Our overseer will tend to him. You can come along with us now."

Thor's smile froze on his face as he heard Willow's sharp intake of breath. Her annoyance at Leah's obvious flirtation and her fear of what was to happen to her while he dined reached out to him without the need for any words. He wanted her to accompany him for his peace of mind as well as her own, but he knew that wouldn't happen too easily if at all. Before he could leave Willow, he had to know just what would happen to her. "Who is this overseer? I need to speak with him first."

Leah pouted. Her fingers flexed against his arm. Neither moved Thor. He stood still as a statue, offering a benign smile and waited. Leah's eyes narrowed with her surrender.

"Papa!" she called, never taking her eyes off Thor. "Where's Lucas?"

"He's around here somewhere." Davis finally acknowledged Grady. "Have you seen your pap since you came back?"

"We passed him in the fields on the way back in," Grady answered. "He should be here directly. What should I do about this here runaway?"

Davis opened his mouth to speak. Leah jumped in before he could say a word. "Papa, can't that wait? We have a guest, and we must be hospitable."

"Propriety takes precedence this evening," Davis informed Grady. "Put him in lock up, and rest up, Grady. You'll need your strength for later." He faced his daughter. "Leah, leave Mr. Magnusen alone with his boy. I 'spect he has instructions that a young lady doesn't need to hear. Come along now."

She reluctantly released Thor's arm and obeyed her father. "Don't make us wait too long, Mr. Thor. You hear?"

He gave her a bland smile. "Loud and clear."

Father and daughter disappeared inside the mansion, and Thor exhaled the breath he'd been holding. He waited until Grady escorted Big Nat off the porch to the rear of the house before speaking to Willow. The dread that reflected in her large black orbs touched his soul. He ached to hold her within the circle of his arms, reassuring her with his touch and warm words of encouragement. Once again, that was something he couldn't do. No matter how much he wanted to. He frowned and searched his mind for another form of consolation.

"Don't worry about me," she whispered, her lips barely moving. "I'll be fine."

"I won't stay inside long. I'll come and get you as soon as possible," Thor said, not surprised that she could read his thoughts. "Just remember to keep quiet and keep that hat on your head."

"I will. You better go. That young girl means to have you for dessert."

He shook his head. His fingers brushed against hers in a quick, light caress. "She can't. I'm already taken."

————◦◦◦————

Supper on a Southern plantation seemed to be a grand affair. Thor couldn't be sure if the Davises put on airs for the sake of having a guest or if every meal was presented with exorbitant flair.

Servants smartly dressed in clean uniforms of black bottoms and crisp white tops whether female or male moved briskly around the table, refilling glasses and replacing empty bowls with full ones. Two young boys, maybe twins, stood on either side of the table. They held wide fans and kept a continuous flow of air blowing in the dining room. During the course of the meal, Thor often glanced at them. Their shoulders should have drooped, and their movements should have slowed. After a couple of hours, they gracefully continued their tasks. Thor admired their ability while distressed over the necessity for it.

"It's getting late, Papa," Leah said, casting a sidelong glance at Thor.

Underneath the table, her slipper-covered foot grazed his shoe. From the heightened color of her cheeks, Thor doubted the move as accidental. The girl's bold behavior surprised him. *Aren't women supposedly demure and chaste during this time?*

Willow's response to him contradicted that thought, but Thor rationalized it by evidence of Willow's passionate nature. Besides, this girl just barely looked old enough to drive. Jailbait was not his idea of sexy.

Willow was his kind of sexy, and lucky for him, she was definitely old enough.

He removed his foot from Leah's vicinity and pulled the timepiece from his pocket. Although nightfall darkened the sky completely, the hour wasn't too late. Maybe Davis would postpone whatever punishment he had in store for Big Nat to a more favorable hour. One preferably after he and Willow had spirited the man away.

"I suppose I am wearing out my welcome." The watch shut with a metallic click. The noise touched his mind. He needed to tell Willow about the timepiece and his theories about time travel.

"Is something the matter?" Davis asked.

"Nothing at all, except that the hour is much later than I thought."

"It's not very late," Leah contradicted. "Why, we haven't even had dessert, yet. Aunty Nitta baked an apple pie. You simply must stay to have some."

Thor glanced at Leah's father. The older man's face held a peculiar expression as he looked from his daughter to Thor. Davis smiled. "The old girl makes the best apple pie. Restaurants in Atlanta buy them from me, and none has ever complained. You cannot pass up a slice."

"But it's late," Thor hedged.

A small part of him wanted to see if he could secure an invitation for the night. At least once on this journey, he wanted Willow to have a decent resting place. Concern for Willow's welfare nagged him. He had to see for himself that she was safe. He ached to hold her in his arms again. That thought pushed him from the table. His chair toppled.

He righted the chair on reflex and spoke directly to his host. "I should be on my way."

"Do you have urgent business elsewhere?" Davis asked.

"No, I'd rather not be a burden."

"You're not a burden," Leah piped in.

"Leah," her father warned in brusque tone. "We would be much obliged if you would accept our invitation to stay the night. I assure you, it would be no trouble at all for you to stay."

One goal accomplished. "I accept and I thank you for your kind offer. However, I must decline the offer of apple pie. I'm allergic."

"I'm sure Aunty Nitta has something else that would be to your liking," Leah offered. "Charlie!" Her voice cracked like a whip. One of the young twins snapped to attention. "Run to the kitchen and tell Nitta we need another dessert."

"That won't be necessary," Thor said before Charlie could hand his fan to his brother. "The supper was quite filling, and I haven't any room for dessert. I appreciate the offer, however. If you would excuse me, I need to stretch my legs for a spell and speak to my…er, boy. How would I go about locating him?"

Leah's mouth opened to answer him, but her father spoke first. "Charlie, show Mr. Thor to the slave quarters. Any of them down there will know where Lucas put him."

———o/o/o———

The slave quarters weren't exactly what Willow expected. She always imagined that something akin to huts or tents housed the captive Negroes. Momentary relief soothed her when the overseer led her to a row of small wooden buildings.

"You don't talk, do you?" the man asked.

Willow shook her head in response, and he grunted. "Old Aunt Sally will have enough to say for both of you."

Chickens created a racket in the back as he strode to the third structure and pushed open the door. An old, wrinkled woman stood at a fireplace, stirring inside a good-sized iron pot. She didn't bat an eye as the uninvited guests entered her candlelit abode. She continued to stir and acknowledged them with a nod.

"Good. You're cooking. This here boy came with Mr. Davis's dinner guest. Look after him," Lucas ordered. He shoved Willow toward the center of the room. "I 'spect he'll be staying the night. Fix up a pallet for him, too."

Sally nodded. Lucas slammed the door after him. Willow peered past the brim of her hat to get a closer look at the quarters and its inhabitant.

The space was actually livable and very clean. A square wooden table occupied the center of the room. Three chairs bordered the table, and Willow wondered if anyone else lived there besides the old woman. An intricately designed quilt covered a bed that rested against the wall adjacent to the door. A wooden chest marked a space at the foot of the bed, and another quilt rested on top it.

Sally worked the pot as if it was a lifeline. Willow felt the old woman's eyes on her with every stir of the wooden spoon. Careful to keep most of her face hidden, she tilted her head to the side to get a better view. Sally's flesh was the color of dark, rich blackberries. Lines fanned the corners of her eyes, and Willow couldn't be sure if they were from laughter or worry. A faded blue rag served as a kerchief around the woman's head, but strands of silver and gray managed to curl around the edges of the cloth. A dark woolen skirt fell to her ankles, and a pair of men's work boots covered her feet.

"Rest yourself at the table," Sally advised. "The cabbage is just about ready."

Willow made a sign that she wanted to wash her hands. Sally pointed toward a pail near the fireplace. "You can dry your hands with that rag over yonder."

Once her hands were dry, Willow sat at the table. Sally finally stopped stirring to give her a hard look. "You can take that hat off. I know you ain't no boy. Ain't nobody coming up in here, and if they do, the chickens out back will put up a fuss. Go on. Take off that hat so's I can see who's at my table."

Willow frowned. She wasn't sure about trusting the old woman. Sally's eyes glowed with intelligence and concern, and Willow's resolve weakened. She removed the hat and met the woman's intense stare. "How did you know?"

"I didn't get to be this old without knowing a man when I see one."

"Think the overseer knows?" Willow shot a worried glance toward the closed door. If the overseer knew the truth, he might become suspicious of Thor and warn Davis.

"He don't know nothing," Sally assured her. "He sees you dressed like a boy, and that's what he thinks. Unless you do something to make him think otherwise."

"No, ma'am." Willow shook her head. "I don't plan to."

Sally set a plate of steaming cabbage in front of her. "It ain't much, but it is filling."

The delicious aroma reminded Willow that she hadn't eaten for hours. Her mouth watered. She grabbed a spoon and dug in, remembering to express her gratitude as she lifted the steaming vegetable to her parted lips. "Thank you."

Sally grunted. "Don't be thanking me. I did it 'cause I was told to, but I wouldn't let a body starve on no account." She carried another plate to the table and sat across from Willow. "Why you in that get up? Do your massa know you ain't a boy?"

Willow wasn't sure what to say to that. Just because Sally's flesh was colored, didn't necessarily mean that Willow should trust her. She chewed her bottom lip as she tried to create a suitable response.

"I 'spect he does. All of 'em do a complete inspection when they get you off the auction block. Don't make no sense for him to let you dress like a boy, though."

Apparently, Sally didn't need an answer. She was fully prepared to come up with her own explanation. Willow sighed in relief and ate more cabbage.

"Hear tell you came in with Big Nat and the overseer's boy, Grady Falls. He almost made it." Sally tisked. "He's gon' pay for it now for sho'."

Digesting those few words, Willow's appetite faded. She lowered her spoon to the plate. "How? What will happen to him?"

"He's locked up now, but they'll take him soon." Sally chewed as she talked. "Big Nat is new here, and he's got to learn a lesson. The Massa be willing to make sure he learn it well. I 'spect floggin'. Something to make him r'member and warn the others not to try the same."

"Flogging?" Willow repeated. Bile lodged in her throat. "When and where?"

"It's too dark for 'em to do it now. They'll want to do it when the sun is shining high in the sky so's everybody can watch and learn," Sally replied. "More 'n likely it'll happen before the noonday meal at the steps of the big house. Floggings happen up there so the massa will have a place to sit. He can't stand for very long, you know."

"No, I didn't know," Willow said under her breath. She twisted the hat between trembling fingers and tried to think of a way to stop it. Informing Thor was a must, but then what? How would they get Big

Nat out of lock up without Davis and his overseer finding out? Where was lock up? Was it accessible or would it be guarded?

"You fit to be tied over this, ain't you?" Sally commented. "When you're young you think of runnin' up north to freedom. When you gets old as me, you knows it don't always work out like that."

"Did you ever try?"

Sally pushed her empty plate toward the table center and sat back. She shook her head. "I thought about it, but never made it off the place. My man did, though. He took off. Don't know if he made it. Imagine he did."

"Why didn't you go with him?"

"I was aiming to, but we had some little ones. I wanted to wait until they were bigger. Turns out it didn't matter no how."

The hairs on the back of Willow's neck stood on end. She sat up straight and leaned toward her hostess. "What do you mean?"

"Massa Davis's daddy was alive back then. He waited 'til my babies were big enough and sold 'em."

Willow's mouth dropped open. "Why didn't you run away then?"

"Why? My man was gone, and so were my chillun. No point in running off. Nowhere to go."

"Maybe you could have found your man."

"And maybe I couldn't have," Sally countered. "It was too late for me then. I should have listened to my man. Grab the younguns and ran off with him. I didn't and paid the price for it. If the Gospel Train call you, I say hop aboard."

—◈◈◈—

The slave quarters, laid out in neat rows, vaguely reminded Thor of a few housing projects he'd seen while doing charity events for the Falcons. Decently constructed buildings created a façade that couldn't possibly correspond with the inhabitants. Oppression could still exist despite the appearance of well-made structures.

Adults conversed outside while their young children played at their feet. Thor read their expressions. Distrust and resignation were plain to see. He could not change their situation.

Realization gnawed at his gut. He hated feeling helpless and lowered his head. His pace quickened. Cackling chickens cried out. He reached the quarters where the overseer placed Willow. Desperation to know her plight plagued him. He forgot his manners and strode in without thinking to knock first. The door slammed shut behind him.

Willow's eyes widened in shock. She blindly adjusted the hat on her head, pulling it low over her face. He felt bad for scaring her and crossed the dimly lit room to face her. "It's me. You don't have to be afraid."

"I heard the chickens and suddenly the door opened," she said in a breathless rush. "I should have kept the hat on."

She pushed the hat from her forehead, and he removed it. "You can leave it off for a little while." He stared intently into her eyes. "Are you okay?"

"I'm fine if that's what you mean. The overseer left me here. Miss Sally shared her supper with me."

Thor stiffened. In his haste to reach her, he failed to notice whether they were alone. He looked around the candlelit room.

"She's visiting a friend. One of the children has a stomachache," Willow explained.

"She knows you're a woman?" He brushed his fingers against her soft cheek. Her body shivered from his caress. Resisting the urge to possess her again became difficult. It couldn't be normal to want someone this much.

"Yes." Her voice dripped over him like warm, sweet honey. "She figures that you must know, too. I didn't tell her yes or no to that."

He nodded. While she spoke, her full, soft lips captured his attention. An invisible cord pulled his mouth to her. She gasped as his mouth closed over hers. Her body became slack. He wrapped his arms around her waist. Her hands clung to him at first, and then pressed against his chest, pushing him away.

"Sorry," he mumbled as he stepped back and released her.

"We have to be careful. I—I enjoy your kisses, Thor."

He smiled. "I know, but you're right. We shouldn't kiss here. Come back with me to the main house."

"I don't think I can."

"If I want you to, you can. And Willow," he added in a low voice, "I do want you to."

Her chest rose sharply as she inhaled. Trembling hands squeezed the hat, and she looked at him through thick, lowered lashes. "I know."

Sweet innocence and remembered passion shone vividly in her coal black eyes. Thor's pants became too tight. He shifted his leg to relieve the pressure. The move only served to inflame him further. This nineteenth-century playing field was dangerous, littered with explosive repercussions, but there was no way in hell, he would be without her tonight. Even if they did not make love, he wanted her near him. He had to keep her safe. He was her only protection.

Palm up, he extended his hand. Her light touch seared him as her fingertips glided across his palm and grasped his hand. With his other hand, he placed the hat on her head. He adjusted the brim, covering her face so that only her kiss-swollen lips were viewable. They left.

CHAPTER ELEVEN

Lovemaking exhilarated Willow.

The heat of bodies joining set her aflame. Her dear friend often hinted at the wonders of married life. Anders's presence always put Eva in good spirits. The touch of his hand made her friend blush and her face glow with excitement. Laying beneath Thor with her nails digging into his perspiration slick backside, Willow understood the fervor of the bond between a man and a woman.

The pace of Thor's thrusts increased. His firm muscles contracted underneath her palms. The rapid strokes brought a low, tingling ache to her thighs, but the pleasure was worth the slight pain. His throbbing member pulsed inside her, sending her closer to the delirious heights of fulfillment. Another hard thrust jolted her straight to ecstasy. She soared through the ceiling high above the clouds and straight to heaven.

"Blessed be!"

Ragged breathing filled the silence as Willow slowly returned to earth. Peace and contentment enveloped them. He rolled onto his back and rose from the palate. The loss of his body heat made her shiver as cool air tickled her bare flesh. He pulled her to her feet and drew her into the bed with him, positioning her on top of him. His hands squeezed her bottom, holding her in place, and she shivered despite the warmth of his touch.

"Cold?" Heavy lidded eyes pierced her and gleamed with satisfaction. He kissed the tip of her nose and didn't wait for her response. Grabbing the crisp cotton sheet, he pulled it over them. "Is that better?"

"It wasn't bad before, but I imagine it wouldn't be seemly to have my bare bottom high in the air without hide or hair of modesty."

His finger twirled a lock of black hair before brushing it against her cheek. "You're modest enough," he murmured. "I had a helluva time getting you into this room with me if I recall."

Their disagreement upon entering the guest room came to mind. Nervously, she chewed her bottom lip. "Are you sure Davis wasn't upset when he saw us coming upstairs? I didn't like the look on his face."

"I think it was customary for a guest to have his . . . um, servant—"

"His slave. I do not like the word much, but that is what I am pretending to be. Your slave. You may as well call me such."

"We're pretending when we have an audience," he responded gruffly. "There's only the two of us right now. You're not my slave, and I wouldn't want you to be."

"Not even in bed?"

The whale-oil burning lamp cast a faint light over the room, but it wasn't so dim that Willow couldn't see Thor's face darken. He stiffened and moved from under her. Concern swept through her.

"What's wrong?"

He sat up and put his back to her. She slid her hand across his muscled flesh. He flinched. His rejection stunned her. She dropped her hand. "Thor?"

"I thought you knew me better than that," he muttered.

"Better than what?" She shrugged to hide her confusion. "I was teasing you."

"It's not funny, Willow." He abruptly stood. The bed creaked upon the loss of his weight. His fingers fumbled with the lantern, filling the room with light and then dimming the flame. "I wouldn't force a woman into my bed. I wouldn't make her submit to me for any reason."

She slid across the bed and stood just behind him. The desire to run her hands over his hard back and broad shoulders was a strong temptation. Fear that he would flinch again compelled her to keep her hands at her sides. "I know you're an honorable man."

"I don't feel honorable," he grunted. He stopped adjusting the lamp's glow to face her. His mouth twisted, and his brow furrowed. He avoided her gaze and took her hands. "Making love with you was wrong."

"Why? Because of amalgamation?"

"What?"

"Because I'm not white and you are," she explained. "Your honor has been compromised because you bedded me."

"My honor has been compromised because I let the wrong head guide me!" His features darkened with disgust. "I wanted you and seduced you even though I knew it was wrong. Hell, to make matters worse, I did it twice! The first time could be written off as plain stupidity, but this second time . . . That's just recklessness that neither of us can afford, especially you."

"Why especially me?"

He pressed his hand against the flat plane of her lower belly. "A life could be forming there as we speak. A helpless baby could be trapped in a cruel world."

"My baby wouldn't be helpless. I would protect my child from this cruel world and teach it like the Browns taught me." She jerked away from him and sat on the bed. "I would love my baby, and I wouldn't expect anything from you."

"Well, you should, dammit!" He dropped onto the bed beside her.

Her bottom lip trembled. Tears choked her voice. "If you d—did-n't want to raise the ch—child with me, I wouldn't want you to . . ."

"Willow." He grasped her chin, turning her head to look at him. "I would want nothing more than to raise our child with you. I would move heaven and earth to do it. In fact…,If I knew how to return to the twentieth century, would you join me? I want to take you with me and not look back."

He wants me with him.

Air lodged in her throat. Her heart swelled, and the tears dried. Endless possibilities swept through her mind. His view of the world filled her with hope for a better future. What if everyone was as open minded as him? How wonderful and perfect would a world like that be? Her thoughts returned to the present. Running away was not an option right now. She had obligations and a serious responsibility to reunite three homeless children with their father.

"What about Big Nat?"

"We'll finish what we started with him and get him back with his kids," he said, "and then it would be you and me, lady, in 1985."

"How?" The question had been on the edge of her thoughts since the moment of his invitation. "Do you know how to return to nineteen hundred and eighty-five?"

He stood and padded across the floor to the wardrobe where he removed the suit jacket. "I'm not sure, but maybe this is it." The garment lay across his arms like a treasured heirloom. When he returned to the bed, he reached inside the interior pocket. "My father gave this watch to me the night before I woke up in 1860. Pop said that Anders found the timekeeper, and it brought him good luck. Cal and I had never seen the timepiece before Pop gave it to me."

Willow took her spectacles from the other pocket of Thor's jacket. After she adjusted the wire-rimmed frames on the bridge of her nose, she reached for the timepiece. The gold covering, intricate design and poetic inscription took her breath away. The beautiful artistry revealed a dedicated person. Light reflected off the covering in a peaceful, yet energetic glow. If this watch held the secrets of time travel, the knowledge would not come as a surprise.

"Love lasts forever," she whispered. "Beautiful." Wonder coursed through her just from holding the watch. Reading the inscription aloud only intensified the sensation. She felt his gaze on her. With a moment's hesitation, she handed the watch back. "How does it work?"

"What do you mean? Can you read a watch to tell time?"

She nodded. "Miss Olivia taught me. I meant how did the watch send you through time? Did Anders tell you how to make it work?"

His forefinger dipped and curved around the words. "Anders doesn't know. He found it in the woods. I don't know how it works or even if it's what brought me here."

The Bible warned that magic was the work of the devil. Was that always true? Mystical forces brought Thor Magnusen to her world. He was a good, kind man, too compassionate to be capable of evil. But that timepiece. . . as easy as drawing water from a creek, the watch brought Thor to her, and it could just as easily take him away. A bucket of dread poured over her. She shuddered.

His large hand closed around her shoulder. "I'll figure out how it works, and when I do, I want you to come with me."

"Would I fit in your time?" Her uncertainty about the watch's powers made her uneasy. Yet, Thor's invitation piqued her interest in his world, and knowing that he wanted her to return with him only fueled her curiosity all the more.

"Nineteen eighty-five is nothing like 1860." He curved his arm around her shoulder and pressed her close to his side. "I have no doubts about you, Miss Willow Elkridge. You would have no problems fitting in. You're so smart and inquisitive. There would be no roadblocks in your way. Nothing would stop you from being whatever you wanted to be or doing whatever you wanted to do." He tilted her chin until their gazes met. "If you could do whatever you wanted, what would you do?"

"I don't know. I suppose I would go to Oberlin College. It doesn't matter if you're Negro or white, or male or female. What about you? What are your dreams, Thor?"

A series of white lines suddenly stretched from his mouth. "My dreams aren't important anymore."

"It's important to have dreams."

"I'm learning that there are other things more important than dreams." He brushed wispy strands of hair from her face. "You're more important than any dream I've ever had. If I could figure this time travel thing out, would you come back with me? I mean it, Willow. Would you?"

Words failed her. A world without Thor saddened her, yet she could not imagine leaving the Browns or her dear friend, Eva. Besides, what would she know about nineteen hundred and eighty-five? Living in 1860 was difficult enough. He said she would fit in, but what if he said that to appease her?

She pulled away from him, straightened her back, and hugged her knees to her chest. "I have to see Big Nat safe with his children."

"And after he is, will you answer my question then?"

"Can't you stay here?" Her breath locked in her chest. Waiting for his response seemed to take forever.

He shifted on the bed until he sat up straight beside her. His legs crossed and he laced his hands together. "We couldn't be together here, at least not safely. I have a family waiting for me. A brother and a father who are probably worried sick. I couldn't just leave them."

"I understand."

"No, you don't." He took her hand and wrapped both of his around it. His warmth spread through her from head to toe. "If there was a way I could let them know I was okay, I'd feel better about staying here. However, the most important thing that sticks in my head is you.

"We can't be together like this without fear or censure. I really don't give a damn what others think of me. I never have, but I do care about your safety. Being together in this time period just isn't safe, and I don't want to be here if I can't be with you."

He raised her hand to his mouth. His lips kissed each fingertip. "Think about it, Willow. You'll have your choice of colleges and not have to limit yourself to just one. Freedom you've never imagined is waiting for you. Besides, this could be your destiny."

"My destiny?" She smiled at the twinkle dancing in his eyes. "What do you mean?"

"Returning to 1985 with me could be the reason why I'm here. I've already saved your life once. Maybe I'm supposed to take you back with me."

"But you're not sure if the watch brought you here or why. How can you be sure my destiny is to return with you?"

"Gut instinct," he said softly. "It feels right when I say it."

"Would you mind if I asked you a question?"

"I'm an open book." He fell back against the pillows and spread his arms. A sensuous flame sparked in his eyes. "You can read me to your heart's content."

Heat flooded her cheeks. His bold, flirtatious manner made her giggle. The laughter only lasted for a short moment. Her question held no mirth. She pointed to the thin, white scar on his right collarbone. Lightly, she pressed her fingertip against the healed wound. His body jerked upon contact, and then he grew still. His eyes became dark and haunted.

"What happened to you?"

"My collarbone was broken."

"I thought as much," she murmured. Her fingers traced the outline of the scar, carefully so as not to cause distress. "How did it happen? Were you in an accident, or did someone do that to you?"

His mouth tightened into a thin line. "Does it matter?"

"It doesn't matter, but you should have warned me that some chapters were sealed shut."

"It's not that," he said quietly. "You can ask me anything. It's just that…well, it's just a scar. I was working and it got broken."

"I never considered what you did for a living," she said with a smile. "What is your trade? Are you a carpenter like Mr. Anders?"

"I built my house, but no, I'm not a carpenter; at least not a professional one. I don't have a specific trade anymore, but once upon a time, I was a quarterback for the NFL."

This sounded interesting! All sorts of images flashed through her mind, but none of them stayed for very long. She couldn't really imagine what a quarterback was or what the NFL did.

"I don't understand. Could you tell me? Would knowing change things?"

He cupped her chin and brushed his thumb across her cheek. She shivered from the exquisite tenderness of his touch. He smiled in response. "I don't think there would be a problem. Football is a professional sport. The NFL, which stands for National Football League, is comprised of football teams from all over the United States. I was the backup quarterback for the Atlanta Falcons."

"The Atlanta here in Georgia?"

"The very same. The football teams play against each other with opposing offensive and defensive sides. The quarterback is an offensive player, and he leads a pack of ten players. The quarterback's job is to get the ball to other members of his team."

"For what?"

"So that his team can score a touchdown or gain more yards."

She noticed from his intense expression that his job meant a good deal to him, but for the life of her, she could not understand why. "Is it a real ball?"

"Yeah." He gestured with both hands. Excitement replaced the disappointment in his eyes. "It's about this wide and this long. The shape makes it easy to grip."

"And doing this football is how your collarbone was broken?"

"I was tackled by a lineman. My collarbone snapped in two, and so did a couple of bones in my arm."

Shock flew through her. Her mouth dropped open. Whatever this lineman was, it certainly was brutal. She clutched his hand. "Blessed be!"

"Tell me about it. That tackle wasn't a thrill. That's for sure."

"When you return to your home, will you continue with this profession? It doesn't sound very safe to me, and surely, there are less violent occupations you could consider."

A warm smile teased the corners of his mouth. "You're worried about me."

"Yes, I do not want you to be hurt."

"How about this?" He leaned toward her, and his voice dropped to a dangerous growl. "I'll think about a change in career if you'll promise to consider coming with me to 1985."

With his face so close to hers, his sweet breath fanned her mouth. Surrender came easily. "I promise."

He removed her spectacles. His hand moved to the back of her head and drew her to him. Her lips parted in anticipation. His kiss was wet, warm, and wonderful. As he lowered her to the bed, her arms closed around him. The soft, tiny hairs on his chest tickled the hardening tips of her breasts. Their hearts pumped in unison. She closed her eyes and prepared herself for the delicious sensations that promised to flood through her body.

All too quickly, his caresses came to a sudden halt and he pulled away. "Did you hear that?"

"No."

"I heard something." He swung his legs over the side of the bed. His bare feet thumped across the hardwood floor. He pulled the door open and stuck his head through the opening. A few seconds passed before he closed and locked the door and returned to her.

"What did you see?" She moved into his open arms.

"Nothing. It must have been the wind."

His mouth claimed hers again, and any concern for unexplained noises disappeared with the taste of his lips on her tongue. The rest of the night was spent in Thor's arms. For that moment, nothing else mattered.

—◦◦◦—

Anders spent most of the night watching over his wife and child and thinking about Brown's dilemma. Brown wasn't bound by blood to take care of Willow. Anders knew the story. Slave patrollers lynched Willow's parents and left her an orphan. Brown had taken the young girl into his home because of a promise to Willow's father, but he allowed her into his heart because she was a lovely person.

Eva told Anders often enough that Willow didn't think he cared for her. Nothing was farther from the truth. He liked Willow well enough and appreciated her friendship with Eva. Country life bored Eva, but Willow's questions about Eva's life in the North invigorated his wife. She enjoyed having a friend her age to chat with while sewing and pouring over those Sears and Roebuck catalogues.

He was never much for book learning, but Eva adored William Shakespeare. Countless times, the two women discussed the English playwright well into the night. Giggles and sighs often accompanied their conversation. The glow that warmed his wife's cheeks created a burning sensation all through him. He supposed he had plenty reasons to be grateful to Willow Elkridge. Her friendship made his wife happy, and that was priceless.

Dorothea awakened with a gusty wail. Eva pulled the squirming babe into the curve of her arm and gave the hungry infant her breast. The greedy display filled him with pride.

A beautiful, contented smile crossed Eva's lips. "She reminds me of you. Loud and red-faced when the hunger pangs strike."

He sat on the edge of the bed and slid his finger between Dorothea's tiny fist. "She's her daddy's little girl."

An overwhelming sensation hit him hard in the gut. Blood rushed from his face. The enormity of parenthood sent him reeling. He dropped onto the bed beside his wife and daughter. The endless sea of responsibilities of raising and loving a child drained him, yet filled him, too.

"It's a powerful feeling, isn't it?" His wife had been watching him closely. "But it's a good one."

"She'll look to us for everything," he said quietly. "She'll learn by what we do, and not always what we say. We'll have to set good examples."

"Yes."

He directed his attention to Eva. "Brown asked me to join him in looking for Willow and Thor. I told him I would think about it. He's coming by here in a little while."

"You're going with him," she said with a knowing smile. "Don't worry about me. Olivia said she'd come by. Dorothea and I will be fine."

"You don't mind if I leave you? I hate to leave you alone."

"I'm not alone. Our daughter is with me. I want you to help Reverend Brown find Willow. I'm scared for her out there and with Thor, too."

"What about Thor?" Anders stepped into his work boots and rose from the bed. He grabbed a rifle and checked to see if it was loaded. It was.

The baby finished breakfast. Eva patted the infant's back until she burped. Eva rocked the baby. "It's a just a feeling. Willow has not had any real attention from men. Thor is a handsome, charming man, and he has been very friendly with her. I wouldn't want her to get hurt."

"Do you think he'd use her?"

"Not on purpose. He reminds me of you; kind, caring, and stubborn. I don't think he'd mean to do it, but things happen despite the best of intentions."

Anders grimaced. "Don't they, though? I will look into it when we meet up with them. Brown will be here any minute." He stopped beside the bed. "Are you sure you'll be fine without me?"

"I'm sure." She took his hand and squeezed. "Go and be sure to tell the reverend that you're all in my prayers. I love you, Anders Magnusen."

"I love you, too."

Leah cornered Thor as soon as he and Willow descended the staircase. The young mistress of the plantation pulled him out of the house before he could protest and had him inside a horse drawn carriage within the blink of an eye.

"Where are we going?" he asked, turning around to stare behind them. Willow's form decreased as the horses carried them down the lane. "I have business to attend to with your father, Miss Davis. I haven't the time for foolishness, and I'm sure your father wouldn't appreciate you being with me without a chaperone."

"My father knows we're together, and Monty here can act as a chaperone even if he doesn't have the proper credentials."

The older black man stiffened as her caustic remark snapped in the morning breeze. Thor saw the tightening of the slave's back muscles and came close to offering an apology. Remembering his situation, he thought better of it and instead asked, "Where are we going?"

"Aunty Nitta prepared a basket filled with breakfast delights. We're having a morning picnic. Papa is busy with Lucas and Grady and would not have time to see you. He suggested I entertain you for a little while."

"How long is awhile?"

Gravel crunched as the horses' hooves pounded into the dirt road. Clouds of dust billowed and wafted inside the open carriage. Thor glanced at the passing scenery. Jumping was a foolish risk. The carriage raced like greased lightning down the dirt road. He grunted and stared straight ahead. "Well?"

"Awhile isn't too long at all. The glen is just ahead," she soothed. "We'll picnic there and once we're done, we'll return to the house."

Thor pulled out the timepiece. It just made eight o'clock. Willow said they planned to punish Big Nat around noon. That gave them four hours. Even a breakfast picnic could not last that long. He sighed and snapped the watch shut.

Leah must have sensed his acceptance. She bounced on the seat beside him and chattered nonstop. While she carried on a one-sided conversation, his thoughts turned to Willow, and he hoped that she'd have an affirmative response for his invitation to join him in 1985. Provided he could ever figure out how to work the pocket watch to get back there himself.

Leah giggled and clutched his forearm. He sighed.

Lord, please let this hour pass quickly.

——— o/o/o ———

The time spent with Leah passed slowly at first. Monty spread a blanket for them and arranged the dishes over it, leaving enough room for Thor and Leah to sit. When the older man shuffled off to tend to the horses, Thor watched him leave with much regret. The last thing he wanted was to be alone with Leah. Willow's comment that Leah wanted him for dessert floated back to him, and he couldn't help but see the truth to Willow's prediction. Leah's flirty behavior left nothing to his imagination. The young woman wanted him, and he was certain she meant to have him. Unfortunately for her, he wasn't so easily had.

"Isn't this lovely?" She speared a piece of ham and extended it toward him. "Go ahead and take a bite. I don't mind."

He plucked the piece from her fork with his fingers. Bacon was his preferred form of pork. Ham was never a favorite, but he popped the morsel into his mouth anyway. Arguing with Leah would no doubt prolong the damn excursion. It would serve him better just to humor her—to a degree—and then get back to the main house as soon as possible.

His stomach lurched at the prospect of consuming ham, and he decided that the faster he consumed the meal, the sooner they'd be on the road again. Grabbing food and shoveling it in, he ate as if his life depended on it.

"Mr. Magnusen?" she questioned. "It doesn't do a body any good to swallow without chewing. Aunty prepares a palatable meal, but please, slow down."

"When I'm hungry, I find it hard to slow down."

"Please, try." She lifted the silver pot and poured a steaming brown liquid into a dainty china cup. "This tea should settle your stomach."

He accepted the proffered teacup and took a sip. The tea was sweet like honey. There was a bitter aftertaste, but overall, he liked it. He emptied the cup and held it out for more.

A tiny smile played around the corners of her mouth, as she willingly obliged his silent request. "Slowly, now."

"Of course," he murmured. He drank more tea and consumed the rest of his meal in a less frenetic pace. As he reached for a teacake, his vision blurred. He blinked to clear it, but there was no change. Leah's gaze didn't stray from him, and her face held a peculiar expression. Seconds later, he became dizzy. Before he could question Leah, his stomach muscles clenched, and everything went black.

————❦❦❦————

As Willow headed for the slave quarters, she tried hard not to think about Thor's unexpected excursion with Leah. She made herself focus on Big Nat and how she and Thor could manage his escape in broad daylight. Rescuing him after his punishment was delivered would force them to remain on or near the plantation longer than either wanted to. The escape would have to happen before noon. She hoped Thor wouldn't be too taken with Leah and her ash-blonde ringlets and pouty pink mouth to remember their goal.

That thought brought her up short. She'd never been envious of another person, even with the injustices society had forced upon her. Nevertheless, she could not deny that her foremost thoughts about Leah were born of jealousy. The planter's daughter pounced on Thor like a starving cat on a field mouse. Willow supposed she could not begrudge the girl for her actions. Thor was a striking man and just the thought of him—not to mention the thought of his touch—caused her heart to pound and her flesh to sprout goose bumps.

Lord have mercy!

She drew in a harsh breath. Even away from him, he had a powerful hold over her. What about his invitation to join him in his world of nineteen hundred and eighty-five? It was sweet of him to offer, but she could not be sure about a proposal such as that. Honor ran deep in him, and he was more than likely feeling remorse for bedding her. Not once or twice. She bit back a smile. But several times. *Blessed be. He is thorough when it came to loving.* Heat burned her cheeks, and she pressed her hand to her face. For just a split second, she didn't watch where she was going and slammed straight into an unmovable body.

Her gaze flew to her unintended victim, and she came close to verbalizing an apology. Grady Falls glared at her with dark, beady eyes, and she stepped back.

His hand shot out and took a firm hold of her upper arm. She tried to jerk out of his grasp, but his grip only tightened. A sinister grin spread across his face, and he snarled, "I hear you're a little spitfire. You'll put a pretty penny in my pocket. That's guaranteed."

Ice-cold fear coursed through her veins. His leering gaze humiliated her, and his touch made her flesh crawl. She tried again to pull free. His fingers bit into her arm. He seemed to have no patience for her attempt at self-preservation.

Willow opened her mouth to scream. He slapped her hard across the face. Bells rang in her ears. Her cheek burned from the assault. Tears stung her eyes. Wrapping his sinewy arm around her waist, he lifted her from the ground and tossed her into the back of a wagon where Big Nat's unconscious form already lay. She moved to crawl toward the prone man.

"Not so fast." Grady grabbed her.

He bound her wrists behind her back with a rope, looping it through the railing on the wagon and shoved a soiled handkerchief into her mouth. "There. That'll hold you."

Ice cold fear transformed into stark terror. She had no idea where Grady was taking her and Big Nat. Common sense warned her that this impromptu excursion wouldn't be a ride on the Freedom Train. Twisting and turning, she squinted in hopes of spotting Thor racing across the grounds to help her.

She did not see him.

Grady slapped the reins against the horses' back. The wagon wheels rolled with a sad creaking sound and carried them off the plantation. Inside, her heart wept, and she prayed for God to save them.

—◦◦◦—

A relentless hammer pounded a sadistic beat inside Thor's head. He rolled onto his side with a loud groan. His head hadn't hurt that badly since his freshman year at college. Waking up with a hangover was standard for the fraternity he pledged. Well, it was standard until Cal found out about it and punched him hard in the gut with a promise to tell their father if he ever caught Thor like that again. Thor never did, and waking up free of mind-bending headaches felt pretty damn good.

The rhythmic pounding increased and he moaned. Slowly opening his eyes, he wondered what happened to his state of sobriety.

"Ouch."

The shining light of the noonday sun nearly blinded him. He turned his back to the glare and slowly sat up. Glimpses of pink and white fluttered beside him. The antebellum getup startled him at first, and then he remembered. He jumped to his feet in one move and growled at the preening young blonde.

"What the hell did you do to me?"

"Now that's a fine how do you do!" she pouted. "I saved you. You should be thanking me instead of yelling, my dear Thor."

She reached out for him. He slapped her hand away. She jumped. The simpering expression on her face switched to one of burning hatred.

Thor was unmoved. "I won't ask you again. What was in that tea?"

Her doll-like face twisted into a hard mask. Returning his stare, she blew on the hand he smacked. "The tea just made you sleep. If you hadn't drunk it all, you wouldn't have been unconscious for so long."

A fleeting image of Willow came to mind. His body tensed and he knew something wasn't right. Alarm shot through him like a lightning rod. The fear must have shown on his face because Leah tipped her head back and laughed.

"Your precious little bed wench will put her good skills to use."

His hands clenched into fists at his sides. "What do you mean?"

"That little darky you brought with you? The one you pretended was a boy. I saw you when you came back with him from the slave quarters. I suppose I should say her."

She paused for effect. Thor seethed. "Get on with it," he bit out.

"I heard you together last night. Rutting around like filthy pigs! You could have been with me! But you wanted that damned black ni—"

He grabbed her upper arms, pulled her to her feet, and put a halt to her vicious tirade. "Why did you drug me? What did you do to her? Tell me!"

"You thought you were smart. Sneaking on my daddy's plantation, hoping to steal that big buck! Well, it won't happen now. He and your wench are well on the road to another plantation. I sold them, and you'll never get them back."

He thrust her away from him. Spinning on his heal, he strode to the horse. Monty tried to block his path, but Thor told him, "Don't make me hurt you."

The old man stepped aside and Thor ripped the leather straps from the horse, freeing it from the constraints that tied the beast to the carriage.

"I'll tell my Papa everything if you run away from me!" she cried. "He'll come after you. You know what they do to advocates of negrophilism down here! Thor! You'll hang for it."

He swung onto the back of the horse's bare back and spared her one searing glance. "And you'll burn in hell," he predicted in a cold voice. "I'll pray to God for that."

He dug his boot heels into the horse. Clouds of dirt and gravel swelled around him. Thor thundered down the lane, leaving the screaming girl in the dust.

—◦◦◦—

Uneven rolling of the wagon made Willow sick to her stomach. The filthy rag in her mouth didn't help matters either. She closed her eyes and tried to think of a solution.

Something nudged her shoulder. She rolled onto her side and tilted her head back. Big Nat was awake and anger darkened his brow. Nothing covered his mouth and he asked in a harsh whisper, "That young massa sold you?"

She shook her head.

"You said he was different and worked on the Gospel Train. You can never be too sure about that." He edged toward her until his face was just inches from hers. "Hold your squirming. I'll get that hanky from your mouth."

Willow lay perfectly still. Big Nat's face swam before her. His teeth bit into the handkerchief and pulled. The rag fell. Tears of relief wet her eyes. She had not realized how painful the obstruction was or how dry it made her throat. She swallowed hard to ease the parched feeling.

"Thank you."

He seemed embarrassed by the show of appreciation. His gaze focused on something just beyond her shoulder, and then he looked at her again. "You're welcome."

Willow squinted at Grady in the driver's seat. He sat without a bit of tension in him. Loose, happy, and free. *Damn him.* Angry tears burned the backs of her eyes.

"You know where he's taking us?" Big Nat asked, casting a brief glance in the white man's direction. "Did he say?"

She nodded. "He sold us to a slave breeder on the other side of Atlanta."

"Shit."

Willow nodded in agreement, but did not repeat the word. She'd heard about slave breeders and knew exactly what that meant for her. Constant fornication without her consent in the hopes of creating a child. She shuddered to think of it. Thor was her only lover, and despite his tenderness, she was still left sore. Thor's loving brought her immense joy, so the pain was bearable. Lying with someone else would not be the same. She felt dirty just thinking about it.

Big Nat's face swam in front of hers again. His dark brown eyes bored into her. "It's only one of him. We'll find a way to run off from him."

Willow wanted to believe him. She had been praying for rescue, but as the miles passed, she stopped. Nothing but a miracle could save them now.

Big Nat's eyes narrowed and his body became tense. "The wagon's slowing."

Grady guided the horses off the dirt road into a grove of trees. The rocking motion stopped, and he hopped down. He swaggered to the rear of the wagon. His crude gaze latched onto her.

"I've been thinking. It wouldn't be right for me to sell you without knowing for myself how you fared."

Grady reached for Willow. Big Nat lunged at him. As if on reflex, Grady struck him across the forehead with a sap he had hidden at his side. The blow knocked Big Nat out cold. Grady dragged Willow from the wagon.

Her prayers had indeed fallen on deaf ears.

He threw her into the bushes. When he crawled between her legs, she released a bloodcurdling scream. Grady backhanded her. Eyes rolled back, Willow fell into complete darkness.

CHAPTER TWELVE

Natural instinct and athletic skill—not to mention fear—kicked in and made Thor an accomplished horseman in minutes. Just like during his days on the football field and the practiced play went off balance, he forced himself to quickly adapt.

In the back of his mind, Willow's training came to mind. The reins wrapped around his hands. Leather straps pinched his flesh. His palms whitened from the intensity of his grip. The beast must have sensed his desperation and galloped down the road as if the hounds of hell snapped at their heels.

Golden leaves and sharp branches slapped against Thor's face and neck. Roadside travelers resembled a blurry mass of brown and white. A crossroads appeared in the distance. A trio of white men carried full sacks on their backs. Thor tugged on the reins. The horse slowed. Another tug brought the animal to a stop. One of the men dropped his sack and wandered over. In exchange for information on the nearest slave-breeding plantation, Thor offered a gold piece. Money talked. A large spread only a few miles from Atlanta housed the most likely hellhole. The man drew a map on the road. Thor memorized the directions and sped off. Man and beast raced against time and didn't ease up until recent wagon wheels tracks stretched before them on the dusty road.

The horse slowed to a steady stride. A warning voice echoed inside Thor's head. *What if Willow's captor isn't alone?* Enough rage to annihilate a battalion burned in his veins, but one mistake... *No*, he thought. *Doubts and fears have no place at a time like this.* Willow trusted him, and he promised to take care of her. Reneging on that deal was not an option.

The element of surprise gave him all the edge he needed, and Anders's pistol provided an incredible ally.

The wagon tracks veered off the road and into several rows of maple and oak trees. Thor followed the markings and readied the firearm. Bullets filled all six chambers of the revolver. Modern guns fired in quick secession. This relic bore no resemblance to his father's hunting rifles. The hammer on this pistol had to be cocked before every shot, which meant his aim would have to be perfect the first time.

He spotted the wagon parked beside a large oak. The horse headed steadily toward it. Big Nat's large frame soon came into view. The steady rise and fall of the man's chest showed that he was only unconscious and not dead.

So where the hell is Willow?

A cold knot hardened like ice inside his gut. Shaking hands clutched the reins. He guided the horse deeper into the woods. Predatory male laughter cut the silence. The still forest vibrated with a menacing presence. The sound of physical confrontation mingled with the cold-blooded heckling.

A feminine scream curdled the blood in his veins. The hairs on the back of his neck stood at attention.

Willow!

Thor slid from the horse in one fluid motion. With the pistol cocked and ready, he rushed through the bushes.

The scene before him played out like a bad B-movie of a dirty, nasty man overpowering the damsel in distress, but this was no celluloid fantasy.

With his pants around his ankles, Grady Falls covered a squirming Willow. She kicked and struggled, never lying still for long. Grady, the filthy sonuvabitch, raised his hand in the air. The upswing motion empowered his ringing slaps to her face.

Blinding fury seized Thor. Weight pounded his chest. His breath came in ragged spurts. Coherent thought failed him, and his reflexes took over.

He uncocked the revolver and slammed its butt into the base of Grady's skull. The man's body jerked wildly. His heavy weight hovered above Willow, still threatening despite his unconscious state. Thor quickly caught his shoulders and threw him to the ground. Twigs and dry leaves crackled from the force of Grady's fall.

Thor got his first real look at her. A tattered shirt revealed the full curves of her breasts. Dark purple bruises covered her arms and chest. Tears of anguish filled his eyes. A woman driven by compassion and dedication didn't deserve this. No woman did. If they lived a hundred years, he'd never be able to make this up to her.

"Willow." His hoarse whisper broke the silence. Shrugging out of his jacket, he knelt beside her, careful not to move too fast or too loudly. "Everything will be okay. I'm here now. Willow, can you here me?"

Her body curled around her. She seemed oblivious to the blood trickling from her mouth and the vivid scratches on her arms. Her head turned. The eyes that often regarded him in a mixture of awe and pleasure looked through him. Unintelligible noises came from her barely parted lips.

"Willow, ssh…" He reached for her hands.

Her entire body flinched. A shrill scream pierced his eardrums. *Oh, God.*

Nothing in life prepared him for a moment like this. Stark terror and roaring anger contorted her beauty into a horrified mask. He moved in front of her. With an unsteady hand, he cupped her face.

"Willow, it's me. It's Thor, love. I promise I won't hurt you."

His assurances meant nothing. The earsplitting screams continued. Water pooled her eyes. Tears spilled down her cheeks. The droplets drenched his hand. Each one drowned a piece of his soul. He gulped for air, but the sinking sensation was unrelenting. A self-deprecating curse tore from his gut. He ducked his head low. The feeling of helplessness shamed him.

The cries subsided into hiccups. Hysteria faded into understanding. She covered his hand with hers, splaying her fingers across the back of his hand. In the next moment, her arms flew around his neck. She slammed her entire weight against him, and he crushed her to his chest.

"Thor! You came!"

Sobs wracked her slender frame. Unshed tears stung his eyes. He blinked to hold them at bay. This moment belonged to her. His hands rubbed her back in circular motion, reveling in the warmth their connected bodies generated. Relief at finding her in time halted his speech.

"I—I'm so sorry. That sounds so inadequate…"

"I was so scared." Her confession came after her tears stopped. "He was tr-trying t-to . . ."

"I know." He pressed his mouth to her forehead. The slight kiss made them both shudder. "Ssh," he murmured. "It's okay now. It's okay."

"He was taking us to a br-breeding plantation. He said he wanted to make sure I was pr-prepared."

"Sonuvabitch." If the blow to his head didn't kill Grady Falls, Thor planned to see that a good ass-kicking would do the trick. Right after he was sure Willow was okay to move.

"I thought he was going to kill me," she added. "He kept hitting me. I didn't think he'd ever stop."

Her quiet words reminded him of her injuries. He held her at arms length to re-evaluate her wounds. Blood trickled from a split lip and swelling began to close one of her eyes. He cleaned the blood with the hem of his shirt. A raw steak would have to take care of her eye. He hoped they'd find one somewhere. The wild mass of her black hair created an interesting halo around her head. He tenderly brushed the unruly mane away from her face.

"I must look a sight." She tried to duck her head, but he would not let her. "Thor, don't."

"You're beautiful." His mouth curved into an appreciative smile. "There's a little bruising around the edges, but you're still a raving beauty."

She accepted the compliment without protest. Her one good eye narrowed to a slit as she tried to look around the woods. Thor realized she needed her spectacles. He reached inside the jacket draped over her shoulders for the eyeglasses. The timepiece brushed against his fingers, and he pulled it out first. When he reached inside again, he found the spectacles and gave them to her.

Willow pushed the glasses up her nose. "How did you find us?" She peered around his shoulders. "Did you see Big Nat? Is he okay?"

"He's on the back of the wagon. I didn't check him too closely, but I know he's breathing."

Thor glanced at the watch. Time passed quickly. Since abandoning an enraged Leah in the glen, the hours flew by. The image of hiking back to Pleasant Hill in all her finery and clutching her bag of deception made him chuckle. Then he remembered the reality of the times. Monty, her driver, probably had to carry the spoiled brat on his back, her rantings screeching the poor old man's ears off. By the time she reached daddy dearest, Thor and Willow's misdeeds were embellished to gigantic proportions. Warren Eugene Davis was a man who would stop at nothing to avenge his precious daughter. Snarling dogs and gun-carrying men were probably already hot on their trail. Apprehension crept along his spine. They did not have another moment to waste.

He stood and extended his hands to Willow. A loud crack echoed inside his head. Once again, his world went black.

—◦◦◦—

A kaleidoscope of images danced before his eyes. Most were jumbled and blurred. Thor tried to focus, but the shapes would alter, leaving him confused. Only one image remained unchanged.

The face of a beautiful woman with chocolate brown skin and large black eyes haunted him.

In a warm, husky voice, she called his name. The sound of her voice set him aflame. Flames of desire burned hot, but somehow, succumbing to passion was all wrong.

Urgency rippled through him. With a pang, he realized danger loomed all around her. Hands grabbed at him, but he pushed them aside. A surge of energy awakened him with renewed vigor. Her name tore from him.

"WILLOW!"

"Thor!"

The hands grabbed him again. His hand balled into a fist, and he pulled his arm back. Seconds before his fist connected with flesh, he recognized the face of his older brother directly in front of him and the voice of his father on his left. Thor lowered his hand to his side. He stared at his family in wonder.

"What are you doing here?"

Cal's mouth dropped open. Unintelligible words spurted from him until he was finally able to say, "Knucklehead!"

"The doctor said we'd have to give him time. Wandering around for days . . . Of course, he's disoriented." Bo pushed Cal aside and reached inside the Bronco for Thor. "Come on, son. You've been out in the sun too long. Let's get you inside the cabin."

Thor jerked free of his father's hold. "I can't go with you. I have to find Willow. She needs me. Leah and Grady sold her to a breeding plantation. I told her I'd protect her."

"It was just a dream, Thor." Bo closed his hand around Thor's arm in an unyielding grip. "You can let go of it now."

"It wasn't a dream! I was there. Grady tried to rape her, and I stopped him. Oh, God . . . Grady. If that no good sack of shit lays a hand on her, I swear I'll kill him!" He tore out of his father's grasp and pushed himself from the Bronco. His footsteps pounded the ground as he headed for the surrounding woods. "WILLOW!"

"He's really lost it," Cal said.

"Enough!" Bo growled. He grabbed Thor and shook him roughly. "Listen to me! You were dreaming."

Stunned, Thor's breathing slowed. He looked beyond his father and brother to their surroundings. The Magnusen fishing cabin stood only a few feet away. Weathered and worn from generations of use, the building appeared the same from all his memories. He wandered away from them until he reached the old creek. The same watering hole where he met Willow, except this one was dry. Weeds blanketed the bank, and everything was the way he remembered it from childhood.

The back of his neck throbbed. His head spun. *How could the last few days be a dream?* Willow was real. 1860 was real. *Dammit, I met my great-great-grandparents, and they were real!* His knees shook. Clutching his head and the memories that didn't make sense, he surrendered to the ground.

"It wasn't a dream," he said quietly. "I was there, and she was real."

"Uh huh," Cal said. "Yeah, let's go back to the cabin. Get you some water, and put you into bed. Everything will make sense after you get some rest."

"I don't need rest. I know I was there."

Bo knelt in front of Thor. His brows creased with worry. "Where, son? We've been looking for you for days and filed a missing persons report with the sheriff's office. If the highway patrolman hadn't called us, we'd still be looking."

He answered with quiet assurance. "Right here at this cabin in 1860."

—◦◦◦—

"You don't believe me." Thor looked from his father to his brother and back again. They wore the same expressions: indulgence, love, and concern. He removed the ice pack from the back of his neck and threw it down on the wooden tabletop. "I'm not making this up. Look at me! Look at this bump. Look at these clothes! Where would I get clothes like this?"

"From the old trunk over there," Cal answered, pointing to the wooden case. "We must have seen that old suit a hundred times growing up. You just put it on and went for a walk."

"Cal, look at these pants and the shirt! They're practically brand new! If they were sitting in the trunk for over a hundred years, they'd be moth eaten for God's sake!"

"Don't use His name in vain," Bo warned.

"But Pop." He crossed to his father and thrust the hem of the shirt under the older man's nose. "See that blood. It's fresh."

"You bumped your head."

"It's Willow's blood, not mine. Besides, my skin isn't broken so it couldn't come from me. I swear to you it's Willow's." He hitched a harsh breath. "That bastard Grady beat her badly. She has bruises everywhere, and her bottom lip is split."

Speech became difficult, but he pressed on. "I made her so many promises, and now, she's all alone. With that lowlife piece of shit!" His voice cracked.

Thor turned his back to his family and strode to the fireplace. The photos on the mantel caught his attention. One of Eva and Anders stared back. Their stoic faces accused him. His head dropped in shame.

"Time travel is impossible," Cal said quietly. A chair scraped across the floor and heavy footsteps thumped across the wooden floorboards. "It doesn't happen in real life. The idea of it can be a good escape, but you gotta come back to reality. I'm only saying this because I love you." He wrapped his arm around Thor's shoulders and hugged him. "Maybe it's time you talked to a professional."

"I don't need a shrink." He rubbed his hand over his face and sighed. When he looked at his brother, he said, "I haven't lost my mind, but I will if I don't find a way to get back there. Willow needs me, and I'm not about to let her down."

———

"You don't believe me," Willow stated quietly.

Her hands clutched Reverend Brown's jacket as the horse they shared galloped toward home. Anders shared his horse with Big Nat, and they followed close behind.

"Thor was with me. He didn't leave me alone."

"You were in a horrible situation," Brown replied over his shoulder. "That man threatened you in a most grievous manner. It wouldn't come as a surprise if your imagination took hold. Nobody would fault you."

"I didn't imagine it, Reverend. Thor was holding out his hand to me to help me stand, and that horrible Grady Falls hit him on the back of his head." She paused to catch her breath. "Thor's face drew up with the pain, and then he was gone. Didn't you and Mr. Anders see him? We have to go back and see if we can find him."

Brown closed his hand over hers. "Willow child, we saw no sign of him. We saw Big Nat coming to on the back of the wagon and we saw a stray horse, but there was no sign of Thor out there. There's just no way we can go back. By now, they'll know that Big Nat is missing and will become suspicious about you and Thor. We have to keep going. I 'spect that Thor has done the same."

"He wouldn't just leave me!" she protested. "He was there! He gave me back my spectacles, and he gave me this coat to wear. He's hurting and needs help. If they find him, you know they'll string him up. I beg you, please, don't leave him."

Deep sobs shook her. She buried her face against her adoptive father's hard back. He reached behind himself and patted her arm.

"Don't cry, child."

"I can't help it, Reverend," she choked. "I love him. If they kill him, I'll want to die, too."

"You shouldn't speak like that." Reproach hardened his voice. "You haven't known him long enough to love him."

"What does time have to do with love? You don't know him like I do. He's a special man who comes from a special place. He wanted me to go back with him, but I didn't believe he meant it. Now I wish I'd told him yes."

The horse hooves played a rapid cadence as they raced through the woods. Brown spoke over the rhythmic beat. "What special place? Where did he want to take you?"

"To his home."

"In Atlanta?"

"He never really said. The place didn't matter. The time made all the difference. He said that I didn't have to go to Oberlin. I could go to any college I wanted and be anything I wanted. He said that my dreams could come true. The only dream I want to come true is to find him again and to know that he's safe."

"What do you mean by 'time?'"

Willow sighed. If he didn't believe that Thor vanished right in front of her face, how in the world would he believe that Thor traveled back in time? "You'll think I'm telling tall tales."

"Try me."

She trusted Reverend Brown with her life. When she thought of a father figure, his pale features came to mind more often than Elijah's earth-toned complexion although she loved her slain father dearly.

The Browns loved her. Reverend's fierce over protective behavior was born out of that love. He wanted to shield her from the ills of their society and from immoral men who would take advantage of her. She sensed he admired Thor's willingness to help The Cause, but felt he still harbored suspicions as to Thor's motives. He couldn't see what she saw in Thor, and she doubted if he'd believe his claims of being from the future. She was not sure what to do.

"You can tell me anything, Butterfly."

Willow smiled through her tears at the use of her parents' pet name. Elijah had called her by that name instead of using Willow. Her father often said she reminded him of a graceful flying creature, and one day, he wanted her to spread her wings and fly. Reverend Brown had used the name, too, but stopped after her parents died.

Willow guessed the reverend thought it would remind her of them. She missed the sound of the name, and hearing it again brought back many memories, the good ones and the bad. Then she realized that he'd been a constant force through all of it. Of course, she could trust him with the truth.

"Thor is from the future." Her admission came softly. "He was born in 1957. When he came here, the year was nineteen hundred and eighty-five in his world."

Brown was quiet for quite some time. "Do you believe him?"

"He showed me proof. I wasn't sure at first, but what I saw is nothing like anything I've ever seen or heard about, and he's different. Haven't you noticed, Reverend? His ways are different. He uses words and phrases that are strange to me, but seem natural for him."

He nodded. "Did he say what brought him here? To us? Now?"

Willow paused. She remembered the pocket watch and the awesome energy that surrounded it. If the timepiece did indeed bring Thor forth, how would the reverend view it? Would he look upon Thor with more censure than he already used? Would his religious fervor cause him to accuse Thor because of the watch's possible abilities?

Perhaps, she said too much. It was too late to take back her words, but she could try to protect Thor.

Willow shook her head. "He wasn't certain. He fell asleep at the creek near the Magnusen cabin, and when he woke up, there I was. He hasn't told me too much about the future. He is afraid anything he says will alter his time. I think I understand his reasons, but I couldn't help but be curious."

"I imagine so," he said. "Did he say why he was at the cabin?"

"He didn't go into detail, but he's related to Mr. Anders and Miss Eva." She leaned close to his ear and whispered, "He's their great-great-grandson."

He exhaled a low whistle. "Well, I'll be."

"Do you believe me?" Despite her misgivings at speaking out of turn, Willow felt lightheaded and giddy with anticipation. "Do you think it's possible?"

"I already know that you do." A smile came through in his voice. "I saw the resemblance with him and Anders right off. Come to think of it, he has a bit of Eva in him, too. The foreheads are just about the same. I don't know, Willow. It seems to me it goes against God and nature."

"Not to me. Only God can perform a miracle such as that."

—◦◦◦—

"So, she's a black girl?"

Thor gave his father a strong look. "Willow is a woman. She is not a girl. The life she's had has made her anything but childlike. Slave patrollers killed her parents in 1847, a few weeks before her eighth birthday."

"I don't recall anything about that. Don't remember Grandpa mentioning anyone by that name. He should have known her, considering she was so close to his Ma, Eva."

Cal rolled his eyes. "You're indulging this trip into the *Twilight Zone*? I can't believe it."

"I don't give a damn what you believe."

"That'll be enough out of both of you," Bo advised his two sons. "I can't say that I don't believe it, and I can't say that I do. What Thor's said... I don't feel right about disputing."

"Why not?" Cal rose from the sofa and planted his hands on his hips. "Where's the proof?"

"Look at his pants and the shirt. We've seen them in the trunk, and we know they're Anders."

"So?"

"Right about now, I'm wondering who the true knucklehead is," Bo growled. "Calvin, look at the material! It isn't worn or threadbare. As Thor said, if he put on the old pair, there would be moth holes all through it. These pants look and feel like new."

"And that was enough to convince you?"

Thor gritted his teeth. Irritation set him on edge. They were discussing clothes when Willow's life hung in the balance? The nitpicking wore out his patience.

"Who cares? Either you believe or you don't. Right now, I really don't give a rat's ass." He looked at his father. "Sorry, Pop. No disrespect, but this is driving me crazy. I'm not making any of this up, and I'm not losing my mind. Willow Elkridge is real. I really met Anders and Eva. And I *really* need to get back there!"

"Well, what brought you back, or is that forward, in the first place?"

Thor's eyes narrowed as he assessed his brother's sincerity. He saw no humor in Cal's eyes and heard no mockery in Cal's tone. He supposed Cal, the great thinker of the family, decided to consider the improbable.

"I don't know what brought me back or what took me there. I think it was the pocket watch, but I'm not sure."

"Well, what were you doing?" Cal stooped in front of him. "Were you thinking about the past? Did you have a beer instead of breakfast? Were you asleep? Awake? What?"

"When I woke up in 1860, I was sitting where the creek used to be. You know, where it has dried up. Anyway, Willow was there getting water." His lips curved into a faint smile. "Her braid fell straight down her back to her waist. She has a smile that could melt steel and a heart the size of Texas. If she was sold into slavery because of me. . ."

"Get a hold of yourself," Cal advised, patting his brother's shoulder. "We'll find out what happened to her."

"How?"

"I'm a History professor, knucklehead! We'll go back into town, and I'll stop by the university library and do some fast research. I can find it for you in no time."

"I don't have that kind of time. I have to go back as soon as possible. Driving back to Atlanta will take too long."

"I have an idea," Bo said. "We can do the research here."

"How?" Cal asked.

"We can pull out the old trunk again and see what turns up. If Thor really traveled back to Anders's day, there'll be proof of it in there."

CHAPTER THIRTEEN

Floorboards creaked from the weight of her worry. Mindless of the activities around her, Willow paced in front of the fireplace. The swooshing of her skirts failed to deafen the roaring turmoil in her heart. Almost an hour ago, Reverend Brown left her at the Magnusen cabin while he and Anders hurried to reunite Big Nat with his children. They planned to direct the runaways to their next Station and later return with Olivia, leaving the three women together as there was safety in numbers. Then the men would double back to where they found Willow in the hopes of locating Thor. The plan seemed sound to Willow, and she wanted nothing more than to join them on their search.

"Won't you rest?" Eva implored. "You haven't eaten anything since you've come back. There's a pot of stew on the stove. Stir up a bowl and sit down."

Willow paused at the window. She adjusted the spectacles on the bridge of her nose and pulled back the curtains. Her other hand rested on her flat midsection, trying to soothe the nervous fluttering inside. "I couldn't eat a bite. I doubt if anything would stay down. Would you like a bowl for yourself?"

"I'm fine." Eva waited a moment before she added, "Looking out that window won't make the time move any faster. Wouldn't you like to peek at little Dorothea and maybe hold her awhile?"

"I'm sorry, Miss Eva." A faint smile of contrition parted her lips. "My mind hasn't been my own with so much worrying. Of course, I'd like to hold her."

Eva stood and nodded toward the rocking chair in a silent invitation for Willow to sit. She did and Eva placed the sleeping child inside the cradle of Willow's open arms. The baby settled there with a small amount of squirming, and Willow was enthralled. She'd never held such a small infant before.

Maternal yearnings replaced the nervous fluttering inside her lower belly. She remembered Thor's warning that she could be with child.

His child.

Her heart raced with untold emotion. An image of a little boy with skin the color of milk-sweetened coffee and large round eyes the color of a dark blue midnight sky flashed before her eyes. What wouldn't she give to experience the joy of giving birth to a child of her own—hers and Thor's.

"It's amazing how having a child changes you. I can see it on your face. You want one of your own."

"She's precious. I'm so happy for you and Mr. Anders." Willow tore her gaze from Dorothea's sleeping form to look upon the child's mother. Tiny white lines that Willow hadn't noticed before stretched from the corners of Eva's eyes. Eva's ivory complexion appeared ashen from strain. "The reverend told me the delivery was difficult. How are you now? Maybe you should lie down a spell."

"I think I will." Eva limped to the bed and gingerly sat. She shifted until she lay across the bed on her side, facing Willow and the baby. "This feels nice. I didn't want Anders to worry, but I'm sore all over."

"You should have mentioned it earlier. Rest yourself. Little Dorothea and I will be just fine."

"I'm not sleepy. Whenever you want to rest your arms, you can lay the baby right here." She patted the empty space beside her on the bed. "In the meantime, I want to hear all about your adventure."

Willow's eyebrows arched. "You weren't keen on me going with him as I recall," she teased.

"Now that you're back safe and sound, I can have a change of heart. I'm praying that Anders and the reverend will find him."

"So am I." Willow sighed deeply. A sharp pain shot across her midsection, and she winced. The rush of air awakened the baby, who responded with a soft cry. Despite her own discomfort, Willow gently rocked the infant until she fell asleep again. "If I knew what happened to him, I could rest a little easier."

"What do you think happened? Of course, if you'd rather not say, I can respect your privacy."

"I can tell you, but I'm not sure if you'll believe me. The reverend seemed to take me at my word, and that surprised me."

Eva pulled the quilt around herself and snuggled deep in the covers. "This sounds mysterious."

The constraints of worry loosened, Eva's curiosity eased the tightness in Willow's chest. "I suppose it is in a way. I think I may know where Thor is, but then again, I'm not sure. Maybe he went home. Just as mysteriously and just as quickly as how he arrived."

"You're not making a lick of sense."

"What I'm about to tell you won't make any sense, and it will seem impossible. Thor asked me to keep this to myself, but I don't see how I can now in light of his disappearance." As the words began to flow, her confidence grew. "He's from the future, Miss Eva. Thor Magnusen isn't just a relation of Mr. Anders. He's your great-great-grandson."

Eva bolted upright as if lightning struck her. "I don't believe I heard you correctly."

"You heard me just fine. I said he's from the future; from nineteen hundred and eighty-five to be exact."

Intense disbelief touched Eva's pale face. "A dose of laudanum would do you a world of good. I should have realized those bruises on your head—"

"The blows to my head have nothing to do with what I'm telling you. Thor told me this the first day he came, and he spoke a little more about it while we were on the road. I don't believe he spoke out of turn. He was telling the truth."

"B—But that's impossible."

"Is it?" Willow remembered the objects he showed her. The vibrant colors on his photograph came to mind. Brilliant, intelligent blue eyes shone vividly in contrast to his ruddy face. The image was perfect as the man himself. Surely, that alone provided proof of his origins!

Expression uncertain, Eva chewed on her bottom lip. "You believe he's my grandson."

"Yes. He looks so much like Mr. Anders, and he has your compassion. Can you not see the resemblance?"

"I suppose I can, it's just hard to believe. Maybe if you told me more of what he's told you, I'd be able to understand."

Willow repeated what Thor told her about his life, and as she reached the conclusion of her recount, Reverend Brown and Anders arrived with Olivia. The men stayed long enough to gather food and ammunition. Willow didn't ask to accompany them. While talking to Eva, she decided to stay with the women. She was not sure why. It was just a feeling she had. She would do better to stay there.

After the men left, Olivia handed Dorothea to her mother and drew Willow into the circle of her arms. Her hands rubbed the younger woman's back in warm, brisk strokes. Her voice shook with tears. "We were worried sick about you. How could you run off and do such a foolhardy thing? Do you realize what could have happened to you? My God! What *almost* happened to you?"

"I'm sorry, Miss Olivia, but I did what I felt was right," Willow said as their hug ended.

Olivia's finger lightly stroked Willow's swollen eye and other bruises. "Look at your face, child. Sit down and let me look at you."

The examination was thorough. The older woman's gentle touch did little to alleviate the pain of Willow's wounds. Thor's disappearance far outweighed the importance of her injuries.

"I didn't want to worry either of you, that's why I just took off. Those children need their father, and he needs them. What happened when Big Nat and the children were reunited? Were they surprised?"

"You are always more concerned about others than you are about yourself. Do you realize that your ribs are badly bruised? Eva, where's your scrap material or an old shirt? I need to wrap her up before more damage is done."

The new mother directed Olivia to the chest of drawers. "Look in the bottom drawer. A few of Anders old shirts are in there. They are worn through in some places, but they are clean. Willow, you should have told me you were hurting." Eva moved to stand. "Let me help."

"Lay down," Olivia commanded with a faint smile that softened her demand. "I can take care of her. Besides, you need your rest, too."

Olivia tore a shirt into strips and instructed Willow to remove her outer garments. Wearing only chemise and drawers, Willow pulled the hem of the chemise to her breasts while Olivia wrapped the strips of material tightly around her torso. Rivulets of pain shot through her.

Perhaps this was worse than the actual beating. Willow sucked in air instead of crying out.

"You'll venture across lots instead of putting your welfare into proper consideration," Olivia fussed. "Some obstacles are not meant to be crossed, Willow. What you did was dangerous! Look at how that filthy beast beat you. My Lord! Did he do worse?"

"Worse than beat me?"

Memories flooded her mind. Grady's hot, tobacco scented breath blew hot in her face. His coarse, rough hands pinched and grabbed in the same places Thor had tenderly caressed. Bile rose to her throat and threatened to choke her. She swallowed hard. Salty tears filled her eyes, and she tried to blink them away. They fell down her cheeks anyway.

Silence filled the cabin. The two other women stood still. Their eyes searched Willow's face. Eventually, Eva turned away. The older woman finished tying the bandage. Her love burned brightly on her pale face. She cupped Willow's face, thumbing away her tears.

"I am so sorry."

"H—He didn't," Willow explained. "He tried to, but Thor stopped him."

"Are you sure? You can tell me. Neither Eva or I will breathe a word of it to anyone."

"We wouldn't say a word." Eva stepped forward. Sympathy glowed from her warm eyes.

The depth of their caring shook her to the core. Their affection for her had always been obvious. Feeling the enormity of their love made her steps falter. Olivia brought the rocking chair for her to sit. Willow sank onto the padded seat and slowly rocked. The gentle swaying motion soothed her as much as their thoughtful presence. The words soon fell from her lips.

"I assure you that he did not succeed in forcing his attentions upon me. I resisted, so he beat me. Then Thor arrived and knocked him senseless."

"Well, God bless him," Eva said.

Once spoken, Willow needed to free her mind of the disturbing assault. Her spirits demanded rejuvenation. Her thoughts turned to more pleasant occurrences. "How was the reunion of Big Nat with the children?"

"We'll get to that in a moment." Olivia's mouth tightened into a thin line. "I'm sure there is more you haven't mentioned, and it wouldn't be right of me not to ask. You were on a plantation and witnessed the atrocities we've been fighting against." She patted Willow's hand. "Do you understand now why Mitchell doesn't want you to take a too active role in the movement? He was protecting you and doing it the best way he knew how."

"I know, Miss Olivia, and I understand, but I'm not a child. I saw their faces, spent time in their quarters, and heard their tales. I'm pained by it all, but it hasn't defeated me. I want to work harder in trying to help. I can't turn my back on them now."

"You have the sensibility of a mule." Olivia blinked back tears. "You could have been killed."

"But I wasn't. Moses has made plenty of journeys, and all her trips have been successful."

"Harriet Tubman grew up on a plantation!" Olivia snapped. "You grew up in a loving home, and that makes a difference. She knows how to handle herself and how to move on and off without notice."

"I can learn how to do the same."

Olivia's grip on Willow's hand tightened. "I would prefer that you didn't. I've saved some money, and I brought it with me. Mitchell and I talked about it. We want you to go to Ohio and enroll in Oberlin College as soon as possible."

Willow jerked free of Olivia's grasp. She stood abruptly and the chair rocked violently on the floor. Pain ripped through her at the sudden movement. She ignored the discomfort.

"I can't leave now! What about Thor? If he didn't go back to…well, he could be out there somewhere. I cannot leave without knowing what happened to him! I couldn't do that."

"Thor?" Eva spoke quietly. "You've talked about studying at Oberlin for as long as I've known you. Now you would give up the opportunity because of him? I warned you about Thor, Willow. He's handsome, charming, and kind, but you and he could never find happiness together."

Willow folded her arms around her waist and jutted out her chin.

"Maybe not here."

"This is foolishness, talking about that man. Oberlin will give you opportunities. Running on and off plantations can get you killed. Enough!" Olivia threw up her hands. She went to the stove and with a shaky hand filled three bowls with stew as she spoke. "You wanted to know about the reunion. It was the most beautiful thing." Her words flew from her mouth in rapid succession. "I wish you could have seen it. Big Nat gathered all three of those children inside his arms and hugged them tight. I swear, even your Anders," she said, glancing over her shoulder at Eva, "had something in his eyes as he watched them. Big Nat thanked us for taking care of his children, and then Mitchell sent them on their way. Before they left, Big Nat asked me to thank you."

She set three bowls on the table and took the sleeping infant from her mother. "It's your turn to eat. I'll lay her in the crib."

"Thank you."

Olivia cradled the baby in her arms. "It's no problem at all. Now that I've said my piece, I'd like to hear the rest of it, Willow. I imagine you've already told Eva the gist of your journey."

Willow and Eva exchanged glances. Olivia's sudden change in tone was not a surprise. The older woman often banked her anger with a gentle voice and a quick change in conversation. Willow expected there would be more to follow.

"I've told her a good deal of it, Miss Olivia. Did the reverend say anything to you?"

"You mean about Thor being from the future? Yes, he told me a bit about that."

"Do you believe it's true?" Willow had to know before saying anything further.

"As you explained to Mitchell, miracles happen." Olivia placed the baby in the crib and joined the two women at the table. "I'm not one to say something can be done unless it can be proven to me that it can't. He appeared to be a courteous young man, but his mannerisms were unfamiliar to me. He speaks with the accent of a Southerner, yet his ideals were the same as some of our Northern friends. Now it would seem that there's a reason for this. Mitchell wasn't sure what to make of it, but it would seem to me that Thor is not of our time."

Willow found speech difficult. She wanted her family and friends to believe her, but she wasn't prepared for them to do so. The Browns' newfound determination to further her education at Oberlin created a new diversion. Her nerves rattled with tension and stretched across a taut line. She wasn't sure if Olivia truly believed her or was preparing to wage another argument.

"She says he's my great-great-grandson," Eva said quietly. "He's not one of Anders's cousins like I thought. It's strange when you think about it, but I don't think it's a lie. He's stubborn like Anders, but there's gentleness to him, too. You've already told me about his brother and father, but I'd like to know more. What does he say about the future?"

"He wouldn't say much about it," Willow answered, "except that I would have a better life there. I could go to any college or university I wanted, and I could do whatever I wanted. Oberlin would not be my only option in nineteen hundred and eighty-five. I would have choices. He asked me if I would go back with him."

"What did you say to him?" Olivia asked.

"I didn't give him an answer," Willow answered. "I wish I had."

—◦◦◦—

The horses galloped through the woods at a break neck speed. Anders gripped the reins and hunched forward. His thoughts raced as fast as the horses' hooves pounded the ground.

Admitting he was wrong had always been a sore spot. Going back on his opinions didn't sit well with him either. However, worry refused to let him escape the facts. Thor's disappearance bothered him. Although they didn't see eye to eye, Anders admired the other man's stubborn willfulness. It reminded Anders of his own unyielding trait, and maybe being pigheaded would keep Thor safe until they arrived to aid him.

"There aren't many places he can hide between Canton and

Atlanta." Brown interrupted Anders's musing. "Besides he's on foot, and that'll slow him down some. It may take a few days, but we will find him."

"If someone else hasn't found him already." The starlit night provided enough light and he clearly saw the shadows of worry darken the older man's face. "What would they do to him? For aiding runaways? I know what the law says, but what will really happen?"

"You guessed right. They wouldn't follow the law. Most of the South is drawn tight as a drum. They'd want to make an example out of him."

"Would they kill him?"

"Maybe."

Anders barely had time to process Brown's quietly spoken warning before the hairs on the back of his neck stood on end. His horse tensed, and he wondered what spooked them both.

Then he heard it. Rapid pounding ripped into the earth and shook the ground. His gaze cut to the reverend again. "What in the world?"

"Posse. They're coming fast, too."

They turned toward the woods to avoid the rushing riders. The yips and barks of hunting dogs filled the forest. No matter which path they took, the sounds came louder and stronger.

"They're chasing *us*!" Anders shouted over the clamorous activity. "Why?"

"I don't know, and I don't aim to find out."

The horses rushed forward. The large beasts seemed intent on escaping the dogs' snapping jaws. The men yielded to the horses' determination, also straining and pushing the horses harder.

Their efforts failed them. The dogs, trained just for this purpose, gained on them and circled Anders. Their ferocious snarls kept the trapped men in place while the dogs' yelps alerted their owner to their location. A group of angry, white men on horseback soon surrounded them.

"Magnusen!" One authoritative voice called.

"Yes?" Anders responded. "What's this about?"

"Stolen property. I'm Warren Eugene Davis and nobody takes what's mine without answering to me."

"What are you talking about? I haven't stolen anything from you. I've never seen you before in my life."

"I have witnesses that will say differently. Grab him and his friend, too."

Two men came toward Anders. Anders reached for his rifle. The loop of a rope circled around him. He bunched his shoulders and tried to pull free. The more he struggled, the tighter the rope cut into him. Finally, someone tugged on the rope and pulled him from the horse. He fell to the ground, landing beside Brown, who was also bound by rope.

"The Davis plantation is where Willow and Thor found Big Nat," Brown said low enough so that only Anders heard him. "He thinks you're Thor."

—◦◦◦—

Windows rattled loudly as pounding shook the cabin. Eva snatched Dorothea from the crib and held the tiny babe to her chest. On the other side of the room, Olivia grabbed a rifle and headed toward the door. Willow's hand shot out, closing around her adoptive mother's forearm.

"You can't go out there!"

The wooden door shook in its frame as the pounding increased. "Mrs. Magnusen! It's Hammond Phelps, ma'am. "

"What do you want?" Olivia yelled out before Eva could respond. "It's too late for calling."

"I know it is, ma'am, but it's important."

Olivia checked the rifle, and then handed it to Willow. Willow's hand shook from the weight of the firearm and from fear. Her heart beat a rapid cadence in her chest. Her body felt ice cold all over. "What do you suppose he wants?"

"I'll find out," Olivia said. "Keep the rifle on him through the window."

Olivia slipped out the door before Willow could protest. Filling her lungs with a deep gulp of air, Willow forced her racing heart to slow to a normal pace. She pushed fear to the back of her mind. She had fired the rifle before, but its kick was strong. She needed her wits about her and hands steady in case Olivia needed her protection from the blacksmith.

Willow pushed her spectacles up her nose and positioned the rifle on her hip. Her eyes narrowed as she made out the shapes of Olivia and Hammond on the porch. The conversation seemed to be serious indeed. Hammond gestured wildly, and Olivia's head nodded in time to his gesturing. A moment later, Olivia returned to the cabin with Hammond fast on her heels.

"What's wrong?" Eva asked as soon as they crossed the threshold.

Olivia paused a moment before she answered. Willow watched the older woman closely. Lines of worry etched from the corners of her eyes. Tiny, white lines framed her mouth that had thinned into a grim line. Her pale hands trembled visibly. Whatever Hammond told her, the news was not good.

Willow lowered the butt of the rifle to the floor and stepped toward the older woman. "Miss Olivia, what is it?"

"I knew it was you," Hammond said in a rush, "a few nights ago with that fella who looked like Magnusen. There ain't too many colored boys in these parts, and none of them smell like honeysuckles. Everybody knows you and Miss Eva spend a good deal of time together. I wondered where y'all were off to in the middle of the night like that."

He stopped talking as if he was waiting for her to answer his unspoken question. Willow shook her head in reply and asked, "What happened tonight, Mr. Hammond? Did something happen in town?"

"It wasn't in Canton. I was delivering some horses and was on my way back when I saw Anders and the reverend. I would have helped, but I was too far away. Besides, there were too many of them."

"Too many of what?" Eva asked.

"Slave patrollers, I reckon. They roped Anders and the good reverend off their horses and dragged them down the trail."

Willow's heart lurched. She reached for Olivia, who clutched Willow as if her strength came from their linked hands.

"They're holding Anders and Mitchell on charges of aiding slaves in escaping," Olivia said. "Hammond heard the name Davis mentioned."

"We have to do something!" Eva cried.

"Where did they take them?" Willow asked.

"I ain't quite sure," he replied. "I 'spect they went back to the Davis place. I came straight here to tell y'all. From that distance, I couldn't tell if the man was Anders or that other fella, but I knew it was Brown. I was gonna come to your place after I stopped here, Miss Olivia."

"Thank you, Hammond," she responded in a distant voice. "So no one knows you're here?"

"No ma'am. I didn't make no stops nowhere and came directly here. I figured you'd want to know. Besides, the sheriff is down by the Etowah River. I can ride down there and tell him now. Reverend Brown and Anders got lots of friends who'll be willing to help. I'll drop in on a few of them before I go to the river."

Hammond headed toward the door. Olivia called out to him before he crossed the threshold. "Thank you again, and please, whatever you do, don't let any strangers know you saw Willow here."

He dipped his head in a quick nod. "I won't say a word to a soul. I understand, Miss Olivia. I won't say nothing."

After his departure, Olivia closed the door and locked it. "We don't have much time. We must move quickly."

"We have to help them!" Eva cried. "Oh, my dear God. They'll hang them for helping runaways. I just know it."

"Don't talk like that!" Olivia snapped.

"What are we going to do?"

Guilt attacked Willow on all sides. If she hadn't decided to find the children's father, Thor wouldn't have gone with her. He was lost to her somewhere, possibly in the next century, and Reverend Brown and Anders's lives were at risk. Willow did not want to imagine either of the men subdued by lifeless sleep. She couldn't.

"Although the meetings were secret and to be held in confidence," Olivia said, "others may know we were helping runaways. We can't be sure they'll hold their tongues if questioned."

"Big Nat and the children are long gone by now, aren't they?"

Olivia nodded and squeezed Willow's hand. "They should be at the next station by now. It's you I'm worried about. Child, we have to hide you, and we have to do it *now!*"

—◦◦◦—

The inside of the cabin resembled the aftermath of a tornado. Old clothing, worn books, and other Magnusen heirlooms littered the floor. For several days, Thor, his brother and his father ripped the cabin apart. They left no stone unturned in the search for something—anything— to help Thor in his determination to return to the past.

Thor left Cal and their father in the bedroom and ambled to the living area. Behind him, their voices rumbled. Thor knew he wasn't alone in his frustration.

If only he could remember what triggered his voyage to the past. The answer seemed to rest on the tip of his tongue. Yet, the harder he tried to force the memory, the more his mind drew a blank on the answers. Cal said that the blow to Thor's head caused his amnesia. Thor didn't care what caused the memory loss. He just wanted it fixed!

The urge to strike out seized him. His right hand balled into a fist. There was a space on the wall that would have to do. He reared his arm back and prepared to swing with all his might when he spotted it. The old trunk sat on the floor. Piles of clothing lay strewn across it from Thor's assault an hour ago. A tiny voice inside his head urged him on.

Look one more time.

He lowered his arm and relaxed his hand. Another search wouldn't hurt. He crossed the room, knelt in front of the chest, and pulled everything out again.

Cal entered the room and perched on the arm of the sofa. "Weren't you just in there? You're wasting time. There's nothing here."

"There's got to be. If it's not in this trunk, it's in this cabin. I know it is."

Thor dug inside his jeans' pocket and pulled out a pocketknife. He flipped it open and moved his hand inside the trunk. Cal's hand shot out and gripped his arm.

"What the hell are you doing? You can't just go ripping into that. Besides, I called Sonia when you were tearing into it the first time."

Thor rolled his eyes. "You called your research assistant? You always think the answer is in a book. Sometimes, it's not."

"Yeah, and sometimes, it is. Don't be such a smartass, knucklehead. Take a minute. Relax—"

"I can't relax!" Thor postponed his plan to inspect the lining of the trunk to look at his brother. "It's eating at me."

"Like when you got sacked and couldn't stop watching the tape? Over and over again?"

Thor's eyes narrowed. His voice grated dangerously low. "If you woke up the next morning and couldn't read another book, how would you feel?"

"It's not the same thing." Cal dismissed the question with a wave of his hand.

"Bullshit."

The brothers were quiet for a moment. The rush of Thor's ragged breathing filled the room. He was mad enough to spit. Cal's needling tried his patience. One more crack and he would forget they were brothers.

"What's got you so juiced about going back in time? Is it really the girl?"

"Her name is Willow." Thor shifted to a sitting position on the floor. He rubbed his thumb along the length of the pocketknife's blade. It wasn't too sharp, and the mechanical movement gave him time to collect his thoughts.

"You said her father was a free black man, right?" Cal scratched his forehead. "I remember reading about a few who settled near the river."

"Her father would have been in that group," Thor said. "He met her mother when Brown helped her on the Underground Railroad. They fell in love, Brown married them, and they settled in the mountains not too far from here. They had Willow and were happy until slave patrollers came along and killed them."

"Sounds like a tragic love story."

"It was." He remembered holding Willow in his arms as she told him about her parents. She had admitted she didn't remember as much as she'd like, but what she did remember eased the loneliness she sometimes felt. No doubt the brutal abduction and murder of her parents overrode the pleasant memories for a traumatized eight-year-old child.

Thor folded the pocketknife up and shoved it inside his pocket. He felt Cal's gaze boring into him, so he glared back.

"What?"

"You care about her," Cal said quietly. "You've hooped and hollered enough to raise the dead, talking about overseers, slave breeders and plantations. But you left out how much this Willow means to you."

Thor's cheeks burned. "She's a remarkable woman."

"I would say she's more than just remarkable; at least, to you. You should have told us you're in love with her."

"In love?" Thor's eyebrows shot up. "I care about her, but . . . love?"

"You said you asked her to come with you to 1985 to be with you. If you don't love her, why in hell would you ask her to do something like that?"

"She can't have the kind of life she deserves in 1860! She can't go anywhere for fear of being enslaved, and if she goes to college, she only has one to choose from! Willow's life would be a helluva lot better here in 1985."

Cal's mouth twitched. "Oh, so your reasons are purely selfless? So, um, if she had said yes and she was here now, what would you have done?"

"That's a moot point," Thor bit out.

"I disagree," Cal countered. "Let's say you go back to eighteen-sixty, find her, and this time she wants to come with you. You figure out how to work the time travel whatchamacalit and then, wham!" He slapped his hands. "You're in 1985 again and she is, too. What do you do then? Drop her off at the university and leave her there? Good-bye and good luck?"

"Stop being an asshole."

"I'm trying to give you something to think about! You can't just ask a woman to give up the life she knows and the friends she loves to be with you without having something to offer her."

Thor nodded. "I know, and I would have something."

"Like what?"

"I played pro ball for six years. I have some money. I can provide for her."

Cal shook his head. "Women need more than money."

"How would you know?" The bantering lessened the tension that gripped him and Thor chuckled.

Cal's deep laugh joined in. "Okay, wiseass. Maybe I don't know from personal experience. Think about what I said. She'd have to cross a century to accept your invitation. Next time you see her, be sure you mean what you say."

"Do you have a problem with her being black?"

Cal's laughter ceased. A frown wrinkled his brow for a split second and then rapidly disappeared. His smile was wide and knowing. "I'm sure I'd get along with anybody who got your mind off football. Nah, little brother. I don't give a damn about her skin color."

"What about Pop?" Thor nodded toward the hall.

"You're asking about us, but what about you? Does it matter to you?"

"No."

Cal reached out and thumped Thor's forehead. "Well, that's all that matters."

"I found something!" Bo's voice boomed down the hallway. He entered a moment later with a stack of faded envelopes clutched in his hand. As he joined his two sons, he thrust the mail toward his youngest son. "They're addressed to you. Open them!"

CHAPTER FOURTEEN

October 19, 1860

Dearest Thor,

There still has been no word about you, so I trust that you safely returned to your family. I pray that your fate has not taken the same turn as your relation, Mr. Anders and my dear Reverend Brown. We continue to pray that they will be saved from the hangman's noose, but as the days continue to dawn anew, the sentiment toward those who aid slaves in escape has become worse. We fear for their lives and are praying that a miracle, similar to the one that delivered you onto us, will liberate them from the imprisonment that keeps them away from home.

Miss Olivia continues to insist that I remain hidden. I am safe here, but very lonesome. On her last visit, she said that some of our neighbors have asked about me, and she told them I left for Oberlin College. As soon as it is safe to do so, I suppose I will. Davis and his men are looking for me, and Miss Olivia believes that it is best I remain hidden here.

I have asked Miss Eva to keep these letters in a safe place for you. The three of us have discussed your ability to transcend time, and we are of the belief that it is possible that you will indeed find these letters in your cabin one day. A part of me believes this may be fanciful thinking and that you were only a figment of my far-reaching imagination. Then I remember the warmth of your smile and the gentleness in your eyes, and I know that you were real—

"Willow?" The hidden compartment in the wall opened and Olivia stuck her head inside the door. "I come bearing supper, fried chicken, biscuits, and a slice of apple pie. I'll bring a bucket of water up before I leave."

The older woman swept into the room. A hand-woven basket swung heavily back and forth against her skirt. The delicious aroma of Willow's favorite foods filled the tiny room. Olivia placed the food on the small table where Willow was writing. She closed her hand over Willow's shoulder and squeezed. "How are you? You've kept busy writing and haven't had any trouble?"

Her adoptive mother's gentle touch helped soothe the loneliness of confinement. "None at all. The nights are quiet, and the animals talk to each other during the day. I miss you. How are Miss Eva and the baby? Has there been any more word on the reverend and Mr. Anders?"

Olivia sat on the bed adjacent to the writing table. A grim line settled on her mouth. New streaks of gray colored her russet-brown hair. Overnight, she aged, and Willow knew without the woman saying anything that the word about the men wasn't good.

The scraping of Willow's chair on the hardwood floor broke the silence. She joined Olivia on the bed. Immediately, her arm wrapped around the older woman's thin shoulders. Contrition weighed heavily on Willow's soul. A lump rose in her throat.

"I'm sorry."

"Don't start apologizing." Olivia slipped her arm around Willow's waist. "This isn't your fault. That Davis is a spawn of Satan! He's determined to set an example with Mitchell and Anders. Some of the elders of the church are protesting. Mr. Edwards wired his lawyer cousin in Pennsylvania. We're hoping he can get here in time to put a stop to this nonsense."

"What about the sheriff? He's known the reverend for years. Can't he help them?"

"He tried, but Davis has the politicians working for him, too. After what happened at Harper's Ferry, they want to keep this quiet and not risk Anders and Mitchell becoming martyrs the way John Brown did."

A single thought formed inside Willow and tore at her. An overwhelming sense of dread filled her at the notion, but she had to know. "So they mean to hang them?"

Tears glittered in Olivia's eyes. "There's no doubt about it."

"They shouldn't hang for what I did."

"They shouldn't hang at all. Nobody should; not for standing up in the face of evil, amoral practices. Lord help us all. I feared one day our actions would be discovered, but I never thought the outcome would be such as this."

"It doesn't have to end like this." Willow rose from the bed to look down at her. "If I turn myself in, Davis will let them go."

Olivia shot up from the bed like a lightning bolt and reached for Willow. Indignation blazed from her. Her long, slender fingers cut into Willow's upper arms in a viselike grip. "No! Do you hear me? You will not do any such thing!"

"But it's my fault! I went to Davis's plantation to get Big Nat, and I helped him go free. Don't you see? Mr. Anders and Reverend Brown lives are threatened because of me. I have to make this right, Miss Olivia."

"Child," she said, cupping Willow's cheek, "you can't. If you surrender to Davis, they'll just add another rope to the tree. They wouldn't spare Anders and Mitchell's lives because they have you. Please, promise me you'll stay here and not do something as foolish that."

"I feel wrong about hiding." Willow moved out of Olivia's grasp. "You and the reverend cared for me as if I were your own. What kind of person would I be if I sit back and do nothing while he suffers for my actions?" Guilt and frustration waged a war inside her. She spoke with earnest conviction. "Neither he nor Anders deserves this fate. Honestly, nor does anyone who's ever liberated a person from bondage. Miss Olivia, surely you understand that putting my life above his or Anders is cowardly and hypocritical."

"It's neither." Olivia pointed at the table. "Sit down and have your dinner. I'll bring your water up to you after I feed the chickens."

The resolute command grated on Willow's nerve endings. She was so sick and tired of being told what to do! *When and where will my life belong to me?* The answer came easily. *Nineteen hundred and eighty-five.* The year, so far into the future, beckoned with endless promise. Thor's handsome face and low, rumbling voice haunted her thoughts as much as the unpleasant turn of events, sending her, Anders and the reverend into captivity. Although hers was self-imposed, the situation was no less dreadful. She sighed and rubbed her temple.

Olivia's watchful gaze remained on Willow until she sat and smoothed a napkin onto her lap. Soon after, the partition creaked close. Alone again, Willow tossed the napkin onto the plate. She dipped her pen into the vat of ink and concluded her letter to Thor. When Olivia returned to the secret room, the letter was sealed inside an envelope.

"Please ask Miss Eva to put this one with the others."

"Of course." Olivia slipped the envelope inside the pocket of her skirt. Her arms closed around Willow. "Never in all my years did I think you would have use of this hideaway. It pains me to leave you here alone."

"It isn't so bad," Willow said, ending the hug. "I'm fine."

"You're worried as are we all. You must not fret. God's plan will be followed."

"I wish I knew what it was."

Olivia gave her a faint smile. "So do I."

—◦◦◦—

The stack of open letters lay on the grass beside Thor. Whenever a gentle breeze blew, the pages rustled softly, and he reached down and pulled the century old stationery closer to him. The letter he held in his hand was the last one in the pile. His fingers trembled slightly as he moved to the second page. Inhaling a deep breath, he rubbed one hand over his face while the other one gripped Willow's letter. His voice was hoarse and unsteady as he read the letter aloud.

"Then I'll remember the warmth of your smile and the gentleness in your eyes, and I'll know that you were real. My greatest wish is that wherever or whenever this letter finds you, it will find you well and content.

"We talked about the different roads a life can take. You called it destiny. Like so many things about you, I believe that to be true, too. Perhaps, my destiny has called me. I cannot permit Mr. Anders or Reverend Brown to suffer the consequences for my actions. I will surrender myself to Davis and accept my destiny.

"I'd rather die for my own actions than sit back and do nothing while Miss Olivia and Miss Eva lose their husbands. I cannot imagine living my life knowing that I did nothing to try to correct this. Maybe Davis will accept my surrender and maybe he will not. If it means death, then so be it.

"Miss Olivia has confused my ideals with those akin to a martyr. Nothing could be further from the truth. Guilt and despair gnaw at me. You mentioned that you might have saved my life, but what if I was not meant to live beyond that moment? Well, since then I have lived, and I have loved. Maybe now, I must settle my account for the precious days of life you spared for me. Forever yours, Willow Elkridge."

Anguish fell on him like a dead weight. No wonder his great-grandfather never mentioned her. Willow was lynched before the child was old enough to know her. Hot tears filled his eyes and guilt pierced his soul. The promise her life held was dashed away, and it was all because of him. If he could find a way to get back there, he would make things right.

But how?

He glanced around the woods he knew so well. The remnants of the creek where they first met lay not twenty feet away. The branches that shaded him as he listened to her hum hung high in the sky. The world she inhabited was his world, but it was a world one hundred and twenty-five years in the past.

How in the hell am I supposed to help her?

That damned movie made everything seem so simple! A little suggestion here and a punch in the mouth there, and bam, the future's taken care of. The guy made out at the dance, kissed the girl, and everything turned out just damned peachy in the end.

Where is Willow's happy ending, dammit?

Shit! Where is mine?

He gathered, folded, and stuffed the letters inside their proper envelopes. His hands did the mindless tasks while his thoughts spun, seeking resolution. In the movie, the kid had a fancy car and a tank full of plutonium that sent him back in time. Maybe Thor had a time travel device, too. Maybe he triggered something. That had to be it!

"But what?"

"Thor?"

He turned sharply. His father's face frowned with concern. Thor waved at Bo and released the air he'd been holding. For a second there, he didn't recognize his father's voice. It sounded an awful lot like Anders.

"You've had the letters for quite some time." Bo sat on the grass beside him. "Did you find what you were looking for?"

"Yes and no. It's not what I expected."

"What's not?" Bo pointed at the envelopes clutched in Thor's hand. "Do you mind?"

He handed all the letters except the last one he read to his father. "The pages are faded, but her handwriting is easy enough to read. Eva did a fine job of hiding them."

"They weren't always there, you know," Bo said slowly. "I searched that closet and banged on the walls like you wouldn't believe. There was nothing there. Then today the board was loose. What do you make of that?"

Thor didn't know what to say, and then the voice of his older brother rumbled behind them. "Maybe it means that time is parallel. Check the date on those letters. I'll bet she didn't start writing them until after we started looking around the cabin."

"You mean it's October nineteenth for Willow, too?" Thor opened the last letter and read the date. His heart raced with excitement. He jumped to his feet.

Cal stepped back. "What's wrong with you?"

"Just answer the question! Is the date the same for her, too?"

"Yeah, that's what I think it means." Cal's eyes narrowed with suspicion. "Why?"

Thor thrust the letter under his brother's nose. "Look at the date. She wrote the letter today. The nineteenth!"

Cal nodded. "Yeah, so?"

"That means there's still time to stop her."

"Stop her from what?"

Thor's excitement warred with exasperation at Cal's slow ability to understand him. "She says here that she's gonna turn herself over to that planter and his people. They're holding Anders and the reverend for helping Big Nat escape. They're determined to hang them and Willow's just as determined that they don't stand trial for the stuff we did. If she turns herself in, they'll kill her, but if I can figure out how to get back there, I can talk some sense into her and stop it from happening!"

As he folded the letter and put it inside the pocket of his jeans, his family stared at him in wonder.

"How are you planning to do that?" his brother asked.

"However I can. Look, I still don't know how or why I went back in the first place, but I know Pop finding these letters today wasn't just a coincidence. She and I talked about destiny. She thinks she knows what hers is, but she's wrong."

"Now hold on there." Cal blocked his path. "You can't just go running back in time half cocked and thinking with the wrong head—"

"This isn't about sex."

"I was out of line. Sorry. You know what I mean, take some things into consideration. Maybe Willow's destiny is for her to die for her beliefs. You must be careful, tampering with history, little brother. So far, we're still here, but if you do the wrong thing, you could wipe out the entire family."

"I don't plan to let Grandpa Anders swing from a noose."

"What are you planning to do?"

"I haven't thought it all through yet, but I'll figure it out. The first thing I gotta do is get back there."

"Slow down." Bo rose from the grass. "Listen to your brother. I read some of those letters. You made a big impression on her. Let's suppose you save them all and Willow comes back with you. What happens then?"

"That's something she and I will decide."

"Family is important, Thor. Never forget that." Bo moved to stand just inches from his son. "Like I told you before and I'm sure you know now from personal experience that Anders is a strong man whose family meant the world to him. He loved them and for him, love was stronger than pride. Your life changed a good deal when you couldn't throw ball anymore. Everything you dreamed of and wanted was gone.

"Like you, Anders suffered a big setback when he didn't find gold in the hills like he thought he would. The life he planned for Eva and their children wouldn't be the one he dreamed of. He did not fulfill the promises he made to her when she agreed to leave New York and her family, and that pained him deeply. That old watch changed him and came to symbolize a different way of life for him, Eva, and their small family.

"Don't go meddling in the past and in Willow's life if you can't accept that dreams don't always come true. You may get there in time to save her, and you may not. If you're not willing to face the consequences and to be careful, stay here."

Bo's words seeped deep inside Thor, right to his core. Everything his father said was true. Dreams hung on a whim sometimes, but like the engraving on the watch said—love lasts forever.

"I'm willing, Pop," he said, his expression solemn.

"But do you know how to go back there?" Cal asked.

The answer seemed to be on the tip of Thor's tongue. He closed his eyes briefly. The key to unlock the past seemed to hang on the other side of a door inside Thor's mind. If he could just push the door open, he would know what to do. He squeezed his eyes tight. Blood pounded his forehead. The answer was right there.

"The watch!" he cried, opening his eyes. "Pop, it's the timepiece! The gold watch you gave me the first night we were here. I stayed up all night, fixing it. The next morning, I took it with me when I went for a walk. Then I took a nap and woke up in the past! I gotta find that watch!"

"Wait, Thor." Bo dug inside his pocket and pulled out the antique timekeeper. He handed it to his son. "There was a letter inside that wall for me, too. It told me just how important this old watch is."

Thor threw his arms around his father and hugged him tight. "Thanks, Pop!" When he released his father, he looked at his brother. "Drop me off where the Browns' place used to be. I'll show you the way. That's where Willow is, and that's where I need to be."

"Pop, you drive," Cal said. "I'm going with him."

Bo shook his head. "No, Thor has to do this alone. Besides, your destiny lies on a different path."

"Say what?"

"Ask him later!" Thor started to jog toward the cabin and the truck that was parked in front of it. "Let's go!"

Cal's Bronco covered the rough terrain from the Magnusen cabin to the old Brown spread at top speed. The beauty of the autumn day blurred in their haste to reach the former Underground Railroad depot. Thor's heart raced as the familiar landscape of the old Brown homestead came into view.

"This is it," he murmured almost to himself. Willow was there, waiting for him.

With minimal words and mostly gestures, he instructed Cal where to go. In his mind's eye, he made out the two-story house with its white-rimmed chimney and the nearby barn where Brown housed his rousing Gospel Train meetings. Right upstairs, Willow hid in the tiny chamber where countless runaways had found sanctuary. His heart lurched. He had to get to her before she turned herself in. The truck slowed, and without waiting for Cal to shift the gear into park, Thor bounded from the passenger side and landed with both feet on the ground.

"Shit!" Cal grumbled. The truck came to a halt with a loud screech. The engine died, and two doors opened and slammed shut. "Wait a minute!"

"I don't have time to wait!" Thor shouted over his shoulder. "You said time's parallel. That means I have to get back there now!"

"One second won't hurt."

Thor whipped around. The three inches that made Thor shorter than his older brother barely registered as the two men stood nose to nose. The wild beat of anger thumped loudly in Thor's chest. He was better equipped to handle this trip back in time. Why in hell was Cal meddling now? Willow needed him!

"That's enough," Bo said, stepping between his sons. He pressed his hands against their chests. "Step back and stop this. You're acting worse now than you ever did when you were kids. Thor, there was a time when you listened to your brother, and Cal, a little compassion never hurt."

"I'm compassionate," he mumbled, his expression sullen. "I don't get why the knucklehead won't listen."

"Maybe because he's in a *hurry*." Bo gave Thor his full attention. "You know enough about the time period to know you can't go in there half-cocked. You gotta have a plan, son."

"I know, Pop. My plan is to get back there and talk some sense into her!"

"And after that?" Cal asked. "Preventing her from turning herself in could jeopardize the family line. We don't descend from Anders and Eva's first child. Their son is our great-grandfather. If Anders dies, the second kid won't be born. That means all of us will cease to exist: Pop, Aunt Greta, me, and you, little brother. I know you want to save your girlfriend, but you must think about Anders. He *cannot* die!"

The erratic beating of Thor's heart slowed to normal. Cal's warning made sense, and the anger he felt toward his brother faded. In the back of his mind, he knew he couldn't let Anders or Brown take the rap for what happened, but thoughts of stopping Willow took precedence.

This last minute wake-up call reminded him of the enormity of his task. The game that ended his career came to mind in a flash. The lineman sacked him because his eyes had been on the soaring football instead of on the opponent's defensive players. He paid for that mistake by losing his ability to throw, and that error only affected Thor. If he didn't pay close attention on his return trip to eighteen-sixty, his entire family would suffer the consequences.

He exhaled a shallow breath. Maybe he wasn't cut out to handle this after all. He looked from his brother to his father and back to Cal again. "Maybe I'm not the one who should go back. You're the history professor. You'll know what to do."

Cal's hazel eyes widened. He glanced at their father. Bo shook his head, and said, "It's not for Cal. You can do it, Thor. A little self-confidence never hurt a man either."

"Yeah, little brother, you helped free Big Nat from that planter. Rescuing Anders and Brown should be a piece of cake."

Thor rolled his eyes. "Yeah, right."

"I know I'm right," Cal quipped. "You can do it. If you can't think of something off the bat, use one of the playbooks. God knows you got at least a thousand football plays memorized. Quarterbacks are the thinkers on the team. Don't be such a knucklehead. Use your brain."

Cal pulled Thor into a hug and patted his back as he released him. "You can do it, Thor. Now go out there and play ball!"

Thor's lips curved into a half smile. Their encouragement went a long way. He didn't make it to the pro level by being a half-ass quarterback. He could do it all. Paying attention would be the key. His mouth parted into a full-blown smile. He saluted his family, pulled the watch from his jeans, and ran into the woods toward the space that once held the Brown home.

—◦∽◦—

The plate of fried chicken, biscuits, and apple pie sat cold on the table. Willow paced the floor, waiting for time to pass. She glanced at the food. The distance into town was long. Food provided strength. Her stomach rumbled from lack of sustenance, but the thought of taking a bite made her throat constrict. Her skirts swooshed across the floor as she turned her back to the food. She could not eat now. The food would have to wait.

Willow paced the floor for several more turns along the length of the wall. The lack of windows made the time of day uncertain. She wished now she had asked Olivia just so she could have a point of reference. So far, no one had ventured to the Brown home while Olivia was away. Maybe Willow could slip out to see if it was dark enough for her to leave. She pondered the possibility of visiting the creek where she and Thor first met. If he found and read her letters, he might attempt to return to her. The thought of one glimpse of him lessened the weight of sorrow in her heart.

The compartment slid opened easily enough as she pulled on the inside latch. Gathering her skirts in one hand, she stepped through the doorway and entered the Browns' bedroom. Speckles of dust filtered the air where the waning beams of sunlight streamed through the curtains. She edged closer to the window and adjusted the spectacles on the bridge of her nose. The beauty of the woods was a welcomed sight. Remaining hidden away in a windowless room created a whole new appreciation of nature's splendor.

Everything was still and quiet. Even the birds ended their songs as if they too were grateful for the peacefulness of the woods.

Willow inhaled a deep breath and wrapped her arms around her waist. This was the last time she would be able to take a moment to look through a window and watch as golden leaves fell to the ground.

Sadness brought tears to her eyes, but determination forced her to blink them away. Her decision was made. This was the only way to repay the debt owed to the man who raised her. Cold despair settled in the darkest depths of her soul. Overburdened with guilt, Willow turned to retrieve the uneaten food from the secret room.

Something heavy landed on the porch. Her nerve endings stood on end. Instinct told her to run to the hidden room, but her feet refused to obey. Holding her breath, she moved closer to the bedroom door and listened. She hoped it was a squirrel or another small animal in search of refuge or food.

The front door creaked on its hinges, and Willow's hope that it was a small animal was dashed. The movements of the intruder were slow and measured. Had it been Olivia, she would have moved quickly and with purpose. Whoever was out there was hesitant about trespassing. Still too afraid to move, Willow whispered the Lord's Prayer under her breath.

"Dammit!"

The muttered curse traveled down the hallway, and Willow was sure she knew that voice. Should she dare hope? It couldn't be him; not possibly.

The floorboards protested loudly underneath the weight as the heavy footsteps plodded closer to the Browns' bedroom. Willow looked around for a weapon. A letter opener lay on the table beside the bed. She scurried across the room and grabbed it. Just then, the door opened.

Time stood still as Thor Magnusen filled the doorway. She barely noticed his attire, albeit similar to what he wore when they discovered each other in the woods that first time. What registered to her first was that he was real and not a figment of her imagination. He was there, returning her unwavering gaze and in the next moment, crushing her to his hard chest. The letter opener fell to the floor. Her arms flew around his broad shoulders, and she held on for dear life.

"Blessed be. I thought I'd never see you again."

"I made it in time," he mumbled against her brow. His hold tightened. His arms held her close to him as one of his hands roamed her back and the other wound inside her thick mass of hair. "Dear God, Willow, it feels so good just to hold you again."

The hand in her hair tilted her head just as his mouth slanted over hers. His tongue bathed her lips with sweeping strokes until her lips parted. With unrestrained passion, he plunged inside her mouth. Willow's knees weakened. Her fingers dug into his solid flesh in an unconscious move to regain her balance.

Pleasure shot through her everywhere their bodies touched. The hand that roamed across her back slipped down to her backside. His fingers flexed and squeezed her, pressing her against his aroused flesh. A low moan rumbled from him and into her mouth. The troubles that plagued her left the forefront of her mind. Wanton flames of desire consumed her.

He dropped to the bed and pulled her into his lap in one swift movement. His fingers fed the roaring fire of passion as they trailed her cheek, neck, and breast. Clothing presented no barrier. His thumb circled her nipple, the peak hardening upon contact. The thin fabric of her dress slid across her heated flesh in sensuously slow motion. His mouth nuzzled her neck and moved lower. Her lower belly contracted as he unbuttoned her top and suckled her. Pleasure shot through her. The touch and scent of him restored her senses. She feared never seeing him again. Holding him close was sheer joy.

"Blessed be!"

—◦◦◦—

Thor couldn't resist Willow's cry of pleasure. He drew her deeper inside his mouth, his tongue swirling around her pebble hard nipple. Her fingers threaded his hair and held him to her. The grip was so tight he could barely breathe, and yet it was worth it. Tasting her again was worth everything, but there was one thing he couldn't risk. He planted another wet kiss onto her swollen flesh before lifting his head. Her glasses were foggy and he removed them. He set the spectacles on the bedside table. With only the slightest bit of hesitation, he buttoned her blouse. All the while, his eyes remained locked on her ebony eyes, glassy with desire. Her breathing slowly returned to normal, but the desire in her eyes only dimmed slightly.

God, how I want you.

"That was quite a welcome back," he said, his voice a husky murmur that he hardly recognized.

"Where were you?" Their fingers laced together after he finished buttoning her top. "Did you go back to your time?"

"Yeah. I'm not sure how or why it happened, but the watch took me away from you. I'm sorry I left you alone."

"I never thought you left intentionally." She frowned. "And it brought you back?"

"Yes." He pulled the timekeeper from the pocket of his shirt. "When I woke up in 1985, I couldn't remember how I got there. All I could think about was getting back to you. I didn't know how special the timepiece is."

"It's very special. I don't understand its magic, but I'm glad you had it. Grady would have killed you."

"I hated that the watch took me away from you like that," he argued. "So suddenly. I was worried sick that he hurt you, and then my Pop found your letters—"

"You found them!" Her features lit up with excitement. She clutched his shoulders. "We hoped you would. Oh, my God! This is amazing!"

"Yeah, it is. Eva must have hid them in the wall. Pop found them and gave them to me. Thank you for thinking of me."

"I can't help but think of you." She reached for her spectacles and rose from his lap. As she slid the glasses on, she added, "I'm glad you're alive and well. Now you have to go back to your pa and your brother. You can't stay here. It isn't safe."

"You can't get rid of me that easily."

"Thor, you don't understand. This is all my fault."

"Your last letter is here in my pocket. I know you're planning to turn yourself in, and I understand why! Many people will die before slavery ends, but dammit, you won't be in that number! I won't let you!"

"Mr. Anders and Reverend Brown will hang for stealing Big Nat off Davis's plantation. The owner of the plantation from where the children ran away has joined in with Davis, and he wants the same punishment. I cannot let them hang for what I did." Shame washed over her face as she turned away. Her shoulders slumped in defeat. "Maybe those awful men won't release Mr. Anders and Reverend Brown if I turn myself in, but I cannot live with their deaths on my conscience without trying to do something to stop it."

"So, you're willing to risk it all? Of all the hotheaded, impulsive, and downright dumbest things I've ever heard of!" He grabbed her shoulders and spun her around. Guilt evidently had her bound tight. If only he could shake some sense into that beautiful head of hers. "Are you listening to yourself? You're all set to die for nothing."

Her expression hardened. Anger danced in her eyes. He ignored it all.

"You actually believe they won't let the others go if you surrender? Anders and Brown are the examples for the community. You'd just be icing on the cake." His jaw tightened. "Who's to say that they'll put a rope around your neck? Maybe they'll decide that the breeding plantation is the best place for you after all. A live, capable body is more profitable than a dead one."

"Don't." She tugged, trying hard to free herself of his gripping hold.

"I bet you never thought of that. No, I can see from the fear and disgust in your eyes that it never crossed your mind."

Tears streamed down her milk chocolate cheeks. She swirled away from him. Her shoulders shook violently. Sobs filled the room, and he went to her. Tentatively, he rested his hands on her shoulders. She tensed upon first contact, but when he didn't release her, she slowly relaxed. Eventually, he curved his arms around her waist. Her shaking back leaned against his chest until her sobs became quiet.

"There's always another way," he murmured near her ear, "around an obstacle. I learned that in football, and the same is true for real life. The watch sent me to you, practically at your feet. I know it wasn't to watch you die."

"I don't know what else to do. Reuniting Big Nat with his children wasn't supposed to end like this."

"It's not over, yet. We can find a solution. I thought you trusted me."

She hiccupped once. "I do trust you."

"Prove it." He turned her around to face him. His thumbs wiped the wetness from her face.

"How?"

"Give me time to come up with a way to free them."

She frowned. "They don't have much time. The pro-slavery crowd is clamoring for their justice to be served. They want to show everyone what happens when white men help slaves run away."

Thor closed his eyes for a moment and nodded. "I know. It's gonna get worse before it gets better, but I know there's a way Anders and Brown can be saved. Trust me to find it."

Indecision marked her features. Thor read the uncertainty in her eyes. Finally, she shrugged and smiled. "I trust you, Thor."

Those words filled him like manna from Heaven. He crushed her inside his arms and hugged her. He never realized that her trust in him meant so much.

CHAPTER FIFTEEN

"How long will it take?" Willow watched Thor as he looked around the room.

"I'm not sure," he said. "Probably not long. Do you have anything I can write with? A slate would work."

"Yes," she answered. "It's in my room."

She turned away from him, and she felt him move behind her. Her pulse raced unexpectedly. Reverend Brown was the only man to come into her bedroom. Having Thor right on her heels as she crossed the threshold felt intimate and reminded her of the passion they shared only a short while ago.

Sharing herself with a man without benefit of marriage was something she never imagined wanting to do. She never thought she would want to be with anyone that way. Love never crossed her mind, so neither did marriage. Not until Thor entered her world. She was not foolish enough to think he'd propose marriage, but she couldn't ignore the love she felt in her heart whenever she looked at him.

She glanced over her shoulder. He stood near the door, the expression on his face was uncertain. Perhaps he was hesitant about entering her room. She beckoned. Uncertainty fled from his face. A warm smile touched his lips as he stepped forward. Intense heat flared inside her. Her flesh tingled just from looking at him.

Willow opened the trunk at the foot of her bed. The large wooden chest contained only a few keepsakes. The slate and chalk rested on top her parents' quilt. She handed him the writing utensils. "I hope this helps."

"Thanks."

Their fingers touched. Excitement rippled from her fingertips to every nerve in her body. Invisible warmth connected them. Passion and its desire for fulfillment threatened to re-ignite. The realization shook her to the core.

Without a word, he took her hand and led them from her bedroom to the dining table in the front room.

"The temptation was killing me."

The confession left Willow speechless. Should she confess that the mere touch of his skin on hers made her long for their bodies to join as one again? Should she tell him that the future seemed hopeful whenever he smiled at her?

She already confessed too much in the letters she wrote to him, thinking she would never see him again. In an unguarded moment, she admitted the depth of emotion she felt for him. Surely, he wouldn't expect her to tell him more.

The light in his eyes seemed to dim as the seconds passed, and they stared at each other. His lips parted as if he would speak, but he slowly closed them shut. He released her hand and moved to the table. He set the slate before him, closed his right hand around the chalk, and promptly went to work.

A wealth of troubles made her rich, it seemed. Thor was upset, and she didn't doubt it was something she did. He must have read her eyes and guessed her thoughts. When the words of love fell from her lips, she was not so overcome with passion to notice that he hadn't said the same. Not that she expected him to. He found her beautiful, intelligent, and he cared for her. None of that meant he loved her.

I'm thankful for it, she told herself. Desire would fare him better than love, and she would do best to remember the same. The realization should have empowered her, but all she felt was sad. Releasing a deep sigh, she turned away from him.

"Willow, could you come here?"

She went to him and looked at the slate. It was void of words or drawings, but the chalk on the sleeve of his shirt gave evidence of his work. Her eyebrows lifted inquiringly. "Yes?"

"Do you know where they're holding Brown and Anders?"

"Yes, at the jail in Canton. The sheriff is holding them until the justice comes to town...provided that Davis doesn't force his hand."

He grabbed the back of the chair closest to him and pulled it from the table. He patted the seat. "Sit down. I need you to describe the building for me."

She sat beside him and tried her best to ignore his pine-coated scent or the way the silky brown hairs dusted his forearm. With the pad of her index finger, she edged the spectacles up the bridge of her nose and directed her gaze to the empty slate. "What do you need to know?"

"How big is it? Does it have two stories or one? How many windows? Is there more than one exit?"

Her eyes widened. He wanted to know everything! She swallowed hard, and her brows knit into a frown. "I have never been inside. We've passed it in town, and once the reverend went inside to speak with the sheriff. Miss Olivia and I waited for him on the wagon."

"What could you see from outside? How tall is it?"

"Oh, well, the building is only one story tall. It looked to be slightly larger than Miss Eva's cabin. There are two pane-glassed windows in the front, and another on the south side. I don't know if there are more."

Thor drew lines onto the slate. The outline of the jail began to take shape, and Willow admired his artistic ability.

"Does this look about right? What about the exits? Is there more than one door?"

Stray tendrils brushed her cheeks as she shook her head. "I'm not sure about that. I only saw one. There could be a back door, but I don't know."

He slid the slate across the table to her. "Do you know where the jail cell is? This is the front." He indicated with his forefinger. "The back is here. Did Brown ever say?"

"I can't say for sure, but I think the cell is here."

He nodded and retrieved the slate. Chalk screeched on the slate as he quickly revised his drawing. "Does the sheriff have help? Any deputies?"

"Sometimes his son helps him, but I think he moved to South Carolina. From what Miss Olivia has told me, Davis and his men are standing guard at the jailhouse, too. They have guns and rifles with them."

"How many men does he have with him?"

"I don't know. She never said."

"That's okay. I'll cross that bridge when I come to it."

"What do you aim to do?" She glanced from the drawing to him. "Do you mean to sneak inside?"

Lines in the corner of his eyes crinkled as he smiled. "That's the plan. Did Olivia ever say how many men were helping Davis?"

Expectation transformed to worry. She didn't like the idea of Thor going against those men without help. Truth be told, even if he had help, she wouldn't want him to risk his life. "She didn't say, but I reckon they're the same ones who hunted Big Nat down. Don't forget they have rifles. You can't take on all those men by yourself."

"You were aiming to."

"I was wrong about that."

"You were," he said with calm assurance. "Promise me you won't change your mind and run out as soon as my back is turned."

"I would never do that!"

His mouth quirked. "You tried to do it before."

His hand closed over hers, trapping them on the table. His thumbs drew tiny circles on the back of her hands. Her insides quivered and her anger dimmed. Surely, it was sinful how her body and mind betrayed her at the simplest turn. *Blessed be!* Only his hands touched her. Why was she so powerless to resist him?

"I won't." Willow sucked in a deep breath and inclined her head in a slight nod. "I promise."

His responding smile squeezed her heart. She offered him a faint smile, and he released her and turned back to his drawing.

The scratchy whispers of chalk on slate filled the cabin. Willow paced the floor, pausing to glance at the clock on the mantle, and Thor's hunched shoulders. He appeared to be deep in thought, but time was passing them by. Only God knew if the justice had arrived and Anders and Brown's fate was already decided.

She crossed the room in long strides and stood just behind Thor. He didn't react as she peered over his shoulder, and she doubted if he remembered she was still in the room. His right hand moved the chalk rapidly over the slate. Tiny circles and small x's filled the lower half of the hand-held chalkboard. He drew lines from the circles and the x's toward the outline of the jailhouse. It all looked like child's play to her. How could they use that nonsense to rescue Mr. Anders and the reverend?

The question lay on the tip of her tongue, but Willow held back. She and Thor already had their fair share of disagreements. Laying the groundwork for another one served no purpose. She moved to the rocking chair near the fireplace and waited. An act of trust had never been more difficult.

—∽∾∽—

"If Hammond is willing to help, this should work perfectly." Thor admired the play he'd written on the slate. There were a few kinks needing adjustment, considering he was not sure where the cell actually was and whether or not there was a rear exit, but overall, the plan was a damn good one.

He expected Willow to check out what he had done. She peered over his shoulder once before, and it took all his restraint to not lean against her softness. *Time for that will come later*, he advised his raging hormones. The promise of fulfillment banked his desire somewhat, and he finished writing the play a minute or two later. He frowned. Why hadn't she responded?

Grabbing the slate, he stood. The open window caught his attention. Daylight was beginning to fade. In order for his plan to work, he needed to arrive before it was too dark.

"Willow…" He turned as her name fell from his mouth.

At first, his gaze rolled past the rocking chair. She sat so still. Had she fallen asleep? The last few days hadn't been easy for any of them. A mountain of guilt weighed heavy on her shoulders. If only he could make her understand, none of this was her fault. Compassion as fierce as hers had no business suffering regret.

He edged closer. To his surprise, she opened her eyes wide. The spectacles lay forgotten in her hands. Sorrow dulled the softness of her expression.

Witnessing her open emotions humbled him. He coughed once to get her attention. Luminous black eyes captured his. She didn't bother to mask her fears. They remained, unchanged.

"I finished." He placed the slate on her lap. Urgency took a big leap inside his gut. His jailbreak plan was foolproof.

"What is it?" She pushed the eyeglasses onto the bridge of her nose. "It almost looks like tic tac toe."

"That's close. It's a game plan, like what I used in football."

"I don't understand."

"These are the men guarding the jail." He pointed to the symbols on the slate. "Hammond and the other men will distract them, and I'll move in here."

Lines darkened her brow. "Are you sure this will work?"

"Sure? No, I'm not sure, but I have to try something. This is better than nothing. If it all goes according to plan, no one will get hurt."

She studied the slate a few moments longer. "I suppose anything is possible."

"Yeah." Her lack of enthusiasm nagged at him. He refused to let insecurities set in now. His family was counting on him. The plan had to work.

He took the slate and reached for her hand. "You'd better stay in the secret room until we come back."

"No, I can't sit here, waiting and worrying. I'm coming with you."

"Willow—"

"Most of my life, the Browns have shielded me from everything. Maybe if they had not tried so hard to protect me, I wouldn't have fought so hard to be free. I cannot wait in the background anymore. Whatever happens, I need to be right there, beside you and helping. You said that in your time I'd have countless freedoms. Let me experience the same. Here and now."

Arguments rose to his mouth. He fought against voicing his concerns. She had every right to be there when everything went down. Taking that from her would make him almost as bad as those wanting to enslave her.

"Let's go."

—◄◊◊◊►—

"Hang 'em high!"

The cries for death rang loudly in Thor's ears. Bile lodged to his throat. He swallowed it down. His grip on Willow's elbow tightened as he guided them around the outskirts of the crowd. They left their horses behind the dry goods store. Using the buildings as cover, their footsteps took them quickly toward the jail. With each step, Thor questioned Willow's presence. If the community was already yelling for Anders and Brown's death, he shuddered to think what they'd do to Willow.

"Hey!"

A hand clamped around his shoulders. Fist clenched, Thor whipped around, ready to fight. Tension filled him. His resemblance to Anders would be obvious. He should have thought of that, too.

"It's me. The blacksmith, remember?" Hammond released Thor and acknowledged Willow with a quick look. "Follow me."

"Where?" Thor asked.

"Over yonder. I got something to show you."

"What is it?"

Hammond's eyes glittered with fortitude. "Help."

———— *ᔕᕈᔕ* ————

"Hang 'em! Hang 'em high!"

The chants seeped inside the jailhouse, floating through the building straight to the single cell where Anders and the reverend waited for their sentencing. The acrid scent of death hung low in the air, suffocating with its heavy weight. Anders's stomach clenched. If they intended to execute them, he wished they'd get on with it. The suspense was driving him mad.

He hurled himself from the cot and rushed toward the bars that separated the cell from Sheriff Gibson's outer office. His knuckles turned white as he gripped the iron dividers. "What's taking so long?"

"What's your hurry?" Brown asked from behind him.

"I'll see about clearing them out and quieting them down," the sheriff said. He lifted the rifle from across his desk and stomped toward the door. Calling over his shoulder, he added, "When a crowd's riled up like that, there's usually no stopping 'em."

Before the door slammed shut, Anders caught a glimpse of the swarm of people surrounding the building. The sight disturbed him. Bloodthirsty faces glared back. Their cries rocked the slight wooden structure and pounded angrily in his head. He turned away. Defeat draped over him like a thick, constricting blanket. The iron bars supported his back as he sank to the floor.

A loud sigh carried across the cell. Anders glanced at Brown. The older man rose from his reclining position on the second cot and sat on its edge. His green eyes hinted at regret.

"I bet you wished you never joined me."

Anders's mouth tightened. The thought crossed his mind several times. If Davis and his gang had their way and Anders died from the end of a rope, then his Eva and little Dorothea would be without a provider. His greatest fear would be realized. He promised Eva's family he'd provide for her, but he couldn't do that from a grave. Anders grunted. *Hell, yeah, I wish I hadn't come.*

"Truth be told, I wish you weren't here," Brown said. "I could have handled Grady Falls on my own and brought Willow and Big Nat back safe and sound. You may not believe me, but I never thought it would end this way. For me maybe, but definitely not for you. If it's any consolation, I'm sorry."

"You're sorry?" Anders's eyes narrowed. "It's a little late for apologies."

The reverend's mouth twisted into a rueful smile. "I suppose it is."

"You think they'll wait for the justice to show up? In the two years I've been here, I never heard Canton as rowdy as this."

Brown rose and moved toward Anders. His fingers tapped a strange beat on the bars. "That's not Canton. The slaver has his folks out there to liven things up. If the sheriff hadn't come up to us on the trail and brought us all back here, Davis would have strung us up by now. He's determined to get his way."

Anders snorted. "Looks like he won't be disappointed."

"Things have a way of changing. Don't be convinced of doom and destruction. Have faith."

"I have faith, but there comes a time when a man knows that all the praying in the world can't change the inevitable."

—◦◦◦—

Awestruck, Willow stared at the small group of Brown's followers, congregating inside the blacksmith's barn. Nervous energy crackled the air. Urgency drove her further into the crowd. Thor walked beside her. His hand at her back provided a constant source of comfort, but the raised voices and thunderous expressions threatened to counteract that.

All present had attended Brown's meetings either faithfully or on occasion. She never questioned their loyalty. Few dared risk communicating with a known abolitionist unless the cause meant something to them.

These men's hearts were in the right place. None present wanted to see the reverend and Anders die. It was quite a sight and definitely tolled on the ears to listen to the abolitionists unite so vocally. She was pleased to finally bear witness.

Simon Edwards stepped forward. Normally, he was quiet, working with Brown and the other abolitionists behind the scene. He was only a few inches taller than Willow, and his balding scalp contradicted his youth, being that he was only twenty-five years of age. His desire to speak surprised her.

"My cousin is coming—"

"We can't wait that long!" The shout came from Tom Milton, a middle-aged farmer with a fearless disposition. "We have to act now."

"There ain't enough of us to take on all of them," Simon said in his own defense. "Besides, they have rifles."

"Here's mine!" Jacob Blakely, another farmer five years Simon's senior, raised his firearm in the air. "Hammond's got one, and Tom could rustle up another one."

"Sure could!" Tom agreed. "No more pussy-footin' around. That slaver aims to lynch our Reverend Brown, and I ain't about to stand for it."

"The Good Book says 'thou shall not kill'—"

"Ain't nobody arguin' about the Bible, Simon," Jacob said. "We're talkin' 'bout the reverend and seeing that he gets out of here alive. Anders's wife just had a baby. Are you planning to take care of them if Anders gets kilt today?"

Anguish tore through Willow. Her footsteps faltered. Thor's arm slipped around her waist. He pulled her close, forcing her to lean on him.

"None of this is your fault," he whispered against her ear. "We'll get them out of this."

She longed to tell him she believed, but the words wouldn't come. The crowd noticed them, and the moment was lost.

"He's got a plan," Hammond announced. He grabbed the slate from Thor and raised it above their heads. "Take a look at this."

The men closed in around them.

"How is this supposed to work?" Jacob asked. "What's all them x's and o's about?"

"The letters represent the different teams. Um, I mean the groups. Us versus them," Thor answered. Taking Willow's hand, he pushed through the crowd until he stood beside Hammond. He pointed to the slate and the objects he referred to. "Look at it like this. *They* represent the o's, and *we're* the x's."

Willow paid close attention, but his nearness made it difficult. His fingers stroked hers at odd moments, and she wondered if he did it on purpose to distract her with desire. If so, it worked.

Tom Milton shouted a question that made bells ring between her ears. The sudden call interrupted her wandering thoughts and drew her back to Thor's drawing.

"That's a good question," Thor replied. "Each man will have two of Davis's men to contend with."

"But they're armed," Simon said. "Some of us don't have rifles and such."

"And some of us *do*!" Jacob said. "I'm ready for 'em. An eye for an eye!"

"Yeah!" The crowd joined in with their approval.

Hammond waved his hands in the air. "Keep it down. They don't know we're meetin' like this."

"Hammond's right," Thor agreed. "The element of surprise will work more in our favor than those rifles. It'll be better if you kept them here. They'll only get in the way when you tackle your men."

"Tackle?" Tom asked.

"Yeah, it's when you throw 'em to the ground. That's called a tackle. Put your shoulder into it and aim for the middle. They'll be on their backsides in seconds and will never know what hit 'em."

"But what if they turn their firearms on us?" Jacob asked. "I ain't planning to face something like that empty handed."

Willow sighed. That rifle was Jacob Blakely's third arm. The firearm would have to be ripped from Jacob to prevent the other man from using it.

"The guns won't be necessary." Thor's jaw clenched. He spoke through gritted teeth. "Leave them here."

"What will we do with Anders and the reverend after we get them out?" Simon asked. "Breaking them out of jail will have the law on us for sure."

"We can take care of Sheriff Gibson," Jacob said. "He won't be a problem."

"I won't be a party to hurting the law!" Simon declared.

"Edwards, come on," Tom said. "Ain't nobody talkin' about killin' him."

"But won't breaking them out make them look guilty?" Simon asked.

"Keepin' 'em in will make them dead!" Jacob said. "I like this plan. I say we do it. Come on, y'all. Let's go!"

"Not so fast!" Thor shouted. "He raised a good point. We can't take them and run."

"Yeah! There ain't too many hidin' places around here," Hammond said. "Soon as they find 'em, Davis and his men won't wait for the justice. They'll just string 'em up." He patted Thor's shoulder. "It was a good plan, but we gotta come up with something else. Got any ideas?"

"What are the charges against Anders and the Reverend?" Thor asked. "Exactly."

"Slave stealing," Simon piped in. "Davis keeps yelling about the

Fugitive Slave Act. He says it's a matter a law, and the reverend and Anders must be punished."

"Slave stealing?" Thor's eyebrows crinkled. "Wouldn't they need proof of that?"

"Yeah."

"Do they have proof?"

The men shook their heads. A few said, "Not that I know of."

"The baggage was forwarded on to the Promised Land," Tom said. "Anders and Brown were alone when Davis trapped them. Ain't that right, Hammond?"

"Sure is," Hammond answered. "They were just out riding from what I could see. Besides, nobody but a fool would try to steal slaves in broad daylight."

"And nobody but a fool would accuse them," Thor said. "Has anything been said to the sheriff on their behalf? Doesn't he have the authority to release them if the charges are unjustified?"

All heads turned to Simon. Willow often heard him mention his lawyer cousin on numerous occasions when he found the courage to speak up, so naturally everyone looked to him as legal advisor.

Simon's face flushed beet red. "I—I suppose so."

The heads moved as a group again until they faced Thor. His lips turned into a faint smile.

"You can't talk to the sheriff," Willow said, "not with Davis present. He's seen you."

"So." Thor shrugged. "Seeing me will clear up the confusion about Anders. He'll see us both together and know that Anders isn't the man he wants."

"But then he'll want to lynch you instead." Fear closed around her heart. She could barely say the words. "He'll want you to die for disrespecting his daughter."

"There's no law that says a man can be lynched for saying no to a woman," Thor said. "Besides, I never stole a slave while I was on his property. None of us is guilty of the charges he has accused Anders and Brown of. I don't know why I didn't think of this before. . . Grady Falls took Big Nat off his plantation and you along with him, and without my permission. I think I'll press charges against him instead."

"Can you do that?" she asked, unconvinced. This plan seemed logical and sound to her; certainly more so than the drawing with its x's and o's. Worry refused to give her rest. Davis had a large group of supporters with him. The man loved his daughter, and Davis had taken Thor in without hesitation. She was sure the sight of Thor would send Davis into a fit of rage. Suddenly, she was not so sure about this plan either.

"You're worrying too much," Thor said.

"I don't want you to die."

The men curved a trail around them as they filed toward the door. A few looked pointedly at their joined hands, and Willow tried to tug free. Thor would not let her go.

"Let them look," he said. "I care about you. I don't care who knows it."

She shook her head sadly. "You forget where you are. You can fight for a Negro's freedom, but you are not free to care for one. Not the way you care for me."

"That's debatable," he murmured, "but not now. Will you please wait here while I go to the jail? I won't be able to think straight if I'm worried about you. I'll ask the rifleman to stay with you; not to watch you, but as protection."

Against her better judgment, she agreed. "I'll stay here."

A warm, sensuous smile parted his lips. "I'd kiss you, but I'm afraid I wouldn't know when to stop 'cause God knows I wouldn't want to. See you soon."

Thor strode to Jacob. After a brief discussion, the two men turned to her. Jacob's expression was crestfallen while Thor's look held longing and determination. She waved at him, and he smiled again before leaving the barn with the other men.

Rifle in hand, Jacob moved to her side. "That's one good man."

Willow nodded. "He sure is."

CHAPTER SIXTEEN

Davis's beady eyes bored into Thor with hatred. Thor returned the stare, relieved that Hammond and Tom stood nearby to watch his back. He glanced at his great-great-grandfather and the reverend. Their faces wore stoic masks as they stared straight ahead. No doubt, his sudden return surprised them. Thor drew in a long breath and directed his speech to the sheriff.

"As I said before, I'm a distant relative of Anders. Some say we could almost pass as twins."

The sheriff shrugged. "What does this have to do with Mr. Davis's charges?"

"Davis has confused Anders with me, and I believe he knows it. He's trying to get back at me by hurting my family."

"Are you admitting to stealing slaves from this gentleman?" Sheriff Gibson asked.

Thor glanced at Davis. The man's pale face colored to deep crimson. Something Thor said riled him. The lying jackass had better prepare himself because more of that was on the way.

"No, Sheriff, I'm not admitting to that because Mr. Davis's charges of slave stealing are false. Well, in regards to Anders, Reverend Brown, and me. We didn't steal anyone or anything from him—"

"That's a lie!" Davis jumped from his chair and knocked it over in the process. He stormed across the room to Thor. His hands shot out to grab him. The sheriff raised his rifle between the two men, and Davis stepped back.

"We'll have none of that. If it happens again, you'll find yourself in that cell."

Davis's eyes cut to Gibson. "You forget who you're talking to."

"I know you, or rather your kind," the sheriff said, "but I'm the law here. You'll sit down and listen or you'll answer for it."

Davis grunted, but offered no further comment. He returned to his seat and continued to stare daggers at Thor. Fury vibrated from the other man. Thor ignored it. Handling his own emotions was hard enough without concerning himself too much with the planter's obvious rage.

"As I was saying, I haven't had the time or the inclination to steal anything from Mr. Davis. The fine Southern gentleman offered me the sanctuary of his home. He even was so kind as to allow his daughter to give me a tour of his plantation. In light of such hospitality, only a fool would try to bite the hand that's fed him. No, Sheriff, I state the truth when I say that I did not take anything from this man. I am also telling the truth when I tell you that Anders and the reverend couldn't have done the deed either."

"Do you have proof of that?" Gibson asked as Davis huffed.

"I have witnesses, Sheriff. Anders's wife just gave birth to a beautiful baby girl. Anders and the reverend were there for the blessed event. Both Mrs. Magnusen and Mrs. Brown can vouch for them. Besides, I know who the guilty culprit is, and I am surprised that Davis is ignorant of this knowledge."

"Why would you say that?" Gibson's expression appeared thoughtful, as if the story intrigued him, and he hung on Thor's every word.

Thor bit back a smile. He had the sheriff in the palm of his hand, and Davis would have no argument to the contrary. Thor was sure of it. "Because the slave stealer is the son of Mr. Davis's overseer. I found Grady Falls in the woods with my boy and with one of Davis's large field hands. While I attempted to reclaim my property, Falls jumped me from behind. The blow left me confused, and I've been wandering around in the woods ever since."

Thor rubbed a finger over the lower part of his head until he found the bump. He lowered his head toward the sheriff. "See that. That's where the thieving bastard clobbered me. Damn near killed me." He straightened and looked around. "Where's Falls now? I got a word or two I wanna say to him, and I want him held on charges of trying to steal from me!"

The sheriff glared at Davis. "Well? Where is he? You got a couple of dozen men out there, bring him in."

Davis stiffened. "He's not out there," he muttered.

"Where is he?"

"He's on a business trip for me. I don't know when he'll be back."

"That's mighty convenient." Sheriff clucked his tongue. "Where did you send him?"

"Different places. I don't see how that matters. You cannot take *his* word over mine! I aim to see justice is done!"

"So do I!" Thor yelled back. His fist pounded the desk for effect. "Get Falls back here!"

"I ain't talkin' about Falls," Davis snarled. "You know damned well who I mean."

"You sure as hell can't be talking about me," Thor countered, his voice dangerously low.

"My daughter—"

"Do you really want to bring her into this?" Thor asked quietly. "She tried to poison me. I'm willing to let bygones be bygones, but I can change my mind." He looked at the lawman. "Sheriff, in addition to Grady Falls, add Miss Leah—"

"Enough!" Davis stood. "You've disrespected my daughter once. You won't do it again." He kept his dark gaze trained on Thor as he said to Gibson, "Charges dropped."

Davis turned on his heel. The planter's boots clomped across the floor. Storming out the jailhouse, he called to his men, "Saddle up! We're headin' back!"

Relief took Thor's breath away. His plan worked. He pulled it off!

"You're free to go." The sheriff unlocked the jail cell and opened the door. "Sorry about the mix-up. I didn't know Miss Eva gave birth. Congratulations, Anders."

"Thank you." Anders turned to Thor. "Thank you, too. I knew you weren't gone for good."

"I'm glad I wasn't."

Brown patted Thor's back. "You did good, Thor. Real good."

"Thank you, sir."

Hammond called from the doorway, "Y'all got a way home?"

"We can double up," Thor told him. "I have a horse and Willow does, too. It won't be a problem. Thanks, Hammond."

The young man smiled and paused at the threshold to allow Willow entry. She rushed to the reverend.

He closed his arms around her and hugged her. "I'm free to go. Thor told that sour-bellied planter a thing or two, and it's over now. Let's go home."

Thor and Anders followed them outside. The night held a strange feeling, almost surreal. Upon Davis and his men's departure, the town had settled, returning to its normal routine. A few of Brown's supporters lingered to congratulate him and Anders on their victory. Half an hour passed before the quartet finally reached the two horses.

The reverend joined Willow on one horse while Anders rode with Thor. They left town in silence. A sensation of camaraderie settled over them, reminding Thor of how good his pro team felt after they won a game. A party usually followed, and they celebrated well into the night. This feeling went deeper than that. He did more than throw a successful pass or score a touchdown. He saved lives. His chest swelled with overwhelming emotion.

"What went on with you and that planter's daughter?"

Anders's low voice came right behind Thor's ear and jarred him from his thoughts. "Nothing really. She was interested in me romantically and wasn't too happy when her feelings weren't returned."

"You said she tried to poison you."

"I exaggerated a little bit there. She slipped a drug in my drink to knock me out."

"You said she had feelings for you. Then why would she do something like that?"

"She was angry."

Thor didn't mean for his response to sound blunt, but he didn't want to go into details to satisfy Anders's curiosity. The other man didn't recognize Willow as a woman the same way Thor did. An explanation would only irritate them both. Thor decided to let things be. Knowledge of the whole truth was none of Anders's business.

"Did she see you with Willow?"

"Of course, she saw me," Thor bit out. "Willow was with me down there. You know that."

"You know what I mean." Anders grunted. "With the way you're waltzing around the question, I can guess the answer. That Davis girl didn't like losing a white man's affection to someone like Willow."

"You mean to a black woman, and yeah, Leah didn't like that I preferred Willow's company to hers."

"Is that all you prefer? Just her company?"

Thor's grip on the horse's reins tightened. The mare protested with a loud snort. His hand stroked the horse's mane as he soothed the horse with cooing noises. "I think we'd better drop this conversation."

"She's a pretty girl," Anders continued as if he hadn't heard the warning in Thor's voice. "Smart, too. She has a lot of spirit, and even though she tries to hide it, I know she doesn't like me. She adores Eva, and that's enough for me. But when it comes to you...Willow shines like a brand-new penny on Easter Sunday."

Thor gritted his teeth. "What are you getting at?"

"You want her," Anders said bluntly. "But you know you can't have her; at least not permanently. If you care about her at all, you'll let her go. Some men think there's nothing wrong with bedding a Negress, but I think it's ungodly—"

"Because she's not white?"

"No, because knowing a woman, any woman without benefit of marriage, is wrong in the eyes of the Lord. I don't talk about religion much. The reverend and I don't agree on too many things," Anders admitted, "but when it comes to the Bible and the Lord, Reverend Brown is a good authority. He doesn't want Willow hurt, and whether you believe it or not, neither do I. She's a special girl, and she's been hurt enough. Don't add to it."

"I don't want to hurt her, but I can't just let her go either."

"Thor—"

"No, hear me out."

"There's nothing you can say that can change things," Anders insisted with a hint of impatience. "You and Willow cannot be together. Society won't allow it. The folks in these hills are generous to a fault, but they wouldn't stand for it. You'd be shunned and the Browns would be, too, because they raised her. For everybody's sake, you must accept it and move on."

"What if—"

"There are no what ifs. Only what is. You can work together for the fight to end slavery, but that's all. You cannot be together as man and woman."

Thor swallowed hard. Anders was right. He and Willow couldn't be happy in 1860, but 1985 presented a different possibility. Being without her was unimaginable. Living near her and not being able to hold her would be a merciless kind of torture. His invitation to join him in 1985 went unanswered when last he asked her. Thor fully intended to ask her again and hoped this time, she'd say yes.

Anders became quiet with his declaration, and Thor welcomed the silence. The lack of conversation gave him time to think about Willow. He'd already mentioned the future and its unlimited range of choices. She could pursue any goal, and he would assist her wholeheartedly. Financial and emotional support were hers for the asking. He would be there for her as long as she wanted him.

What if she doesn't trust me?

Her trust in him seemed lacking. Without trust, there was no way in hell she'd go with him to 1985. She would have to give up the Browns and her friends to be with him. Cal said he needed to offer her more than money and a college education if he planned to bring her back with him. Thor hated to admit it, but maybe Cal was right. Then there was Anders's warning.

Making love with Willow wasn't the brightest thing he ever did. Without protection no less. *That was just brilliant. Shit!*

He glanced to his right. She and the reverend were engaged in a deep discussion and neither noticed him. He couldn't help but think that right now she could very well be pregnant with his child.

Thor couldn't leave without her with that possibility hanging over his head. Like all Magnusens, family meant a lot to him. Returning to the future, wondering if he left a child behind in the past, went against his very soul. He refused to do it. If she wouldn't come with him, he'd have to stay with her.

—∽∾∾—

Willow rested her head against Reverend Brown's broad back and closed her eyes. The steady beat of the horse's hooves nearly lulled her to sleep, but Brown's recount of Thor's speech in front of the sheriff kept her captivated. She wanted to know everything.

"What did the sheriff do then?"

"He pushed the barrel of his rifle between them. Davis wanted to knock Thor flat on his backside for speaking the truth! Gibson wasn't having it."

She sighed. "I wish I could have seen it."

The reverend patted her hand where it gripped the sides of his overcoat. "Some things aren't for the eyes or the ears of a young woman. You shouldn't have been in town at all."

"I couldn't stay hidden, worrying about you both. I'm sorry they hurt you."

"Cuts and bruises heal, child. It's of no consequence. I know the dangers of my calling, and I'm prepared for it. You're too young to sacrifice."

"I'm not a child," she gently reminded him.

"I know. You and Thor did a good thing, going after Big Nat. Those children appreciated it; he did, too. I'm proud of you."

His quiet statement left her speechless. He was so angry with her before. She never expected him to say her actions pleased him. And he was proud of her, too? Tears of happiness welled in her eyes.

"Thank you."

"A stubborn old fool like me doesn't deserve thanks. Elijah asked me to look after you. Olivia and I have done the best we can. I wish we could have done better." His deep voice faltered, and he took in a deep breath. "We always loved you like you were ours. From the first time we saw you, just a tiny little thing lying in Bessie's arms, our hearts opened to you. I just want you to know that."

The tears spilled and flowed freely down her cheeks. "I always knew, and I've loved you, too."

He laughed suddenly. "Listen to us. A person would think our actions never showed the truth." He squeezed her hand. "Olivia and I always knew, child. Always. We've been saving up for you to go to that school in Ohio. Oberlin would be a fine place for you to further your education. There's only so much we can teach you from Olivia's collection of Shakespeare. We want you to follow your heart."

"What if my heart is pointing in a different direction?"

His back stiffened, and he released her hand. "Not to Thor."

"I care about him, Reverend. He asked me to go with him."

"To the future," Brown grumbled. "What did you tell him?"

"I didn't give him an answer. When he asked, I wasn't sure if he meant it."

"And you're sure now? What kind of life can he give you in his future?"

"Freedom to live the life I want. He said that in nineteen hundred and eighty-five choices for me are limitless. No one would bat an eye at seeing him and me together. He said I could have a life that would make my parents proud of me. You and Miss Olivia, too."

"I don't know what to say about this. It sounds like you've already made up your mind."

"I haven't, but I have been thinking about it. What he's told me is better than anything I've ever dreamed."

"Would Olivia and I see you again?"

"I think so," she said. "That's where Thor went after Grady Falls knocked him in the head; back to his time."

Brown turned his head to the left toward Thor and Anders. Willow's gaze drifted in that direction, too. She understood the reverend's misgivings. Her concerns were the same. She'd miss the Browns and Eva terribly.

Willow expelled a low breath. Why did life have to be filled with complications? Before Thor came along, she knew exactly what she wanted and where she wanted to go. Oberlin College promised fulfillment of all her dreams and goals. She could pursue a degree while aiding in the Northern abolition movement. Thoughts of having her own family were put on hold. It was something she would consider later.

Just looking at Thor brought the thoughts to the forefront of her mind.

Her gaze wandered as her hand let go of Brown's coat to press against her flat belly. Right this very moment, a new life could be forming inside her. The notion both excited and terrified her. She directed her attention to Thor again and found him staring at her. The moon provided enough light for her to note the expression on his face. He looked as confused as she felt.

Suddenly, gunfire broke the silence. The horses neighed in protest and reared back. Willow clutched Reverend Brown to keep from falling. Then a voice rang out, consumed with venomous hatred and self-righteous indignation.

"Get down off them horses!"

The group of travelers sat still. Their heads turned in different directions, searching for the owner of the voice. The light from the moon and stars revealed only so much. Anyone hiding in the trees would be impossible to see. The reverend patted Willow's hand.

"Do as he says."

Brown slid from the saddle and caught Willow as she jumped down. Anders and Thor joined them in the middle, with the horses walling them in on both sides.

Brown called out, "Who's there? If it's money you want, you'll have to try elsewhere. We have no worldly goods here."

"I have money," Warren Eugene Davis spat as he stepped from behind an oak. "I didn't come here for that."

"What did you come for?" Thor asked. "We agreed to let bygones be bygones. Stop it now before someone gets hurt."

"Hurt?" Davis repeated, his voice thick with sarcasm. "You say that word to me after what you did to my daughter. What kind of a fool are you? I could kill you where you stand."

"No!" Willow cried and crossed in front of Thor. He gripped her shoulders and tried to push her away. The heels of her boots dug into the ground, and she wouldn't budge.

"Move!" Thor growled.

"No!"

"Listen to her! She knows I come for you both."

"You sonuvabitch!" Thor tried to circle around Willow. She blocked him with her body.

Brown called out. "They're not going anywhere with you."

"You're right about that." Davis cocked his pistol and aimed. "She's going straight to the devil while he wallows in hell on earth."

The click of the trigger echoed in the forest. Thor grabbed Willow around her waist just as the reverend jumped in front of her. The shot rang out suddenly like the crackle of lightning on a clear, spring day. Brown crumbled to the ground at Willow's feet. She screamed and fell to her knees.

Another click sounded and something heavy fell on top of her. Her spectacles fell from her face. The images blurred. A second emission of gunfire reverberated around her. Hands pushed her face down. The rapid-fire noises ceased and silence hung in the air. Willow shuddered.

Thor's scent filled her senses. He breathed heavily against her ear. "Are you okay? Were you hit?"

"No. You?"

"I'm fine. Here are your glasses." He shoved the spectacles into her hands and slowly rolled off her. "Anders?"

"I'm here. How's Brown?"

She pushed the glasses on and looked around. Reverend Brown lay sprawled on the ground right beside her. She went to the reverend and cradled his head in her lap. Blood poured from the open wound in his chest. He stared at her with a peaceful smile on his face. Her hands moved frantically, tugging on his shirt and overcoat.

"No, child," he said in a barely audible whisper. "Let me be."

"I have to stop the bleeding!"

"It's too late," Brown whispered. "Be still, and listen. Don't you hear it? Angels on the wings of doves; simply beautiful."

"No." Her body shook with sobs. "I don't hear anything. Be quiet. We will take you home, and Miss Olivia will patch you up. Good as new."

His head shifted from side to side. "Ssh, it's alright, Willow. Tell Olivia I love her. I love you, too. Be happy, child. Follow your heart."

His eyes closed, and his head fell to the side for the last time.

CHAPTER SEVENTEEN

"Ashes to ashes, dust to dust," Willow said, her voice hoarse, "is how the saying goes. You never really know what it means until you have to face it."

She and Thor knelt at the grave of Reverend Mitchell Brown. The peaceful tranquility of the woods reminded her of the home she left behind. For a brief moment, she closed her eyes, inhaling the essence of her new world and reconciling it with the old. The scent of pines trees wafted gently in the early fall morning. Birds engaged in conversation. Their happy chirping aided in lessening her sorrow. Golden rays glowed as the sun made its usual ascent into the wide, blue sky. A cool breeze blew brown and red leaves, causing them to swirl in front of the headstone. A shudder went through her. Thor wrapped his arm around her shoulders, instantly warming her.

"It's colder than usual this morning," he said. "We can head for the cabin anytime you're ready."

His words registered in the far recesses of her mind, but she wasn't ready to act on his suggestion. Before she could say hello to his time, she had to first say goodbye to hers.

With Davis's whereabouts unknown and his hatred running rampant, necessity screamed for them to make haste. She had little time to bid Olivia and Eva farewell, nor was she allowed to pay her respects to the man who forfeited his life for her. Now that they were safe from Davis's quest for vengeance, she needed to make peace with her past.

"When my parents went away and never came back, it was easy to believe they were just gone someplace else. A place I could not visit just yet, but it was a beautiful place. Peaceful and free from hate." She paused, drawing in a deep breath.

"It's different this time. I watched him die. I felt it. 'Ashes to ashes...' You cannot truly comprehend the meaning until you are face to face with it is what I'm trying to say."

"You're saying it well. When my mother died, it was hard for me to grasp it. Thinking back, I still see and feel the loss through a child's eyes. I never imagined someone else would understand."

"I do."

"I know."

A companionable silence stretched between them. After awhile, peace settled over her. She glanced at him and nodded. "I'm ready."

—◦◦◦—

The Magnusen cabin held up remarkably well in the twentieth century. After one hundred plus years, the building aged, yet Anders's fine craftsmanship hadn't diminished. The cabin obviously weathered the different seasons and the many years since 1860, but the building had grown, too. Anders's additions expanded to at least three or four new rooms. Just that sight alone was enough to convince her that they really did it. Thor brought her to the future. Her fingers tightened around his. Sadness faded as anticipation took over. She could not wait to see the other changes that time had brought.

"That's it," he said, watching her closely, "Anders and Eva's home. As you can see, it's not quite what you remember. The changes may feel weird at first, so if you feel overwhelmed just tell me. We can do this at your pace."

"I'm fine." Her voice sounded distant and awestruck even to her own ears. Overwhelmed failed to cover half of what she was feeling. She never once doubted his origins, yet the very notion hinted at fantasy…until now.

A large structure with windows all around blocked their path to the cabin. Her eyes widened. She stopped suddenly and pointed. "What's that?"

"Oh. That's just Cal's dirty Bronco."

"A Bronco?" The word tumbled from her. She wasn't sure what it meant, but somehow, the term seemed to fit. "What does your brother do with it?"

"He drives it almost like a carriage. Really, it's more like a wagon. Most people use it to haul big stuff, but Cal only hauls books."

Her hand hovered near one of the windows. She longed to touch it, but wasn't sure if she should. Thor nudged her with his elbow.

"Go ahead, but be careful. He hasn't washed it in months, and God knows what's stuck to it."

She pressed her forefinger against the window and trailed a small path down the side. When she pulled her finger away, dirt covered it. She sniffed. The smell was no different from the dirt she was used to. Craning her neck, her curious gaze missed nothing. It was unlike anything she ever saw in Canton. "Where are the horses? Where does he hitch them?"

His responding warm and affectionate laughter rippled through the air. "He doesn't need horses. The Bronco runs on gasoline. He puts the key into the ignition, and off he goes. You'll ride in it when he takes us home."

"You don't live here?"

"Nah." He tugged her hand, leading her up the cabin's steps. "I have a place in Stone Mountain. It's not too far from here." He paused at the door. His voice softened. "I think you'll like it."

His voice, low and seductive, seeped under her skin, and her body betrayed her. Desire burned a path of fire through her before she could protest. Her breath quickened as her mouth became slack. Thor's eyes darkened and his face swam before her. Her eyes closed. In an instant, his mouth claimed hers in a sweet kiss, which ended earlier than she wanted when the front door squeaked open and boisterous voices welcomed Thor home.

"Welcome back, son!"

"Wow, knucklehead! You actually did it."

The two men towered over Willow. Their open stares glowed with friendly curiosity. The older one had shining blue eyes whose shade was the same as Thor's. The younger one, who stood a few inches taller than Thor, had intelligent, hazel eyes and a wide smile. The older man took her hand and pulled her inside.

"I'm Bo, Thor's father. You must be Willow."

"How do you do, Mr. Magnusen? I've heard a good deal about you."

"I've heard a lot about you, too," he said with a smile. "Please, just call me Bo. Mr. Magnusen makes me feel old."

She blushed. Thor was the first white man she ever addressed by his first name. Doing the same with his father would take some getting used to. In her time, elders were treated with respect. His father's offer explained Thor's openness with her and the runaway children. For them, the display of etiquette was unnecessary. The treatment of others conveyed respect more than spoken words.

A finger tapped her shoulder. She glanced up into hazel eyes that crinkled with good humor.

"I'm his brother, Cal. I'm not sure if I want to know if you've heard about me."

She laughed. His family was friendly and funny. She understood why Thor was so open to her when they met. Candor came naturally to him.

"Nice to meet you."

"And please, call me Cal."

"It's a pleasure to meet you, Cal." She nodded toward his father, "Both of you."

"Are you tired?" Bo asked. "Would you like something to eat? We caught a mess of fish and were about to fry some up. Have a seat, Willow. Thor, you can just set that bag down over there. Cal and I want to hear everything, but not with you hovering by the door. Come in and close the door before the flies trail in after you."

Cal pointed to a long, plush object that took up the center portion of the living room. It reminded Willow of a settee, but the one the Browns' had wasn't nearly as long. She sat and found it surprisingly soft. Her fingers traced the intricate patterns of flowers and leaves that covered the furniture while her bespectacled gaze stared in wonder. The cabin was huge!

Cal sat on a chair across from her and continued to stare. Without looking away, he asked, "Pop, you don't need help with the fish, do you?"

Thor kicked his brother's foot as he passed him to sit beside

Willow. "Leave her alone."

Heat flooded Willow's cheeks. "He's not bothering me. I 'spect he's just curious."

"Finally, someone who understands me. It's about time."

Laughter bubbled in her throat. Sensing Thor's annoyance, she raised her hand to suppress a giggle, but her efforts were wasted. Thor grunted an unintelligible response, and then Bo called from the kitchen.

"Mind your manners, Cal. Don't pick her brain all at once. Thor, come and help me with this recipe. I can't read your Aunt Greta's hand-writing; nothing but chicken scratch."

Thor's hand closed around Willow's waist and squeezed. "Will you be alright without me?"

"I'll be fine. Do you need help in the kitchen? I can help your pa…"

"Nah, it's okay. He called whom he wants. He'll probably give me the third degree," Thor muttered. His eyes narrowed on his brother. "She's been through a lot the last few days. Leave her alone."

"Thor, I'm fine." Her voice held an edge to it. His protective demeanor warmed her heart, but she did not want him to be impolite to his family on her account. There was no excuse for bad manners. "I'm sure he's just as curious about the past as I am about the future. We'll be fine."

The muscles in his jaw flickered. "Okay."

Thor crossed between Willow and Cal, and as soon as he was gone, Cal began his inquisition. "What was it like?"

"What are you referring to?" His intense stare was startling. If any-one else had looked at her so closely, she would have been embarrassed and nervous. Because Cal was Thor's brother, she felt relaxed. Besides, his expression contained no malice, mostly interest.

"Eighteen-sixty. What was north Georgia really like? I have read books that say everybody was for secession. Would you know if that was true?"

"I know that the books exaggerate if that's what was written. Not everyone wants to separate from the union. Many are afraid they'll lose contact with friends and family." She slid to the edge of the large settee. "Could you tell me what will happen? They don't really secede, do they?"

Cal's gaze cut briefly toward the kitchen. "He didn't tell you?"

"He said that if I know too much the continuum will be damaged."

"The time space continuum?" Cal's eyebrows shot up.

"Yes, I believe that's what he called it. What is that?"

Cal smirked. "Something he got from a movie."

"What's a movie?"

Cal left the chair to sit beside her. His arm spread across behind her, and he crossed one leg over the other. "You have a lot to learn. Let's make a deal. I'll tell you about everything that happened since 1860, and you'll tell me about your life there."

His offer was sweet and unexpected. His willingness to help touched her. "Thank you."

"You don't have to thank me," he said with a shrug, "but I'll accept it anyway. Changing centuries is going to be a major adjustment. Pop and I are willing to do whatever we can to make things easy. I'm sure you know you can count on Thor, too. He cares about you, Willow. He may not be good about saying it, but his actions will prove it." He took her hand and closed it between both of his. "Welcome."

—◈◈◈—

Cal's hand closed around Willow's and Thor's gut clenched. What was going on over there? Why was his brother being so chummy with Willow? Jealousy had never been a part of Thor's life until now. His heart hammered inside his chest, and he moved to exit the kitchen and tell his brother a thing or two!

"So you brought her back."

Bo's quiet voice and firm hand on his shoulder halted Thor's planned attack. He glanced at his father, read the understanding in the older man's eyes, and drew in a harsh breath.

"Cal's welcoming her into the family. There's no more going on over there than that." The older man added pepper and salt to the cornmeal batter. He jutted his chin toward the stove. "Is the oil hot enough?"

Checking the frying pan helped to cool Thor's temper. He grabbed the potholder and reached for the cast iron skillet. The adventure in time suddenly hit him like a ton of bricks. He remembered watching Willow flip hot water cornbread in a pan just like this one. Could it be this was the same one? *Whoa.* It was almost too much for him to handle. He set the skillet back over the burner and stepped back.

"How long have we had that?"

"What? The stove? Pa bought that before Mama died. I 'spose it's time we got a new one. It's not getting hot enough?"

"No, Pop, it's fine. I was asking about the skillet. I think I've seen it before. What I mean is, I think I saw Willow use it. Have we had it that long? How could it last?"

"Stuff was made with better materials back then, son. We've had the cast iron skillets and pots ever since I can remember. If you saw it with Anders and Eva, then we've had it that long."

Thor sighed. Resting his forearms on the counter, he leaned down and looked up at his father. "This is crazy, Pop, but I know it happened. I went back in time. I met my great-great-grandparents. I helped with the Underground Railroad. It's hard to believe I did those things."

"That's not all you did." Bo rolled the thick batter into round balls for hushpuppies. "You brought Willow back with you."

"I wouldn't have come back otherwise." He made quick work of washing and drying his hands. "I couldn't leave her there alone, and if she hadn't agreed to come with me, I would have stayed there."

Bo placed a tablespoon of rolled batter into the popping oil. The cornmeal crackled in the hot oil. The smell of hushpuppies filled the kitchen. "She means that much to you?"

"Yeah, she does."

"I have something for you." Bo wiped his hands on the dishtowel and left the kitchen.

In his father's absence, Thor finished preparing the hushpuppies and fried the trout in another cast iron skillet. From the living room,

Willow's husky voice and Cal's deeper tones drifted to him. He sucked in his breath and told himself that he was glad she and Cal hit it off so quickly. The sooner she had friends, the more relaxed she'd be in her new environment. It wasn't as if he wanted her to depend solely on him for companionship, or was it?

His father returned before Thor could question himself further. Bo beckoned, and Thor joined him at the kitchen table. A faded envelope rested on the table and a leather pouch sat on top of it. Bo handed the pouch to Thor. "That's for you."

"What is it?"

"Open it." Bo picked up the envelope and tapped it against the table. "I was told to give that to you."

Thor emptied the pouch's contents into the palm of his hand. A small diamond ring with a gold band glittered under the glow of the tubular fluorescent lights. His mouth dropped open. With his thumb and forefinger, he picked up the ring.

"Where did you get this? Who told you give it to me?"

"Anders told me. It was in the letter addressed to me that told me how important that old timepiece is. He wanted you to have the ring."

"Why? I can't wear this, and I can't sell it. It's a family heirloom."

"It was Eva's," Bo confirmed. "He said he wanted you to have it and when the time comes, you'll know what to do with it."

Later as they gathered around the dining room table, Thor pondered Anders's gift. A diamond ring meant serious business. It symbolized a lasting commitment, reminding him of the words engraved on the watch. Did he have the dedication of his father and Anders to make a promise like that to a woman and mean it? Although he truly cared for Willow and wanted her with him, his invitation to join him in 1985 was not entirely selfish. She could thrive in his world whereas danger and limitations filled hers. The loss of her family and friends ran deep, but he had no doubts that he and his family could provide whatever support she needed.

≈∽∾∿≈

"Thor said you wanted to go to Oberlin." Cal passed a platter of corn on the cob to Willow. "Atlanta has plenty of good colleges. I teach History at Emory. You should come sit in on one of my classes."

"Is that allowed? I don't expect you to give me special favors."

Thor poured lemonade into her glass. "Anyone can observe a class. I'll come with you. You like Shakespeare, they have a good English and Drama department, too. We'll get a catalogue and you can decide what you want to do."

"In the meantime, we need to get her established here," Bo said. "She'll need a birth certificate—"

"Not to mention school records for when she enrolls at the university," Cal added.

Thor felt Willow stiffen. Her food lay untouched, and her eyes held a faraway look. He reached out and covered her hand. To his surprise, her flesh was cold and clammy. He recognized the signs of being shell-shocked immediately.

"Hold on, everybody. This is her first day. We can take care of that stuff later. Let her get used to everything first."

"They're just trying to help," she said quietly. "I didn't realize how much was required."

"It sounds like a lot," Bo said, "but it isn't. My sister can help us with most of it. She worked with Doc Phillips for years and before that, she was a midwife."

"When it comes to enrolling in college, I can help with the admission forms and whatever else you'll need." Cal eagerly volunteered. "You're a bright young woman. With a good coach, you will ace the admission exams. You have no reason to worry. Magnusens take care of their own, and you're one of ours now."

—◦◦◦—

Willow clutched her small carpetbag of belongings as Thor gave her a tour of his home. The design was unlike any she had ever seen. Thor called it split-level and explained it to her. She nodded at his words but could not think of a suitable response. The travel through time exhilarated her at first, but that feeling wore off during dinner. Now she felt overwhelmed, missed her home, and wondered if she made a mistake in coming.

"That's the kitchen," Thor said, pointing. "It has more gadgets and fun stuff than the one at the cabin. There's a microwave, dishwasher, fridge with an ice cube maker, and a self-cleaning oven."

He stopped talking and she looked at him. Her brows drew together, and she assumed the confusion she felt was evident.

His cheeks reddened. "Sorry about that. This is new. You don't have to grasp it at once. Anything you want to know, just ask and I'll tell you."

"Mister—Cal said the same. He gave me this." She pulled out a slip of paper.

He took the note and frowned. "This is his telephone number. I guess he thought I didn't have sense enough to give it to you."

"No!" Willow said that more sharply than she intended. She inhaled a deep breath. Her rattled emotions were getting the best of her. She needed some time alone to adjust to all the changes and to understand what her life would be in this strange, new world. "I'm sorry. He just gave it to me. I think he was being nice."

Thor folded the paper and handed it back to her. A muscle worked in his jaw. His mouth opened as if he would respond, and then just as suddenly, his expression changed. A charming smile that left her breathless came to rest on his mouth. With one hand, he grabbed her bag and slipped the other hand around her waist. His maneuvering led them to the bottom of a narrow staircase.

"Upstairs are three bedrooms and two bathrooms. I'm not much on decorating, but I think you'll like the master bedroom. There's a huge walk-in closet. The bathroom has a sunken bathtub with whirlpool features, and the shower is state-of-the-art, too."

He continued to rattle off more words as they ascended the staircase. Willow did not interrupt him. His nervousness was impossible to ignore. The good Lord knew she was fit to be tied, too. Maybe a good night's rest would calm them both.

Their short journey paused at the end of the hall. He kicked the door on their left opened and ushered her inside. After placing her bag on a chair near the door, he took her hands and led her around the room.

"The closet is through that door. My stuff is in there, but I don't have that much. You don't either. We can go to the mall in the morning and get you some new things. Over here is the bathroom I was telling you about."

He pulled her into a room that was the size of her old bedroom. Mirrors lined the walls. All sorts of contraptions filled the space, and if Thor did not have a firm grip on her hand, she would have bolted.

"You'll get used to it, Willow. It's the same as an outhouse, except it's better. You don't have to go outside."

"What's this?" she asked, pointing at a round, white stool. "Is it a chair?"

"Um, in a way." His voice vibrated with humor. "It's a toilet…where you can relieve yourself. Think of it as an indoor outhouse."

Her cheeks felt hot, and she looked away. "I understand."

"This is the bathtub." He pointed to what looked like a hole in the floor. As he knelt, he gestured for her to do the same. "This turns it on. You can adjust the temperature. Hot is on the left. Cold is on the right."

Water poured from the spigot. Willow reared back in surprise. *Miss Olivia would have loved this!*

"I don't have nice smelling soap. Just the usual stuff for me, but I imagine you'll like something nice." Longing deepened his voice and darkened his eyes. "Something sweet like honeysuckles. We can find that at the mall, too."

His stare mesmerized her. Her heart throbbed with an erratic beat. She leaned toward him without realizing it. The first taste of his lips thrilled her, but it was the sweeping of his tongue across hers that shook her to her core.

Thor pulled her against the solid wall of his chest. Her hands clutched his arms, as his strong, steady hands roamed over her. Low moans growled in his throat. The vibrations seeped into her veins. His mouth and probing tongue trailed kisses from her ear down her neck.

She fought to regain control over her senses.

His touch inflamed her and created a fire deep inside. She wanted to surrender, but then the image of Reverend Brown flashed into her mind. Pressing her hands against his chest, Willow pulled away. Tears pooled into her eyes and streamed down her cheeks. He dried her face and tenderly kissed her cheek.

"I'm sorry. You just got here. You're probably tired and just want to relax."

Thor reached around her and stopped the water. He stood and helped her to her feet. "I'll grab some towels for you. There's a fresh bar of soap in the cabinet. Go ahead and take a bath." At the door, he paused to look at her. "Would you like some music?"

"I don't know."

"I'll bring a radio, too. Take your time." He offered her a faint smile. "I can shower in the other bathroom."

—◈◈◈—

Thor didn't wait for Willow's response. He closed the door and rushed to the hallway linen closet before he lost his head again.

Just great, a tour and a seduction wrapped up in one, inexpensive package!

What was I thinking? She'd think all he wanted was a bed wench as Leah Davis had so eloquently phrased it, he thought bitterly. *Dammit!* If he wanted her transition to go smoothly, he'd better start thinking straight.

Thor grabbed fresh towels and a portable radio then headed for the bathroom in the master bedroom. He knocked and waited for her call.

"Yes?" The closed door muffled her reply.

She sounded skittish. He couldn't blame her. He nearly took advantage of her on the bathroom floor for goodness sakes!

"I have the towels and the radio. May I come in?"

He heard the distinct sound of splashing water, and then she called out, "Yes!"

234

Restraint chanted inside his head like a mantra. *Hand over the towels and get out!* Against his best intentions, his gaze cut straight to Willow.

She sat in the bathtub, looking both regal and delectable. Her hair piled high on her head, but damp, ebony tendrils freed themselves and clung to her cheeks and neck. Droplets of water covered her shoulders and the swell of her breasts. The familiar tightening in his pants reminded him that he was only human after all.

Consideration came at a high price. Averting his gaze, he set the towels on the lid of the toilet, placed the radio on the sink, and backed out of the room. As the door closed, he distinctly heard her sigh. No doubt from relief at not being molested by him again. He groaned. He never needed a cold shower more than he did at that moment.

The frigid downpour proved to quell his burning desire, but it took fifteen minutes to do it. By the time Thor stepped from the shower, he shook from head to toe. The effort was worth the torture. If he were lucky, he'd be too damned cold to put the moves on Willow again.

Yeah, right.

He dried himself with fast, brisk strokes and pulled on boxers, pajama bottoms, and an old T-shirt. When he returned to the bedroom, he wondered what Willow would wear to bed. The image of her in one of his old football jerseys made his chest swell.

God, I bet she'll look beautiful. The jersey would stop at mid-level of her creamy, chocolate thighs. He emitted another groan.

Cut it out!

The empty bed stopped him in his tracks. "Willow?"

The curtains at the balcony billowed into the room. He went to the sliding glass doors and padded barefoot outside. Willow stood with her back to him. A white cotton nightgown covered her down to her ankles. Her long, thick black hair fell loose to her waist in waves. Thor resisted the urge to slip his fingers through the thick mass and instead closed his arms around her waist. He released a sigh of relief when she leaned against his chest. She shivered and his hold tightened.

"Are you okay? I thought you'd be in bed by now."

"I'm tired, but I don't think I can sleep. Not yet, at least."

"Is something wrong? I am sorry about what happened in the bathroom. I should have waited."

"It's not your fault. I wanted you to kiss me." She paused and released a deep sigh before she kept on. "Where do you sleep?"

Her tone made his throat constrict. He swallowed hard. "In that bed in there. Why?"

"Where will I sleep?"

Thor slowly released her and moved to rest his hip against the balcony's railing. "I thought you'd sleep with me. Where do you want to sleep?"

"I can't share your bed, Thor."

A thousand voices screamed inside his head to ask her why not, but he closed a door on those voices. She had her reasons. It was enough that she returned with him, he refused to make demands on her. He wouldn't. "There are two other bedrooms. You can choose one of them."

She finally turned to face him. A small beam of light streamed in from the bedroom, revealing just enough of her expression. The firm set of her jaw spoke volumes. Her mind was made up. He saw her chin tremble. Her mind was made up, but there was still some indecision. He wondered what the hell happened in such a short amount of time?

"You're not angry?" she asked.

"Should I be?" He folded his arms across his chest and sighed. "I don't think I have a right to be. You are free to sleep wherever you want, Willow. I can't be angry about that."

Silence lingered between them for several moments. His thoughts ran at a rapid pace, trying desperately to decipher what was going on inside her mind and realizing that there was no way he could know unless she told him. He hated feeling powerless.

"Cal said he'll tell me everything that happened since 1860. Do you think he could find out what happened to Warren Eugene Davis?"

"Sure, Cal's good at research. Why do you want to know about Davis?"

"What if he comes back and hurts Miss Olivia?" Her voiced trembled. "He was mad about his daughter. M—Maybe killing the reverend won't be enough for him."

Sobs shook her body. On impulse, his arms encircled her. "Ssh. I'm sure Davis went back to his plantation to lick his wounds. Besides, Anders and Eva left some letters. There was no mention of Davis. Don't worry about that. Would you like to see the letters?"

Willow sniffled and snuggled closer to Thor. "Later. Would it be alright if we stayed like this for a little while?"

His hands stroked her back in sweeping circles. "It would be just fine."

CHAPTER EIGHTEEN

The trip to the mall gave Willow a firsthand view of 1985. She was not sure if she liked it. Everything was so loud and moved so fast. Thor's truck raced down the interstate as he called it at a speed that made her stomach somersault. She clutched the seat until he took her hand and told her to hold on to him.

"Would you like to go back home?" he asked as they left his truck in the parking lot and headed for the large, looming square box of a store. People jostled past them and Willow's arm closed in tight around Thor's waist. "Willow?"

"I didn't know it would be like this." She summoned strength to release him and walk without touching him. "Atlanta bustles, doesn't it?"

"Yes, it does."

He held the door open for her. Once inside, he reclaimed her hand. His touch was soothing and she welcomed it. The store was nothing like Canton. The outside only hinted at the massive size of the building. And the lights! There were so many that her bespectacled eyes needed time to adjust.

People moved around them of all different colors, shapes, and sizes. Most of their clothing resembled the Magnusen men's attire. The openness of the women appalled her. Their pants clung to their bottoms like a second skin while their tops exposed far too much of their bosom. She raised a protective hand over her modestly covered chest. If Thor was used to these types of woman, what must he think of her?

They visited at least ten different shops, never leaving until they made at least one purchase. The sales total always rung her ears. The price of a sweater in1985 could feed a nineteenth century family for months! He never mentioned the opulence of his time nor did he flinch at the prices, only calmly reaching inside his wallet and retrieving a small card to give the salesperson. As the purchases grew and the totals increased, she wondered how she could ever repay him. Finally, she dug in her heels.

"We have enough."

His brow knotted as he looked through the bags. "Are you sure? I don't know everything a woman needs, but I doubt if we have everything here. What about underwear?"

"Blessed be, Thor! I can sew that on my hand!"

"You don't have to," he said with a teasing smile. "There are stores that specialize in women's unmentionables. If you'd rather I stayed out here and wait for you, I will."

"You're laughing at me."

"No." His smile transformed into a flirtatious grin. "I'm enjoying this. I never thought I'd enjoy shopping with a woman, but this isn't so bad."

"I'm glad you're enjoying yourself."

His laughter faltered. "Aren't you?"

"I suppose." She thought about everything she'd seen. So many objects made life easier. Adjusting to his world promised to be a challenge. Thor's presence made everything better, even with his merciless teasing. She smiled. "I am. Thank you, Thor."

"You're welcome." He pointed to a nearby store with a frilly pink awning. "You can find what you need in there. Give me your bags. I'll wait here." He placed their bags near a bench and reached inside his front pocket. "Here's some money. If it's not enough, come and get me. Okay?"

Willow's hand closed around the bills and she slipped inside the store. A couple of women, one Negro and the other white, milled around a center table near the doorway. Their clothing was less revealing than others she encountered. For once, she breathed a sigh of relief, glad that she accepted the pair of pants and T-shirt he bought on the way to his home. Finally, she felt like she fit right in.

A white woman with spiky blonde hair and a ready smile approached. "I'm Laura. How may I help you?"

"I need to purchase unmentionables," Willow whispered.

"Unmentionables? Like bras, panties, slips? Stuff like that?"

The words were foreign to Willow. She almost wished that Thor had joined her. Her brows knitted together. "I suppose."

"Well, I'm sure we'll have everything you need. Follow me."

A quick lesson ensued. She quickly learned what a bra was and how it worked. It was certainly less restrictive than a corset! Willow chose underwear in every color and in different types of material. Cotton reminded her of home, but silk felt so nice against her skin.

Laura tallied the purchases and Willow handed her the ball of bills Thor had given her. "This isn't enough," the sales clerk said, leaning toward Willow so that the other customers could not hear. "Do you have any more?"

"Thor has. He's sitting outside. I'll be right back."

Thor returned with Willow with a cheeky grin on his face. "Should I cover my eyes?" he teased.

Heat flooded her cheeks. "No, it's all bundled now."

He pouted. "That's too bad."

"Blessed be!"

His responding laughter rippled through her. Willow basked in his attention and noticed that other women were not immune to his charm. Their gazes followed him through the store. Some nudged each other and a few made suggestive comments. She moved closer to him as he paid Laura for her purchase. While Thor chatted with the saleswoman, Willow listened to the conversation behind her.

"The Falcons messed up when they let him go. Look at that tight end. Damn."

"Oh, he could be my tight end any time. I bet he's wild in bed. Look at those hands. I've seen him hold a football. I could only imagine what they'd feel like on me! It must take a lot to keep a man like him satisfied. Do you think Little Miss Unmentionables is up for it?"

The women giggled and moved away. The women's coarse words weren't difficult to decipher. Her throat constricted with humiliation. If these shameless women had no problems hiding their interest, perhaps refusing to share his bed was a mistake.

Thor turned away from the counter. "Is it okay for me to carry this?" He held out her purchase. "Or should you do the honor?"

"You're teasing again." His usual gentle teasing calmed her. A sliver of humor echoed in her voice. "I suppose you can carry it if you want."

"Why, Miss Willow, I'd be honored."

They left the shop and moved through the crowd of other shoppers. This time as they moved through the shopping mall, she noticed how other women stared at him. Thor was a decidedly handsome man. Of course, other women would think so, too.

"Blessed be," she muttered. *Must they be so blatant in their appreciation?*

"What's wrong?" he asked. "Have a seat." He pointed to a table with a couple of chairs around it. "Did the saleslady upset you?"

Willow sat and Thor claimed the seat beside her. He set their bags on the table, took her hand, and waited.

"She was hospitable." She looked down at their joined hands. "Did you hear what those women were saying about you? They said you have a tight end."

Crimson colored his cheeks and then he laughed. "Did they really? Nah, I didn't hear them."

"That's disgraceful."

"Not really. I don't mind. It's just talk."

"Is everyone so forward with private opinions?"

"That's the way things are in 1985. People are open and honest."

"Everyone?"

"Yeah." He squeezed her hand. "Are you ready to go? I was thinking about putting some steaks on the grill for dinner. How does that sound?"

"It sounds good I guess."

He placed a quick kiss on her lips and stood, grabbing as many bags as he could carry and waiting for her to get the rest. They left the mall. During the drive back, she pondered his comments about honesty and openness. He'd been blunt since the day she met him, and that coincided with his statement. She realized that if his feelings for her ran deeper than responsibility and just simply caring about her, he would have said so. Tears stung the back of her eyes, and she told herself to forget about it. He cared. That would have to be enough.

—❦❦❦—

Excitement bristled in the air. The overhead lights of the large auditorium faded to black. As the curtains parted, revealing a sparsely decorated stage, Thor glanced at Willow. Enthusiasm illuminated her dancing black eyes. She sat on the edge of her seat, charged and ready for the show to begin. The university's production of "Hamlet" received rave reviews, but Thor had a feeling that her excitement at seeing her first play would mark his memory far stronger than the actors on stage would.

Instinctively, he reached for her. Bursts of adrenaline soared through him at the touch of her hand. The sudden charge reminded him of the rush of football games and running onto the field. Nervous energy had pumped inside his veins. Whether they won or lost, the true victory came in how they played the game. When he lost the desire to play, he never believed anything would replace that heady sensation. Two actors came onstage, and Willow turned to smile at him. In that moment, he realized how wrong he'd been. Sensations exploded inside him every time she looked at him.

"This is better than what Miss Olivia and Miss Eva described," she whispered. She took his hand and ran it along her forearm. "Can you feel that? Goosebumps! Blessed be!"

"I feel it." His fingers grew bold in their exploration of her soft flesh. They trailed under her sleeve toward her shoulder. A different kind of energy pulsed between them. He leaned close to kiss her cheek.

"Thor…" A faint moan came from her parted lips, then she shifted from his embrace. Her arms wrapped her middle. An invisible barricade seemed to drop between them. Her gaze never strayed from the play. She jutted her chin toward the stage and whispered, "The ghost is coming."

No, it's already here.

He kept his thoughts to himself and feigned interest throughout the next couple of acts. Once his attention diverted from her, her enthusiasm returned, totally captivating him with its exuberance. He heard her breath catch several times and watched as she clenched her hands in her lap.

Living with a woman who drove him crazy with desire, but refused to share his bed could have made him certifiable. Somehow, he toughed it out. She did not want to have sex so he had to respect it. He even understood it, sort of. Adventure and abnormal circumstances brought them together. They needed stability, and if she believed abstinence would give them that, he had no argument to challenge it.

With a brand new birth certificate and impeccable school records, Cal helped her enroll at his university and even obtain a scholarship. She spent far more of her time with his brother than Thor liked. His father patiently listened to his rants of frustration, then reminded him that she was going through a big adjustment and to take it slowly, give her time.

Thor gave her time all right, but he was furious as hell that she gave most of hers to Cal.

The auditorium lights blinked twice before blaring to life and signaling intermission. He rubbed his eyes to lessen the sting of the sudden glare. Willow lightly touched his thigh.

"Do you have a headache?"

"No, I'm fine." He lowered his hand to his lap and glanced around the emptying room. A concession stand waited in the lobby. A cold soft drink promised to cure his dry throat. "Let's stretch our legs. We can get a drink or something."

"I'm not thirsty but I'll join you."

He took her elbow. To his relief she didn't move away. As they stepped into the aisle and headed to the lobby, his hand dropped to her waist. A thousand warnings sounded inside his head. He listened and resisted the urge to pull her closer to his side. Her body strained toward his, contradicting her request for less physical contact, but Thor was a man of his word. When their relationship became physical again, it wouldn't be because he seduced her.

The theater-goers crowded the counter. Thor led them to the end of the line behind three young black women. Their conversation sparked with a lively discussion about the play. He chuckled softly at one comment regarding the costumes. Three heads turned and three pairs of eyes locked on him. Then they looked past him and broke into smiles.

"Willow!"

"Why didn't you tell us you were coming tonight?"

"What do you think of the play?"

Their obvious familiarity stunned him. Willow's responding peal of joy surprised him even more. It never occurred to him that she'd formed outside friendships so quickly.

"Hello, girls," she said, moving ahead of him to join the trio. "I didn't know. The tickets were a surprise. The play is astounding. I love every minute of it."

One of the women glanced from Willow to Thor. She gave Willow a questioning look. "Who surprised you with the tickets?"

"Blessed be!" Willow pressed a hand to her mouth. "I apologize for not making the proper introductions. This is Thor Magnusen. He surprised me with the tickets. He and Professor Magnusen are brothers. Thor, these are my friends: Dionna Thompson, Kendra McAdams, and Dawn Jensen. We're in the same study group for English Literature."

"Oh, the study group," he murmured. The women eyed him with open curiosity and a small hint of suspicion. He forced a smile and extended his hand. Each one took his hand in a firm grip. "Nice to meet you, ladies."

"The same here," Kendra, the shorter of the two women, said, "It's nice to finally put a face with a name."

He would have liked to respond in kind, but he didn't want to lie. Willow never mentioned the young women. Yet as they stood together and spoke with easy openness, he knew she valued their friendship. He wondered why she never told him about her friends and what other secrets she concealed.

"Malcolm is still working on your Motown compilation cassette," Dionna said. "He's the DJ for Jordan's party this weekend. Otherwise, he would have been here tonight."

"I forgot about Jordan's party. Was it to celebrate his birthday?"

Thor frowned. "Are Malcolm and Jordan more study buddies?"

The tightening of Willow's mouth conveyed she heard the note of irritation in his tone. "Yes, they are a part of our group."

He nodded once. An angry retort came to mind, but he held his tongue. It was pointless to voice his frustration. The young women resumed their conversation. He listened to part of it. Willow's responses captured his attention more than anything else.

The weeks following the mall shopping spree changed them. They lost the easy companionship that bound them in 1860. Adjusting to the twentieth century took a good deal of her time. At first, he envisioned making the adjustments with her. Somehow, it didn't happen that way. He hoped a night at the theater would resurrect the bonds. Watching her respond to strangers as if they were lifelong friends burned him and made him question his part in her life.

He took too much for granted, believing he could give her everything she needed. Watching her connect with others who shared the same beautiful skin as hers revealed how misguided his beliefs were.

The overhead lights blinked. Willow's friends rushed to the restroom, and they returned to their seats. Tension filled the silence. He searched for a solution but found none. His confidence stood on shaky ground. Losing her was not an option.

But I can't force her to stay.

"You didn't quench your thirst," she said. "There may be time. The auditorium is still lit."

"I'm fine," he replied, surprised that she remembered. "According to the program, we have another intermission."

"Thor!"

A heavy hand closed over his shoulder. He recognized his former coach's voice immediately. Seven years had passed since he followed Bart Michaels's guidance. Of all the places to run into his college football coach! He rose and shook the other man's hand in a hearty shake.

"Coach Michaels, how are you?"

"Surprised to see you here. Did you lose a bet with Cal?"

"No, I'm here with my gir—my friend, Willow Elkridge. She's a student here and loves Shakespeare." Thor reached for her hand. "Willow, this is Bart Michaels. He was my coach at Georgia Southern University. What are you doing here?"

"Nice to meet you." Bart gave Willow a polite smile. "Would you believe my daughter goes to Emory and is in the play?" Bart laughed softly. "She wouldn't hear of being an Eagle, but at least she's still in Georgia. I saw the game. Sorry about what happened. I called several times but never got through. What are you doing now?"

Thor stiffened. *God, how I hate that question.* He shrugged. "I'm reviewing my options."

"Yeah," Bart said, all-knowing, "right. Well, I'm the head of the Athletics Department at University of Georgia and in need of an assistant football coach. Interested?"

"Are you offering me a job?" The swift offer caught him off guard.

"Yes. What do you think about that?"

Willow's fingers tightened around Thor's hand. She remained silent during the entire exchange, but he strongly felt her interest. Months ago, he would have balked at the idea, but the expression on her face changed his mind. Excitement burned in her olive black eyes. Somewhere deep inside, she still cared. Hope flared to life inside him. Refusal died a lonely death on the tip of his tongue.

"I've never coached before."

"I wouldn't offer the job if I didn't believe in you. Thor, you were one of the best quarterbacks I ever coached. Why the Falcons used you as backup never made a lick of sense."

"But that tackle—"

"—could have happened to anybody," Bart said. "Your whole life can't be summed in one moment. Being coached by someone who made it to the NFL would benefit the kids. I think you'd benefit, too. Besides, what else do you have to do?"

Put that way, Thor's arguments crashed and burned. "I'll give it a try."

"Here's my card with my home and office numbers. Call me and we'll set up a time for you to come in." Bart's smile was wide and sincere. "I'll see you soon. Enjoy the play."

CHAPTER NINETEEN

Gravel sputtered in the driveway and the familiar beat of Jim Croce filled the quiet. Thor rose from his favorite recliner and watched from the door. Agony tore through him. Seeing Willow chat with Cal stung his pride. In addition to her friends, his brother had replaced him in her life.

She climbed from the Bronco, rear first. His body hardened. A pair of stonewashed jeans clung to her curvaceous backside. Denim never looked so good.

Have mercy.

She breezed past him with a mumbled greeting. The airy scent of honeysuckles assailed his nostrils. *Lord, she smells good, too.*

Cal waved at him then ripped out the driveway. Thor slammed and locked the door. The clang of pots and pans greeted him as he joined her in the kitchen.

"How was your day?" He shoved his hands in pockets and leaned in the doorway. A hint of accusation and envy put an underlying steely edge to his tone. "You're home late. Did you have a test?"

"Would you like chicken or steak tonight? Baked potato or rice?"

"You don't have to cook. Let's just order a pizza."

Her busy movements stopped in mid-air. She whipped around, a lovely smile on her face. "Pizza? With the works? Pepperoni, sausage and anchovies?"

"Yeah, even with anchovies." Her smile worked to ease his doubts. He mustered a smile. "Wanna make the call?"

She nodded. After she stuffed the cookware into cabinets, she made a beeline for the kitchen telephone. The number for the local pizza delivery was taped to the fridge. She turned away from him as she dialed the number and placed their order. When she was done, she grabbed the dinnerware from the cupboard and headed toward the table.

Thor intercepted as she came in range. He took the plates from her and plopped them on the table. "We can do that fancy stuff later. You were telling me why you were late."

Willow sidestepped him and leaned against the counter. Her arms folded across her chest. The toe of her shoe traced the outline of the tile, and she looked more at the floor than at him. "I took a test at student health. Cal waited around for me."

"That was nice of him. What kind of test?"

"My monthly curse hasn't arrived, so I went to a doctor to find out why."

"A monthly curse?" Thor sputtered. "What is that?"

Her eyes rounded like saucers behind her glasses. An expression of pure mortification crossed her features. "You *know!*"

Realization dawned. "Are you talking about your period? Menstruation?" Thor's heart raced with anticipation. "It didn't come? What did the doctor say? Are you pregnant?"

"I don't know. She examined me. She said when she knows she'll call."

"Did you tell Cal?"

"Yes. He waited for me while she gave me the test."

"You told Cal and not me?" he asked through gritted teeth. "I should have been with you, Willow. Not Cal."

"You were busy." She spun on her heel and rushed out of the kitchen before Thor could react. Seconds later, a door slammed on the floor above.

—◦◊◦—

"Blessed be!"

Willow flung herself across the bed. The springs of the mattress creaked once in protest, but quickly sprung back into place to accommodate her. Tears of anger stung her eyes. Her fists pummeled the bed in frustration.

What was wrong with her? They found letters from Eva, informing them that a horse threw and killed Warren Eugene Davis and freed Olivia of his threats. Life was a near dream. She was going to college, learning new things, and making friends. Everything was so close to perfect that she could cry.

Everything except her relationship with Thor.

She rolled onto her back and groaned. The image of his hurt face flashed before her eyes. He had every right to be upset. Her palms flattened against her abdomen. If she was carrying Thor's child, he should have been told first, but she couldn't bring herself to mention it.

What happened to them? They talked so freely in the beginning. Making love with him, as he phrased it, was the closest thing to Heaven she ever experienced. His touch was so tender and exhilarating. Shivers darted up her spine just thinking about it, and her lower belly tingled. She shifted onto her side and raised her knees to her chest.

The direction of her thoughts was sinful, yet she was hard pressed to stop it. She grabbed a pillow, holding it to her chest the way she longed to hold Thor.

That was not to be.

He probably regards me as a hypocrite, she sadly thought. In her world, social values were stricter, yet, she gave herself to him without one word of protest. She never told him why because at the time she did not know the reasons herself. A few weeks of studying psychology helped her understand.

Sharing her body with him made up for the possibility of losing him later. For a short break in time, they could be together freely without censure or concern for right or wrong. The era's unfriendliness toward interracial relationships bound them together in a whirlwind of emotion that transcended everything else. When she gave herself to Thor, Willow felt true freedom for the first time in her life, and it was breathtaking.

Returning with him to his world with its plethora of liberation seemed to degrade the passionate connection.

"Liar," she muttered. That wasn't the whole truth. *Be honest,* her mind badgered. She refused to share her body with Thor again out of fear. What if he only wanted her because of the anomaly that brought them together?

From a large assortment of women's circulars, she learned that the exotic captivated men. What could be more exotic than a woman of another race from an antiquated period?

Her eyes filled with tears. She swallowed the sob that lodged in her throat. Surely, she could be accused of the same. Thor was handsome, kind, and gentle. He flirted with her outrageously, and she soaked up his attention like the sponge he kept on the kitchen sink consumed water. It wouldn't be fair of her not to recognize the similarities in their situation. One thing made all the difference. She loved Thor while he just felt responsible.

The doorbell chimed downstairs. Pizza. The argument diminished her appetite, and the thought of tomato sauce, mozzarella cheese, black olives, and anchovies turned her stomach. She didn't want the food anymore. Besides, the large pie wouldn't go to waste. Thor could devour the thing without missing a beat, and she doubted if he would miss her company.

She rose from the bed and crossed the room to her stereo. The radio was set to her favorite easy-listening station. Having music at her fingertips was a true blessing.

The Patti Austin and James Ingram duet filled the room as she gathered her textbooks. Her melancholy faded as the music relaxed her. Then suddenly, loud voices roared from downstairs. A crash followed. The books fell from her hands as she raced from her room to see what happened and to make sure Thor was unharmed.

—◦◦◦—

Thor's chest heaved with every breath he took, and his shoulder throbbed. His right hook connected with Cal's jaw with such force that it reawakened his old injury. Surprise by his actions, he spun away from Cal's accusing stare and rubbed his shoulder.

"What the hell is wrong with you?" The sound of movement mingled with his words and Thor guessed Cal pushed himself off the wall. "I told you there's nothing going on! We're just friends. You need to listen!"

"Seeing is believing."

"What the hell! *Seeing*?" Cal's voice dripped with sarcasm. "Just what the hell did you see?"

"She's with you a lot more than she's with me."

Cal grabbed Thor's arm and whipped him around. "That seems to be your choice, brother. From now on, you can take her to class and you can pick her up. I did it because I wanted to help, but if you don't appreciate it, then by God, you can do it yourself."

Thor wrenched his arm free of his brother's grasp. Resentment blazed a trail of fury through him. His lips parted, an insult on the tip of his tongue, but the rebuttal remained silent. He closed his mouth and glared angrily at Cal.

"What?" Cal demanded. "You have nothing to say?" Blood trickled from the corner of his mouth, and he pressed his fingers against the wound. "Pop would be disappointed with both of us if we don't settle this thing right now. Hell, I wouldn't be too thrilled either. I care about Willow. She's a living, breathing history lesson, and she's not shy about answering my questions. More than that, she's nice and easy to get along with. But that doesn't mean I want her."

"Right."

"There's a word that's coming to mind right now, but I promised someone I wouldn't use it." Cal snorted. "You're taking the Magnusen trait of stubbornness to another level."

"You took her to student health."

"Yeah, because she asked me."

"Why did she ask you instead of me?"

"I don't know. Maybe it's because she's not sure if you really care about her. I told you before you brought her here. A woman needs more than a roof over her head and food on her table."

"I suppose she told you what she needs," Thor sneered. "I suppose you fulfilled those needs, too."

"There's no getting through that thick skull. How do you feel about her? From the less than brotherly greeting I received for dropping off her notebook, I would imagine you have it bad."

Thor swallowed hard. Leave it to Cal to voice aloud what Thor hadn't been able to admit to himself. He was so in love with Willow that making a fool out of himself became the norm. "Yeah, it's bad and that ain't good."

The doorbell rang again and Thor went to answer it. While he and the deliveryman exchanged money and a cardboard box of pizza, he heard Cal call out.

"Willow, wait!"

Thor closed the front door and then an upstairs door slammed hard, rattling the living room windows. "What happened?"

"She overheard us. She was crying. I'm leaving before another dam bursts. If you need me, you have my number."

"Thanks, Cal. Sorry about your lip."

"What's a split lip between brothers?" He shrugged. "You have a good woman up there. You should let her know how much she means to you. G'night."

Thor took the staircase two steps at a time. He knocked on Willow's bedroom door. A muffled voice told him to come in. He did and his stomach flipped when he found her packing.

"What are you doing?"

"I have overstayed my welcome," Willow explained in a hoarse whisper. "Kendra needs a roommate, and she asked me if I was interested. I told her I would let her know."

"You don't want to live with me anymore?"

She shook her head without bothering to look at him. "Not if you don't want me here. I heard you say it was bad, and I don't want to make you unhappy."

Her voice broke, and he crossed the room in two steps to reach her. Despite her weak protests, he gathered her in his arms. "You misunderstood. Having you here isn't bad. That's not what I meant."

"You were fighting with Cal, and that was because of me," she said tearfully. "I don't want to be the cause of dissension between you." She rested her hands against his chest and pushed. "It's better if I go."

"No!" His hands locked around her waist. "It's not better. It would be awful. I'd hate it."

"You're just saying that."

"No, I'm not. I mean it. I don't want you to leave."

Fat tears rolled down her cheeks. "You just want me here because you feel responsible for me."

Thor cupped her face and tilted her head so that their gazes met. Tears filled her eyeglasses so he removed them and lowered his head close enough that only a breath separated the tips of their noses. "I do feel responsible for you, but that's not why I want you here."

"You think I may be with child and that's why—"

He pressed his forefinger against her mouth, and her words stopped. Her lips quivered beneath his caress. His stomach clenched in response. His jeans suddenly felt too tight. He fought a hard battle against the raging desire that demanded immediate attention. Removing his finger from her mouth, he exhaled a sharp breath and quickly said the words he wanted to say a long time ago, but never had the courage.

"I don't want you to go because if you do, I think I'll just die again." Her eyes widened, and she opened her mouth to speak. He continued before she uttered a sound. "I don't mean in the literal sense, but I guess if you don't have much to live for, it doesn't matter. You saved my life, Willow. You showed me that there's more to life than the rush of adrenaline on game day. I thought I loved football, the roar of the crowd and everything that went with it. It meant so much to me for so long that I associated myself with it, and when I couldn't do it anymore, I didn't know what to do with myself. Losing football hurt, but I swear to you, it can't compare to the thought of losing you.

"When I returned home to Pop and Cal and left you behind to deal with Grady Falls, I completely lost it. They can tell you; I was totally messed up. The very idea of Grady putting his hands on you made me want to kill him. The fear of not knowing how to get back to you made me want to die. I can't bear the thought of anything hurting you, and knowing that I've caused you pain lately makes me mad. I am sorry, Willow."

"You don't have to apologize."

"Yes, I do. I'm bad at this. With football, you get a playbook to tell you what to do. When you fall in love, you get nothing but a bad case of stubborn stupidity."

"You don't have to say that. I know that you care for me."

"But just caring isn't enough for you. You deserve more. I should have said it a long time ago, but I thought you knew. I tried to show you, but I messed up somehow. I wanted to give you the world when I brought you here with me. Instead, I just gave you a world of heartache."

"I didn't come here because I wanted the world. I came because I wanted to be with you."

He exhaled. "Well, I don't want you to go. Please, don't leave. Stay with me."

"I want to…"

"Before you say anything else," he said, leading her to the bed, "have a seat. I have to get something. Don't move."

Willow watched his retreating back until he slipped out the door and then she drew in a deep breath. Although she was seated, her legs felt wobbly.

Thor loves me. Blessed be! It did her heart good to hear the words.

He returned to the room with a bounce in his step. Crimson darkened his tan face. His eyes sparkled with a secret. He balled his right hand into a fist, and as he knelt on one knee at her feet, he placed both hands on her thighs.

"I don't have a speech prepared. I learned that winging it sometimes works, so that's what I'll do."

"What are you doing?"

"I'm asking you to marry me. I don't have much to offer, but what I have is yours. I love you, Willow, and want you to be my wife."

A soft gasp escaped her. His declaration caught her off guard. A marriage proposal? "Blessed be."

"Is that all you have to say?" The corner of Thor's eyes crinkled as he teased her. He opened his balled hand and lifted a ring from his palm. "I have a ring. Pop gave it to me the day we came back. It was Eva's. If you say yes and let me slide this on, the engagement can be official as of this moment."

Willow bubbled with joy. A warm glow shot through her. She extended her hand. "Yes!"

Thor slid the ring on faster than a speeding bullet. His mouth closed over hers in a devouring kiss and not much later, he took her to heaven.

EPILOGUE

Canton, Georgia
October 2005

Thor couldn't sleep. Lovemaking usually tired him out, but tonight not even Willow's unrestrained passion tuckered him. The idea of watching the DVD again refused to let him rest. Careful not to wake his sleeping wife, he rolled out of bed. He pulled on his robe and wandered downstairs.

His hands glided over the railing. Since his marriage and the birth of his first child, the cabin underwent a number of changes. Thor was mindful of Anders's original design and workmanship, taking great pains to match it.

The second floor was efficient, yet spacious. He and Willow decorated it in an old country style with oak furnishings and warm, thick quilts in every room. Cal and Pop teased them at first, but weren't shy about offering their suggestions.

A window here and the den over there. The cabin became the family's preferred vacation spot, and Thor made sure his children knew the history of it and appreciated the Magnusen legacy.

He turned on the lamp beside his recliner and grabbed the remote. With one push, the large screen digital television roared to life, and with another push, the DVD player did, too.

A velvet carpet of green covered the football field. Two sets of players sized each other up over the fifty-yard line. The Falcons had the ball this go 'round and the quarterback threw the sweetest pass Thor ever saw. Even though he knew the outcome of the game, the Falcons whipped the Eagles twenty-four to eighteen, his breath caught in his throat. The pass set a record, and that quarterback did his heart proud.

"How many times do you plan to watch that?" Willow asked, surprising him as she hopped onto his lap. "You've seen it at least ten times already and the game was yesterday! You'll wear the disc out."

He pulled her close to him and snuggled. "It's okay. I made copies."

"Olivia will be mortified."

He shrugged. "She'll get over it. It's not everyday my little girl scores the pass that wins the homecoming game."

"She's sixteen. If you pull that DVD out the night her date picks her up for the prom, I'll take care of you myself."

He growled, and his lower body twitched with renewed vigor. "That sounds promising."

She giggled and rested her head against his shoulder. Her hand slipped underneath his robe. Sensual caresses teased his chest. He flattened his hand over hers and shook his head with mock warning.

"Your three children are upstairs fast asleep. What would they think if they knew their mother was initiating a forward pass?"

"They'll think she's happy and very much in love."

"Still?" He cocked an eyebrow and regarded her closely. "After twenty years?"

"Yes." Her voice was a wanton mixture of silk and huskiness. "And you?"

"You don't have to ask. I love you, Willow Elkridge Magnusen, and each day that passes, I know that our love will last forever."

ABOUT THE AUTHOR

Dominiqua Douglas discovered the joys of writing through fan fiction. Readers' responses, awards, and encouragement prompted her to focus on her own original work. Her desire to learn more about the craft prompted her to join Romance Writers of America, which provides a wealth of information for unpublished and published writers. When she is not writing or reading, she enjoys listening to 80s music, designing websites, watching movies, traveling and delicious chocolate.

Dominiqua loves to hear from her readers. Please send a self-addressed stamped envelope for a personal reply to the following address:

P.O. Box 1963
Grenada, MS 38902

Dominiqua's email address is dominiquad@aol.com and her web-page is located at **http://www.dominiqua.net**

Excerpt from

ENCHANTED DESIRE

BY

WANDA THOMAS

Release Date: February 2006

PROLOGUE

The young man stood statue still.

His mind told him to run, but he was unable to make his body move. He felt as though he was passing through a dream, an unreality of his own making, even though his mind was fully aware of the signs of life going on around him. The sun beamed down hot on top of his head while cars whizzed by, their back wind tousling his glossy black hair as the squeaky squawk of a female voice and intermittent beeps came from a radio in the car that was parked a few feet away. When his startling blue gaze rose and he saw the birds soaring in the sky above him, he wished with all his heart that he could grow wings and fly off with them.

He looked down at the man lying on his back in the street and squeezed his eyes shut, blocking out the pool of blood that surrounded his head. He clenched his fists as a loud scream reverberated inside his mind. *What in God's name had he done?*

"Dexter, let's go!"

He heard the voice of his friend Carlos and opened his eyes, but he still couldn't make himself move.

"Santangelo, get in the car! We can't stay here!"

Carlos grabbed his shirt from behind and began dragging him back, while Dexter struggled to get away. The man needed help; someone had to help him. "B-but w-what about-"

"Ain't nothin' you can do for him, he's dead! Come on, man!"

Dexter pulled away and looked down at his hand. It began to shake uncontrollably and tears welled in his eyes. Sunlight glinted off the shiny black metal and the heaviness in his hand suddenly became unbearable. Releasing his grip, he watched the gun fall to the street. When it hit the paved road with a loud metal clank, his lips began to tremble with his efforts to hold back a sob. He glanced again at the man lying in the street and felt the weight of his crime land heavily on his shoulders.

He'd done a lot of things wrong in his short life, but this was by far the worst. He had committed an unforgivable sin. He was a killer, and knowing that he'd taken the life of another human being would haunt him for a very long time, possibly forever.

His friends called out to him again and Dexter looked up at the car parked by the side of the road a few feet away. A young boy stood by the open door, his dark eyes widened in terror. Dexter swallowed, his throat aching with unshed tears. The boy was an exact replica of the man lying in the street. He had to be the man's son.

"I'm sorry," Dexter murmured too softly for the boy to hear. "I didn't mean to do it."

This time when Carlos grabbed him, Dexter didn't struggle. Emotionally drained, he was too weak to fight. The last thing he saw as his friend dragged him away to their car was the eyes of the boy. Eyes that had narrowed and, despite the tears running down his brown face, blazed with hate. Eyes that he would remember for the rest of his life.

CHAPTER 1

"That's it!"

The explosive yell rent the early morning air a split second before a large, brown hand wrapped around Tyreese Johnson's throat. Lifted bodily from the ground, Tyreese found his feet dangling, his back pinned to the brick wall behind him, and his attention wholly focused on the enraged, black glare of Detective Christopher Mills.

Tyreese tried to nod his head. When that didn't work, he darted pleading dark eyes to Christopher's partner, Donny London. Donny turned his back and crossed burly arms over his chest as he ostensibly surveyed the empty street in front of him. Tyreese Johnson was on his own.

Christopher used his other hand to grab Tyreese's chin and switch his attention back to him. He was cold, tired, and was not going to put up with any more of Tyreese Johnson's nonsense. "I've been up all night and I've had enough of your shit. Now, are you gonna play ball, or am I gonna kick your ass from here to the corner of Colfax?"

Christopher tightened his grip, his expression growing fiercer by the second. Tyreese struggled against the force of the hand holding him firmly against the wall, but only succeeded in almost choking himself. His slightly glazed eyes widened in disbelief. The man staring up at him was someone he'd never seen before, and his expression emphatically stated that Tyreese might possibly end up a dead man if he didn't give up what he knew, and quick.

The problem was that Tyreese didn't know anything. He was hurting and had been looking for a quick fix. He'd sought out the man because Mills was usually good for a bill or two. That is, if the information proved useful. If not…well, Tyreese didn't even want to walk that road. With the grip on his throat making him dizzy, Tyreese scanned his brain, searching for at least one tidbit of information that would pacify the man who could, with a flip of his wrist, snap Tyreese's scrawny neck.

He tried to swallow and found that he couldn't. "Okay, Mills," he finally rasped. Christopher loosened his hold. "I got something I think you can use."

Christopher relented by letting Tyreese slide down the wall as Donny faced the men again.

"A shipment arrived this week with Santangelo's name on it."

Christopher's gaze narrowed to black slits. "How do you know?"

Tyreese made a show of rubbing the front of his throat and taking in deep gulps of air. Christopher pushed him into the wall. "Spill it, Reese!"

Tyreese mashed himself flat against the hard surface, putting as much space as possible between himself and Christopher Mills. "I was there, man. I saw the whole thing. Five crates—marked household goods. They came by truck and went direc'ly into Santangelo's warehouse."

Christopher reached into his back pocket for his wallet. With slow deliberation, he pulled out a twenty and watched a smile dent Tyreese's hollowed cheeks. "What else?"

Tyreese swabbed a dry tongue along swollen lips as he eyed the money. "Nothin' else, Mills. I swear. They unloaded the crates, stashed them behind some boxes, and I waited until they split before gettin' my black ass outta there. Santangelo's people don't 'preciate folks droppin' in on their private parties and I seen what they do to uninvited guests." Tyreese swiped the back of his hand over his mouth, then looked down at the sidewalk. "I don't know nothin' else, Mills," he mumbled.

Christopher took in the addict's bedraggled appearance and a shiver of disquiet ran down his spine. Drug addiction was a powerful master and it had taken down too many educated, successful men like Tyreese. Just a few short years ago, Tyreese Johnson had been on the fast track to the top in the DA's office. His life had come crashing down the night his wife found him in bed with another woman and, with revenge on her mind, leaked news of his twice a day *minor* habit with crack cocaine to the press.

By the time the media finished crucifying him and his divorce became final, Tyreese had lost his job, his friends, and all of the material possessions he'd accumulated. His addiction to crack had taken everything else, including his self-respect, pride, and dignity. Instead of the two-story, palatial palace in Douglas County Tyreese had once called home, he now spread his blanket in abandoned warehouses or sought warmth on the steam-heated manhole covers alongside the light-rail station at 14th and Stout.

Christopher had tried many times to help Tyreese overcome his addiction, but the man never stayed clean for more than a couple of months. With a shake of his head, Christopher lifted one of the man's skinny, dried up hands, and placed the money inside his palm. He smiled. "Thanks, Reese. What you've told me will be a big help."

Tyreese returned the smile, showing drug-stained teeth. He crushed the money in his hand. "Glad I could be of assistance, Mills. Only next time, keep yo' hands to yo'self." Tyreese pulled at the edges of a faded army jacket, patted down matted black hair that hadn't seen a comb in months, and stood a little straighter. He moved with caution around Christopher Mills, though. Ambling away, he began conversing with someone only he could see. "What I tell you, man? See what happens when you try and help a brother out? They try and jack you up. So, you take it from, T. Don't never let nooobody—"

The rest of his words were lost as Tyreese rounded the corner. Christopher and Donny looked at each other, shrugged, and headed for the black Jeep parked by the curb. Donny settled his broad frame into the passenger seat and buckled the seatbelt. "Why'd you give him the money, Mills? He didn't tell us anything we didn't already know."

Christopher started the engine and checked the side and rearview mirrors before steering the Jeep into the street. He'd seen Tyreese leaving the warehouse the night Santangelo's latest shipment had arrived. It was a good thing Reese had left when he did, because Christopher also knew what happened to someone found in the wrong place at the wrong time. "I'm aware of that," he said to Donny, keeping his eyes focused on the road and the happenings in a neighborhood awakening to begin another day.

Soon the business owners and their employees would lift the bars on the windows and doors and start preparing to greet their customers. Those like Tyreese—the drug addicts, the pimps, the prostitutes, and the homeless—who roamed the streets under the auspices of darkness would disappear for a few hours.

Donny's brows furrowed as he surveyed the long city block. "Then I don't understand. Why did you give him money when he had nothing new to tell us?"

Christopher knew why he'd given up the dough. Guilt. Guilt for taking his anger out on Tyreese when he was actually mad at someone else. It wasn't Tyreese's fault that Manette Walker hadn't bothered to return even one of the many telephone calls he'd made to her house or to the boutique. He didn't look at his partner as he responded, "Just wanted to make sure Reese was still being up front with me. It pays to check up on your informants every once in a while."

Donny nodded, comprehension clearing the wrinkles from his forehead. He mulled over Christopher's words, then tucked the lesson away for use another night. "By the way," he said. "I traded off for a day shift tomorrow."

"Oh," Christopher said without any real interest in the young man's plans.

"I invited Chief Diggs to dinner to thank him for his help in getting me on with the department. He and my father grew up together, you know."

"So you've said."

"Yeah, even though Dad's no longer with us, I think he'd be happy to know that one of his best friends still thinks enough of him to help his kid out."

"Hmmm," Christopher responded.

"Carl Simmons will be there, too, I think. Hey, maybe you could join us, Chris."

Christopher restrained himself from commenting on Donny's tendency to name drop. Carl Simmons was the head of the local MET operation. MET, an acronym for Mobile Enforcement Team, was a federally-sponsored program that aided local police departments with the identification and arrest of criminals known to be involved in illegal drug-related activities.

Donny had transferred to the Denver Police Department after having some strings pulled by higher-ups. The man was flashy, too flashy for Christopher's taste. He could also do without Donny's daily update of his financial profile, which he'd increased considerably from a small inheritance received from his father. His bragging and boasting, expensive threads, and flamboyant black Camero had alienated the other officers. Their refusal to work with the cocky kid was the reason Christopher had gotten stuck with Donny four nights out of the week.

For Christopher, a man who liked to work alone, having the kid hang on his tail was tedious. It also didn't help that Donny was foolishly unaware that while who he knew could be important to his career, his on-the-job-performance would be the determining factor as to whether or not he remained on the force. A lesson he might learn sooner rather than later if he didn't stop flaunting his wealth in the faces of the other officers.

"No thanks. I have a couple of things to wrap up tomorrow."

"Well, maybe next time," Donny said.

Christopher sucked his teeth. "Yeah, maybe."

Shelby Reeves looked up when the bell over the door tinkled. Setting her cup of tea on the table, she crossed the room and walked up the three steps leading to the ready-to-wear store of Exterior Motives. A frown settled on her face as she watched her friend and business partner enter the shop.

Normally, the air around Manette Walker crackled with energy and her cheerful, bubbly personality drew smiles from everyone she encountered. Today, Manny didn't return the greetings from the sales associates already stationed on the floor, and she moved through the shop without her usual clamor. When Manny stopped to straighten a rack of silk blouses, Shelby saw the downward tilt of her mouth and the glum expression on her face. Concerned, Shelby watched Manny resume her trek to her office in the back.

Shelby sighed, went back for her tea, then made her way to her private office. Sitting behind her desk, she sipped from her cup and considered her options. She could try to talk to Manny, but now was probably not the best time. Though it didn't happen often, when Manny was in a bad mood, Shelby knew it was not wise to approach her unless she wanted to find herself on the wrong side of Manny's lightning quick temper.

That knowledge, though, didn't deter Shelby's need to know, and she was leaning toward taking the chance. However, the telephone on her desk rang before she could move from her chair. Shelby set her cup down and picked up the receiver.

"Exterior Motives, this is Shelby Reeves, how may I help you?"

"Shelby, its Chris."

She leaned back in her chair. "Christopher, how are you this morning?"

"Tired, Shel. Has Manny made it in yet?"

Her lips twisted as she contemplated her response. Since Shelby was sure that Christopher was the reason behind Manny's despondency, perhaps she didn't have to wait to satisfy her curiosity after all. "She's here, Chris, only she doesn't appear to be doing too well."

"Why, what's wrong with her?"

"Physically she's fine," Shelby said, in an attempt to ease the worry she'd heard in his voice. "It's just that Manny seems...well, down in the dumps."

"Oh." Christopher chuckled softly. "You had me worried there for a sec, Shel. Manny's probably upset because I had to cancel our date on Friday, and I pulled a lot of overtime this weekend so I didn't get a chance to see her."

Shelby had known Manny since college. Her friend was not the type of person who would let something as trivial as a broken date upset her. Manny was the type of person who had no problem chewing up and spitting out anyone who crossed her, unless that person was someone Manny cared for. Then, Manny would absorb the hurt and hold it inside until the wound healed itself. As much as Shelby wanted to believe Christopher, something else had happened to upset Manny.

Then too, Christopher was also a reserved person. Shelby knew she'd gotten as much information as she was going to get out of him. "Oh, okay, Chris," she said. "Then hearing from you should definitely cheer her up. Hold on and I'll put you through."

The ringing telephone didn't interrupt Manny's concentration on the sheet of numbers on the desk in front of her. The fingers on her right hand continued to fly over the calculator's keyboard, while her left index finger punched a button on the telephone.

"Call for you on two."

"Put them through to voice mail."

"But, Manny¾"

"Shelby, I'm busy. These figures from last week's sales are not jiving. I can't take the call right now."

"But, Manny¾"

"It's probably just a salesman and I don't have time to listen to his pitch. Just send the call to voice mail."

"Manny, it's Christopher."

Continuing to manipulate the calculator, Manny frowned when the number on the display still didn't match the number circled in red on the report. She began entering the numbers again.

"Christopher Mills," Shelby added when Manny didn't respond.

Manny automatically reached for the phone, and then, as if she'd touched a hot flame, just as quickly snatched her hand back. Christopher Mills was not a person she wished to speak with, especially not after what she'd witnessed last Friday after he'd cancelled their date with the excuse that something had suddenly come up.

Manny gripped her hands together, a physical sign of her internal struggle. It had taken a long time for her to accept Christopher Mills into her life. Just when she'd decided that he was the only man for her, she found out that he'd lied.

"Manny, are you still there?"

She took a deep breath exhaling loudly. It did not stop the wobbly beat in her chest, halt the trembling of her lips, or ease her desire to pick up the phone just to hear the sound of Christopher's voice. "I'm busy, Shelby. Send the call to voice mail."

Manny punched the button ending the connection and went back to what she was doing before Shelby interrupted her. When the numbers still didn't add up, Manny shoved the papers across the desk and leaned back in her chair, staring blankly into space, which was how Shelby found her when she entered the office a few minutes later.

"You should have talked to him."

Startled by the unexpected voice, Manny's body pitched forward and she nearly fell out of the chair. She braced her hands against the edge of the desk, righted herself, and fixed her stare on Shelby as she walked into the room. "Talked to whom?"

Shelby sat in the yellow wingback chair and smiled, despite the gloom in the air. "Christopher."

Manny blinked several times, which was the only indication of how much hearing his name affected her. "Oh him," she said flippantly, accompanying her tone with a shrug meant to convey that the name meant nothing to her. Inside her chest, her crying heart told a different story and its beat rattled out of control like a drum gone wild.

"Oh him," Shelby mimicked with sarcastic undertones. "Yes, him. Why don't you want to talk to Chris, Manny?"

"No reason, other than I don't have the time to waste right now."

"Waste!" Shelby blew out an impatient breath. "Christopher took time out of his day to call you, Manny Walker. The least you could have done was pick up the phone and say hello." Shelby set the cup of tea she'd brought with her on the desk and settled back in the chair. "What's the matter, Manny?"

"Nothing." Swinging her chair around, Manny turned her back to Shelby and reached for a tissue from the box sitting on the oak credenza behind her. She blew her nose, deposited the tissue in the trashcan, and turned back to her friend. She tried to smile, but when she felt her lips quiver, Manny gave up the effort. She looked down as her gaze turned watery.

Shelby, more than concerned now, leaned forward. "Manny, what is it?"

Manny's shoulders lifted on a sigh. Seeming to put whatever was on her mind away, she looked at Shelby again. This time, she did manage a smile. "Nothing's wrong, Shel. I'm just a little tired, that's all."

Unconvinced, Shelby continued to study Manny and decided to try another approach. "Didn't you have a date with Chris on Friday?"

Manny's gaze hardened and froze. "I was *supposed* to have a date with Christopher, but he cancelled it."

"Why would that upset you? This is not the first date Christopher has cancelled. He was probably calling to explain."

Manny shrugged. "He can call, but it won't make any difference. I'm through with Christopher Coltrane Mills!"

"But why? You've been seeing Christopher for a long time, longer than anyone you've been with since I've known you. I thought the two of you were happy together."

"That's what I thought, too, but apparently Christopher Mills doesn't want to be with me anymore. He's made that very clear, and that's fine with me because I don't want to be with him either!"

Shelby rose from the chair and moved around the desk. She pulled Manny up by the arm and smothered her friend in a hug. She'd been so sure that things would work out this time and that Manny would find the love she'd been seeking for far too many years. "Oh, Manny. I'm so sorry."

Manny pushed away and resumed her seat. Picking up the telephone messages on her desk, she casually flipped through the pink pile. "I'm not. At least this time I found out before I committed my heart. Men are dogs and I hate every last one of them."

"I guess," Shelby replied half-heartedly, as she sat on the edge of the desk and folded her arms under her breasts. If not for her husband, she might feel inclined to agree with Manny. Life with Nelson Reeves wasn't always a calm sea, but she had no reason to complain. Nelson was the find of her life and she'd hoped that in Christopher Mills, Manny had finally found her lifetime mate. However, despite Manny's drastic transformation—to Shelby's knowledge, the first she'd undergone for any man—it seemed that Christopher was not the one either. Only this time, Shelby wasn't so sure she agreed with the conclusion she'd drawn. Something in Manny's voice gave her pause to consider the matter a little further. "Did Christopher tell you why he wanted to break off your relationship?"

"He didn't have to tell me, I know why."

Shelby frowned. "I don't understand, Manny."

"What's to understand, Shel? Instead of keeping his date with me on Friday, Christopher decided to spend his free time with another woman."

"If you didn't see Chris on Friday, what makes you think that he was with someone else?"

Agitation marred Manny's face as her eyes shifted around the room in a struggle to keep her composure. How did she know? She knew because she'd seen him with her own two eyes. After he'd called to cancel their date, she'd decided to keep their reservation and go to dinner alone. Entering the restaurant, she'd immediately spotted

Christopher sitting in a cozy corner with his arm around the shoulders of another woman. Frozen by shock, she'd watched the two of them exchange whispered comments before the woman had kissed him on the cheek.

While she and Christopher hadn't yet declared undying feelings of love for one another, Manny had felt strongly that their relationship had been moving in the direction of something permanent. Now she knew that he was a low-down, two-timing cheat, and Manny wanted nothing more to do with Christopher. The tears welled again and when one overflowed the brim and rolled down her cheek, Manny lost her battle to restrain her emotions. "Because I saw him with her!"

Manny dropped her head and hid her face in her hands. Shelby watched her, momentarily at a loss for what to do. In all the years she'd known her, she'd never seen Manny Walker cry, and her quiet sobs pulled at Shelby's heartstrings. Shelby leaned over and wrapped her arms around her friend. This was all her fault. She was the one who'd encouraged Manny's interest in Christopher Mills and she was responsible for the agony her friend now suffered. In trying to quell her tendencies at matchmaking, Nelson had told her to stay out of it, but Shelby hadn't listened. She'd thought Christopher to be a solid, strong, and dependable man—the kind of man Manny needed to help her settle down. Apparently, she didn't know Christopher Mills as well as she'd thought.

When Manny's tears subsided to soft hiccups, Shelby reached for the tissues. She plucked several from the box and handed them to Manny. "I know it hurts, Manny, but we'll get through this. If Chris has been two-timing you, then he's not worth another second of your thoughts. You just forget about him."

Manny sniffed. "That's a lot easier said than done, Shel. I really thought Christopher cared for me. He was so kind and patient with me and all the things he did—like calling just to say hi and rubbing my feet after a long day at the shop. He even brought me flowers and cooked dinner for me. Have you ever had a man do that for you,

Shelby?" Manny looked down at the desk, dejection evident in the slump of her shoulders. "Of course you have; you have Nelson."

"You'll find another man, Manny, and he'll do all those things for you again. But the next time, it will be real and he'll treasure you the way you deserve to be treasured."

"But I love Christopher!"

The shock of Manny's words quickly registered on Shelby's face. Since her wedding, she had noticed a marked improvement not just in Manny's attitude, but also her appearance. Manny had traded her eye-popping, original outfits in favor of more traditional and sedate attire. Solid-colored pantsuits and longer skirts matched with silk blouses had replaced fur, spandex, and the other odd and glittery apparel that had once dominated Manny's wardrobe. She had swapped her snakeskin boots and her spiked heel collection for low-heeled pumps, sling backs, and flat, leather sandals. She no longer covered her face in heavy, almost clownish makeup, but now used only a light face powder, a little mascara, and colored lip-gloss. Manny had even removed the wildly colored braids from her hair in favor of styles more suitable for her age.

After years of trying, to no avail, to help Manny improve her outer appearance, Shelby had silently approved of her friend's new look. Now she knew the real reason behind the changes. Manette Walker was in love.

This morning though, Manette looked more like the Manny of old. A thick layer of foundation hid the smooth, tan brown color of a beautiful, heart-shaped face. Garish purple eye shadow and the long, black false lashes sank rather than enhanced her chocolate brown eyes. Manny had used a heavy hand with the blush that stained her cheeks and with the orange lipstick rimming her mouth. The eye shadow and lip color matched the deep purple sweater and bright orange miniskirt that covered Manny's slender frame. She'd painted her fingernails orange and styled her black hair into spikes that poked out all over her head.

Everything about Manny's appearance said she was screaming for attention. Examining her, Shelby finally saw the answer she'd been seeking since she'd met Manette Walker. As much as Manny professed to want a man, she used clothes and makeup as a shield to keep men from getting too close to her.

If not for the metamorphosis she'd personally witnessed, Shelby never would have figured it out, because Manny was so adept at guarding her feelings. She'd dropped that shield and exposed her true self for Christopher Mills, something he apparently hadn't wanted, and now Manny Walker had gone back into hiding.

Regretting the role she'd played in getting the two of them together and feeling her fury rise toward Christopher Mills, Shelby helped Manny up from the chair. She reached into the bottom drawer of the desk and took out the purple purse. "Manny, I want you to take the day off—in fact, take the week. Go somewhere special and pamper yourself."

"I can't, Shel," Manny protested. "I have a meeting with the buyers this morning and I need to close out the accounts for month's end."

Shelby's tawny brown eyes glittered as she assessed her friend. "What you need is time away from here. You're way overdue for a vacation and you need some time to heal."

Though Manny took the purse Shelby held out, she hesitated. "Are you sure, Shelby? I mean, this thing with Chris is not that big a deal. I'm just feeling a little low right now, but I'll get over him, and I would never let my personal life interfere with my performance in the store."

"I know, honey. But today, I'm the boss and I'm ordering you out of our shop." Shelby watched as Manny gathered the rest of her things, then walked with her to the door. "I'll call you later and see how you're doing, okay?"

"You're a good friend, Shel, but don't worry about me. I'll be fine. In fact, I think I'll head to Boulder and visit the family for a few days."

Shelby nodded. Manny shared a close and loving relationship

with her family and right now, her friend needed all the extra love she could get. "That's a good idea. Call me when you get back in town."

Shelby returned to the boutique and went into her office. Lowering herself in the chair, she set her cup on the desk and turned her mind to planning the payback she would deliver to Christopher Mills for hurting the best friend she had in the whole world.

LOVE LASTS FOREVER

2006 Publication Schedule

January

A Lover's Legacy
Veronica Parker
1-58571-167-5
$9.95

Love Lasts Forever
Dominiqua Douglas
1-58571-187-X
$9.95

Under the Cherry
   Moon
Christal Jordan-Mims
1-58571-169-1
$12.95

February

Second Chances at Love
Cheris Hodges
1-58571-188-8
$9.95

Enchanted Desire
Wanda Thomas
1-58571-176-4
$9.95

Caught Up
Deatri King Bey
1-58571-178-0
$12.95

March

I'm Gonna Make You
   Love Me
Gwyneth Bolton
1-58571-181-0
$9.95

Through The Fire
Seressia Glass
1-58571-173-X
$9.95

Notes When Summer
   Ends
Beverly Lauderdale
1-58571-180-2
$12.95

April

Sin and Surrender
J.M. Jeffries
1-58571-189-6
$9.95

Unearthing Passions
Elaine Sims
1-58571-184-5
$9.95

Between Tears
Pamela Ridley
1-58571-179-0
$12.95

May

Misty Blue
Dyanne Davis
1-58571-186-1
$9.95

Ironic
Pamela Leigh Starr
1-58571-168-3
$9.95

Cricket's Serenade
Carolita Blythe
1-58571-183-7
$12.95

June

Cupid
Barbara Keaton
1-58571-174-8
$9.95

Havana Sunrise
Kymberly Hunt
1-58571-182-9
$9.95

Bound For Mt. Zion
Chris Parker
1-58571-191-8
$12.95

2006 Publication Schedule (continued)

July

Love Me Carefully
A.C. Arthur
1-58571-177-2
$9.95

No Ordinary Love
Angela Weaver
1-58571-198-5
$9.95

Rehoboth Road
Anita Ballard-Jones
1-58571-196-9
$12.95

August

Scent of Rain
Annetta P. Lee
158571-199-3
$9.95

Love in High Gear
Charlotte Roy
158571-185-3
$9.95

Rise of the Phoenix
Kenneth Whetstone
1-58571-197-7
$12.95

September

The Business of Love
Cheris Hodges
1-58571-193-4
$9.95

Rock Star
Rosyln Hardy Holcomb
1-58571-200-0
$9.95

A Dead Man Speaks
Lisa Jones Johnson
1-58571-203-5
$12.95

October

Who's That Lady
Andrea Jackson
1-58571-190-X
$9.95

A Dangerous Woman
J.M. Jeffries
1-58571-195-0
$9.95

Sinful Intentions
Crystal Rhodes
1-58571-201-9
$12.95

November

Only You
Crystal Hubbard
1-58571-208-6
$9.95

Ebony Eyes
Kei Swanson
1-58571-194-2
$9.95

By and By
Collette Haywood
1-58571-209-4
$12.95

December

Let's Get It On
Dyanne Davis
1-58571-210-8
$9.95

Nights Over Egypt
Barbara Keaton
1-58571-192-6
$9.95

A Pefect Place to Pray
Ikesha Goodwin
1-58571-202-7
$12.95

Other Genesis Press, Inc. Titles

Title	Author	Price
A Dangerous Deception	J.M. Jeffries	$8.95
A Dangerous Love	J.M. Jeffries	$8.95
A Dangerous Obsession	J.M. Jeffries	$8.95
A Drummer's Beat to Mend	Kei Swanson	$9.95
A Happy Life	Charlotte Harris	$9.95
A Heart's Awakening	Veronica Parker	$9.95
A Lark on the Wing	Phyliss Hamilton	$9.95
A Love of Her Own	Cheris F. Hodges	$9.95
A Love to Cherish	Beverly Clark	$8.95
A Risk of Rain	Dar Tomlinson	$8.95
A Twist of Fate	Beverly Clark	$8.95
A Will to Love	Angie Daniels	$9.95
Acquisitions	Kimberley White	$8.95
Across	Carol Payne	$12.95
After the Vows	Leslie Esdaile	$10.95
(Summer Anthology)	T.T. Henderson	
	Jacqueline Thomas	
Again My Love	Kayla Perrin	$10.95
Against the Wind	Gwynne Forster	$8.95
All I Ask	Barbara Keaton	$8.95
Ambrosia	T.T. Henderson	$8.95
An Unfinished Love Affair	Barbara Keaton	$8.95
And Then Came You	Dorothy Elizabeth Love	$8.95
Angel's Paradise	Janice Angelique	$9.95
At Last	Lisa G. Riley	$8.95
Best of Friends	Natalie Dunbar	$8.95
Beyond the Rapture	Beverly Clark	$9.95
Blaze	Barbara Keaton	$9.95
Blood Lust	J. M. Jeffries	$9.95
Bodyguard	Andrea Jackson	$9.95
Boss of Me	Diana Nyad	$8.95
Bound by Love	Beverly Clark	$8.95
Breeze	Robin Hampton Allen	$10.95

Other Genesis Press, Inc. Titles (continued)

Broken	Dar Tomlinson	$24.95
By Design	Barbara Keaton	$8.95
Cajun Heat	Charlene Berry	$8.95
Careless Whispers	Rochelle Alers	$8.95
Cats & Other Tales	Marilyn Wagner	$8.95
Caught in a Trap	Andre Michelle	$8.95
Caught Up In the Rapture	Lisa G. Riley	$9.95
Cautious Heart	Cheris F Hodges	$8.95
Chances	Pamela Leigh Starr	$8.95
Cherish the Flame	Beverly Clark	$8.95
Class Reunion	Irma Jenkins/John Brown	$12.95
Code Name: Diva	J.M. Jeffries	$9.95
Conquering Dr. Wexler's Heart	Kimberley White	$9.95
Crossing Paths, Tempting Memories	Dorothy Elizabeth Love	$9.95
Cypress Whisperings	Phyllis Hamilton	$8.95
Dark Embrace	Crystal Wilson Harris	$8.95
Dark Storm Rising	Chinelu Moore	$10.95
Daughter of the Wind	Joan Xian	$8.95
Deadly Sacrifice	Jack Kean	$22.95
Designer Passion	Dar Tomlinson	$8.95
Dreamtective	Liz Swados	$5.95
Ebony Butterfly II	Delilah Dawson	$14.95
Echoes of Yesterday	Beverly Clark	$9.95
Eden's Garden	Elizabeth Rose	$8.95
Everlastin' Love	Gay G. Gunn	$8.95
Everlasting Moments	Dorothy Elizabeth Love	$8.95
Everything and More	Sinclair Lebeau	$8.95
Everything but Love	Natalie Dunbar	$8.95
Eve's Prescription	Edwina Martin Arnold	$8.95
Falling	Natalie Dunbar	$9.95
Fate	Pamela Leigh Starr	$8.95
Finding Isabella	A.J. Garrotto	$8.95

Other Genesis Press, Inc. Titles (continued)

Forbidden Quest	Dar Tomlinson	$10.95
Forever Love	Wanda Thomas	$8.95
From the Ashes	Kathleen Suzanne	$8.95
	Jeanne Sumerix	
Gentle Yearning	Rochelle Alers	$10.95
Glory of Love	Sinclair LeBeau	$10.95
Go Gentle into that Good Night	Malcom Boyd	$12.95
Goldengroove	Mary Beth Craft	$16.95
Groove, Bang, and Jive	Steve Cannon	$8.99
Hand in Glove	Andrea Jackson	$9.95
Hard to Love	Kimberley White	$9.95
Hart & Soul	Angie Daniels	$8.95
Heartbeat	Stephanie Bedwell-Grime	$8.95
Hearts Remember	M. Loui Quezada	$8.95
Hidden Memories	Robin Allen	$10.95
Higher Ground	Leah Latimer	$19.95
Hitler, the War, and the Pope	Ronald Rychiak	$26.95
How to Write a Romance	Kathryn Falk	$18.95
I Married a Reclining Chair	Lisa M. Fuhs	$8.95
Indigo After Dark Vol. I	Nia Dixon/Angelique	$10.95
Indigo After Dark Vol. II	Dolores Bundy/Cole Riley	$10.95
Indigo After Dark Vol. III	Montana Blue/Coco Morena	$10.95
Indigo After Dark Vol. IV	Cassandra Colt/	$14.95
	Diana Richeaux	
Indigo After Dark Vol. V	Delilah Dawson	$14.95
Icie	Pamela Leigh Starr	$8.95
I'll Be Your Shelter	Giselle Carmichael	$8.95
I'll Paint a Sun	A.J. Garrotto	$9.95
Illusions	Pamela Leigh Starr	$8.95
Indiscretions	Donna Hill	$8.95
Intentional Mistakes	Michele Sudler	$9.95
Interlude	Donna Hill	$8.95
Intimate Intentions	Angie Daniels	$8.95

Other Genesis Press, Inc. Titles (continued)

Jolie's Surrender	Edwina Martin-Arnold	$8.95
Kiss or Keep	Debra Phillips	$8.95
Lace	Giselle Carmichael	$9.95
Last Train to Memphis	Elsa Cook	$12.95
Lasting Valor	Ken Olsen	$24.95
Let Us Prey	Hunter Lundy	$25.95
Life Is Never As It Seems	J.J. Michael	$12.95
Lighter Shade of Brown	Vicki Andrews	$8.95
Love Always	Mildred E. Riley	$10.95
Love Doesn't Come Easy	Charlyne Dickerson	$8.95
Love Unveiled	Gloria Greene	$10.95
Love's Deception	Charlene Berry	$10.95
Love's Destiny	M. Loui Quezada	$8.95
Mae's Promise	Melody Walcott	$8.95
Magnolia Sunset	Giselle Carmichael	$8.95
Matters of Life and Death	Lesego Malepe, Ph.D.	$15.95
Meant to Be	Jeanne Sumerix	$8.95
Midnight Clear	Leslie Esdaile	$10.95
(Anthology)	Gwynne Forster	
	Carmen Green	
	Monica Jackson	
Midnight Magic	Gwynne Forster	$8.95
Midnight Peril	Vicki Andrews	$10.95
Misconceptions	Pamela Leigh Starr	$9.95
Montgomery's Children	Richard Perry	$14.95
My Buffalo Soldier	Barbara B. K. Reeves	$8.95
Naked Soul	Gwynne Forster	$8.95
Next to Last Chance	Louisa Dixon	$24.95
No Apologies	Seressia Glass	$8.95
No Commitment Required	Seressia Glass	$8.95
No Regrets	Mildred E. Riley	$8.95
Nowhere to Run	Gay G. Gunn	$10.95
O Bed! O Breakfast!	Rob Kuehnle	$14.95

Other Genesis Press, Inc. Titles (continued)

Object of His Desire	A. C. Arthur	$8.95
Office Policy	A. C. Arthur	$9.95
Once in a Blue Moon	Dorianne Cole	$9.95
One Day at a Time	Bella McFarland	$8.95
Outside Chance	Louisa Dixon	$24.95
Passion	T.T. Henderson	$10.95
Passion's Blood	Cherif Fortin	$22.95
Passion's Journey	Wanda Thomas	$8.95
Past Promises	Jahmel West	$8.95
Path of Fire	T.T. Henderson	$8.95
Path of Thorns	Annetta P. Lee	$9.95
Peace Be Still	Colette Haywood	$12.95
Picture Perfect	Reon Carter	$8.95
Playing for Keeps	Stephanie Salinas	$8.95
Pride & Joi	Gay G. Gunn	$15.95
Pride & Joi	Gay G. Gunn	$8.95
Promises to Keep	Alicia Wiggins	$8.95
Quiet Storm	Donna Hill	$10.95
Reckless Surrender	Rochelle Alers	$6.95
Red Polka Dot in a World of Plaid	Varian Johnson	$12.95
Reluctant Captive	Joyce Jackson	$8.95
Rendezvous with Fate	Jeanne Sumerix	$8.95
Revelations	Cheris F. Hodges	$8.95
Rivers of the Soul	Leslie Esdaile	$8.95
Rocky Mountain Romance	Kathleen Suzanne	$8.95
Rooms of the Heart	Donna Hill	$8.95
Rough on Rats and Tough on Cats	Chris Parker	$12.95
Secret Library Vol. 1	Nina Sheridan	$18.95
Secret Library Vol. 2	Cassandra Colt	$8.95
Shades of Brown	Denise Becker	$8.95
Shades of Desire	Monica White	$8.95

Other Genesis Press, Inc. Titles (continued)

Shadows in the Moonlight	Jeanne Sumerix	$8.95
Sin	Crystal Rhodes	$8.95
So Amazing	Sinclair LeBeau	$8.95
Somebody's Someone	Sinclair LeBeau	$8.95
Someone to Love	Alicia Wiggins	$8.95
Song in the Park	Martin Brant	$15.95
Soul Eyes	Wayne L. Wilson	$12.95
Soul to Soul	Donna Hill	$8.95
Southern Comfort	J.M. Jeffries	$8.95
Still the Storm	Sharon Robinson	$8.95
Still Waters Run Deep	Leslie Esdaile	$8.95
Stories to Excite You	Anna Forrest/Divine	$14.95
Subtle Secrets	Wanda Y. Thomas	$8.95
Suddenly You	Crystal Hubbard	$9.95
Sweet Repercussions	Kimberley White	$9.95
Sweet Tomorrows	Kimberly White	$8.95
Taken by You	Dorothy Elizabeth Love	$9.95
Tattooed Tears	T. T. Henderson	$8.95
The Color Line	Lizzette Grayson Carter	$9.95
The Color of Trouble	Dyanne Davis	$8.95
The Disappearance of Allison Jones	Kayla Perrin	$5.95
The Honey Dipper's Legacy	Pannell-Allen	$14.95
The Joker's Love Tune	Sidney Rickman	$15.95
The Little Pretender	Barbara Cartland	$10.95
The Love We Had	Natalie Dunbar	$8.95
The Man Who Could Fly	Bob & Milana Beamon	$18.95
The Missing Link	Charlyne Dickerson	$8.95
The Price of Love	Sinclair LeBeau	$8.95
The Smoking Life	Ilene Barth	$29.95
The Words of the Pitcher	Kei Swanson	$8.95
Three Wishes	Seressia Glass	$8.95
Ties That Bind	Kathleen Suzanne	$8.95
Tiger Woods	Libby Hughes	$5.95

Other Genesis Press, Inc. Titles (continued)

Time is of the Essence	Angie Daniels	$9.95
Timeless Devotion	Bella McFarland	$9.95
Tomorrow's Promise	Leslie Esdaile	$8.95
Truly Inseparable	Wanda Y. Thomas	$8.95
Unbreak My Heart	Dar Tomlinson	$8.95
Uncommon Prayer	Kenneth Swanson	$9.95
Unconditional	A.C. Arthur	$9.95
Unconditional Love	Alicia Wiggins	$8.95
Until Death Do Us Part	Susan Paul	$8.95
Vows of Passion	Bella McFarland	$9.95
Wedding Gown	Dyanne Davis	$8.95
What's Under Benjamin's Bed	Sandra Schaffer	$8.95
When Dreams Float	Dorothy Elizabeth Love	$8.95
Whispers in the Night	Dorothy Elizabeth Love	$8.95
Whispers in the Sand	LaFlorya Gauthier	$10.95
Wild Ravens	Altonya Washington	$9.95
Yesterday Is Gone	Beverly Clark	$10.95
Yesterday's Dreams, Tomorrow's Promises	Reon Laudat	$8.95
Your Precious Love	Sinclair LeBeau	$8.95

ESCAPE WITH INDIGO !!!!

Join Indigo Book Club©
It's simple, easy and secure.

Sign up and receive the new releases
every month + Free shipping and
20% off the cover price.

Go online to www.genesis-press.com
and click on Bookclub or
call 1-888-INDIGO-1

Order Form

Mail to: Genesis Press, Inc.
P.O. Box 101
Columbus, MS 39703

Name _____

Address _____

City/State _____ Zip _____

Telephone _____

Ship to (if different from above)

Name _____

Address _____

City/State _____ Zip _____

Telephone _____

Credit Card Information

Credit Card # _____ ☐ Visa   ☐ Mastercard

Expiration Date (mm/yy) _____ ☐ AmEx   ☐ Discover

Qty.	Author	Title	Price	Total

Use this order form, or call 1-888-INDIGO-1

Total for books _____

Shipping and handling:
  $5 first two books,
  $1 each additional book _____

Total S & H _____

Total amount enclosed _____

Mississippi residents add 7% sales tax